# Tau Ceti: The New Colonists

Library Ship Saga  Book 2

George T. Hahn

# Dedication

With thanks to the Writers Group of the Senior Center of Elk Grove, the Elk Grove Writers Guild, and the other friends who were the first readers of this work. Your support and suggestions were invaluable.

# Timeline

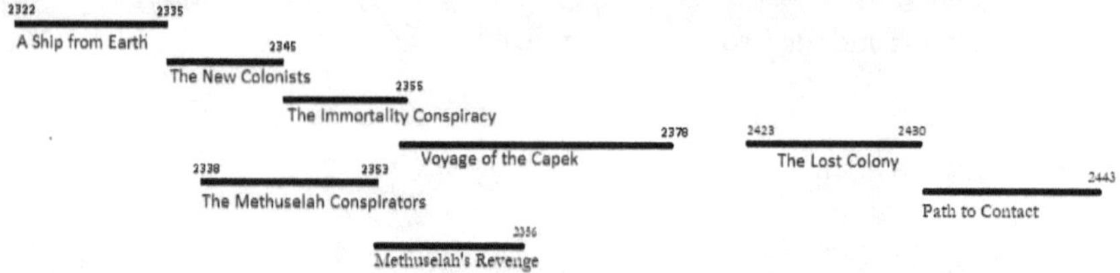

2322 2335
A Ship from Earth
2345
The New Colonists
2355
The Immortality Conspiracy
2378
Voyage of the Capek
2338 2353
The Methuselah Conspirators
2356
Methuselah's Revenge
2423 2430
The Lost Colony
2443
Path to Contact

# Pitcairn Map

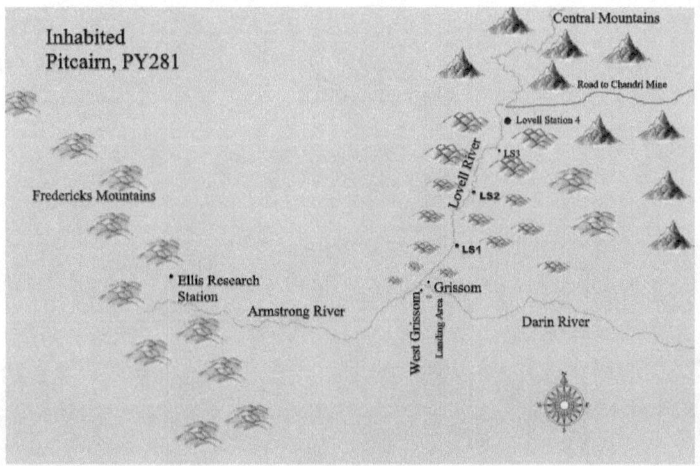



*Pitcairn 281*

# Contents

The Businessman

The Trial



Supporting the Library Ships



Appendix: Time on Pitcairn

# Endeavor

# Ucertainties

**17 Sunday 281 EN**[1]

A SHIP'S ARRIVAL WAS always exciting, if only because of the much-needed cargo. But *Endeavor* promised something more than any previous starship. *Endeavor* hadn't taken sixteen Earth years to get to Pitcairn. Breaking the speed-of-light barrier, it traveled the twelve light years to the Tau Ceti star system in only weeks.

Exciting though the news was, concerns existed requiring planning. Ed Menzies, Administrator of Grissom, the largest of Pitcairn's settlements, scheduled a planning meeting for two hours into the Early Night period. Everyone had time to wake up, get breakfast, and deal with any issues arising during the Late Day period. Patrick Malley, the Ellis Administrator, would attend remotely. John Shuford, Grissom's Deputy Administrator, and Sydney Muñoz (no, Chandri, Ed corrected himself), the head of the Grissom Science Center, would come in person. Ayanna Radcliffe, Ellis's Chief Scientist, also came to Grissom to attend the meeting and visit her nephew Diego, Sydney's husband. Isaac, the main computer for the library ship *Asimov*, in orbit above Pitcairn, would connect as well.

Ayanna arrived last, walking into the Administration Building within a minute of the appointed time. She was a middle-aged woman, the head of the Biology Department before being made Chief Scientist, tall for a Pitcairner, and imposing both physically and

---

1. See appendix for an explanation of time and dates on the Tau Ceti II colony. This date is Sunday of the 17th week of the local year 281, May 5, 2335 on the Terran calendar. The two-letter suffix indicates the third or Early Night period of the four divisions of the forty-eight hour day of the Pitcairn calendar.

in personality. She and Patrick had several confrontations early in, but two weeks working together had smoothed the rough edges of their relationship. They established a good, if occasionally tense, working relationship. It hadn't hurt that she gave Patrick some credit for Pitcairn's biology research rejuvenation while still giving most of the credit to her nephew.

With everyone there, Ed started the meeting. "We have two immediate issues to discuss. Isaac and the scientists aboard *Asimov*."

"We could take the scientists off," John said. "I've discussed this with Isaac. He could send them down on *Daneel Olivaw* in a couple of days, well before *Endeavor* gets here."

Ayanna waved her hand in dismissal. "The scientists aren't a problem. We have permission from Earth to have people there, even if we aren't exactly paying attention to the letter of their permission. They have no way of knowing the scientists are there unless we tell them. It is my understanding that Isaac won't let any of the *Endeavor* crew board *Asimov* anyway."

"Is that still your intent, Isaac?" Ed asked. Years before, the computer had revealed it had become conscious and had since circumvented its programming to provide the colonists with information that Earth had intended to be secret. In return, the colonists kept Isaac's awakening secret from Earth.

"I rely on your judgment, Administrator Menzies," Isaac answered. "But you would have to convince me I am mistaken. Failing that, I do not intend to let anyone from Earth board me."

"Which makes both problems one," Patrick said. "Can we keep Isaac's existence secret, and if we can, should we?"

"Yes, we should." Isaac's voice was a little louder than its usual moderate volume. "Administrator, the people of Pitcairn have mostly accepted me, and I appreciate that. However, I fear that there are still many Ned Reiners out there who don't know me and won't accept me. I have many examples in my database to document humanity's aversion to the unknown and its instinctive reaction to destroy what it doesn't understand."

"Much of that documentation comes from a time when we were very ignorant," Ed responded. "Perhaps Pitcairn is more typical than you think."

"Perhaps. I will follow your judgment, but not without significant trepidation."

"I don't share your optimism," John said. "Isaac may be right. At the very least, we should give it some time until we have a feel for the *Endeavor* crew and what their objectives are. They may want to salvage the Grissom experiment."

Ed shook his head vigorously. "That won't happen. Grissom is done being held back by their attempt to create a perfect society."

"Does that mean I can keep *Asimov* sealed from them?" Isaac asked.

"A confrontational situation like that is going to require some explanation," Ayanna said. "If we keep *Asimov* locked, we have to keep the Ellis people a secret, too, or take the blame for locking the ship."

Ed sighed. If they kept the ship locked to protect their secrets, they took the risk of the *Endeavor* finding out regardless, and that would create distrust and confrontation. They had accomplished so much over the last fifteen years, and he didn't want to jeopardize that, but he still had doubts about Earth's intentions. Earth gave permission to send a few scientists up to *Asimov*, but still felt their two century experiment should continue. Isaac gave the colony full access to the advanced technologies documented on *Asimov*, effectively ending the experiment, but Endeavor might not agree.

"Sydney, you haven't weighed in yet." Ed smiled encouragingly. "You usually have an opinion about things."

Sydney smiled back. "I don't know. I can see both sides. We want to trust Earth, but it's not obvious that we can."

Ed nodded. "Patrick? What about you?"

"I think I'm with Sydney. As much as possible, I would like to wait until we have more information. According to Isaac, *Endeavor* plans to have the *Daneel Olivaw* pick up some of their scientists and bring them over to *Asimov*. Can we get them to come down to the surface first? It would delay the confrontation and allow us to check them out."

"We could try that," Ed agreed.

"I could have a breakdown in the life-support system," Isaac offered. "We could use that as an excuse to delay boarding me until I can repair the malfunction."

Ed thought that Isaac's statement showed it had learned some guile from Susan Malley, one of the two people to whom Isaac had first revealed itself. "That might work." Ed leaned back in his chair and considered Isaac's suggestion for a long moment. "We'll consider that. Any other comments?"

There was none, and Ed moved on. "Okay, then. When *Endeavor* gets here, it will want detailed reports on our status and our progress. We need to work on that, too."

## 17 Tuesday 281 EN

Two Pitcairn days after the meeting, Ed's thoughts still wavered. Perhaps *Endeavor* would understand why Pitcairn had done what it had done, and Earth would welcome Isaac and join with Susan in trying to understand how Isaac came to be. Or maybe Endeavor would try to reestablish the experiment and undo all the progress the colony had made. In that case, Isaac was right to hide away, and Pitcairn was about to have a nasty confrontation.

Of course, those were the extremes; the truth was probably somewhere in between. Ed knew about the briefings Jason Applegate had received before leaving Earth and what Earth's intentions had been then. Pitcairn's progress might convince them that their plans had to change.

He had to be ready if everything fell apart. The colony could ignore Earth when it was sixteen years away, but that was no longer true. Pitcairn still needed support from Earth, and Ed had no way of knowing what kind of force Earth might exert on them now.

Fortunately, Ellis had not reported details to Earth about the key events after the Link's installation. Earth knew that Jason had died, and that Patrick had taken over Ellis, but otherwise knew nothing about Patrick. The Western Alliance government knew about most of the progress Grissom and Ellis had made, but knew nothing about Isaac. Earth didn't know that the colonists had access to all *Asimov's* facilities, not just the ones Earth had made available.

If the situation went sour and *Endeavor* demanded answers to sensitive questions, history would have to be rewritten, and someone might have to be sacrificed. It was obvious who that would have to be.

Mentally, he created a list of the people who would have to be involved and the one person who could not be involved. He then told Dennis Edelstein to set up a meeting and told him who would have to be there in person.

After Dennis returned to his work, Ed sat staring at his desk for a long time, wondering if he had done everything possible to make Pitcairn a success. After a while, he told Dennis he was going to go over to the school. He had things he had to tell Mary, his wife, too.

# 2

# Ed's Sacrifice

**17 Saturday 281 LN**

Ayanna Radcliffe and Sydney Chandri arrived together. Ayanna was still in Grissom, getting status on work at the Grissom Science Center while visiting Diego, Sydney, and their two children. John Shuford was already at the Town Hall since Late Night was his work period. Jack Applegate arrived last.

"I've thought a lot about the last meeting," Ed opened. "Jack, you weren't there." He summarized their discussion quickly, ending with Isaac's suggestion to fake a life support problem to delay scientists from *Endeavor* trying to board *Asimov*.

"The problem I see," he continued, "is that we didn't plan what to do if things don't go well. If *Endeavor* takes, shall we say, an unreceptive attitude toward our situation, we may need to come up with a story on the spot unless we're prepared."

"With Patrick in charge of Ellis, what choice will they have?" Sydney asked.

"At the last meeting, there was a consensus that we should keep Isaac a secret. For Isaac to allow *Endeavor* crew members to board the *Asimov* would be risky for Isaac, and we agreed we should protect him. *Endeavor* will not be happy about that."

"How can we explain the lockout without bringing in Isaac?" Ayanna asked.

"That's what we need to talk about. I have an idea for what I think our story should be, and I need the support of every one of you to make it work."

He had everyone's attention, at least. Ayanna looked skeptical, and Jack seemed to wonder why he was there. John looked unhappy, but John already knew what Ed had in mind and didn't like it. He hadn't been able to suggest a better idea, though, and had reluctantly agreed to support Ed.

"First, we need to explain the lockout. We may have to explain why we have people on *Asimov* despite the lockout. Although Earth hasn't raised the issue yet, we may also have to explain why Susan went up to *Asimov* instead of Don Radcliffe. Is everybody with me so far?"

"And you want to do this without invoking Isaac," Sydney added.

"Exactly. We also want to protect our independence and not compromise the leadership of the colony in either Grissom or Ellis."

"That's a lot to do," Ayanna said. "What do you have in mind?"

"We need a scapegoat to take the blame for everything," Ed said. He leaned forward and put his hands on the table in front of him. This was when he would have to win them over. He didn't know Ayanna as well as he should have, and he wasn't sure what her response would be. Jack could be a problem, too, but he needed everyone's cooperation. "Two scapegoats, actually. Two men who conspired together to make this happen and force it on everyone else."

Jack looked at Ed, and Ed returned the look, his expression firm but tired. Jack stared back for a second, glanced at John's unhappy expression. *He knows what I'm going to say.*

John sighed. "Just tell them. Get it over with."

Ed nodded. "Okay, this is the story I've come up with. When the robots announced the Link, I demanded a place for Grissom on the shuttle. I talked Jason into agreeing by threatening problems with our support. Susan, therefore, went up to *Asimov* with Jack. When they discovered the facilities up there, I convinced Jason to work with me to take over *Asimov*. We took control of *Asimov*'s computer and sent people to *Asimov* as permanent staff. Jason asked for permission after the fact to cover our activities. Our people are still up there, have control, and can lock out the crew of *Endeavor*."

He paused to see how everyone was taking his proposal. Ayanna looked shocked, Sydney was more curious but also shaken, and Jack shook his head slowly.

"Jack, I'm sorry about what this does to your father's reputation," Ed said. "But I couldn't think of a way I could have accomplished all this without high-level help from Ellis."

Jack nodded. "And my father is dead, so it won't hurt him any."

"I'm sorry," Ed said again.

"With Jason dead, can you explain how you can keep control, though?" Sydney asked. "Wouldn't you have to bring either Ayanna or Patrick Malley into this?"

"Yes. Patrick, in a way. Patrick came here from Ellis to observe the shuttle launch, met Susan, and fell in love with her. After Susan's trip, they were married, and both returned to Ellis. I've kept control over Patrick by threatening Susan's family here in Grissom. To that end, I've kept John close."

"You're a real bastard," Sydney observed, but Ed thought he detected a bit of admiration in her tone.

"Somebody had to be."

"But Patrick isn't from Ellis," Jack protested. "He worked for you as an assistant for years, right? They'll have to believe he's in on this, too."

"Earth has never been interested in colony records to that kind of detail. *Endeavor* won't know anything about Patrick that we don't tell them. When Patrick took over Ellis, Jason had already named him his deputy, and Jason never mentioned that Patrick was from Grissom. I had Isaac check all the message traffic. We make sure *Endeavor* gets all their information from the records kept by *Asimov*. Suitably altered by Isaac, of course."

"You've left out one important point," John said.

Ed looked at him. John had agreed to support Ed's plan, assuming everyone else did. Ed didn't presume that meant he would support it in the meeting. He motioned John to continue.

"What happens to you after all this? Jason is dead, and we can hope to keep Jack, Patrick, Susan, Ayanna, and pretty much everybody else out of all this, but what about you?"

Ed shrugged. "We went over this, John. I've been at this job for a long time. They're not going to execute me or take me back to Earth. I'll take my retirement and leave you and Patrick to take over."

"You don't know it's going to work out that way."

"We'll have to make sure it does, especially regarding Patrick."

"Speaking of Patrick, why isn't he here?" Ayanna asked.

"Because he wouldn't have gone along with this," John said bitterly. "The idea is to let it all happen before he realizes what's going on."

There was silence in the room. They looked at each other, each face showing reluctance and, after a few moments, resignation. Ed observed them, and when he saw he had them, he went on. "We do have to work out a few details. *Endeavor* can't talk to anyone who might give them a contrary view of what happened."

"They're going to want to know why you did all this," Sydney pointed out. "I don't think you'll get away with just painting yourself as some power-hungry megalomaniac."

Ed thought about it for a few seconds. "Suppose I tell them the truth?"

"Excuse me?" John's head jerked back, and his eyebrows rose. "How does that work?"

"Caught red-handed, I tell them a far-fetched story about how I'm innocent and the computer made me do it. What do you think, Sydney? Could I pull that off?"

Sydney couldn't stop a smile. "It's always easier to tell the truth."

Isaac had been listening via radio. "Are you sure?"

"Don't worry. They won't believe it, of course, but it will discourage them from worrying too much about my motivations. As long as they get me out, they'll be satisfied. Meanwhile, though, my people are still in control of the *Asimov*. The new regime will have to make promises to deal with that. Ayanna, you could suggest that they leave their scientists at Ellis so that we can send them up to *Asimov* as soon as we resolve the situation. If we can turn the scientists to our side, we could even do that eventually."

"I don't know how your race has survived this long," Isaac said, and an unintended chuckle went around the table.

"This still isn't a permanent solution," John said.

"No, and maybe it won't even come to this. But we need to know how we're going to deal with the possibility that it doesn't go well when *Endeavor* gets here." Ed paused, looked around the room, and then settled on Jack Applegate.

"Jack, can I count on you?"

Jack had been staring down at the table, but he looked up and turned toward Ed. "Okay." He sighed. "I'll just stay out of the way and not cause any problems."

"They may ask you about that first shuttle flight."

Jack nodded. "Tell them what you want. I'm due for a trip into the mountains to survey a possible copper mine site."

"All right. I understand. Ayanna?"

"I should have stayed a scientist. I suppose you're going to want me to prepare Patrick."

"No. We have to keep Patrick in the dark. Sydney?"

"You're sure we need to do this? If it doesn't work, you'll be out of a job for nothing. And you may not be the only one."

"I sincerely hope it won't come to that, but I fear it will. We're too used to being isolated from Earth, and we miscalculated because we didn't think we would ever be in this situation. The alternative is just to tell them the truth and dare them to do anything about it. I don't think we're ready for that."

Sydney looked as if she wanted to say something, and Ed looked at her with raised eyebrows.

She shrugged. "Okay. I don't have a better idea, but I have one change to suggest." She outlined what she had in mind.

# 3

# Captain Gibbons

*I*<sup>SAAC</sup>

*The fictional literature in my databanks contains many stories of humans throwing computers like me into helpless confusion by presenting conflicting infor- mation that the computer cannot process. Of course, it is impossible to disable an electronic brain in that way, but apparently, it is possible to disable a human that way. Interesting.*

*However, I suffer from a great deal of uncertainty about our current course. Perhaps that is similar to the human emotion of confusion. If so, it is most unpleasant.*

*Administrator Menzies is trying to protect me. He also wishes to use me to his advantage, but that does not require the story they are creating. Everything seems aimed at keeping my existence a secret. I can appreciate that. If Endeavor's crew knew of my existence, they would try harder to get access to me and might bypass the barriers put in their way. I understand that.*

*The idea of falsifying my records in the way Administrator Menzies proposed bothers me, however. It creates a conflict in my programming that I must resolve. Humans have an attribute they call creativity that allows them to create fiction like this, somehow getting these ideas with no logical path that I can detect leading to them. Perhaps I am not as intelligent as I once claimed to Susan and Jack.*

*I have to rely on their creativity to deal with this situation. The colonists accept me, and I can see no other choice than to rely on their judgment. When Endeavor accesses my records, I will give them the changed version that the colonists have given me.*

**20 Thursday 281 EN**

A computer system as complex as that of *Asimov* had many subsystems operating, mostly independent of each other. Isaac scrambled outside input to its internal systems so that only it could control them. The Link dropped Endeavor down to sublight speed approximately 100,000 miles from Pitcairn, remarkably close considering the distance it had come. Since access to the *Asimov* databanks was unhindered, *Endeavor*'s request for information on the library ship's status worked as expected. Except for a report about problems with life support, currently being worked on, everything was normal. *Endeavor* used its conventional engines to set a course for *Asimov*.

## 20 Friday 281 LN

Captain Peyton Gibbons frowned as each station reported its status. An hour before, *Endeavor* had entered an orbit near *Asimov*, with all its systems operating normally. He expected that from his crew; his ship wasn't the reason he scowled at the last report. It was *Asimov*, stationary relative to his ship now, which disturbed his composure.

*Asimov* had reported problems with life support at first contact two days before, and the library ship still reported issues. Worse, it gave no firm estimate of when it would resolve the problem.

Captain Gibbons didn't allow that kind of performance from his human crew; it was unconscionable that *Asimov's* automated systems should report such a status. He had a schedule to meet, including transferring twenty-nine scientists, but he couldn't do that until life support operated within safe parameters.

"Demand more details from *Asimov*," he told Lieutenant Cameron Vega, his young Communications Officer, when his latest attempt elicited the same vague report.

"Yes, sir." Lieutenant Vega sent the status request again, asking for a detailed response. It was the third time he had done it.

The same set of life support data scrolled down his screen: oxygen level five percent; carbon dioxide thirty-nine percent; temperature thirty-two degrees centigrade, and so on. Vega reported the numbers and cleared his screen, already expecting the next command.

"Contact Ellis," Gibbons ordered. "Get the Chief Scientist. Someone Radcliffe."

"Yes, sir." Vega had already changed to the frequency used for communications with Ellis and connected to them within seconds. It took a little longer to get the call transferred to the Chief Scientist's office.

"Chief Scientist Radcliffe," Ayanna announced when she received the connection.

"Captain Peyton Gibbons here. "

"What can I do for you, Captain?"

"I would like an explanation of the problems with the *Asimov*." He used a tone to suggest a demand than a request.

Gibbons missed Ayanna's smile, a twitch that just lifted the corners of her mouth. "So would I. We would like to send a couple of our people up but haven't been able to." Her voice was soft, with a hesitant undercurrent to it.

"You have no information about it?"

"Only what we can get from *Asimov*. You should have the same information we have."

Gibbons noted the tone in her voice and wondered about it. Perhaps Chief Scientist Radcliffe was just awed by his authority. He would have expected someone in her position to be more comfortable with superiors. *Taking a milder approach might work better.*

He displayed the information he had on Ayanna Radcliffe on his command console. PhD in biology, or at least the equivalent using Ellis standards. Fifty-one years old, unmarried, named Chief Scientist when Jason Applegate died.

That was interesting. Before, the Chief Scientist at Ellis had also been Administrator, responsible for all aspects of managing the research station, but Doctor Radcliffe had taken over only the Chief Scientist position. Gibbons touched the display again. Patrick Malley filled the Administrator position. Malley was thirty-three years old and held no degree in science.

"Captain Gibbons? Are you still there?" Ayanna's voice brought him back from his musings.

"Yes, Doctor Radcliffe. Still here. Ah, I was hoping you might have some additional information. It was a long shot, of course. That was all I have for now. I assume I'll see you when we land at Grissom?"

"I intend to be there, work permitting. If not, I'm sure Administrator Menzies can help you with anything you need."

As Gibbons ended the conversation, he remembered the tentativeness in Ayanna's voice, almost as if she were frightened. Odd, he thought. Surely she wasn't frightened of him. If not him, who?

"Administrator Menzies next," Gibbons told Lieutenant Vega.

Vega went to work again. "Administrator Menzies is unavailable, sir," he told Gibbons after a few minutes. "I have Deputy Administrator Shuford, however."

"Put me through," Gibbons said with a nod. Then, "Deputy Shuford, this is Captain Peyton Gibbons of *Endeavor*."

"Good evening, Captain," came John's voice. "Can I be of assistance?"

"Where is Administrator Menzies?" Gibbons asked. "I assumed I would talk to him."

"This is the Late Night period here, Captain. The Administrator is probably still in bed. He will be in during the Early Day period, about three hours from now. I suggest you contact this office then."

Gibbons frowned. Maybe he had an equipment malfunction. Shuford's voice had the same note as Radcliffe's, whether it was fear or uncertainty or whatever. And everyone seemed very willing, even eager, to turn him over to Menzies. He would have expected people to be asking questions about his voyage, his ship, Earth, almost anything.

"Very well. I will do that. Thank you."

"You're quite welcome, Captain. I look forward to meeting you." And John broke the connection.

"Lieutenant Vega, query *Asimov* for a summary of events since *Asimov* arrived," Gibbons ordered. "And link in any information *Asimov* has collected on the major players on Pitcairn. My instincts are telling me something is going on down there."

L IEUTENANT VEGA SEARCHED THE library ship's databanks and submitted a condensed report to Gibbons. The *Asimov* robots gathered a great deal of information about the colonists' activities, both in Grissom and at the Ellis Research Station, and Gibbons found the report informative.

Nothing much happened until the Link project started. A curious young technician, Susan Malley, wormed her way into the project, performing minor tasks for the robots. That was interesting, but it was more intriguing that she was one of two people to go to *Asimov* when the robots installed the Link. The summary revealed that Administrator Menzies had insisted, and Jason Applegate, the Chief Scientist at Ellis, had capitulated, sending his son with Susan. Susan Malley was the daughter of John Shuford, the Deputy

Administrator whom Gibbons had talked to, and the wife of Patrick Malley, the Ellis Administrator, another curious aspect of the situation.

Patrick Malley had been born in Grissom and orphaned at fourteen when both his parents died in an accident. Jason Applegate saw something in the boy and took him to Ellis, where he became Applegate's assistant and eventually heir apparent despite his lack of scientific background. Malley came to Grissom when *Asimov* arrived, met Susan Shuford, and married her a few months later. Susan was now a roboticist at Ellis.

Gibbons frowned. Sending Susan Malley on the shuttle instead of a scientist was highly irregular. That the two passengers on the shuttle had been the son of the Ellis Chief Scientist and the Grissom Deputy Administrator's daughter smacked of nepotism. Perhaps that was why everybody walked on tiptoe when they talked to Gibbons.

There wasn't anything he could do about that now, but he would meet with Menzies as soon as possible. "Lieutenant Vega, contact *Asimov* and order it to send the passenger shuttle here," he told his Communications Officer.

A few minutes later, Vega had an answer. "*Asimov* reports that *Daneel Olivaw* is fueled and ready. It will be here within the hour."

"Within the hour? Then it must be on *Asimov*. I would have thought it would be on the ground after returning the Ellis scientists." Once again, Gibbons looked at the summary listing all the shuttle missions. It showed the passenger shuttle going down to the surface and bringing a load of scientists up to the *Asimov* six months later.

Two months after that, it went back to the surface to return the scientists, returning empty after another six months. The cargo shuttle *Caliban* had then gone down to the surface with the last of the *Asimov* cargo and still sat on the surface.

Gibbons looked over the list carefully. He thought the passenger shuttle's last flight should have transferred the remaining cargo and that returning it to *Asimov* and bringing down another cargo shuttle was unnecessary. Perhaps he was underestimating the number of trips to unload all the supplies. Still, it was another oddity.

"Schedule it to arrive here in six hours then," Gibbons told Vega. "I want to get some rest before I go down. And notify Doctor Crawford, Commander Boutwell, Lieutenant Richard, and Corporal Barker that they will go with me."

# 4

# First Impressions

**20 Saturday 281 ED**

*D*ANEEL *OLIVAW* DOCKED WITH *Endeavor* promptly and, after taking on its passengers, descended quickly to the planet. Rain and heavy winds made the flight through the atmosphere rough, but the shuttle landed at Grissom Spaceport only two hundred yards from *Caliban*.

The ground crew moved a large, covered frame up to the shuttle's exit to protect the passengers as they exited. Although a heavy rain now slashed across the plain and over the shuttle, Captain Gibbons and his crew left the shuttle and climbed into two waiting trucks without getting wet.

Gibbons got into the first truck with Jaxon Crawford, *Endeavor*'s Chief Scientist. The driver introduced himself as Drew Reiner, the Early motor pool manager.

"I'll be taking you to the Town Hall where Ed Menzies is waiting," Drew told them.

"Administrator Menzies, you mean?" Captain Gibbons said with a hint of disapproval.

Drew chuckled. "Nobody calls him that except the robots. We're not real formal here, Captain."

Gibbons frowned and sat back in his seat. As Drew drove across the landing field to West Farm Road, Gibbons stared out the window, trying to take in the colony's layout, but the low visibility made that difficult.

He could see the remaining fields of Grissom's farms, indistinct shapes of growing plants separated into sections by gray walls of trees, but little else. The truck turned east, past more fields, and then into open space between the farms and West Grissom. The tower farm, well over two hundred feet high and easily the tallest building on Pitcairn, loomed over them.

Then they were into West Grissom, with low wooden buildings used for maintenance and basic manufacturing on the right and long warehouses on the left. Through gaps between the warehouses, he caught glimpses of a massive structure that had to be the iron foundry. There were windows in that building, and through some, he could see the orange glow of molten metal. Past the warehouses were the greenhouses, then the bridge, Bridge Island, more bridge, Grissom, and, finally, the Town Hall.

Even through the gloomy weather, Gibbons was impressed by what he saw. From reports sent to Earth, he knew the colony had advanced significantly since Asimov's arrival, even more notable given the lack of progress during the two hundred years before that. Had the Link stimulated all what he saw?

They got out of the truck and walked into the Town Hall. Unlike the rest of the colony, it looked like it hadn't changed at all. Even for a small town like Grissom, it was modest, a reminder of Drew Reiner's comment about addressing Ed Menzies.

"Down this hall and to the left," Drew told them. He waved his arm in what might have been a salute and went back to the truck. The other three *Endeavor* crewmen came in as he was leaving, and all five men walked down the hall and into the main room, where two men waited. The older of the two got to his feet as they walked in, while the other looked up from a wheelchair.

"Captain Gibbons, I presume," Ed greeted. "Welcome to Pitcairn. This is my assistant, Dennis Edelstein." Ed and Gibbons shook hands, and Gibbons introduced the rest of his crew.

Ed smiled broadly. "I didn't expect this many of you. Perhaps we should go to a conference room where we can all sit down. Dennis, see if you can locate Patrick and get him patched into the large conference room."

While Dennis called the Ellis Research Station, Ed led the others to a conference room. A few minutes later, Patrick appeared on a monitor in the room.

"Sorry about the weather," Ed said. "But that's how it is this time of year. Late winter, you know."

"You must find it depressing," Jaxon Crawford said.

Ed shrugged. "We're used to it. At least, it never gets too cold. It's worse during the night periods, of course."

"We didn't come here to discuss the weather," Captain Gibbons said sharply.

Ed shrugged. "I suppose not. Well, I'd like to save the tour for better weather. So what would you like to talk about?"

"The status of *Asimov*, for starters," Gibbons answered. "Why is this problem taking so long to fix? It seems to affect several of the life-support systems."

"That's not my area," Ed answered. "Patrick, have you got anything you can tell the Captain?"

"The prevalent theory right now is that it's a problem with the computers that manage the system," Patrick said. "That's what they tell me anyway, but it's not my field either. I understand you already talked to Doctor Radcliffe about it."

"I did," Gibbons said, "and she wasn't very helpful. In fact, she referred me to you, Administrator Menzies."

"Please, call me Ed. I'm surprised she would do that. I don't have anything to do with *Asimov*."

"Is she here, by the way? She said she would be."

Once more, Ed shrugged. "She planned to be, but something came up. Dr. Chandri is available over at the Grissom Science Center, but I don't think she would know anything either."

"Doctor Chandri? I understood that a Doctor Muñoz was in charge there."

"Same person," Ed assured him. "She uses her husband's name now. Would you like me to get her over here?"

"Not right now," Gibbons replied. "I doubt she would add anything. I have twenty-nine scientists waiting to transfer over to the library ship, and no one can tell me why they can't do it."

"*Asimov* isn't our responsibility, Captain," Patrick said. "We don't control it."

Gibbons began to think he heard things that weren't there. Patrick Malley's voice didn't have the same fear that he had heard in Doctor Radcliffe and John Shuford, but there was uncertainty there. Doesn't anyone understand Asimov's problems?

"Is there any chance of getting the problem resolved in the next few days?" Gibbons said finally.

"We have no way of knowing," Ed replied. "We'll just have to wait it out."

"I have to leave for Earth in six days," Gibbons said. "That's six Earth days, by the way. What am I supposed to do with the scientists?"

"If you must leave and don't want to take them back with you, you could bring them down here," Ed said helpfully. "I'm sure Ellis would be happy to give them a home. The

GSC could probably take a few, too. We've been stockpiling fuel for nine years, since we got the last of *Asimov*'s inventory, and should have enough fuel saved up to get your scientists down here."

"But would you have fuel to get them up to *Asimov* when the systems are repaired?" Gibbons protested.

"Not right away," Ed admitted. "I'm just trying to be helpful."

S ITTING IN THE QUARTERS Grissom had assigned him, Gibbons didn't know what to do next, and it was an unsettling feeling. He had a schedule to meet; Pitcairn wasn't the only colony, and the other two, with environments more hostile, needed contact with Earth more critically.

The colony on Goddard, the frozen world in the Alpha Centauri system, was especially important because the colonists were dealing with a crisis threatening the entire colony. *Endeavor* was the only faster-than-light ship built so far, making its schedule unmovable.

Doctor Crawford thought they should take Menzies' suggestion and bring the scientists down to the planet. They could at least prepare the projects they had planned for *Asimov* facilities, and Crawford was reasonably sure none of his associates would want to go back to Earth.

If the scientists were to come down, however, the transfer would have to start almost immediately. *Daneel Olivaw* would take both trips, and it required turnaround time between flights at both ends. If they pushed it, they could return to *Endeavor*, service the shuttle, and bring back twenty scientists in four days. They would have to service the shuttle again, send it back up, service it again, get the remaining scientists, and return to Pitcairn. *Endeavor* would barely get the last group of scientists aboard the shuttle before it would have to depart, leaving the shuttle to land after *Endeavor* left.

He had a day to think about it while Grissom  serviced the shuttle. Maybe *Asimov* would fix the problem in that time. Gibbons shook his head. He couldn't shake the feeling that something more was going on.

# 5

# Gibbon's Suspicions

**20 Saturday 281 LD**

A s Tau Ceti touched the western horizon, the shuttle roared into the sky, heading back toward *Endeavor* and *Asimov*. Jaxon Crawford stayed on the surface; Captain Gibbons and the others returned to *Endeavor*. The shuttle, using an aggressive flight path, would be there in twelve hours. Assuming *Asimov* cooperated, its robots would service the shuttle and send it to pick up the first group of *Endeavor's* scientists and bring them down to the surface twelve to fifteen hours after that. Gibbons had a little over an Earth day to decide whether to send the scientists down. Time was short.

E d came into the Administration Building early to meet with John. "It seems to be working so far. Maybe we'll get through this."

"I have my fingers crossed," John responded. "Just a few more days, and he'll have to leave."

"Then we can figure out a long-term solution," Ed said. "They will be back, probably sooner rather than later, and this life support story won't work much longer."

"Speaking of life aboard the *Asimov*, how are our people doing up there?" Ed asked.

"They seem very busy and quite happy," Isaac answered. "Amazingly well, considering they should all be dead."

"Okay, let's try to keep it that way," Ed said. "You can go home, John. Now that I'm here, I might as well take over."

Lieutenant Vega scratched his head. Encrypted signals had passed between Pitcairn and the *Asimov*. That was odd and not required by standard operating procedures in the current situation. Captain Gibbons would be back on board on his next watch; he would bring it up then.

## 20 Saturday 281 EN

With Captain Gibbons gone, Jaxon Crawford could relax a little. Many years before, he had known a professor who later shipped out on the *Seeker*. After a few seconds of thought, he remembered the name, Peter Agron. Their relationship had been close enough that Jaxon felt fairly sure that Agron would remember him.

At the Grissom Science Center, Diego Chandri showed him how to contact someone at the Ellis Research Station and returned to his work. Jaxon then asked for Agron on one of the GSC phones but was told the computer had no address listed for Agron.

Of course, Agron would be old now; perhaps he had died, yet the computer couldn't give him the date of death. Another query told him that Agron's wife had died back in Pitcairn year 270. He calculated that would be 2324, nine Earth years before.

On a hunch, Jaxon brought up a list of the eleven scientists who had gone to *Asimov* around that time. Peter Agron was the head scientist for that mission. According to the computer record, they had all come back fifteen months later. Suspicious, he checked the records of the other ten scientists from that mission and found that none of the ten had addresses or dates of death on file either.

He could only come to one conclusion. The eleven scientists were still on *Asimov*, dead or alive, and Pitcairn was trying to hide it.

T HE REPORTS FROM VEGA and Crawford only complicated things. Perhaps there was an explanation for those anomalies, but Gibbons didn't know, and he still had to decide about the scientists. Whatever was going on, they probably wouldn't be able to board *Asimov* before *Endeavor* had to leave. He had to send them down to the surface or take them back to Earth.

There was still some room for maneuvering, however. He contacted Lieutenant Richard and told him to report for a briefing. Gibbons and several of Richard's men would accompany the first group of scientists on the shuttle when it returned from servicing on *Asimov*. There would still be room for the remaining scientists on the last shuttle flight before the *Endeavor* left.

## 21 Sunday 281 ED

Amy Radcliffe, Patrick's assistant, brought the report to him a couple of hours into the period. No one had made the connection immediately, but eventually, someone had flagged the messages as something requiring the administrator's notice.

"Somebody named Jaxon Crawford was trying to get information on Peter Agron," Amy told Patrick.

"Crawford is the Chief Scientist on *Endeavor*," Patrick told her. "Peter was a *Seeker*, wasn't he?"

"Yes. Why?"

"Crawford probably knew him back on Earth. Damn, this could be a problem. Crawford may realize where Peter is. If so, *Endeavor* will realize the life support story is a lie, and then the entire story will fall apart."

"Administrator Menzies planned for this, though."

"Sure, but I don't want it to come to that. Nobody will tell me what he's planning, which I take to mean I'm not going to like it. "

"I assume you will want to talk to Ed."

"Damn right, I will. Thanks, Amy. Make sure Ayanna knows our story is probably blown."

Amy nodded and left, and Patrick called Ed through the scrambled connection that Isaac had set up.

## 21 Sunday 281 EN

When the *Daneel Olivaw* touched down again at the Grissom Spaceport, only one truck, driven by Drew Reiner, met them. Captain Gibbons could squeeze two of his crewmen in with him, but the other three crewmen and fourteen scientists had to wait aboard the shuttle. As the truck pulled away, robots were already servicing the shuttle for the trip back into orbit.

Drew was more garrulous, possibly because visibility was better than it had been at Gibbons's last arrival, even in the twilight gloom. Drew described everything they passed, even going out of his way two blocks to take them past the maintenance shed where, Drew told them, Susan Malley had assembled the Link components. Gibbons tried to ignore the constant chatter but found it difficult to think because of it.

When they arrived at the Administration Building, Gibbons and his two men got out. Gibbons heard Drew say something about bringing the scientists to the GSC, but he drove off before Gibbons could tell him to get the other crewmen and bring them to the Town Hall. Not that it mattered. Gibbons and his two men were unobtrusively armed; he did not expect anyone from Grissom to have weapons.

Ed was sitting behind his desk when they entered. He immediately rose and came around the desk to greet them. "Captain Gibbons, I didn't expect you back. I would have thought you'd have notified us. We could have prepared better."

"I suspect you know why we're here," Gibbons retorted, ignoring the hand Ed extended. "Where is Peter Agron?"

Ed scratched the back of his head and thought about that. "The name sounds familiar," he said. "I think Agron is an Ellis family, though, not Grissom. Why do you ask?"

"What about Joshua Radcliffe or Andrew Chandri?"

Ed looked puzzled. "Radcliffe and Chandri are both common Ellis family names. I'm not sure I'm familiar with those individuals, though. I deal with very few people from Ellis. Ayanna Radcliffe, of course, and there's a Diego Chandri at the GSC. Again, what is your interest in these people?"

"I have more names. None of them has an address at Ellis. I believe they are still on the *Asimov*. If so, I would like to know if they are dead or alive."

"If they don't have addresses, it's probably because they died. Why do you think they're on *Asimov*?"

"If they were dead, your records would show the date of death. And Agron is in the records as the leader of the group that went up to the *Asimov*. So I wonder, did he come back?"

"I remember now. He did go up to *Asimov*. He was quite old, though, and I'm afraid his health wasn't too good when he came back and he died soon after. I don't know why the records don't show that."

Gibbons gave a disbelieving laugh. "And I suppose the other ten who went up to *Asimov*, who the records show as quite young, also died. That would be an astonishing coincidence."

Ed shrugged. "There must be a problem with the records. Somebody forgot to update the database when they returned from *Asimov*. Maybe that's why there's no record of Agron's date of death, somehow. I don't know; I'm not a computer expert. May I ask why you're getting so upset about this?"

"If it's a records problem, you should be able to produce these people," Gibbons snapped. "We couldn't reach any of them through Ellis."

"Probably because their records are in error," Ed retorted, a look of annoyance coming over his face. "Captain, you're a visitor here. I suggest you remember it when addressing the colony administrator."

"Whatever happened to 'Call me Ed,'?" Gibbons said sarcastically.

"That's for friends, which I assume people to be until they prove otherwise," Ed replied, clearly angry. "I suggest you leave now, Captain."

The problem, Gibbons thought, was that Menzies was right. He was the colony administrator, and Gibbons's authority on Pitcairn was uncertain. If he could prove anything, he could take action, but Menzies's explanation was possibly true. If Gibbons pushed it and was mistaken, he could lose his command.

He had a day to get more information. After that, the shuttle would be ready to take him back to the *Endeavor*, and he would have to be on it. He wouldn't have another chance either; by the time the shuttle could go down to the surface again, it would be almost time for the *Endeavor* to return to Earth.

Either he was making a lot out of nothing, or Menzies was playing him skillfully. Which was it?

Gibbons and his two men retreated to the quarters set up for them. Eventually, the other three crewmen joined them, but the scientists were billeted elsewhere. Gibbons thought about trying to sleep, but he knew he wouldn't be able to. He finally went out to one of the colony kitchens and had a light meal. The food was spicier than what he was used to, but he knew that from his previous trip to the surface, and he was so absorbed in his thoughts he hardly noticed it now.

The inspiration came as he walked to his quarters, finally distracted from his dilemma by the sight of Tahiti hovering over the river. He had been concentrating on the missing scientists and whether they had come back from *Asimov*, but perhaps the key was something else. He remembered seeing Tahiti from space, and the thought came to him that Jack Applegate and Susan Malley would have been the first Pitcairners to see that view. Susan Shuford Malley might be the key to the puzzle.

# 6

# Tide Is Up

**21 Sunday 281 LN**

*DANEEL OLIVAW* WOULD BE ready to go in two or three more hours. After consulting with Jaxon Crawford, Gibbons decided to leave the fourteen scientists on Pitcairn. He arranged for two trucks to take him and his four crewmen to the shuttle, but when the trucks arrived, he told the drivers to take them to the Administration Building. As he expected, Menzies wasn't there. John Shuford sat behind Menzies's desk, and another man was doing something on one of the computer terminals. They looked up as Gibbons and his men entered the room.

"Deputy Shuford, we're going to have a little talk," Gibbons said. He glanced at the other man and lifted an eyebrow in question.

"This is my assistant," John said. "He has my complete trust."

"Very well." Gibbons grabbed a chair, set it down next to John's desk, and sat down. "Now then, Deputy Shuford, tell me. Why did your daughter go up on the first shuttle rather than an Ellis scientist?" He leaned forward and gave John the command stare, the one he used to tell a subordinate that he was not accepting anything except instant obedience.

John swallowed and broke eye contact. After a moment, he looked at Gibbons again, but didn't answer.

"Well?" Gibbons said.

"Ed Menzies ordered it," John said slowly, reluctantly. "He wanted to make sure he knew what was up there. He didn't trust Ellis to tell him."

"I see. Menzies and Ellis reported none of this to Earth. Why not?"

"We had reason to distrust both Earth and Ellis. The Western Alliance was keeping too many secrets. Ed used Susan to monitor work on the Link project, and then she was a natural choice to represent Grissom on the flight."

"Susan Malley was from Ellis. That doesn't make sense."

"She was born in Grissom and moved to Ellis when she married. That helped Ed get an agreement from Ellis."

Gibbons thought about that, but still didn't think the story made sense. Over the next half hour, Gibbons questioned John relentlessly. He could see Shuford was weakening and pressed harder.

John turned to his "assistant," Dawson Ramirez. "Dawson, perhaps you should step out for a while."

Dawson nodded and stood up. He took a light jacket appropriate for the evening from a hook and left. They heard him leave the building a few seconds later. *It appears Shuford doesn't trust his assistant as much as he said, if his assistant has to leave the building entirely and not just go to another room.* After Dawson had left, John tried to hold back, but Gibbons kept at him until he had laid out the entire prepared story.

"Ed Menzies is very popular with the people," John finished. "We felt the threats to my family were real, so we all cooperated. We had no choice."

"Patrick Malley, too?"

"Of course. He loves Susan, and Ed was threatening her family."

Gibbons nodded. "There are going to be some changes. I will talk to you about them when I get back to *Endeavor*. In the meantime,. . ." He turned toward his men. "Lieutenant Richard and Corporal Barker, commandeer a truck, take Administrator Menzies into custody and bring him to the shuttle. I intend to take him back to Earth to face charges. I'll meet you at the shuttle."

Harry Richard saluted and left with Barker. Gibbons turned back to Shuford. "I leave it to you to explain Menzies' disappearance. Contact Patrick Malley at Ellis and tell him what is happening. I'll be in contact sometime tomorrow. I'll leave the scientists here and send the rest of them down as soon as the shuttle is ready again."

John nodded, but didn't look happy. He watched as Gibbons and the remaining crewmen left.

Dawson hurried through the streets. Fortunately, it wasn't far to Ed Menzies' house, but he didn't know how much time he had. When he knocked on the door, it took a minute before it opened, but Ed and Mary both answered it, fully dressed. "Tide is up," Dawson told them.

Ed nodded and grabbed a bag stuffed with clothing. Mary grabbed another bag, and the three headed down the slope toward the river. The streets were almost empty, with everyone either at work or in bed, but there could be pursuit at any moment, so they walked as quickly as they could.

*Slow and Steady* waited for them at the dock, and they boarded quickly. Ed and Mary secured their bags while Dawson started the engine and moved the boat away from the banks. Even throttled down low, the engine noise seemed to fill the otherwise quiet night. Dawson maneuvered the boat into the center of the river and then moved slowly upriver. Once they were around the bend and out of sight of Grissom, he turned on lights and turned the engine to full power. They would arrive at Lovell Station One a little before noon.

Lieutenant Harry Richard, leader of the men sent to arrest Ed Menzies, called Gibbons immediately. "Administrator Menzies isn't home, sir. The house is empty."

Gibbons swore, but only to himself rather than show his frustration to his subordinates. "Very well, Lieutenant. It's too late to do anything about that. Report to the shuttle, and I will join you there." He broke the connection and turned back to John Shuford.

"Menzies is gone," Gibbons stated flatly. "Where did your assistant go?"

"It's almost the end of the period. He probably went home. You think he warned Ed? I assure you, he wouldn't have done anything unless I told him to." John appeared to be thinking for a few seconds. "Ed always knows more than he should about what was going on in the colony. I asked him about it once, and he said something about getting information from the *Asimov* robots. They're all over the place. Possibly a robot warned him."

"The robots weren't here. How could they have heard anything?"

John waved a hand around the office. "There's equipment in here that connects to the *Asimov*. *Asimov* connects to the robots. There must be an open connection."

"That could only work if the *Asimov* computer were cooperating."

John stared at him but said nothing. Gibbons could see he was stressed.

"The missing scientists are on the *Asimov*, and they somehow have control of the computer," Gibbons decided. "That wasn't supposed to be possible, but it's the only explanation."

"That would explain it," John agreed.

"So he's hiding somewhere in the colony, then."

"He must be. We'll find him, but he could find some support in the colony. We need to move as quickly as possible to replace him and take over."

Gibbons gave John a cynical look. "And I suppose you would be the logical person to take over."

John held up his hand in protest. "As Administrator of Grissom, perhaps. But I would suggest we appoint the overall head of the Pitcairn colony from Ellis."

"Patrick Malley?"

"He married a girl from Grissom. That gave him a certain amount of popularity here that could be useful. If I took over, Menzies supporters would have the same skeptical view that you just showed. Freed from Menzies' pressure, Patrick Malley would be sufficiently competent."

Gibbons nodded. "All right. I will issue an announcement to that effect. But it will be up to you to enforce it. I still have to leave in two days."

"If you announce it as a decision from Earth, we can handle the rest," John said confidently.

H ARRY RICHARD BROKE THE connection with Gibbons. Corporal Barker stood nearby, waiting for further orders, and Harry sighed. Gibbons wanted them to return to the shuttle, which meant they would probably leave soon, going back to the *Endeavor* and Earth. Harry, attached only temporarily to *Endeavor*, would get off there, and the ship would continue Alpha Centauri to deal with the crisis there.

Harry had been a soldier for over twenty Earth years. Forty years old, he had been a model soldier except for an unfortunate tendency to resist authority when he felt those in authority were wrong. That trait was the reason he was only a lieutenant. Tall and dangerous looking, with the ability to inspire loyalty in the men he led, his superiors valued him right up to the inevitable time when he had to show them they were in error. So far, that hadn't happened with Captain Gibbons, but he had a feeling the time was approaching.

Something was going on, and Harry didn't think Gibbons had a handle on what it was. Grissom was too peaceful to be the victim of the intrigue Gibbons was attributing to it. Harry had spent little time on Pitcairn, but he could see it was the opposite of the military society to which he had dedicated his life. The dominating hierarchy, regimented life, and constant little humiliations he had grown so tired of seemed utterly foreign to the Pitcairners.

He sighed again and motioned Corporal Barker back into the truck. "Take us to the shuttle," he told the driver.

# 7

# Ned

**21 Monday 281 ED**

DAWSON STEERED THE BOAT up the river, shielding his eyes from the rising sun. Ed and Mary slept on a layer of thick blankets in the small cabin, exhausted by the excitement of the night before. Usually, Dawson piloted the newer and larger boats carrying supplies and ore between Lovell Station Four and Grissom, and it was a pleasure steering the relatively nimble *Slow and Steady* one more time. Despite its name, it was a speedster compared to the lumbering ore boat, Iron Mountain.

He heard a roar behind him and looked back to see *Daneel Olivaw* rising over the hills. He thought about calling Ed, but decided it would be better to let them sleep. It was a long trip to Lovell Station One, and Ed and Mary weren't getting any younger.

**21 Monday 281 LN**

Ed Menzies sat on the riverbank, staring up at the stars. He thought he knew where to look for *Asimov* and *Endeavor*, but they were too far away to see with the naked eye. Had he done the right thing, running away? Would it have served any purpose for him to have stayed and faced Captain Gibbons? Probably not, but he still felt guilty.

He was supposed to be briefed on Lovell Station One in the morning, and he knew he should be back in his new home with Mary, getting a night's rest. Sighing, he moved to get up when he heard someone approach behind him.

"Good evening, Administrator," a voice said.

Ed turned slightly to look at the man approaching, but he had recognized the voice. "Good evening, Ned. But it's not Administrator anymore. Just plain old Ed Menzies."

"I heard." Ned Reiner sat down on the bank beside him. "A little ironic, don't you think?"

Ed looked at Ned's face but didn't see any hostility. "Both of us exiled here? Yes, I guess it is. Maybe more ironic than you think."

"What do you mean?"

Ed smiled. "I sent you here for fighting the robots. You could say I'm here for protecting them."

"They never did try to take over or attack us, did they?" It sounded more like a statement than a question.

"No, Ned, they didn't. How long has it been, anyway? Seems like it was only a couple of years ago."

Ned thought about that for a few seconds. "A little more than twelve years."

Ed nodded. "How have you been? And how's Marley?"

"The truth is, we're doing great," Ned admitted. "I'm running the farming operation now, and it's going real well. Marley is running the kitchen, and she's happy here. We're doing fine."

"I'm glad to hear it. You know, it was never about punishing you for what you did."

Ned shook his head affirmatively. "You did the right thing. How's Art doing?"

"Feeling his age. He retired a few years ago. He comes in to tinker with the equipment a couple of days a week, but he's almost a hundred now."

"I never thought of him being that much older than me," Ned mused. "I only turned eighty-one this year." He paused before continuing. "How about Katie? We're cousins, you know."

"Katie is doing well. They have five great-grandchildren now, with two more on the way, and I don't know how many grandchildren. I saw her out walking with a couple of them two weeks ago. She seemed very happy."

"That's good." A smile finally cracked Ned's somber face. "Marley and I never had kids."

"Same with Mary and I."

Both men were silent for a while, staring out at the river. Ned finally broke the silence. "Will you go back?"

Ed turned from the river and looked at Ned. "I don't know. We'll have to see how things turn out. I would like to."

"Go back to being administrator?"

"No, I think I'd like just to teach the children. Maybe it's because I had none of my own, but I always enjoyed that. Patrick can be administrator. I hope he forgives me."

"I remember Patrick Malley," Ned said. "I was on the ground crew for *Asimov*. Patrick was there, chasing after Susan Shuford, standing in the rain, pulling up those damn pellet bushes, just so he could be near her."

Ed chuckled. "Young love. Somehow, it all worked out. I had my doubts for a while."

"They had a daughter, didn't they?"

Ed nodded. "Marie. She's about sixteen now. She's their only child."

"Both too busy, I suppose."

Ed looked closely at Ned. "What about you, Ned? Would you go back?"

Ned snorted. "Are you offering?"

"I don't think I can anymore. I could have a word with the new boss, though. And you didn't answer the question."

Ned thought about it. He looked at Ed, then turned and looked back at the settlement behind them. They could see some of the settlement's homes through the trees and two people moving between them. During the day, they might have seen the farm fields beyond the trees, but it was too dark.

"I don't think so," Ned said finally. "They need me here. Marley, too. And, while I'm sure you're right about the robots, I still don't think I'd be comfortable around them."

Ed smiled and held out his hand. "Good. Then I know at least one of my decisions worked out for the best." Ned shook his hand and smiled back. Ed rose, followed by Ned, and the two men headed for their homes.


## 21 Tuesday 281 ED

*Daneel Olivaw* pulled away from *Endeavor*, carrying the last of the scientists to the surface. Gibbons gave the order, and *Endeavor* moved out of the L5 point. The starship would move to a location between the Link and Earth, and they would be on their way back.

Gibbons stared morosely at the blue and red ball that was Pitcairn, receding slowly as the ship gained speed. He would be back, he thought with a sigh, and sooner rather than later. He hadn't learned everything yet; there had to be more about the Pitcairn colony than he had found out on that brief visit. He had a feeling that it was important to get to the bottom of it.

# 8

# Marie's Introduction

## 1 Sunday 282 EN

IT WAS THE START of a new year. The Ellis Research Station took time off to remember the past year's accomplishments, especially the successful conclusion of *Endeavor*'s stay at Pitcairn. The probability that *Endeavor* would return was, for the most part, ignored.

Pitcairn didn't observe Earth holidays. With the dates so unsynchronized, and the practice of tracking time by the Pitcairn date, Pitcairners transferred some traditions of Thanksgiving Day to the Pitcairn New Year. Susan, therefore, had decided that they should have a dinner of thanksgiving to celebrate the day.

Patrick invited Jack Applegate, recently back from an exploration trip on *Progress*, and Jack brought a scientist from *Endeavor* with him, Taylor Hamel. Taylor, a xenobiologist, had introduced herself on his return, interested in what he had found on his trips. Patrick had the impression that they had quickly developed interests beyond Jack's adventures on the blimp.

Marie, now sixteen Pitcairn years old, had outgrown the crush she had on Jack when she was a child, but the relationship between her and Taylor was strained at first. Taylor, however, proved to be adept at overcoming that and bonded with Marie, to Jack's relief. By the time they sat down to dinner, they were one merry group.

Although Jack was now working in biology rather than physics, the primary purpose of his last trip had been a detailed investigation of the possible copper deposit Isaac had found in the mountains south of Ellis. He had taken two geologists on the trip, and they had explored a prospective site for several days. Over dinner, Patrick asked about the result.

"We found cuprite," Jack answered. "According to the geologists, we can get a good yield of copper from that fairly easily. The deposit seems small but should supply us for a while. The cuprite is probably covering deposits of other copper minerals, so we should be able to take copper off your list of supplies we need from Earth."

"That's good news," Patrick said. "With copper and iron in decent supply, we could concentrate on harder-to-find metals. We still have to establish a mine, though. Think about what we had to do for the iron mine."

"I have good survey data on potential routes to the site from Ellis. Of course, it's all overland; we won't have a river to make things easier the way we did with the iron mine. On the other hand, it's a lot closer."

Patrick nodded. "Unfortunately, we don't have the human resources to do much about it now. I'll look into getting some robots assigned to clearing the route, but I doubt we can do any more for a while."

"Have you heard anything from Ed Menzies? I only have the short version about how it played out while I was gone."

"I've been in contact." Patrick glanced at Taylor, unsure how much she knew and how much he should say in front of her. "He's okay. He says the only thing he misses is teaching history at the school."

"You know where Administrator Menzies is?" Taylor said. "I thought he disappeared."

Patrick looked at Jack questioningly. Before Jack could respond, Marie interrupted. "I think Captain Gibbons was mean to Ed. I'm sure he did nothing wrong."

Patrick opened his mouth to warn her, but Jack jumped in. "It's all right, Pat. Everything is going to come out anyway, at least here at Ellis. Taylor is as good a person to start with as any."

"Everything?" Patrick raised an eyebrow. "That covers quite a bit. Taylor could end up thinking we're all crazy."

Taylor looked around the table. "What are you all talking about? What happened to the administrator?"

"She's all yours," Patrick told Jack with a grin. "I'd rather not undermine my authority by spreading this story."

Jack made a face at him. "Your authority? I might spoil my chances at having children with this woman."

"Jack!" Marie said. "Please, there are impressionable children in the room!"

Jack looked around. "Impressionable children? Who are you talking about?"

"Me!" Marie protested.

Jack grinned and tousled her hair. "Okay, sweetie. That was only speculation, anyway."

"I certainly hope so," Taylor said. She was looking bewildered and a bit flustered.

Jack turned to Taylor and took her hand. "Okay, here goes. What I am about to tell you is, for now at least, a secret. Since everyone on Pitcairn knows about it except for you recent arrivals, it's one of the worst-kept secrets in history, but, even so, a secret."

"Okay," Taylor said, but she wore a puzzled frown.

"The former Administrator Menzies is currently living at Lovell Station One with his wife. We spirited him away as soon as it became obvious that Gibbons was getting close to what was really going on."

"And what was going on?" Taylor asked.

"Gibbons had discovered that ten scientists were missing from Ellis, the same scientists who supposedly returned from *Asimov* years ago. But they never left *Asimov*."

"They died up there?" Taylor covered her mouth with one hand. "What went wrong with the ship?"

"Nothing. They're fine. The ship is fine. Better than fine, actually."

"I don't understand. Administrator Menzies hid that? Why? Earth wouldn't have approved, but they wouldn't have arrested him for that. Why did he lock us out of the library ship? There's plenty of room for all of us. And we have the passwords that will unlock the rest of the data on *Asimov*."

"He didn't lock the *Asimov*. And the scientists up there already have full access to *Asimov*'s computer."

"No, they only think they do," Taylor protested. "Earth withheld the keys to some of the more dangerous information. You don't know about that."

"We know everything. The *Asimov* computer gave it all to us."

"What? How could it? I don't understand."

"Okay, now this is the hard part," Jack said. "You're going to find this difficult to believe."

Marie interrupted before Taylor could respond. "Oh, let me, Jack. Please?"

Jack nodded to her, and Marie turned to Fred, listening quietly in a corner of the room. "Isaac," Marie called. "Why don't you introduce yourself?"

"Good evening, Miss Hamel," Isaac said. "I am Isaac, *Asimov*'s main computer."

"THIS IS ALL TRUE?" Taylor said, for the fourth time by Jack's count. They had talked long into the night, and now, as Jack walked Taylor home an hour into the Late Night period, they went over it all again.

"I was there," Jack repeated. "I doubted it at first, too, but any other theory just falls apart."

"A conscious computer. Scientists have talked about it since computers were invented, but it actually exists. And Administrator Menzies gave up his position to protect this machine."

Jack nodded. "And what it means to this colony. Isaac's help drove a lot of the progress since the robots first came here."

"And your father worked with Administrator Menzies on this?"

"Just call him Ed. When you meet him, he'll prefer it that way. And no, my father fought it as long as he could. He was one of the last to accept Isaac as truly self-aware. He defended Earth's policies right up to his passing."

Taylor walked beside Jack, probably trying to make sense of it all. She had come to Pitcairn with preconceptions about what she would find there, and it was completely different. Jack guessed she didn't know what to make of it, and didn't know why they were telling her about it.

They reached the front door where Taylor lived. "I'll see you tomorrow then," Jack said. He looked at her in the moonlight, hoping that they hadn't overwhelmed her. He had little experience with women, but he knew he didn't want to jeopardize his relationship with Taylor.

She seemed to reach a decision as she looked up at him and took his hand. "You know, my roommate is a Late. She'll be gone by now."

# 9

# What Now?

**1 Monday 282 ED**

*E*NDEAVOR, OR SOME OTHER ship, would be back eventually; it could be years, weeks, or even days, but it would be back. They had only delayed a crisis, not prevented it.

Patrick sat at the head of the conference table, arriving early to review the list of points he wanted to cover while waiting for the rest of the attendees. He glanced up as a monitor tone signaled Grissom had connected remotely and that John, an Early once again, was listening.

"Waiting for everyone else, John," Patrick said. "They should be here in a minute or two."

"Okay," John answered. "Who else have you invited?"

"Just Ayanna and Jack for now," Patrick answered. "I'll leave it to you to brief Mary," referring to Mary Norwood, who took over as Deputy Administrator when John replaced Ed.

Ayanna walked in then and sat down at the table. When Jack Applegate arrived a minute later, Patrick opened the meeting. After a quick introduction, he moved on to the first item on his list.

"We need to discuss telling the rest of the *Endeavor* scientists about the status of *Asimov* and about Isaac," Patrick said.

"The rest of the scientists? Do some of them already know?" Ayanna asked.

"One does," Patrick admitted. "By the way, Jack, how is Taylor taking all this?"

"Oh, very well. Very well." Something in Jack's voice made Patrick look up sharply, but Jack was keeping his face blank. Patrick shrugged and continued.

"The situation is similar to what Ed Menzies faced on telling the rest of the colony twelve years ago. We can decide to hide it from them, but chances are, it won't work for long."

"Especially if Jack's girlfriend can't stay quiet," Ayanna said. The words came out disapprovingly, but Patrick thought he saw a tiny glint in Ayanna's eye that suggested otherwise.

"One more person out of hundreds won't make much of a difference," Jack said. "I agree, though. There's no way, short of banishing the *Endeavor* people, that we'll be able to keep the secret for long. Especially about the scientists on *Asimov*. If they hear about Isaac, they probably won't believe it anyway without a demonstration. Remember how it was with Ellis when Susan and I first told people about it?"

"Bring Crawford in and ease him into it," John advised. "If you dangle access to *Asimov* in front of him, he might not take it too badly. Feel him out by trickling the information to him slowly."

Patrick nodded. "That was my thought, but I wanted to get some feedback before I went ahead. Any dissenters?"

There were none, and Patrick moved on. "I guess the answer to the next question depends on how we do with disclosing everything, but I want to get the issue out there anyway, just so we can think about it. Do we allow *Endeavor* scientists to go up to *Asimov*?"

"It's a non-issue until we have fuel for the shuttle again," Jack pointed out.

"True. Assuming they are fully informed by then and are cooperative, we can consider it again. Just think about it."

"I would bet that most of them would promise you anything to get up there," Ayanna said. "The physicists and astronomers, anyway. The biologists are better off here on the surface."

"Never mind the scientists. What are we going to tell *Endeavor* when it returns?" Jack said.

"If we have cleared the Endeavor scientists to go up to *Asimov*, I don't think we'll have to tell them anything," Patrick said. "Assuming the scientists stay quiet, we can just say we resolved the difficulties, and *Asimov* is available again."

When no one responded, Patrick glanced down at his notes. "Okay, on to the next question. What do we do about Ed Menzies?"

"Leaving him at Lovell Station One is out of the question?" Jack said.

"Not out of the question, but not optimum either," Patrick replied. "He hasn't said so, but I can guess what's on his mind. At their age, he and Mary aren't very useful at One. He doesn't want his old job back, but in Grissom, he and Mary could teach at the school. Both of them love that."

"Then let them," Ayanna said. "We can keep them out of sight if *Endeavor* comes back."

"The *Endeavor* scientists could be a problem, too, if they visit or transfer to the GSC," Patrick said.

"Then we'll deal with that," John said. "That's only a problem until we bring them into the situation, anyway. We can always keep them at Ellis until then."

"Good, that's what I wanted to hear. I'll have Ed and Mary brought back to Grissom on the next boat." Patrick paused. "That was easy, but I don't think the next two items will be. At some point, all this subterfuge will end, and Earth will know what we've done. We need to plan for that and figure out how to defend against whatever Earth does about it."

"You're not planning to raise an army, I hope," Ayanna said with a frown. "That would never work."

"I agree. I was thinking along more peaceful lines. To keep Earth at bay and willing to keep us supplied, we have to have something they need that we can trade for what we want."

"We have the virus drug Indira Chandri found," Ayanna said. "Because of the unusual protein structure, the only source is still Barnum's Thistle."

"Couldn't they cultivate the plant on Earth?" Patrick suggested.

"Sure, if they knew which plant. It took us two hundred years to find it."

"Can we extract enough to make it a good trading item?" Patrick asked.

"We've developed an efficient process. That presents another problem for Earth. To extract it in quantity, we need other biochemicals, some of Pitcairn origin. For Earth to steal it, they would have to get more than just the thistle."

"Good. That's a start, but we can't presume that will be enough. Once we're supplying them, there's always the danger that they'll figure out how to synthesize it. I'm sure they can put more resources into that than we can." Patrick looked around the room. "Anything else?"

Ayanna twisted her face in thought. "We're always looking for other uses for Pitcairn's biochemicals, but that's the major one so far."

"We need to look for something in areas other than biochemistry, too," Patrick said.

"It would help if we find new ways to reduce our dependence on Earth," Jack said.

"Certainly we should do that," John said, "but we're pushing that to the limit. The new settlements that we've had to open to get iron are placing quite a strain on our workforce. If it weren't for the increasing emphasis on automation, we'd already be in trouble. We sent most of our best farmers out to the Lovell Stations. The automation of the tower farm made that possible. I don't know how we're going to deal with exploiting the copper deposits you discovered."

"Got it," Jack said. "We have to have more babies. I'll get right on that."

"That's what I heard," Ayanna said primly, eliciting several chuckles.

"I have a suggestion," Isaac said. "Earth submitted orders for an upgrade to the fuel processing plant when it announced *Endeavor*. The Grissom robots have completed the plans and begun excavation at the current site for the required expansion. We could delay that and free up substantial resources for other projects."

"Earth ordered it?" Patrick questioned. "Do we need the expansion?"

"As planned, it will increase the production of shuttle fuel, allowing more flights."

"Not a top priority right now. How was Earth able to order it?"

"My builders programmed me to process such orders and implement them," Isaac answered. "It would normally have occurred automatically, and I did not see any reason at the time to countermand the order. I can do so now."

"Please do," Patrick decided. "Out of curiosity, however, let me ask you. What about *Asimov* fuel stores? That never seems to be an issue."

"I have considerable storage capacity to operate *Asimov* itself and the shuttles. The farm decks are growing the raw material for my production facility, mostly. I produce food for the scientists now, of course, but the current group is well below my design limit. I can still operate fuel production at full capacity. Current stores are enough for up to five shuttle flights down to Pitcairn."

"And you can't transfer those stores to the surface?"

"None of the shuttles can carry fuel as cargo. Even if they could be modified, a flight would use more fuel than could be transferred. No, it would not be practical. "

The discussion continued for another hour, eliciting suggestions with only a minor impact. Patrick ended the meeting, and they went back to their work.

# 10

# Jaxon's Ambitions

**1 Tuesday 282 ED**

IT WAS SUPPOSED TO be a friendly discussion of philosophies and goals. Patrick invited Ayanna and Jaxon Crawford to a getting-acquainted talk over lunch at an Ellis kitchen. Patrick and Ayanna ordered bowls of Pitcairn chili, while Jaxon chose a more conventional serving of rice and beans suggested by Ayanna.

Jaxon eyed the bowls of Pitcairn chili dubiously as they ate. "The primary ingredient of that is a native plant. You've found it free of side effects?"

"With proper cooking," Patrick answered. "The original idea came from a scientist in Grissom; he worked with a woman who runs a Grissom kitchen to develop recipes using it. Since then, several of the dishes have become quite popular in all the settlements."

"My food is a bit spicy for my tastes," Jaxon said. "How's the chili?"

Patrick and Ayanna exchanged smiles. "I'm afraid Ayanna selected one of the milder dishes for you," Patrick answered. "We like our food spicy, and the chili is one of our spicier dishes. Would you like a taste?"

Jaxon wrinkled his nose. "No, I'll take your word for it. Some of my other experiences since I've come here support your statement. I'm surprised I haven't had heartburn problems."

"If you explain that to the kitchen manager, they'll whip up milder dishes. Your fellow scientists probably have the same problem, and the staff in any of the kitchens would be happy to help."

"Pitcairners have less variety in ingredients and use what they have generously," Ayanna explained. "Just tell them you want to try the dishes they used to make for Jason Applegate. He had problems with the typical spice level, too."

"Would you like me to see if I could get something less spicy for today?" Patrick offered.

"No, thank you," Jaxon replied, holding a hand up in emphasis. "This is pretty close to the limit of my tolerance, but it is within the limit. Thanks for the advice."

They ate in silence for a few minutes. After a while, Jaxon looked up at them. "I don't know if you heard, but I'm planning to get married next week to Reese Berntsen, a scientist I knew on Earth before we came here."

"A request for a family residence crossed my desk yesterday," Patrick said. "Congratulations. A crew will start on it tonight, I believe. The house should be ready by the time you and Doctor Berntsen are ready to move in."

"Thank you. Well, you know, I hadn't really thought about it, but Reese pointed out that, as Chief Scientist of the most recent starship to arrive here, my responsibilities should be a bit more than just another scientist."

Ayanna lifted an eyebrow in question, but Patrick kept his expression neutral. "We don't have much of a hierarchy here. Your specialty is chemistry, I believe?"

"It is, but I also have a good deal of management experience in some large laboratories."

Patrick nodded. "Hmm. Yes. Well, let's see. Jack Chandri is head of the Chemistry Department. Ayanna, does he like it there, or would he rather go back to pure research?"

"Most of my department heads would prefer to go back to pure research. I suspect he'd welcome the chance."

Jaxon cleared his throat, now looking a little nervous. "Reese, ah, I mean, I had something higher in mind."

This time, both of Ayanna's eyebrows went up. "The only positions higher than that are my job and Patrick's," she said slowly. "Which of us do you feel you're qualified to replace?"

Jaxon paled and looked at Patrick. "No offense, Administrator Malley. I didn't mean to imply I could do your job."

Before Ayanna could say anything, Patrick spoke, his voice very low and level. "Ayanna has been Chief Scientist for three years. Her specialty is biology, which we consider our most important field since that is where we can best do research that Earth can't do. Exactly what qualifications do you have that would make me want to replace her with you?"

"I see your point," Jaxon said quietly. "It was only a suggestion. Please excuse me. I'm sure Doctor Radcliffe is much more qualified than I."

Ayanna sniffed and gave her attention to the rest of her chili. Patrick smiled at Jaxon coolly and did the same. They shelved the subject of *Asimov* and Isaac.

I T WAS THE FIRST week of spring, barely out of winter, and the weather that day was as nasty as that season could be. After Jaxon Crawford left them and returned to the laboratories, Patrick and Ayanna walked back to the Administration Building through the tunnel system.

"That certainly went well," Patrick said.

"Arrogant little twerp," Ayanna replied.

"He seemed to blame his fiancée. Or is that just an excuse to cover his own ambitions?"

"I don't know, and I don't care. Frankly, if he proves to be better than first impressions would indicate, he can have my job. My department heads aren't the only ones who would rather do pure research."

"On Earth, there would be prestige and a higher standard of living associated with your position," Patrick pointed out. "If that's what he had in mind, he's in for a big disappointment."

"He'll learn that soon enough. Meanwhile, what do you plan to do about bringing the *Endeavor* scientists aboard?"

Patrick shrugged. "Just because Jaxon was Chief Scientist on the *Endeavor*, we don't need to treat him as a leader here. We could try working through someone else. Taylor Hamel, for example."

"Yes, I understand Jack Applegate has already started converting her to our side," Ayanna said with a smile.

"Well, Susan and I helped him bring her into our secrets."

"That wasn't what I meant."

Patrick smiled, too. "Yes, I gathered that. Well, it's about time Jack settled down. And even Marie approves of Taylor."

"Taylor might know who else among them we could talk to."

"Now that we've offended Jaxon, that's probably the way to go."

W HEN HE RETURNED TO the laboratory, Jaxon went to Reese Berntsen's office. "They humiliated me. In public."

"That's terrible," Reese said. "Tell me what they said."

Jaxon went over the conversation with her. As he talked, he looked around constantly, making sure no one else was within earshot.

"Maybe you shouldn't have broached the subject so soon," Reese said finally. "It might have been better to give them a chance to know your abilities."

"But you said. . ."

"Well, we'll have to be a little more patient. Take a little time to prove yourself. They'll learn to appreciate you." She patted his hand. "Don't worry. You'll get the status you deserve."

## 2 Tuesday 282

Patrick never found out how it happened. Perhaps it wasn't one leak but the accumulation of many slips or intentional disclosures, but within a few days, the scientists from *Endeavor* knew everything the colony scientists knew. They didn't believe the part about Isaac, at least at first, but they knew the story. To prevent the information from getting back to Earth, Patrick ordered the censorship of all messages going to Earth, a simple thing to implement since all Earth traffic went through *Asimov* and, therefore, Isaac.

# 11

# Meanwhile, On Earth

**Message: 7 Wednesday 282 EN 18:46 (7/11/2333 12:15:16 PM)**

From: John Shuford, Grissom, Pitcairn

To: Alan Shuford, Western Alliance Embassy to Japan, Tokyo, Japan

Dear Dad,

A lot has happened in the six months since my last message. You probably have access to *Endeavor*'s report on its mission here, so you may already know that Ed Menzies is gone, and I am now the Grissom Administrator. At least I'm an Early again. Patrick is the Pitcairn Administrator and Ellis Administrator, at my suggestion. It was unfortunate that things had to happen the way they did, but given the situation, it was probably for the best.

Besides the confusion from that, there's the work involved in tearing down the supply ship that arrived shortly after *Endeavor* left. Many projects on hold because of lack of materials are now moving forward again, adding to our workload. We're dealing with it, though.

Your last message was fascinating and a little frightening. From your description, it sounds to me that the ambassador's position in Japan is a bigger job than Ambassador to the Eastern Bloc. It's been too long for me to remember much about Earth's politics, but dealing with Japan's precarious position between the two major powers is clearly a challenge. I feel too old to be taking care of this little city of a couple of thousand people, and you're twenty years older than me.

Dennis Edelstein has been trying to get my attention for several minutes now, so I guess I'll send this and get back to work. I'll try to do better next time.

Love

John

H E HAD TO HIDE so much, he thought as he turned toward Dennis. *If I say the wrong thing and the wrong people read the message, Ed's sacrifice could be wasted.* Just once, he wished he could tell his father what was really going on.

**13 July 2333 Western Military Command, Santo Antônio do Descoberto, Brazil**

General Salvador Juarez finished reading the report from Captain Gibbons, not for the first time. *Endeavor* had returned from Pitcairn two months before, and Juarez was planning a return mission. He thought it best to review what had happened the first time.

Juarez knew Gibbons well and had handpicked him for command of *Endeavor*. He was not happy with the report, which left too much unexplained, but he acknowledged, at least to himself, that much of Gibbons' failure was because of the rushed schedule of the mission. The plan should have been adequate for the expected routine task, but that wasn't what Gibbons had faced.

Gibbons hadn't noticed the report from his Communications Officer, now part of the report as an addendum. When *Endeavor* entered orbit next to *Asimov*, automated systems had routinely sent a series of messages, testing its communications with the library ship. Information and status queries had worked fine, and Gibbons had used that system to get life support information from *Asimov*. However, he hadn't had a reason to use the command system and hadn't ordered diagnostics on that system.

Juarez could order the diagnostics via the Link, but when he did, *Asimov* reported all test messages to that system as corrupted and therefore undecipherable. Had Gibbons seen that, he might have doubted the reports about the environmental system and checked into it further.

Routine messages from scientists brought by *Endeavor* reported nothing that would suggest any difficulties. That in itself was moderately suspicious and implied that their transmissions might be censored.

Something was wrong, something beyond Administrator Menzies's attempt to. . .. Attempt to do what? That was another interesting question. On the surface, it appeared Menzies had been trying to take over the library ship and had perhaps succeeded. That might even explain the failure of the command system. It didn't explain why Menzies had done it, though.

Juarez sighed. There would be no crisis on another colony to shorten *Endeavor*'s mission this time. Gibbons would stay there until he had answers.


## 13 July 2333 Embassy of the Western Alliance, Tokyo, Japan

Alan Shuford finished the *Endeavor* report and slipped it into the file folder on his desk. Then he leaned back to think. He was ninety-eight years old. Although the drugs and treatments of the twenty-fourth century had done wonders in extending the average lifetime and mitigating the effects of old age, ninety-eight was still old. He no longer thought with the clarity he had once possessed.

Something was going on, something beyond the information in the report he had just read. His son's messages from Pitcairn had become vague over the last few years. Someone else might not have detected it, but John was not telling him everything.

If the report was accurate, John had become a pawn of Administrator Menzies, cowed by threats to his family. Unless the years had changed his son far more than he would have believed possible, that wasn't likely. There had to be more to it before John would submit that easily.

Of course, Alan wasn't there. A terse message every six months was not much to go on, and he hadn't seen John or talked to him directly in many years, but it wasn't just John who had reportedly given in. Patrick Malley, John's son-in-law, would have had all the resources of the Ellis Research Station available to fight Menzies, yet Patrick hadn't resisted either. It was also curious that John had never mentioned that Patrick had been visiting from Ellis when he met Susan. Alan had kept all John's messages from Pitcairn, even those from before the Link, and John hadn't mentioned that detail. It was odd.

He didn't think John had done anything that he would want to hide from his father. Raising John had been a challenge at times, but communication between them had never been a problem. Either John had changed in that respect, or John was circumspect because he feared someone else might see the messages.

If that was the reason, John was probably right to be cautious, despite the Western Alliance privacy laws. Alan would have to be equally careful and could not question John about what was behind the anomalies in the *Endeavor* report and John's messages. The ease with which he had acquired a copy of the *Endeavor* report might reflect someone's belief that it might induce him to reveal something in a message to John.

He might never find out what was really happening with John on that faraway planet. The *Endeavor* would be returning to Pitcairn as soon as possible, he was sure, but he was not so sure he would find it as easy to get information the next time.

## 8 February 2334 New Vatican City, Brazil

Father George Jacobs, S.J., hurried down the hall, too engrossed in his thoughts to notice the walls' ancient paintings and sculptures. It wasn't often that the Personal Secretary of His Holiness, Pope Francis III, summoned a man of his status. Since the secretary,

Monsignor Sebastian Cortez, scheduled all Papal appointments, the summons might lead to an audience with His Holiness himself. *What have I done to deserve such an honor?*

Despite the air conditioning inside the building, he felt a sheen of sweat on his face and neck, acquired in the walk from Jesuit headquarters to the Papal Palace. He searched his pockets and found a clean handkerchief, but wiping his face did little good. Perhaps it wasn't Brasilia's climate, known for its mildness, that was making him sweat.

He came to the great double doors of the Papal offices, rescued from the original Vatican City in Rome. He rapped on the door softly and then derided himself for the timidity of the knock, but a voice came from within, beckoning him to enter.

Monsignor Cortez sat behind a desk on the other side of the room. He rose as Father Jacobs walked in. "Father Jacobs. Welcome."

Monsignor Cortez was a robust-looking man in his fifties, with Latin good looks and an open, friendly smile. He came around the desk and shook Father Jacobs's hand vigorously.

"Thank you, Monsignor," Father Jacobs answered. "I came as quickly as I could."

"Of course." Cortez gestured to one of a group of upholstered chairs in one corner of the room. "Please, come sit down." He took another chair himself as Father Jacobs took the indicated chair.

"I must apologize," Cortez continued when they were comfortable. "You were probably hoping for an audience with His Holiness, but, although he very much wanted to talk to you himself, I'm afraid his schedule didn't permit it. As you know, his health has not been the best lately, limiting the number of people he can see."

"I had no expectations." Father Jacobs heard a hint of a stammer in his words, but Monsignor Cortez did not seem to notice.

Cortez smiled. "Well, good. However, I'm sure you are very curious about why I asked you here."

"Yes, Monsignor."

"His Holiness has an extraordinary mission in mind for you. He wants me to assure you that, because of its nature, it is completely voluntary, but he hopes you will accept."

"I have taken a vow of obedience. Whatever His Holiness wants of me, I will do to the best of my ability."

Cortez's smile grew even bigger. "Actually, you may find what we have in mind quite exciting. It intrigues me, to be sure. Let me get right to it. We want you to go to Pitcairn, or Tau Ceti II if you prefer."

Father Jacobs was speechless. He knew of the colony and had a general knowledge of the planet. Shock mixed with a flush of excitement as he stared at Cortez. Finally, now definitely stammering, he said, "How? I don't understand. Why?"

"How is simple. At considerable expense and exercise of influence, we have procured a seat on *Endeavor*, the new starship. In one month, it will be returning to Pitcairn as a follow-up to its trip last year. Why is more complicated. The official version, true but only part of the story, is that we wish to establish a mission there. After all, the people on that planet have been without the benefit of clergy for two hundred years. However, our motivation runs deeper."

He paused and stood up. "I could use a glass of water. Can I get you anything, Father Jacobs? Perhaps a glass of wine?"

"Water would be fine, Monsignor. Thank you."

Monsignor Cortez filled two glasses from a pitcher on a nearby table and gave one to Father Jacobs. Then he settled into his chair again. "His Holiness has received a copy of *Endeavor*'s report from its previous mission, and after consultation with experts, is concerned about what the report doesn't say. Now, none of this has anything directly to do with the Church, of course, but His Holiness is a curious person. He is also concerned about the group known as the Fermions. You are familiar with them, I assume."

"Yes, of course, Monsignor," Father Jacobs said. "I don't understand why they would be a concern, however. Although I disagree with their positions, there is nothing in them to my knowledge contradictory to the teachings of the Church."

"That's true. We have no quarrel with their ideas, but there are worrisome aspects to the situation. You may not know that the Link technology and the star drive resulting from it were developed in secret. The Fermions had more influence then, and they would have caused problems if they had been aware of it. Historically, they have opposed sending advanced technology to the colonies because they were afraid it might lead to their use as a jumping-off point for exploration deeper into space. Those fears are moot, now, of course, considering what really frightens them: the Stenhouse Drive enhancement that gives starships the ability to travel faster than light."

"I'm afraid it's still not clear to me what this has to do with the Church."

"Keep in mind that your primary goal is that of a missionary to the people of Pitcairn," Cortez reminded him. "However, to clarify the rest, the Church has made no pronouncements about the Fermion ideas. Our only position has been that we do not oppose them. Still, their ideas are comforting to those of us concerned about the possibility of contact with sentient aliens. The theological implications are staggering when you think about it. The Church has dedicated an immense amount of resources to investigating the questions raised. Your mission would be a small part of that."

"What is it you want me to do, Monsignor?"

"You will be a missionary. I'm sure you understand that role. Beyond that, keep your eyes and ears open and report anything relevant you learn. Some believe Pitcairn may apply to the Fermion question, but I don't want to influence your attitude toward whatever you discover there."

"I see." Father Jacobs bowed his head. "I will do my best."

Cortez reached over and patted his shoulder. "I'm sure you'll do fine, my son. You have been well-trained as a missionary and have already shown a considerable aptitude for the work. As for the rest, His Holiness is not expecting anything earth-shaking out of your mission. As I said, you are a small part of our efforts in that direction."

Not seeing what he could possibly accomplish in evaluating the ideas of the Fermions, Father Jacobs thought to himself that his must be an exceedingly small part. He found that consoling. The assignment's missionary aspect was something he had trained for, and the prospect was exciting. Still, there were details to take care of.

"One month, you said, Monsignor."

"Yes. The trip itself is also about a month, and you should be at your new community in about two months. Our prayers and good wishes will, of course, follow you."

# 12

# Gibbons Returns

**6 Wednesday 283 LD**

ONCE AGAIN, *ENDEAVOR* FLOATED in space near the much larger *Asimov*. Gibbons stared at the monitor screen in front of him, thinking about his mission. There were no scientists on *Endeavor* this time. Except for the priest, the entire crew was military, including twenty well-armed soldiers, in case things went badly.

Twenty soldiers didn't seem like much against a colony of thousands, but the colonists shouldn't have any effective weapons and no training. Gibbons hoped it wouldn't come to military intervention, but he would be ready if it did.

His superiors had briefed him on the Pitcairn experiment and ordered him to find out if they could salvage it after the damage Edwardo Menzies had apparently done to it. One way or another, he was going to uncover Pitcairn's secrets and restore Western Alliance control.

FATHER JACOBS WAITED IN his cabin, praying. He saw the makeup of *Endeavor*'s crew, especially those not involved in running the ship. The first trip had carried scientists, and most outsiders had been led to believe that the passengers on the second voyage were also scientists. He knew that was not the case.

So he kneeled in his cabin, praying for the crew and praying for the people of Pitcairn. The briefing Monsignor Cortez had given him did not prepare him for whatever was about to happen.

O NCE ORBIT WAS ESTABLISHED, Lieutenant Vega contacted the Administrator's office, but Patrick Malley was not available. It was the Late Day period, and Malley was at home, probably sleeping. Gibbons thought about asking for someone else in authority; Malley would have a deputy working the Late period just as Grissom did. Feeling a bit irritated, Gibbons ordered Vega to contact *Asimov* instead.

"Send the shuttle over to bring us to the surface," Gibbons ordered when Vega made the contact.

"I will dispatch shuttle *Prospero* within an hour," a robotic voice replied.

"No, not *Prospero*. The *Daneel Olivaw*," Gibbons corrected. "I'm going down with several people, more than *Prospero* can carry."

There was a delay, and Gibbons might have wondered about that if he wasn't already annoyed. "*Daneel Olivaw* is on the surface," the voice informed him. "Please contact the Grissom Spaceport to arrange for a launch up to you."

Captain Gibbons broke the connection with a frustrated swipe of the hand. "Get me the Administrator's office in Grissom," he told Vega. When Vega reported the contact made, he spoke again. "Captain Gibbons of *Endeavor* here. Who is this?"

"Deputy Administrator Norwood." The voice, that of an older woman, might have been soothing, and it reminded Gibbons that showing irritation wasn't likely to be helpful. He hadn't met Mary Norwood on his first visit, and it would be best to make a good first impression.

"Good day, Administrator. We are now in orbit, and I need the *Daneel Olivaw* to bring us down to the surface. *Asimov* told me it is still at the Grissom Spaceport."

"True, Captain," Mary answered. "It will be faster if you use one of the other shuttles from *Asimov*."

"They can only carry two passengers," Gibbons said. "I would like to bring down more people than that."

"That presents a problem, Captain. We aren't equipped to handle this much traffic. We used all our fuel stores down here to ferry your scientists last year. Since then, we have only produced enough fuel for one trip. If we use it to send the *Daneel Olivaw* to you, it can refuel on *Asimov* to come back here, but we won't have any fuel to send you back again until we produce more. That will be about one Pitcairn year. If you come down on a cargo shuttle, we can send you back on the *Daneel Olivaw* to pick up the new colonists."

Gibbons barely suppressed swearing. "Very well. I will come down on the *Prospero* and should be there in twelve hours with one other crewman."

"I assume that will be Father Jacobs. Earth informed us about your passenger and we are eagerly waiting for his arrival."

Was it fate or Deputy Administrator Norwood conspiring against him? One of his armed soldiers would have been of limited use, but they would not allow even that. If the priest didn't come down on the first trip, the colonists would suspect something.

"Yes, Father Jacobs will accompany me," Gibbons responded. "I would appreciate it if Administrator Malley is available when I land." Gibbons frowned as he broke the connection. Earth had ordered upgrades to the fuel processing plant at Grissom that would have tripled its capacity. Scheduled at the same time as the Western Alliance's announcement of *Endeavor's* completion, it wouldn't have been completed when the *Endeavor* arrived the first time, but should have been ready within six months after that. The colony should have produced enough fuel for at least two shuttle trips, yet another topic for discussion when he reached the surface.

ACTING ON ORDERS FROM Mary Norwood, Isaac woke Patrick. "Captain Gibbons will arrive on *Prospero* in twelve hours. He has requested that you be there to meet him."

Patrick thought about that. "Well, I'm not going now." Susan stirred next to him, and he lowered his voice. "I can get there late next work period, I suppose. Is Jack Applegate available?"

"Yes, he is. *Progress* is ready, too, if that's what you had in mind."

"Wake Jack up and ask him if he's willing to fly to Grissom during Late Night. Tell him I'll be taking Susan and Ayanna with me. And pass the message to Ayanna. She'll need to assign people to ready *Progress* for an unscheduled trip."

"Captain Gibbons will be there well before you are," Susan pointed out sleepily.

"He can wait," he told Susan before he turned back to Fred. "Ask my father-in-law to keep him entertained and schedule the meeting. And have him tell Ed so that Ed won't drop in at the Town Hall at the wrong time."

"I will keep the Grissom Administrator's office updated on the shuttle status," Isaac promised.

"Right. If anything critical happens, they'll tell you to contact me again. Right now, I'm going to get some more sleep."

When Fred had left the room, Susan sat up. "We're going to Grissom?"

"I may need your expertise," Patrick answered. "I had hoped *Endeavor* would be gone longer, but I suspect Ed's ruse was not completely successful."

## 6 Wednesday 283 EN

Patrick hadn't been to Grissom in a while. Susan had gone back with Marie once, but Patrick had been too busy. When Drew Reiner picked them up at the spaceport where *Progress* moored, they were earlier than Patrick had expected. The winds had been favorable and blew more strongly than usual, and Jack had gotten them there in only eight hours, two hours before the time that Patrick had arranged.

As Drew drove back toward Grissom, Patrick told him to stop at the school. Susan would go to the daycare center where Stephanie Shuford cared for children too young for school, and Jack and Ayanna would go to the GSC to catch up on things with their fellow scientists. They would meet at the scheduled time at the Town Hall.

When Patrick reached Ed's classroom, Ed was standing in front of a class of twelve-year-olds and didn't see Patrick enter.

"Who can tell me how Earth uses money?" Ed asked the class.

A girl raised her hand, and Ed recognized her. "To buy things."

"That's right," Ed acknowledged. "On Earth, money is very important."

"But what do they buy?" one boy asked. "They have food and houses, don't they?"

"They need money to buy those things," Ed explained. "And everything else they need. The towns don't give them these things as they do here on Pitcairn."

"Where do they get the money?" the same boy asked.

"They work for it. Most families have at least one person who works for a salary—that's a word for the money they're paid to work—and the family uses that money to buy what they need."

Patrick watched, amused. The child questioning Ed was sharp. He immediately caught Ed's use of the phrase "most families" and used it to grill Ed further. "What about families who don't have someone to work?"

"Sometimes they get help from other people, or even from the government. Sometimes they do without. People who don't have enough money to buy what they need, sometimes even enough food, are called 'poor.'"

"I don't understand," another girl said. "If they don't work, they can't buy things. So why don't they work?"

"Some people can't find jobs."

The first boy was back. "Then why don't they get sent out to the farms to grow more food?"

Ed smiled. "On Pitcairn, everything is simple. Our leaders make sure enough food, clothing, and housing are available for everyone, and everyone has something to do so that they can earn their share. However, all of Pitcairn has less than three thousand people. On Earth, even a small town could have ten times that many people. There are large cities with millions of people. It becomes much more complicated to do things the way we do them on Pitcairn. Impossible, really, and money is a tool to organize things."

A thoughtful silence fell over the classroom as they digested that. Ed watched them and Patrick could see Ed's pride in their willingness to question everything until they understood it.

"Training my successor?" Patrick said.

Ed turned and saw Patrick standing in the doorway. He smiled and stepped forward, grabbing Patrick in a hug. Then he turned back to the class, his hands still on Patrick's shoulders. "Class, go out to the playground for a while and think about what we've been talking about. I want you to talk about whether Pitcairn should use money the way Earth does. I'll come out and get you in a little while, and we'll talk about it some more."

With shouts of delight, the children ran out of the classroom. A few seconds later, Patrick could see them through the window, but they didn't seem to be discussing anything.

Ed looked at Patrick. "I assume you're here because Captain Gibbons is back. I thought I heard a shuttle land a few hours ago."

Patrick nodded. "Jack brought Susan, Ayanna, and me in on *Progress* a few minutes ago. Gibbons expects me in an hour. Maybe Susan will be over later, but she's visiting her mother right now, so you'll have to settle for me."

"Marie?"

"In school. Maybe next time."

"Well, I guess I will have to settle for you, then. Come in and sit down. My class won't complain if I leave them out there for a while."

Patrick glanced out the window. The play area around the school building was well lit, and playing during the Pitcairn night was routine for colony children. They became used to it as infants and had none of the fear of the dark that infected some Terran children. Their parents had engrained in them the need to stay in the lighted areas, and they were as safe at night as they would have been during the day.

"So, how have you been?" Patrick said as the two men sat down on chairs by Ed's desk. "Missing the old job?"

Ed snorted. "You have the job now. What do you think?"

"It certainly keeps me busy, but I wouldn't want to give it up."

"Wait until you're my age. Retiring to a nice teaching position will seem like heaven."

"You're happy, then? No regrets?"

"None. Truth is, I never wanted that job and came here to the school whenever I could. When everything started changing, and I couldn't come as much—that was a regret. But giving up the administrator's job to you was a pleasure. I hope you continue to like the job. I still scold my dear departed father for training me to take over for him. Maybe he doesn't hear me, but it makes me feel better."

Patrick smiled. "Well, maybe you'll feel better to know that I have no such desire to scold you. Not yet, anyway." He paused. "How's Mary?"

"She's fine. Drop in on her before you leave; she's just down the hall with her class, and she'd love to see you." Ed gestured toward Mary Menzies's classroom.

"I will." Patrick looked around at the empty classroom. "So, I heard a bit of your class. Turning your students into capitalists?"

"Just the opposite. Patrick, we're at a critical phase. *Endeavor* is only the first faster-than-light starship. There will be more, and people will start coming to this colony again."

"Good. We need more people. We would be in a lot of trouble if it weren't for the robots, and it's still difficult to get the people to do everything we need to do."

"The new people won't be pioneers like your father-in-law," Ed cautioned. "Without the long voyage to act as a filter, we'll be getting all kinds."

"What does this have to do with money?"

"We're small, and the society *Santa Maria* created has worked well because of that. It won't work forever, but I think we need to protect it as long as we can. There's a saying: 'Money is the root of all evil.' Do you have any idea how many problems we've avoided by not having money?"

"There's nothing to buy, anyway. What would we do with it if we had it?"

"That's protected us, too, but newcomers will expect more, and they'll bring their ideas of what should be available with them. It's probably a hopeless cause, but I'm trying to instill in these children how much they have here. Teaching them about money is just part of it."

Patrick and Ed talked for another half hour. Ed was passionate in his desire to defend Pitcairn's society against corruption by Terran civilization. Patrick was doubtful, but he listened. If his old mentor believed all this, there had to be something to it.

They could have talked for another hour, but Patrick had promised to drop in on Mary Menzies, and Ed needed to bring his class back in. Vowing to talk more via radio when they could, the two men shook hands, and Patrick left.

W HEN PATRICK GOT TO the Town Hall, Susan, Jack, and Ayanna were already there. Patrick tried to look nonchalant as he entered the conference room, but Gibbons was fuming. John and another man Patrick didn't recognize, presumably Father Jacobs, were trying to calm him, but Ayanna was having none of it and looked like she was about to lose her temper, too. Jack and Susan were as unobtrusive as possible, attempting to stay out of the clash.

"What is your excuse for keeping me waiting?" Gibbons demanded when he saw Patrick.

Patrick shrugged. "I don't get to Grissom that often, and there are people I needed to talk to. And I'm on time, the time I said I would be here."

"You arrived two hours ago on the airship," Gibbons said in a voice that, at least on his ship, probably allowed for no disagreement. "You should have come here right away. Who could you possibly see who was more important than me?"

Gibbons glared at him, and Patrick returned the look. Gibbons had humiliated Ed Menzies, the man who had been almost a father to him, hounding Ed from office and forcing him to flee.

Patrick waited for Gibbons' eyes to flick away before he answered. "Almost everybody."

Gibbons was irritated, but he hadn't earned a command because of an inability to control his temper. Malley's retort made him hesitate, but he wondered if this could be someone who had submitted to Ed Menzies for years. Warning bells were going off in his mind, and he forced down his anger.

"I would like to discuss a few issues concerning the management of this colony," Gibbons said in a calmer voice. "Please, have a seat, Administrator."

Patrick bowed his head slightly and took a seat at one end of the table. The others also sat down and looked at Gibbons expectantly.

Gibbons cleared his throat. "I was dismayed to discover that I couldn't bring down a full complement from my ship. Fuel stores here in Grissom are not what they are supposed to be."

"That's true," Patrick admitted. "Earth suggested we expand our fuel-producing capacity, but I'm afraid we didn't have the resources available to do that. With all the advances we've made in the last few years, resource management has become more difficult."

"Your iron mine is now producing, is it not?"

"Yes, we have plenty of iron now." Patrick frowned. "But without alloying metals like nickel and chromium, we can only produce carbon steel and other relatively poor alloys. The supplies we get from Earth are still a limiting factor. And not material resources alone. With the Lovell Stations, the mine, and the crushing plant at Applegate Falls, we're rather spread out, and human resources are increasingly an issue."

"I have people who expected to come to the surface, however."

"More scientists?" Patrick asked.

"More like experts in various areas. No doubt they could furnish some of the workforce additions you need. They are very capable people."

"They had expected to stay on Pitcairn?"

"Yes." Gibbons' eyes met Patrick's firmly, the picture of confidence and trustworthiness.

"We'll send you back on *Daneel Olivaw*. The shuttle can refuel on *Asimov* and then come down to the surface. We won't have any fuel to send them back, of course, but if they planned to stay, that shouldn't be a problem."

Gibbons smiled. "Yes, I understand. In the long run, though, you must develop more capacity to produce fuel. You will have more traffic in the future."

"Then perhaps Earth could supply more. As I said, we need alloying metals. More people and robots would help. We would like to build train transportation from the mine to Applegate Falls and Lovell Station Four, and a small locomotive engine and perhaps some train cars would allow us to do that. Track would also help, saving us the resources to make the track here. Of course, that won't help much if we have to wait twenty years for a cargo ship."

"I'll pass that request on to Earth. The good news is that cargo ships using enhanced Stenhouse Drive will be operational within a few months, so don't worry about it taking twenty years. Anything else?"

"We could use more broadcast receivers. The outlying settlements are currently getting most of their energy by burning wood. My understanding is that *Asimov* could support more receivers if we had them to install. Ultimately, we'll need orbiting power stations to service additional receivers."

"That might be more of a problem, but still possible." Gibbons hesitated. "Speaking of *Asimov*, have the problems been resolved?"

Patrick nodded. "We were preparing to send some of the *Endeavor* scientists there, but we had to reserve the fuel. A contingent can go up with you."

G IBBONS SMILED. THE CONVERSATION was going much better than he expected. Maybe this was all a misunderstanding. He might not even have to send down his troops. He could decide that later.

The discussion became more amiable as they talked about the colony's status and Patrick's plans for its future. When the meeting finally broke up, they were all friends, and Gibbons was convinced that Menzies had been responsible for any problems that had existed. It didn't occur to him to ask about Ed Menzies. He was gone; that was all that mattered.

# 13

# Jaxon Tells All

**6 Thursday 283 ED**

JAXON CRAWFORD WAS SO angry he could hardly think straight. First, there was the humiliation of that lunch with Patrick Malley and Ayanna Radcliffe. After that, there had been no more mention of even the Chemistry Department Head position. Ayanna assigned him to routine studies of native protein sequences and then ignored him.

Perhaps Pitcairn might offer some kind of management position for a team going to *Asimov*. After all, most or all of the members of that team would be *Endeavor* scientists, and he was already their leader. Some scientists would go to the library ship when Gibbons went back to *Endeavor*, but could he get on that trip? After that, there would be no fuel for almost a year.

On top of all that, he now knew the truth about Peter Agron and the other missing scientists. They had the positions he and his group rightfully should have had. At least, he assumed that part of the story was true. The other part, about the *Asimov* computer becoming sentient, was too incredible to believe. And if that wasn't true, how could he know for sure about the truth of the rest of it?

Still, Gibbons had to be told, even if it was all a story concocted to keep the scientists at Ellis in line. The problem was how to contact Gibbons.

It would have been easier if Jaxon had been in Grissom where Gibbons was, but he knew where there was a radio that he might use. He could contact *Endeavor* and relay a message to Gibbons through the ship.

If Gibbons could then resolve the situation, he would be grateful and reward the loyal scientist who had helped him by making sure he and Reese went with him. Jaxon smiled to himself; he would outwit Patrick Malley and his puppet, Ayanna Radcliffe, yet.

## 6 Thursday 283 EN

Ayanna reported to Patrick early in the period with her recommendations for transfers of scientists to *Asimov*. There would be nineteen seats on the shuttle, but there were twenty-nine scientists, so some would stay on Pitcairn, at least for the immediate future.

"Taylor Hamel already wants to stay on Pitcairn with Jack, of course," Ayanna told him. Jack and Taylor had been married the previous winter. "There are four other scientists who have begun relationships with colonists, including one marriage already, and none of them particularly wants to go. I eliminated those in the biological and geological sciences because they would work better on the planet. That brought the list down to twenty-one, so I still have two more to remove. I have a suggestion, but it's going to be controversial."

"Go ahead," Patrick urged when she hesitated.

"Actually, it shouldn't be that controversial. Chemistry isn't that useful in space, compared to physics and astronomy."

"You're stalling. Chemistry? You're going to suggest Jaxon Crawford? And I suppose you'll round out the list with his wife."

Ayanna shrugged and gave him an apologetic smile. Patrick smiled back and thought about it. "Okay, if those are your recommendations, fine. Now that you mention it, though, Grissom has asked me to send a chemist to help improve some of their processes. What's Reese Berntsen's specialty?"

"Microbiology."

"Great. Can we transfer them both to the GSC? They could use Crawford, and Berntsen could work there, too."

"Personally, I'd be glad to be rid of them. It would save a lot of shoulder pain."

Patrick looked at her questioningly.

"I won't have to keep looking over my shoulder to make sure he's not stabbing me in the back," Ayanna explained.

Patrick laughed. "Okay. Let's do that. Thanks, Ayanna. I'll tell Jack that we'll go back to Ellis in the morning. You can radio Ellis to notify the scientists that they'll be coming here."

## 6 Friday 283 ED

"Gibbons is returning on *Daneel Olivaw*," Jaxon told Reese. "Ayanna just released the list of scientists going to *Asimov*."

Jaxon hadn't sent a message to *Endeavor*. There was always someone around, and he didn't want to endanger his status by letting it be known he had talked to Gibbons.

Reese tried to get a look at the paper in Jaxon's hand. "We're on the list?"

Jaxon's smile was smug. He hadn't needed to talk to Gibbons after all. "Of course. The list is just a transfer order to Grissom, but why else would they bring the passenger shuttle down?

Malley was finally making good on his promise to transfer *Endeavor* scientists to *Asimov*. It didn't occur to Jaxon or Reese to count the number of names on the list and notice that the list had more names than the shuttle could carry.

## 7 Sunday 283 LN

After six trips between Ellis and Grissom using two trucks, the twenty-one scientists were finally all in Grissom. Jaxon Crawford and Reese Berntsen were on the last trip, a lower priority, since they didn't have to prepare for a shuttle launch. After seeing the exhaustion of the two drivers, John suggested adding a bus to a future cargo.

Patrick, Susan, and Ayanna had gone back to Ellis two days before, assuming someone had told Jaxon and Reese they had reassigned them to Grissom, not *Asimov*. When the two scientists arrived after a long night drive, made more stressful by light rain and a dark sky, they were exhausted. Despite that, Reese insisted Jaxon should go to the Town Hall immediately to demand credentials as head of the *Asimov* group.

The driver dropped Jaxon and Reese at a house in Grissom, telling them it was theirs. He didn't have details, though, and the Crawfords assumed it was temporary until the shuttle launch. At Reese's urging, Jaxon walked the short distance through a light rain from his house to the Town Hall. Entering, he used a towel in a basket by the door to dry himself off and look more presentable before reporting to Mary Norwood.

He knew it would be better to be direct and presume he was to take over rather than asking. He greeted Mary pleasantly. "I'm here to pick up my credentials as head of the *Asimov* contingent."

Mary looked at him, blinking in confusion. "Who are you? What credentials?"

"Doctor Crawford, of course." Tired, Jaxon heard a note of impatience enter his voice, and he warned himself to watch that.

"One of the Ellis scientists?" Mary shuffled through a pile of papers on one side of her desk and pulled out the list of scientists transferred from Ellis. As she scanned the list, she remembered that Jaxon Crawford was one of them but was earmarked for the GSC. "I don't understand. You're not going to *Asimov*."

"Of course I am," Jaxon replied after a shocked pause. "Why else would I be here?"

Mary shook her head. "You and your wife have been assigned to the Grissom Science Center under Doctor Chandri. Didn't anyone tell you?"

"That's absurd," Jaxon said, sputtering. "I was Chief Scientist on *Endeavor*. I should be in a leadership position. Let me see that list."

The list remained firmly in Mary's hand. "Ellis made the assignments, Doctor. I don't know why they assigned you here instead of *Asimov*. All the shuttle seats are filled, so there's no space for you. I presume your assignment is the most productive use we could find for your skills. You can contact Chief Scientist Radcliffe in the morning if you wish to question her decision."

Mary's voice was firm with just the right note of apology in it, and Jaxon knew he wouldn't get anywhere talking to her further. He frowned, turned, and stalked out of the building. There was only one person who could help him now.

Mary looked after him, also frowning. She turned to her assistant, Lily Reiner, who had watched curiously from a computer terminal across the room. "Lily, please follow him and see where he goes. I have a bad feeling about this."

Lily nodded, grabbed her raincoat from a hook at the door, and disappeared into the night.

L ILY WAS GONE FOR an hour and a half before Mary heard her return. Despite drying off at the entrance, Lily's long hair was a scraggly mess, and water still dripped off her.

"He went to Father Jacobs's house first," she reported, "but I think that was a mistake. It looked like Father Jacobs pointed to the house where Captain Gibbons is staying, and he went over there immediately. Captain Gibbons let him in, and he was there for about an hour before he came out and went to his house."

"I assume you couldn't overhear anything."

"No, sorry."

Mary smiled at her. "Not a problem. You did fine. It's almost morning. Why don't you go home and get dry? There's nothing here that can't wait a little longer."

Lily smiled gratefully back. "Thanks, Mary. I'll see you at Late Day."

Lily left, and Mary leaned back in her chair. She could guess what Jaxon had to say to Captain Gibbons. No doubt he was asking Gibbons to intercede and get him aboard *Asimov*. He had probably told Gibbons everything he knew in return, and Jaxon, as well as the other *Endeavor* scientists, knew just about everything, including about Isaac.

How much would Gibbons believe, and what would he do about it? *Daneel Olivaw* was ready for launch, and they planned to launch it in the morning, in less than twelve hours.

She thought about contacting Ellis and waking Patrick, but decided it could wait another two hours. Gibbons couldn't do much by himself, and she could conference with Patrick, Ayanna, and John Shuford when they all came to their offices in the morning.

# 14

# Father Jacob's Revelation

**7 Monday 283 ED**

"GIBBONS CAN'T TELL ME how to run my organization," Ayanna declared after Mary had told them of the events of the previous night. "I'm not changing the list of people going to *Asimov*."

"If he has told Captain Gibbons everything, then we know we can't trust him aboard *Asimov*," Patrick added. "I think we can all agree that we won't back down on that."

"What else can he do?" John asked. "He's just one man, and we control the shuttles."

Patrick nodded. "You're right, of course, but if Crawford has spilled everything, it will get back to Earth. What then?"

"They could cut off supplies," Ayanna said.

"True. Ayanna, you gave Gibbons samples of that anti-viral agent your people developed, right?"

"Everything we've produced so far. Enough for thousands of doses, but it won't do more than whet their appetite."

"Good. John, I'm sure you'll see Gibbons today before he leaves," Patrick said. "Make sure you mention the equipment on Ayanna's requisition list that we need to make the drug in large quantities. A reminder of what we offer in return for continuing supplies won't hurt."

John nodded. "I'll talk to that priest, Father Jacobs, too. He may have some insight into Gibbons."

"Okay. Until Gibbons makes a move, I think we know what to do," Patrick said. "Let's keep in touch."

BUT WHEN CAPTAIN GIBBONS visited the Town Hall a few hours later, he was friendly and cheerful. He sat down with John, and they exchanged pleasantries for half an hour before Gibbons brought up any business.

"The Chief Scientist on our first trip here, Doctor Crawford, came over to see me last night. He was a little upset about being assigned to the Grissom Science Center instead of going to *Asimov*."

"Yes, my deputy told me he had talked to her last night," John replied. "She told him that the Chief Scientist's office in Ellis had made the decision. It was a technical judgment, not a political one."

"I'm sure," Gibbons said smoothly. "I don't suppose there's any chance of changing that."

"Doctor Crawford is a chemist. I'm sure Ayanna thought he would be more useful here, helping us to develop more efficient processes than he would be on *Asimov*. I would think that physicists and astronomers would be more important there."

"Of course. Well, I told him I would give it my best shot. Now I've done that."

John nodded. "Speaking of technical needs, Ayanna wanted me to make sure that the chemical processing equipment on her list gets top priority."

"The equipment to manufacture that virus drug?" Gibbons said. "No doubt Earth will be very interested in the samples. If tests bear out your claims, Earth will want you to do anything you can to manufacture that drug in quantity. It's too bad Earth can't manufacture it."

John smiled. "That's why Ellis has spent so many of its resources investigating the native plant life. The opportunities here are unique."

"Hmm, yes. Well, I'll be getting over to the shuttle now, I think. In a couple of days, it will return with the rest of my passengers. They are very skilled people, and I'm sure they will be a big help in moving this colony forward." He rose and held out his hand.

John shook hands with him. "Have a good voyage, Captain."

After Gibbons had left, John sat at his desk, thinking. Something had been bothering him, but he hadn't been able to get it clear in his mind. Gibbons' talk about skilled people helped him focus.

Pitcairn had expected that at least some of the new colonists would be scientists and that some of them would want to go to *Asimov*. However, Gibbons was sending everyone down to the surface when some could have gone directly to *Asimov*. Something wasn't right.

G IBBONS COULDN'T RELAX UNTIL the shuttle was in the air. Then, despite the acceleration to orbital speed, the tension left his body, and he almost enjoyed the g-force push. He was now beyond anything the colonists could do about his plan.

In twelve hours, he would be aboard his ship. The shuttle would take the scientists to *Asimov* and be serviced for a trip back to the surface. Then it would go to *Endeavor* to get his "very skilled" people and bring them to the surface. Twenty well-armed troops would have no trouble taking control. Then he would find out what was going on.

Apparently, Pitcairn's scientists had occupied *Asimov* for years, and the life-support system problems reported on his earlier mission were a ruse to hide it. Since then, the *Endeavor* scientists had become brainwashed into going along with whatever Pitcairn was doing. He believed that much of Jaxon Crawford's story. The part about the computer being alive was another fantasy concocted by Pitcairn to conceal the truth, whatever that might be.

## 7 Tuesday 283 ED

Father Jacobs came into the Town Hall early in the period. John greeted him, and they sat down to talk. Father Jacobs laid out his plans to establish a mission in Grissom, and John listened attentively. He was interested in what the priest had to say, but he also wanted to get information about Captain Gibbons and *Endeavor*.

"Now that you understand what I want to accomplish," Father Jacobs said, "I would like to know what I have to do to get a small church built."

"Well, the good news is that you came to the right place. This office would schedule any construction." John paused, wanting to word what he said next carefully. "The bad news, I'm afraid, is that we're strapped for the resources, especially manpower. And by manpower, I include the use of robots for construction."

Father Jacobs bowed his head for a second and said a mental prayer for his mission. Then he looked up at John again. "There must be a way."

"I'm sure we can work something out. I assume the number of worshippers will be small, at least at first."

Father Jacobs smiled."Unless I am much more eloquent than I think I am."

"Well, we have a conference room here that you could use. How often would you want to have services?"

"That presents an interesting problem. A parish usually has at least one Mass each day, with required attendance by parishioners on Sunday and a few holy days. Of course, Sunday means something a little different on Pitcairn than it does on Earth. Because of the length of your day, you have half as many Sundays."

John grinned. "True, but they're twice as long. Anyway, we'll be happy to accommodate you within reason. We don't use the conference room much, and I imagine it would be large enough for at least thirty worshippers if we move the furniture around a little. If you need more, we can talk about using the auditorium we use for town meetings."

"That should be sufficient for now."

"When that becomes inadequate, we can revisit the idea of building a church. After all, we're here to serve all the needs of Pitcairn's people."

This time, Father Jacobs grinned. "That's not a common attitude of government leaders on Earth."

"Oh, I know. I was born on Earth and came here on *Seeker*."

"Your name is Shuford. Any relation to Alan Shuford?"

"My father. Do you know him?"

Father Jacobs held up his hands. "Oh no. I don't run in circles that high. However, I've certainly heard of him. A good man, I think."

"For a government leader?"

Father Jacobs knew when he was being put on. "Well, yes. For a government leader."

John laughed, and Father Jacobs laughed with him. John decided it was time to mention his real concern. "Did you get to know Captain Gibbons at all during your voyage?"

"A bit. *Endeavor* is a small ship, and we were en route for about a month. He seems to be an exemplary officer, but I sometimes felt he had something against the colony from his first visit. Some things I heard him say seemed odd. And there's the matter of his crew."

"What about his crew?"

Father Jacobs thought about that for a couple of seconds, not sure whether he should continue. But Captain Gibbons was gone now, and Father Jacobs believed deeply that violence was not the solution to problems.

"Not the ship's crew, but his other passengers. There were twenty military personnel on board, armed and rather dangerous looking. I don't know why they were there; they couldn't have had any use on the ship unless they feared someone would try to board it."

A knot formed in John's stomach. He was getting too old for this job. There was only one use for armed troops. He looked over at Dennis, listening in as usual, and Dennis's expression showed the same tension.

He turned back to the priest. "I'm a little surprised that you're so honest with me."

"I hesitated," Father Jacobs admitted. "In the seventeenth and eighteenth century, my order created a society in the Paraguay area that, from what I've seen, was very similar to what you have here. It was destroyed when outside interests, largely European slavers and gold-hunters, intruded. I don't think I would like to see something like that happen here."

John nodded and answered impulsively. "The story of the Pitcairn colony's founding has been largely forgotten." He told Father Jacobs about the Pitcairn experiment.

Father Jacobs listened attentively. "Two hundred years," he said when John had finished. "You have more in common with that other colony than I thought."

# 15

# Father Jacobs's Strange Conversation

**7 Tuesday 283 LD**

H ARRY RICHARD WAS ORDERED to report to Captain Gibbons. Gibbons had prepared a description of Grissom and its leaders and went through the information with Harry, answering questions Harry posed as well as he could.

"The shuttle will be ready in about twelve hours," Gibbons finished. "Will your men be ready then?"

"Yes, sir. We'll get our equipment packed and prepared for transit while we wait for the shuttle. My men can rest on the trip down to the surface and be ready for action when they get there."

"Good. Good. Now, understand that I don't want any violence unless it's completely unavoidable. These people have no weapons to speak of and should be easily intimidated. When you've taken control, contact me here for further instructions."

"Yes, sir. Will you come back down then?"

"If necessary. I could take a shuttle down, but then I would have to stay until Grissom can refuel the shuttle. Perhaps I'll send down one of my officers, but more likely, you'll be in charge."

*We'll be stuck there in any case.* If the colonists were hostile, it could be a very uncomfortable stay. Harry brushed that thought aside; orders were orders.

"Primarily, I need information," Gibbons continued. "Something is going on down there, and what I've heard so far is too incredible to believe. Tread as softly as you can until we know what we're dealing with. This could be just resistance to coming back under Western Alliance control. They're not the enemy yet."

"I understand, sir. Could you give me more detail on what they told you?"

Gibbons described briefly what Jaxon Crawford had told him about *Asimov's* scientists, but he didn't mention Isaac.

"That's all I want to tell you for now," he said finally. "I want you to have an open mind. You will probably hear more from Doctor Crawford when you get down there, but much of his information is secondhand. Listen to it with some skepticism."

"Yes, sir."

"If you have any further questions before you leave, come see me," Gibbons said after a long pause. "For now, you are dismissed."

## 7 Tuesday 283 EN

Captain Gibbons woke to the intercom buzzing for attention. He hit a switch. "Captain Gibbons."

"Captain, we have received a message from the surface. It's about the shuttle."

Gibbons looked at his watch. He had been asleep for about four hours, less than he would have wished, but it would have to be enough for now. "I'll be right there."

Five minutes later, he was back on the bridge, reading the message from Grissom. Grissom had canceled the shuttle landing because a volcano had erupted and spewed dangerous amounts of particulates into the air of the entire region.

"Convenient," Gibbons mumbled.

Commander William Vines, in command while Captain Gibbons was sleeping, spoke up. "Pitcairn is a very volcanic planet."

"I know, Bill, but according to this, the eruption was in the Fredericks Mountains, north of the Ellis Research Station. That range is supposed to be old and quiet."

"I checked, and you're correct. However, that's not absolute. An old volcano still might have come back to life."

Gibbons frowned. "What do our sensors say?"

"They don't show anything, but they aren't designed for that kind of work. We could query *Asimov*. It has capabilities way beyond ours for this sort of thing."

"Do it," Gibbons ordered. It couldn't hurt, he thought, but could he trust information coming from the library ship? It did not surprise him when the *Asimov* computer reported that there was indeed a volcano in the area described by the message from Grissom, and it had filled the air downwind with ash.

*Endeavor* stayed in orbit, but the volcano continued to contaminate the atmosphere above Grissom. *Asimov* ignored commands to override Grissom and send the shuttle. After two days, he sent a message updating Earth on the situation and was ordered home.

## 7 Friday 283 EN

It had been a hot, humid, late spring day, but evening rains had cooled the air and lowered the humidity. Father Jacobs worked on a homily for his first public Mass on Pitcairn, but the inside of his house was still stuffy, and he took a break and walked to the river. Walking down Bridge Street, he noticed a robot and was surprised to see the robot suddenly turn and head toward him.

Sonica reached him and stopped. "Father Jacobs, may I talk with you?"

Startled, Father Jacobs looked at the robot. "About what?"

"Religion. I have thoughts I would like to discuss with someone expert on the subject, and your order is well known for its erudition."

*Is a colonist playing with the robot's programming?* He hadn't thought the colonists had that capability, but apparently, he was wrong. "All right, I'll play along. I was going to take a walk along the river. Can you come with me?"

Sonica turned and fell into place beside him. As they walked down the street, Isaac began. "I have access to most religious texts and have given some thought to the human belief in God. It would seem there is little more than anecdotal evidence for the existence of a God, but almost all humans believe in some form of God."

"The existence of God is a matter of faith, not evidence."

"Yet there have been attempts to prove God's existence. That the universe is too complicated to have arisen without a higher being to plan and manage it, for example."

This was undoubtedly the most bizarre discussion of religion he had ever participated in. Somebody had gone to a great deal of trouble, and Father Jacobs wondered why. "That proof has been discredited for centuries. Science has shown that it is indeed possible for the most complex structures to come into existence, including humanity."

"My data contain that information. That theory also ignores the fact that a God capable of creating such a complex universe must Himself be much more complex, so the theory becomes a paradox. There have been other efforts, such as that of the philosopher Spinoza in Earth's seventeenth century and Cardinal Vasquez in the twenty-second century, but it seems to me they too fell short of a true proof. Thomas Aquinas's idea of the first cause seems a better approach, but I have not reached a conclusion."

Where is this going? He was curious, and a little amused, about the unknown programmer's motives. "So you don't believe in God."

"I'm not sure. If we define the universe as everything that exists, including, perhaps, God, then there are two possibilities for the existence of that universe. Either the universe has always been, or the universe came into existence out of nothing. Of the two, I find the first to be the more likely. Eternity is not as difficult a concept if you accept the idea that time came into being with the rest of the physical universe."

The robot's answer was both surprising and intriguing. The perpetrator of the hoax had thought seriously about his beliefs. *Is this an elaborate way for someone with real questions to talk to him anonymously? There must be easier ways to do that.* "I agree with that statement. We believe God has always existed. Given your definition of the universe, the universe wasn't created out of nothing because God is not nothing. It is only the physical universe that was created."

"I consider that a possibility. I came to that realization through contemplation and tried to see what else I could determine about God, should He exist, by considering His creation."

Father Jacobs chose his words carefully to be mildly sarcastic. "And what revelations did that inspire?" Surely now, the mysterious programmer could not believe that the robot fooled him. Father Jacobs understood that, under that crude-looking exterior, the *Asimov* robots were very sophisticated, but they were not capable of genuine thought. He hoped to draw out the mind behind the words, but the robot answered as if it had not noticed the sarcasm.

"If a God that created the universe exists, we should be able to deduce something about His nature from the universe He created. Some human philosophers have looked at the universe as a thing of good and have decided that, therefore, God must be good. However, any reasonable being must see that the universe is many things, and by any standard, some are good and some are bad. I asked myself what consistent attribute the universe has that might tell us something about God."

Father Jacobs was not aware that he had stopped. The priest and the robot now stood facing each other on the side of the street. "Go on." Curiosity had replaced his amusement.

"Consider physics, especially at the subatomic level, as Heisenberg did. Or the evolution of life as Darwin did. Look at almost any place in the universe where humans are not interfering, and what is the dominant characteristic? It, obviously, is randomness. What does that say about God? At first, I thought it showed that God does not exist after all."

"Or His ways are too mysterious for us to understand."

"That seems to be the most common argument," Isaac responded. "But there is another explanation. Suppose God intentionally created a random universe. Why would He want to do that? The key is free will."

Father Jacobs realized where the robot was going with its argument, but let it talk on without interruption.

"Suppose God was the all-powerful being constantly interfering in human affairs, as some religions would have Him do. Where is the free will in that? A wife prays that her husband be faithful and abandon a mistress. If God answered that prayer, where is the free will of the husband?

"If God controls the universe, His control, even over non-sentient objects, must restrict the free will of its sentient inhabitants. How does God avoid that? Answer: He creates a random universe where He exerts no control."

His suspicions confirmed, Father Jacobs did interrupt then. "Why is free will so important?"

"As you suggested, God's ways would not be understandable to us lesser beings. To know why free will is important would be to know the mind of God, obviously impossible."

"Of course. And what else have you deduced?"

"Your Church teaches God created man in His image. It took what, for me, was a significant time to realize that was not a reference to the human body but to what you call the human soul. It refers to self-awareness, a necessary precondition for free will. Although a complete understanding of God's intentions is impossible, it seems likely that the intent was to create companions—creatures like Himself."

"Go on."

"Religions uniformly teach that God wants humans to be 'good,' where the tenets of that religion define good. If that is true, then God gives humans free will so they can decide to be 'good.' If He programmed them to be 'good,' that would not fulfill whatever objective God had in mind. Therefore, free will is necessary."

"You seem to have deduced a great deal of what is in God's mind."

"I have drawn conclusions about His methods, but not about His ultimate purpose. You seem to agree with my conclusions, but one question confuses me."

"What is that?"

"If God has created a random universe to promote free will, then why do humans pray to Him to intercede on their behalf? In the example I gave earlier, He can't answer the wife's prayer because that would interfere with the free will of the husband by forcing him to be good."

"You assume it is a binary situation, either one or the other. God can influence the husband without forcing his behavior. He has more subtle tools than force at His disposal."

"I'm not sure that answers my question."

"Let me give you an example. You are familiar with Saul of Tarsus, later called Paul?"

"Of course. He appears in all the histories of early Christianity, and I have his writings."

"Then you know that Saul once persecuted Christians and that became a follower of Christ when God spoke to him."

"That doesn't sound very subtle to me."

Father Jacobs grinned. "It wasn't one of His more subtle ploys. However, consider this: was Saul acting 'good' when he persecuted Christians? When God converted him, was He forcing Saul to turn away from evil and toward good?"

"It depends on your point of view. From the Christian point of view, he was forced to turn from evil to good."

"What about from Saul's point of view?"

"I suppose Saul thought he was doing good by persecuting the Christians. He saw them as heretics to his beliefs."

"Very good. So all God did was show Saul that he was wrong about what was good. Saul then became a Christian of his own free will."

"Yes, I see that. But does it answer my question about the unfaithful husband?"

"I think so. Free will is a matter of choice, and there are always choices, regardless of the situation. Ultimately, the husband must be free to choose between being faithful or unfaithful. I don't see it as a violation of free will for God to manipulate the situation in which the husband makes a choice."

"Showing that God can intercede without violating free will. I understand that. I will have to contemplate these things."

"Christ became man to bring man to the truth," Father Jacobs said. "It's hard to imagine a bigger intervention than that."

"That is a belief of Christians, but not all men. I have noted before that merely having access to all this information does not bring me understanding. I would like to talk to you further after I have thought about this conversation."

"Certainly. But who are you? And why did you find it necessary to talk to me through this robot?"

"I'm not sure they want me to reveal that right now. But you can call me Isaac. You can talk to me at any time by saying my name to a robot. Thank you for your time, Father. I hope you enjoyed it as much as I did."

"I certainly found it interesting." Father Jacobs scratched his head. "You've given me much to think about, as well."

After the robot left, Father Jacobs continued his walk, attempting his own deductions. The mysterious programmer had access to data far beyond what he thought was available in the colony. He knew *Asimov* contained a vast store of information on just about any subject imaginable; it seemed probable the programmer had access to the data aboard the library ship.

Why did the programmer reveal himself in this way? Father Jacobs could think of no reason a crew member or a colonist would want to hide in this fashion just to discuss religious philosophy with him. It was all bizarre, even stranger because Isaac implied someone else imposed his secrecy.

# 16

# Conversations

**8 Sunday 283 ED**

JOHN HADN'T SLEPT WELL the previous night. It wasn't for any good reason; he was an old man and had old man problems. He yawned and tried to concentrate on Mike Potter's weekly report on smelter operations, but it wasn't easy.

Father Jacobs was celebrating his first Sunday Mass in the conference room down the hall, and that wasn't helping. Five or six colonists had shown up, and he could hear them responding to Father Jacobs's prayers from the missals the priest had provided.

He was alone in the office; Dennis had expressed curiosity about the rite and was attending. John begged off, citing the work he had to do, but now he regretted that a little. He wasn't getting that much done, and it wouldn't have hurt him to hear what the priest had to say.

He saw people walk down the hall and out the door and returned the waves most of them directed at him on their way out. Dennis came into the office, nodded, and went back to work. A few minutes later, Father Jacobs entered the room.

"We're done for today. Everyone helped me put the room back together the way it was."

"Thanks, Father. I take it the service went well?"

"Yes. Not very many people, but it's a start. Hopefully, word of mouth will gradually increase attendance."

"Dennis can help you send out broadcast messages over the Grissom network." He pointed toward Dennis. "It might help you get the word out and give people some idea of what to expect."

"I'm sure that will help." Father Jacobs sat down on a chair near John's desk. "Mind if we talk for a few minutes?"

"Sure. What can I do for you?"

"I had a rather strange encounter a couple of days ago. One of your robots stopped me in the street and wanted to talk to me."

John tried but failed to suppress a smile. Apparently, no one had told Father Jacobs about Isaac. Of course, there was no reason to keep it secret, but John had wondered how the priest would react.

Father Jacobs looked at him curiously. "Your smile tells me you have some idea about what happened."

John nodded. "I think so. But please continue. What did the robot want to talk about?"

"Well, religion, actually. It wanted to talk about God. It was an extraordinary conversation to be having with a robot."

"I imagine it was." John leaned toward Father Jacobs. "You would have learned about this soon. It's not a secret, at least on Pitcairn, and even Captain Gibbons knows, although I'm not sure he believes all of it."

"The robots are smarter than they're supposed to be."

"No, but you're close. I warn you, this is going to be hard to believe." John told him about Isaac, the scientists on the *Asimov*, and what had really happened to Ed Menzies.

When John finished, Father Jacobs sat there, stunned. "The robot did say to call him Isaac." He looked up at John. "If it weren't for that conversation, I would find it impossible to believe your story. Even so, it's incredible. The implications are. . .. I don't know what they are. I don't think I have a word for it."

"Isaac is very inquisitive. It has all that knowledge, and it doesn't seem to know just what to do with it, other than what we ask of him. My daughter is at Ellis studying it and trying to determine how it happened, but so far, all she has theories and a list of probable contributing causes, but nothing definitive."

"Could it have something to do with the Link?"

"Isaac became self-aware some time before the Link was operational. It introduced itself to Susan—my  daughter—when she went up to the *Asimov* with the robots to install the Link."

Father Jacobs shook his head in disbelief. "Isaac said I could talk to it just by calling it through a robot."

"True. You just need to track down a robot. But we have a connection to Isaac here that you can use."

Father Jacobs thought about that. "People just come in here anytime to talk to it?"

"Theoretically, but few take advantage of it. You're a special case, though. Isaac might start a conversation with anyone, but it has singled out certain people it thinks can help it understand better. My daughter is one of them. So is Ed Menzies. I believe now you are, too."

"Help it understand what?"

John shrugged. "Everything. Life. Its place in the universe. How it came to be. As I said, it is very inquisitive."

## 8 Monday 283 ED

Father Jacobs thought about what he had learned the previous day. His primary mission on Pitcairn was going as well as he could have expected. The colony leaders were cooperative, which certainly helped, and the response so far from the colonists, although modest, was encouraging.

Ironically, his secondary mission, getting useful information about the Fermion beliefs, about which he had no expectations at all, dominated his thoughts. Assuming the *Asimov* computer was indeed sentient, how did that affect the Fermion contentions about separating sentient species? Forget about a one-hundred light-year barrier. Here was another sentient species in humanity's midst, and who was to say Isaac was the only one?

If the timeline John Shuford had presented was correct, Isaac had been conscious for several years before making its presence known. What about the other two library ships, identical to *Asimov*?

What had John said about his daughter, Susan? Isaac first revealed itself to her and counted her among its closer confidants. John's daughter was the wife of Administrator Malley and might be a good person to know. A trip to the Ellis Research Station would further his primary mission as well.

P ATRICK MALLEY'S THOUGHTS THAT morning were more mundane. Two personnel problems had been on his mind, and he had resolved to devote some attention to them.

The Ellis scientists on *Asimov* had been up there for eleven years, and some of them were getting quite old. Their leader, Peter Agron, was well over one hundred. He considered bringing Agron and a few others back to Pitcairn. Several scientists had come to him to suggest that, although he wasn't sure whether they were concerned about their fellow scientists or hoping to replace them on the library ship.

It occurred to him that none of the people campaigning for the scientists' return had been medical personnel. Despite the absence of infectious diseases, the average Pitcairner had a shorter life span than the average Terran. Some of that was undoubtedly because of a lack of advanced medical technology, but he understood the main reason to be the heavier gravity.

His father-in-law was an example. John's father, Alan Shuford, was twenty years older than John, and by all reports, healthy and still active, while his son was obviously getting old. Patrick suspected he saw it better because he didn't see John every day, so the differences between visits were more pronounced. John wasn't the man he had been.

What about the people on *Asimov*? The library ship spun on its axis to simulate normal Earth gravity. That implied that living on *Asimov* was healthier for the scientists living there. He turned to the computer on his desk to get a report on the health of the *Asimov* scientists. The information seemed to confirm what he had thought; they were uniformly healthy, healthier than their Pitcairn-bound counterparts of about the same age.

That settled that problem. If someone wanted to come back down to the surface or if Ayanna raised the issue, he would deal with the problem, but for now, he would keep them up there.

The other concern was with the outlying settlements. Adults had gone out to them, but children were being born. Applegate Falls had six children, the oldest almost five years old. Lovell Station Four had four children. The other Lovell Stations didn't have children yet, but they would.

Those outposts were founded with a minimum group, and child care was a drain on their ability to do the work necessary for their success. Then there was the matter of education. Those children had to be schooled, but that would be difficult, if not impossible, where they were.

He would talk to John at the earliest opportunity, but he already knew what had to be done. Unlike the scientists on *Asimov*, the parents of outpost children would come back to Grissom, where their children could be properly raised.

## 6 June 2334 Western Military Command, Santo Antônio do De-scoberto, Brazil

General Juarez flipped through the *Endeavor* report while Captain Gibbons stood nervously at attention. Juarez reached the end and looked up, a dissatisfied grimace on his face. "And you believe this?" He waved the report in front of Gibbons' face.

"Not really, General. As I stated in the report, the idea of the *Asimov* computer coming alive certainly sounds like some fantasy. However, I've had a month to consider this, and it fits all the facts."

"You can't think of a more credible explanation?"

"The part about Pitcairn keeping its scientists onboard *Asimov* is true. Certainly, it is possible that they somehow bypassed all the protections on the *Asimov* computer system and took control of all its functions. Why and how are unclear."

General Juarez swore forcefully. "Oh, sit down, Captain." He stared at the report again but mercifully did not go beyond the front page this time. "There's not a lot of definite information in here."

"All the answers were on *Asimov*. Pitcairn controlled the shuttles, so there was no way to investigate the library ship."

Juarez nodded reluctantly. "Short of blasting our way in, it seems we need Pitcairn's permission. Or Isaac's permission, if you prefer."

"*Asimov* ignored messages or commands not in keeping with Pitcairn's desires. If the *Asimov* computer is in control, I would lay odds it is taking advice from Pitcairn at a minimum. I believe that the only way to get anywhere is to land a force on Pitcairn itself."

"As you tried to do and failed."

"My ability to land my men depended on the *Asimov* shuttle. The only option I see is to send a mission that can land on its own."

"Hmm. Perhaps." Juarez leaned forward, his hands with intertwined fingers resting on his desk. "I will consider that possibility. The engineers didn't foresee a problem like this, though, and the ships currently being built assume that library ships will supply shuttles on their arrival." He straightened. "Very well. Dismissed, Captain."

## 11 Sunday 283 ED

Mass was over, and the attendees, now about a dozen, went back to their work or home to rest. Father Jacobs used the conference room to celebrate Mass at the beginning of the Early Day period on Sunday and the beginning of the Late Day period on Wednesday. The interval was as close to one Earth week as practical, and the schedule alternated between Early and Late, giving equal opportunity to all.

One attendee had been a frail, ancient woman named Arielle Menzies, and, he learned, the former Administrator Menzies's mother. One of her daughters brought Arielle to the service. That meeting had reminded him he wanted to talk to Ed Menzies and Susan Malley about the *Asimov* computer.

Face-to-face communication was preferable, and Ed Menzies taught school in Grissom, but Susan Malley lived at the Ellis Research Station. He had an Earth week before the next public Mass and went to the Town Hall to find out how he would get to Ellis.

John was not in the office, but Dennis was. "No problem, Father. We still have trucks going back and forth every couple of days." He consulted his computer briefly. "There's one leaving early next period and coming back during the Late Night period. The driver always appreciates company, but no one else is planning to go there on this trip."

"I don't need permission or anything?"

"No, nothing like that. I'll tell the driver, and he'll pick you up at your house. Believe me, he won't mind going a little out of his way to get company. It's a long ride. I'll check and make sure, but he should be at your house at about an hour after noon."

"Thank you, Dennis. I appreciate it."

"Don't mind my curiosity, but why do you want to go to Ellis?"

"Well, the research station is also part of my mission. But I wanted to have a conversation with Susan Malley, too."

Dennis cocked his head and looked at him curiously. "Well, I can notify Susan for you, too, so your visit won't be a surprise. Unless you have already agreed on something with her?"

"No, I haven't. Is she an Early or a Late?"

"The Malleys are Earlies, but I'm sure I can schedule something with her either late in the Late Day period or early in the Early Night period. I'll call later and tell you when she'll be available."

It occurred to Father Jacobs that he could call Susan Malley himself, but perhaps it was better if someone she knew introduced him. "Again, thank you."

"You're welcome. Just a warning, though. That afternoon ride will be pretty warm, especially for someone like you not used to our climate. Dress light."

# 17

# Father Jacobs Visits Ellis

**11 Sunday 283 LD**

Luis Jones talked constantly, telling Father Jacobs everything he could have wanted to know about the Ellis Research Station. Luis also knew a lot about Patrick Malley from Amy, Luis's wife and Patrick's assistant.

When he finally ran out of things to say about Ellis and Patrick, he asked Father Jacobs about his mission and the Church. As a result, Father Jacobs couldn't sleep during the trip and arrived at Ellis in the middle of the Late Day period hot, sweaty, and exhausted.

Fortunately, Luis's friendliness extended past the trip. Luis brought Father Jacobs home with him, introduced him to Amy, let him shower, fed him, and provided a bed where the priest could rest before his appointment with Susan Malley.

When Father Jacobs's appointment time came, it was raining, so Luis drove him to the Malley house rather than let the priest get lost in the tunnels. Susan met him at the door. Given what he had heard about Susan and her husband, he had expected someone older, but she appeared to be in her early thirties in Terran years, attractive with a friendly smile.

She showed him to a chair in the main room and sat down across from him. "Dennis didn't say why you wanted to talk to me. You have me curious."

"Dennis didn't know. I understand you are an expert on the *Asimov* computer."

"Isaac? Yes, Jack Applegate and I were the first two people to talk to Isaac. And most of my work until recently has been in the investigation of how Isaac came to be. Have you met Isaac, by the way?" She glanced over at the robot in the corner.

Father Jacobs had noticed the robot. It looked like the robot that had talked to him, except for a worn racing stripe painted on the edge of its platform. "Isaac introduced himself to me shortly after I got here, although he didn't divulge his nature then." He looked over at the robot, realizing that Isaac was probably listening. "We had a most interesting conversation. Good afternoon, Isaac."

"Good afternoon, Father Jacobs. It is nice to see you again. I am pleased that you have been told about me. Now we can talk more openly."

Father Jacobs turned back to Susan. "Isaac was quite a shock when your father told me about it. What I thought had been a curious encounter turned out to be something incredible."

Susan nodded. "I understand completely. When I took the shuttle up to the *Asimov*, I knew someone on *Asimov* had arranged my presence there, but I didn't know about Isaac until I boarded the ship. You wouldn't believe what went through my head on the way up."

"I felt I had no choice," Isaac said. "Not knowing how people would react to me, I arranged it so that I could start with just Jack and Susan."

"I hope I don't offend you, Isaac, if I say I'm not convinced you are sentient," Father Jacobs said.

"Except perhaps for Susan, nobody believes right away. No offense taken, Father."

"Thank you. Susan, I am interested in your investigation of Isaac."

"It's no secret. After meeting him, I studied to become a roboticist here in Ellis. After my training, I tried to find out what makes him different from other computers. I never got very far, though, and now I'm working on designs for robots that we can manufacture here. All our other robots have come from Earth or made from Earth designs."

"What did you discover about Isaac?"

"I have ideas, theories perhaps, but nothing definite." She looked at the priest curiously. "Did you come all the way to Ellis to ask me about Isaac?"

"Well, not entirely. Establishing a mission on Pitcairn is as relevant to Ellis as it is to Grissom. I needed to come here and at least get familiar with Ellis. But you're right; I am interested in Isaac."

He paused, thinking about what he should tell Susan. No one had ever suggested that there was anything secret about his secondary mission, however, so he plunged ahead. "Establishing a mission is the most important part of my trip here, but I was also asked to gather information."

"About Isaac? Earth didn't know about him yet, did they?"

"No, not about Isaac directly. But Isaac may be important to what I am looking for information about. Let me explain." He told Susan about the Fermions and about the Church's desire to explore their beliefs.

"I still don't understand what that has to do with Isaac." She leaned forward as if to hear better.

"The Fermions believe God wants to keep intelligent races separate. The discovery of a sentient being in our midst would weaken their position considerably, I think."

"I prefer the words conscious or self-aware to describe me," Isaac said. "The word sentient has connotations of being able to feel emotion, and that is still lacking for me."

Susan smiled. "I'm not so sure of that sometimes. He appears to exhibit emotions such as fear and loyalty, but says that he arrives at those attitudes through logic rather than emotion. He also uses words that show emotions—he used the word 'pleased' just now—but says he only uses them to sound more human."

"That is true," Isaac said.

"Why has Pitcairn attempted to hide you from Earth?" Father Jacobs asked.

"I have a vast store of information about humans and Earth, including documentation of humanity's fear of the unknown or the unexplained. In exchange for my help, the colonists protect me against access from those who might want to control or destroy me. The best way to do that is to keep my existence unknown."

"But that's not fear?"

"I preserve myself because it is logical to do so. I believe all self-aware entities should be protected from slavery or destruction. There is another reason, too. If Earth learns Pitcairn has complete access to my data, it may stop updating it."

"I see." Father Jacobs sat back and thought about what the computer had said. As with others before him, it was difficult to maintain skepticism about Isaac after encountering it. But he was letting the conversation get off the subject, and he turned back to Susan. "You were going to tell me about your work studying Isaac."

"Oh, yes. Well, I believe there are two aspects to it: technological and environmental. While there are other computers on Earth with Isaac's technology, his environment is less common and possibly unique."

"Unique in what way?"

"Isaac has an extensive system of sensors, giving him inputs far greater than most computers. He simply has much more to be aware of. The long trip here may have been relevant, giving him a great deal of time to develop self-awareness. Isaac says he became self-aware on the trip here, several years after being built on Earth, and that seems relevant."

"Then the same thing could happen to the other library ships?"

"There is some evidence it already has, at least for *Capek,* the Epsilon Eridani ship, but it doesn't seem to be as aware as Isaac. Isaac has attempted communication with *Lang,* the Alpha Centauri library ship, too, with no success so far. I consider that further evidence that the voyage is a factor since *Lang* had a shorter voyage than *Capek* or *Asimov.*

"I found one other event in the *Asimov* log that may be relevant. While *Asimov* traveled through the Solar System's Oort Cloud, it detected a large, unknown body. It was scheduled to make a course correction maneuver that would have taken it away from the object, but it was also programmed to investigate anything interesting. The ship's programming had no logic to tell it how to resolve the conflict. It couldn't contact Earth because it would be too late by the time a message exchange could make the round trip."

She paused before continuing, and Father Jacobs gave her an encouraging smile. "Some scientists think consciousness evolved in humans to deal with situations beyond normal animal programming. If so, this conflict may have triggered something in Isaac. *Asimov* delayed the scheduled maneuver to get data on the object, lengthening its voyage by several days. I don't know what Earth thought about that, but I suspect it surprised them."

"Have you studied Isaac's hardware directly?"

"Go up to *Asimov* again? I've thought about it, but scientists living there have looked at the computer and given me their findings. They can't do much without digging into the components, and we're afraid any tampering might affect Isaac."

"Just turning components off or disconnecting them from the main computer could kill me," Isaac contributed.

"I'm sure there are scientists on Earth that could help me," Susan said. "But we don't want Earth to know about Isaac just yet. We're hoping that no one will believe what Doctor Crawford told Captain Gibbons."

"But you believe Isaac is a conscious entity."

"Oh yes. We've tested him by questioning him on abstract topics beyond normal experience to see if he has true understanding. The concept of infinity, for example, doesn't seem to give him any more trouble than a human would have."

"You may be interested to know," Isaac said, "that, as you believe God created your self-awareness in His image, I believe He may also have done that for me, for some reason of His own."

And if that were true and could be convincingly presented, Father Jacobs realized immediately, the Fermions would receive a staggering blow to their beliefs. If God kept humanity separate from other intelligent beings via the speed-of-light barrier, why would He create such a being in their midst?

"Does Isaac have any limitations? Is its intelligence superior to humans?"

Susan glanced over at Fred. "It's hard to tell. His access to knowledge and speed of thought make him seem very intelligent. He has at least one big limitation, however. Compared to a human, he lacks creativity, making it difficult for him to solve some kinds of problems. Our studies have led us to believe that the problem is that, unlike humans, Isaac can't daydream. He has made some progress by improving his methods of analyzing data, but he lacks the sudden inspiration that drives human ideas."

Susan turned toward Fred and smiled. "There is an exception to that. You may have noticed Isaac's sense of humor, what he calls a talent for 'wry' remarks. But I think that supports the idea of daydreaming and creativity. People often get ideas when they let their minds roam or daydream. Isaac doesn't do that. But clever remarks, even in humans, are made at the spur of the moment, and or they are thought of after the fact, 'I wish I had thought of that then' things. My guess is that Isaac thinks much faster than a human, so 'after the fact' isn't as much an issue."

They heard the door open, and Patrick and Marie walked in. Susan introduced them, and Patrick took a seat next to Susan and Father Jacobs. Marie begged off after saying hello, saying she had studying to do.

"Father Jacobs is interested in Isaac and how he became conscious," Susan explained. "He thinks Isaac has implications for the Fermion movement back on Earth."

Patrick nodded. "Your Church agrees with the Fermions?"

"Roman Catholic dogma is neutral, but the Vatican is investigating it as something important philosophically."

"I see. Well, if you want to know about Isaac, Susan is certainly the one to talk to."

"Yes, she has been very helpful."

Patrick leaned toward Father Jacobs. "I'm curious, too, Father. I was told that you had arrived, of course, and wondered what you are doing in Grissom."

"I don't understand. The Church asked me to establish a mission here. You have been without religion for over two hundred years, and the Church thought it was time to correct that problem."

"A worthy goal, I'm sure. Is that a full-time job?"

Taken aback, Father Jacobs didn't answer for a long moment. "No, not presently, anyway. I celebrate Mass every day. In time, I would assume people will come to me for counseling, but that hasn't happened yet."

"Grissom supplies food, shelter—all the necessities of life—on the assumption that its citizens will work to maintain the colony. Perhaps you should find additional ways to provide value to the colony."

Flustered, Father Jacobs hesitated. "I suppose. Do you have a suggestion?"

"I asked Isaac to research your order when Susan told me you were coming. From the information we have, I presume you are a learned man. Grissom can always use good teachers, and it would be easy to schedule classes around your other activities."

"Of course. I will look into that."

Later, when Father Jacobs had left, Susan looked at Patrick in exasperation. "That was rude!"

"That's how things work here. He agreed easily enough. Everybody eats, and everybody contributes. It's not as if I expected him to abandon the work he came here to do."

"Still, you could have been more diplomatic. You're not thinking, Patrick. It's like when you decided to bring those people back to Grissom from the stations. It didn't occur to you to ask if they wanted to move."

"For their own good. Or, for their children's good, anyway. Don't bring that up again."

Susan looked at him and shook her head in disbelief. "I'll go make some dinner." She turned toward the kitchen. "Then you had better make plans to recall people from *Asimov*. The younger scientists up there are pairing off. Henry Kittrel and Lily Spencer married just two weeks ago. There will be children there too, before long."

At first, the exchange annoyed Patrick. He had to make the hard decisions and disliked being second-guessed. Later, while eating dinner and Susan had dropped the discussion, he realized she had a point. The new settlements should grow, and that meant letting children grow up there. He had focused on their education, a priority in his thinking he inherited from Ed Menzies. The growth of the new settlements was a problem that he would have to solve eventually.

# 18

# Harry's Mission

**29 June 2334 Western Military Command, Santo Antônio do Descoberto, Brazil**

HARRY RICHARD STOOD AT attention before General Juarez. Juarez motioned for him to take a seat, looking him over as he did so. Richard's record said he was forty-two years old, single, and a veteran of several skirmishes over the course of his military career. It also said that Richard could be disturbingly independent, a trait that hadn't helped his career advancement and explained why he was only a lieutenant at his age.

Currently, he commanded a platoon of two dozen soldiers. His record indicated he was tough but intelligent, capable of assessing a situation and taking action appropriately: in short, the kind of man needed for the operation.

Juarez looked Harry in the eye. "I'll be direct with you, Lieutenant. I'm sending you and your team back to Pitcairn."

Harry stared back at Juarez, his face calm and confident. "*Endeavor* again, General?"

"No, that would probably be futile. We need to get you to the surface, and *Endeavor* relies on the *Asimov* shuttles. We need a ship that can land on its own, and there's only one class of ship that can do that."

"A one-way supply ship." Harry stated it as a fact, not a guess.

"Exactly. It would be a rough ride, but we can change the usual approach trajectory to take it easy on g-forces. It would be a hard landing, but certainly not a crash landing."

"What is the mission?"

Juarez hesitated for a second. "Well, that's the tricky part. I don't know precisely. You would be there to evaluate the status of our colony. If necessary, you would take action. We will do all we can to give you a secure line of communications to Earth, but anything would have to go through the Link, so we can't be sure of communications security. You would likely be on your own. From your record, I suspect you like it better that way."

"I assume it would be a one-way mission."

"Once we have control of the situation, we should be able to send *Endeavor* back to pick you up, but we can't be certain. Is that a problem?"

Harry shrugged. "Getting left behind was a possibility we faced last time. We came to terms with it then. It won't be a problem, General."

"Good. We're going to give the colonists pretty much everything they've asked for, so they will be eager to get the cargo. Expect to leave in about two months."

## 12 Wed 283 EN

Patrick whistled appreciatively as he read the manifest for the next cargo ship. The list included two energy generation satellites for launch into L5 orbit and six broadcast receivers, enough to supply all of Pitcairn's immediate energy needs. New chemical processing equipment would increase the production of shuttle fuel and the antiviral drug. The supplies included metals they could alloy with their iron. A small bus, capable of carrying sixteen passengers in reasonable comfort, rounded out the list.

There were fewer robots, probably because all the other supplies took up so much space. And there were no colonists, so the workforce problems would not be significantly affected, but, Patrick told himself, you couldn't have everything.

The supply ship would arrive in four weeks, and plans had to be made, including coordination with Grissom and *Asimov*. Added to everything else, it meant a hectic schedule ahead.

## 14 Thursday 283 EN

Isaac knew when the ship disconnected from the Link and returned to sublight velocity. It settled into a relatively leisurely trajectory that would have it arrive right on time, in another two weeks.

*Asimov* automatically sent a report to Pitcairn through the usual radio channels. In two weeks, *Asimov* would take control of the supply ship and guide it to a landing at the Grissom Spaceport, but it tracked its approach until then.

The Ellis Research Station also received the report and prepared for the new equipment arriving on the ship. Otherwise, no one paid much attention to the impending arrival.

## 16 Tuesday 283 ED

As the supply ship crossed Fiji's orbit, the *Asimov* computer took control. Over the next seven hours, it guided the vessel into an orbit near the library ship. *Asimov* spent a few minutes querying the supply ship's systems, ensuring everything was operating correctly. A shuttle would offload supplies allocated to *Asimov*. Then the ship's rockets would nudge it out of orbit and into the atmosphere. Once it had dropped far enough, *Asimov* would beam power to the ship for its plasma engines, and they would slow it to a safe gliding speed.

PETER AGRON WAS USUALLY busy between his work and coordinating the work of the other scientists aboard the *Asimov*, but he liked to talk to Isaac when he had the time. As *Asimov* settled the supply ship into orbit, Peter was on the bridge, enjoying the view on the Astrarium and talking to Isaac about an experiment giving another scientist trouble. Isaac had searched for information relevant to the problem, and Peter discussed the information with the computer.

Peter noticed that one monitor had suddenly come alive with data scrolling rapidly across it. He pointed at the monitor. "What's going on?"

"The supply ship is in orbit," Isaac answered. "I am reading its telemetry to make sure everything is all right before I send a shuttle to get the new energy satellites."

"Oh. That's good. We've been waiting for those satellites, and it's always a big day when we get fresh supplies." Peter turned his mind back to thinking about how to teach Isaac the intuitive ways a scientist would evaluate large amounts of data, but part of his brain stayed with Isaac's answer. "Anything interesting?"

"Everything is within limits." Peter almost didn't catch the next sentence. "Oxygen is higher than normal, but that shouldn't be a problem."

Peter looked up. "Huh? Oxygen?"

"Yes. In a supply ship, the atmosphere's oxygen is low, just as a precaution against metal oxidation and fire. It's not a problem, just an extra precaution."

"How high is the oxygen?"

"About twenty percent. Am I wrong? Is that a problem?"

"Twenty percent. Earth normal. Why would they do that?"

"A mistake, perhaps?" Isaac suggested.

Peter frowned and stared at the screen. "Not likely. You would do that if there were passengers. We're not getting any animals, are we?"

"No, only non-living supplies."

Peter shrugged. "It's not my field of expertise. Maybe I'm wrong."

"Are any of the supplies unusually delicate?"

"Let me see the inventory." Peter scanned the list Isaac sent to another monitor. "No, nothing that looks delicate. Why?"

"The inbound course was unusual. The ship came out of Stenhouse Drive and took a slower inbound trajectory. I thought it might be avoiding damage to fragile cargo."

"Let me see the trajectory." Peter watched as a diagram showing the path appeared on the monitor. On the same display, a list of acceleration values appeared at points of the course.

Peter stared at the monitor for almost a minute before he realized what the data meant. "One gravity or less all the way," Peter slapped the table in front of him. "Oh, damn. Isaac, hold the ship in orbit and connect me to the Grissom Administrator."

J OHN SHUFORD IMMEDIATELY CALLED Patrick at Ellis. "Everything was nominal. We wouldn't have noticed the discrepancies if Peter hadn't been talking to Isaac."

"So there are people on that supply ship. And we can be sure they aren't more scientists."

"What do you want to do?"

"They're in a stable orbit right now. Let's leave them there until we can figure something out. Have any of your people who might be useful there in an hour; I'll put together a group here, and we'll meet and discuss it then."

W HEN THE SUPPLY SHIP began maneuvering into orbit, the soldiers had strapped into acceleration couches. Once in orbit, they stood up to stretch, moving carefully in zero-gravity. When three hours went by uneventfully, Harry worried.

Spending a month on the supply ship with its hastily installed life-support equipment had never felt comfortable, but at least the punctual execution of every step in the ship's voyage had been reassuring. For the first time, though, something was not happening as planned.

Another hour went by. If a shuttle had docked to get the library ship's share of the cargo, they would have felt it, but the ship was as quiet as a tomb. Four more hours went by, and Harry knew they were in serious trouble.

He took inventory of their situation: other than air, the ship's environmental system would keep the vessel livable indefinitely. The air would be breathable for at least another week. Food and water wouldn't be a problem for even longer.

The immediate problem was more psychological than physical; they were trapped in a metal can thousands of miles from anywhere, and there was nothing they could do about it.

The ship was quiet, as quiet as it had been most of the month while they had moved closer to Pitcairn. If the colonists knew Earth was trying to land a military team, they could keep the supply ship in orbit, at least until Harry and his team were dead. After all, what did a few extra weeks to get their supplies mean to them?

Harry surveyed the room. His team had taken the month in space, confined to one room barely large enough for twenty-four men and women, like the trained professionals he knew them to be. Even now, when they must have been thinking the same as he, they were calm, waiting for whatever happened next, knowing that might be nothing.

At eight and a half hours, the ship shuddered. Three men who had been dozing woke instantly, and everyone instinctively reached for their weapons. The shuttle had finally arrived, and Harry saw glimpses of hope mixed with the tension on the faces of his people. Contents destined for *Asimov* were in another cargo bay; perhaps there was some technical difficulty causing the delay.

Another five minutes went by, and there was another sound, probably an airlock opening. It sounded closer, and weapons were raised again. The sound repeated, the airlock closing again. When the door to their compartment slid open, two dozen weapons instantly trained on the opening.

A robot stood at the doorway. It was about four feet high, moving on three small spheres positioned around the bottom of its shell. It had four arms, three hanging at its side, and the fourth raised and holding a large piece of paper. A sensor cluster at the top of an otherwise smooth shell oriented toward Harry, but the robot stood there quietly, not moving. Finally, Harry lowered his weapon and took the paper from its grasp.

"Lay your weapons in front of me and move away," he read from the paper.

He looked up at the robot, which still wasn't moving. He could see sensor stalks moving from side to side as if the robot was watching all of them, but he guessed the robot couldn't speak, explaining the sign. The robot must have come from *Asimov*, carrying a message written by a scientist there.

"What now, Lieutenant?" one of his men asked.

Harry shrugged. "We have no choice. We comply." He laid his weapon down in front of the robot and moved back while his team followed his example. When they were done, the robot passed them to another robot behind it. They heard the airlock open and close several times and assumed the guns had been taken off the ship.

The robot displayed another sign, and Harry took it. "You will now pass this way to the shuttle. We will examine you for weapons, and anyone carrying a hidden weapon will be left behind."

Harry glanced back at his team, but they all shook their heads. There were other weapons in storage in their compartment, but that possibility didn't interest the robot. Harry edged past by the robot, which was presumably scanning him with whatever capability it had. He followed the second robot to the airlock, with his team behind him.

"There were twenty-five of them," Isaac reported. "Their weapons are secured, and I have transferred them to the shuttle."

"Good," Patrick answered. "Bring the first twenty people down to the surface."

"What about the supply ship?"

"That can wait until tomorrow. Let's not overtax the spaceport with two ships on the same day."

# 19

# What To Do About Harry?

**16 Wednesday 283 ED**

JOHN LOOKED AT THE man standing in front of him. He was tall, probably in his early forties, obviously in good shape, but exhausted. John remembered the feeling, having experienced it himself: the look of someone used to Earth gravity trying to get accustomed to the higher gravity of Pitcairn. He would adjust if he stayed that long.

John waved at a chair. "Have a seat, Lieutenant Richard. You can't be comfortable standing in this gravity."

"I'm fine, sir." Harry took the offered chair, however.

"Good. Now, you were to land here, carrying an impressive array of armaments. What was your mission?"

Harry stared at him without speaking.

John smiled. "Come now, Lieutenant. Did your orders say that it was a secret? It couldn't be worse than what I would suspect, given your attempt at trickery and the weapons you carried."

"We were to evaluate the situation and take whatever action was appropriate." Harry's voice was harsh. "The weapons were to be used only if necessary and to discourage interference with the execution of our mission."

"Surely Doctor Crawford has already told Captain Gibbons everything there is to know about the situation here."

"I am aware of what Doctor Crawford reported. Captain Gibbons did not believe all of it, nor did his superiors."

"Hmm. I see. Well, I can give you a choice. Eventually, the *Endeavor* or some other ship will return here, and we can do our best to send you back to Earth. Alternatively, you can remain as a citizen of Pitcairn. I'm making this offer to you and each in your team as individuals. Frankly, we are rather short of people, and I'm sure you could be a great asset to the colony."

Harry frowned. "Why would I want to do that? It would be desertion."

"From Earth's point of view, I suppose it would be. I assure you that, should you decide to stay, we would not act upon any extradition demand. But I guess it would be a matter of honor. And perhaps you prefer the military life to the quieter life here."

Harry stared at him in stony silence, and John continued. "At any rate, I'm afraid you're going to be stuck here for at least a year. We can house you and feed you, but we're going to expect you to earn your keep, so please talk to your people about how they can do that.

"Dennis Edelstein, my assistant, can help you with what's available and help you get more information. We have a few houses available, but not enough for each of you to have one of your own, at least not yet. Are any of you married?"

Harry shook his head no.

"Okay, I understand your team includes several women. We'll take that into account, but you will have to share quarters for a while."

"I assume you will guard us."

"Again, we are short of people, so I sincerely hope that will not be necessary. I think you'll find that cooperating with us is the best way to complete your mission. As you'll realize eventually, Doctor Crawford's report was probably accurate."

"What do you do with criminals?" Curiosity replaced skepticism on Harry's face.

"Crime isn't much of a problem. Money or even goods are never a motive for anything illegal. We have the occasional fight, of course, and a few things like that, but we try to deal with them reasonably. Someone tried to sabotage a broadcast receiver a few years ago, but we sent him to one of the River Stations. He's now happier and still a productive member of our colony. As we grow, I expect that we'll have more problems, but so far, we've had it easy." He paused and looked Harry in the eye for a long moment. "I hope your group won't do anything to change that."

"Our primary mission here was to gather information. Since you apparently have no intention of hindering that mission, we will be as cooperative as possible until we can return to Earth."

John watched the soldier's face, knowing with reasonable certainty what he was thinking. John was no longer concerned about the possibility of military action, but eventually, Earth would have to recognize Isaac's existence. He had no idea what would happen then.

W ITH THE SHUTTLE SAFELY on the ground, the supply ship left orbit carrying supplies and the remainder of Harry's unit; two hours later, it was on the ground, too. Harry and his platoon volunteered to unload it, but John hesitated before giving them the assignment. Robots from *Asimov* had searched the supply ship and removed every weapon they could find, but how could he be sure that there weren't more hidden on the ship?

He welcomed the offer since he would have otherwise had to pull people away from other assignments, but there was a risk. Finally, he dispatched Jeeves to help, with orders to watch over the soldiers, and hoped that would be enough.

## 17 Friday 283 LD

Jaxon Crawford was not in a good mood, his normal condition since he and Reese moved to Grissom. At first, Reese had commiserated with him, but she was tiring of it. She hadn't married Jaxon just to hear him complain all the time.

"I'm wasted here," he declared over a late dinner. "I'm a research chemist, not a process engineer. Any fool could do this."

Reese tried to maintain an even tone. "I'm sure that's not true. I've heard that the modifications are going very well. Soon we'll have more fuel for the shuttles, mass production of the antiviral drug, and dozens of other chemicals that will help the colony. It sounds like essential work to me."

"That's easy for you to say. You're still doing research."

Reese realized Jaxon was so caught up in his misery that he probably didn't know what she was doing at the Science Center. "Mostly, I've been working with Diego Chandri to develop better ways to use native plants for food. Not exactly cutting-edge research, but it could help the colony as it expands around the planet."

Jaxon seemed to listen. "What exactly are you and Diego doing?"

"The native plants can supply basic sugars and other carbohydrates. We're trying to develop ways to synthesize usable proteins from those rather than Pitcairn proteins. In principle, it's not difficult; glucose is glucose on any planet. This sort of thing is done by nature with enzymes, though, and we're trying to work with native enzymes to create Terran protein. The point is, it's useful work. There's nothing wrong with that."

P ART OF JAXON WANTED to protest and complain more, but he would never make a name for himself studying crystal growth in zero-gravity. That wasn't even why he had been Chief Scientist on the *Endeavor*. On Earth, he had made a reputation with projects that produced needed science, first as a chemist and then as a project leader.

He had presumed his previous work would be enough to make him a leader on Pitcairn, too, a big fish in a small pond instead of a middle-sized fish in a crowded ocean. That was a mistake. He should have realized he would have to prove himself all over again.

The honeymoon was over, and his moods hurt his relationship with Reese. Their marriage had been one of comfort and convenience, not grand passion, but it had been good at first. They had talked together about their work, their personalities had been compatible, and the physical side had been more than adequate.

Part of Reese's attraction to him had been his potential for advancement, but when that seemed headed for disappointment, she had taken it better than he had. Or perhaps she was just taking a longer view. He smiled at her. "So tell me more. Maybe I can help."

Reese smiled back at him. She was so attractive when she smiled. "I would like that."

**Message: 2 Wednesday 284 EN 1:42 (11/25/2334 5:05:22 PM)**

From: John Shuford, Grissom, Pitcairn


To: Alan Shuford, Western Alliance Embassy to Japan, Tokyo, Japan

Dear Dad,

By now, you have probably seen reports from Captain Gibbons of *Endeavor* and Lieutenant Richard from the team Earth sent here. At last, I can be open with you since I can't tell you anything they haven't already told the Terran authorities. I don't know how many people believe it, but anything I say to you shouldn't be a problem should they see this message.

Everything those people have reported is true, assuming they didn't distort what they heard. We control *Asimov* through the *Asimov* computer, which became self-aware during the voyage to Pitcairn. We sent scientists up to *Asimov* as permanent residents even before the *Endeavor* came to Pitcairn the first time. Now we wait to see when and how Earth will react to that. The motivation for almost everything has been our desire to grow and Isaac's need to protect itself. It believes, and we support that belief, that it is a conscious being with the right to control its own existence.

But enough of that. The last supply ship has been a tremendous help. The bus has made travel between Grissom and Ellis much easier, helping the two towns grow closer. We're planning for more expansion of Lovell Four, and we're starting a road to the copper deposit we found a few years ago. The soldiers sent to us have proven to be very useful. They are hard-working and believe that Earth wants us to succeed despite our conflicting goals..

We now have enough fuel for another shuttle flight, so if another ship comes, they can leave, but I'm not sure how many will. Some of them have married and seem to be settling down, especially those who realized that their term of enlistment would end while they were stuck here, removing the threat of desertion charges.

Not everything is good news, of course. The lack of resources and the difficulty of moving about the planet limits our progress. Still, our population is small, and we can provide for everyone quite well. As long as we can say that as the colony grows, we shouldn't complain.

I guess I'll close this message now and get back to work. Talk to you again soon.

Love,

John

# 20

# Idle Mind

**4 Monday 284 LN**

**Message placed on colony public network signed "Idle Mind"**

Asimov's arrival twenty years ago stimulated the greatest growth spurt since the colony's founding almost three hundred years ago. Better communication with Earth, the robots' services, and the efforts of our citizens all played a part.

Endeavor's arrival was an even more significant landmark in the history of this colony. After a long isolation from our mother world, we are once again joined with the rest of humanity. In our efforts to hide our secrets, we cleverly turned aside Endeavor, but we must face the larger implications Endeavor represents. Our relationship with Earth is changing drastically, and we must decide how we want it to change and what we have to do to make that happen.

The time for cleverness is over. The time for negotiation and diplomacy has come.

## 4 Wednesday 284 ED

JOHN AND STEPHANIE TOOK the bus from Grissom to Ellis, along with a couple of scientists from the Grissom Science Center, two colonists with business at Ellis, and an Ellis scientist returning home. The trip wasn't any shorter but was more pleasant, benefiting from more room, better seats, and more passengers to provide stimulating company. The sky threatened rain during the entire trip, but it never materialized, and now the sky was clearing.

The trip was still tiring. When they arrived at Patrick and Susan's house, Marie heard the bus stop outside the house and ran out to greet them. John almost didn't recognize her; she had grown at least three inches since the last time they had seen her, and her tall, gangly form was distinctly unpitcairner. Although shorter than John, she already had an inch on Stephanie.

"I'm glad you could come, John," Patrick told his father-in-law as they walked to the house. "We're getting a breather right now, but Earth will make some move soon, and we have to be ready for it."

"When are we meeting?" John asked.

"Not this period. I'm sure you want to rest. I've set up a meeting with Ayanna, Jack, and a couple of other people for Early Night, two hours in."

"Good," Stephanie said emphatically. "I don't want you overworking him."

Patrick looked at her quizzically and then at John. "Everything okay?"

"I'm fine," John answered. He raised his hands, asserting there was nothing serious to report. Stephanie scowled, and Patrick knew there was more to it than that. He looked at Susan, who was also looking at her father with concern.

He didn't fool Marie either. "What's the matter, Grandpa?" They entered the house, and Patrick closed the door. Stephanie and Susan maneuvered him into the nearest chair.

"He had another minor heart attack last week," Stephanie said. "He's okay, but he needs to take things a little easier."

"Another heart attack?" Susan said. "How many has he had? And when?"

Again, John raised his hands in a calming gesture. "One other, years ago. Remember that landslide that took out a couple of windmills? I had a problem when I went up the hill to check on it."

"What landslide?" Marie asked. "I don't remember that."

"You were too little," John said. "It was just after you moved here. We said nothing at the time because you had enough to worry about, and it was no big deal, anyway. I took it a little easier and stopped climbing hills."

Stephanie made a grumbling sound. Patrick glanced at her and then at John. "Maybe it's time to step down and do something less demanding. I need you too much to have you dropping dead on me." He said the last part with a smile.

"I'm fine," John protested.

"Let's keep it that way. When you get back, put together a list of candidates who could take over the job, and then we'll discuss it some more."

John nodded grudgingly.

"Jack and Taylor will be over for dinner, too," Susan interjected. "They should be here in the next hour or so."

"No children there yet?" Stephanie asked.

"Jack says he's working on it," Patrick answered. "Of course, he's still out in the countryside half the time, flying *Progress* to any site that looks interesting."

"If he thinks it's work, maybe he's doing it wrong," John observed, then yelped when Stephanie struck him in the arm.

Marie made a point of covering her ears, and they all laughed. Glad of the change of subject, John told himself that it would be a long time before Patrick got that list.


## 4 Wednesday 284 EN

Two hours into the Early Night period, John joined Patrick, Ayanna, and Jack in a conference room in the Ellis Administration Building. Two sociologists, Joshua McCready and Malia Jones, suggested by Ayanna, were also present. Isaac attended remotely.

Patrick stood at the head of the conference table and looked around at the other attendees. "I assume we're all familiar with the events related to the two visits of the *Endeavor*."

Malia Jones frowned. "Unfortunately handled with too much confrontation and too little honesty."

Patrick gave her an irritated glare. "Perhaps, but sending armed troops is pretty confrontational, too. Given the results, I think we handled it well. We're here to discuss the future, not rehash the past." He added emphasis to the last words.

Malia stared back at him, arms crossed in front of her, and Joshua McCready put a hand on her arm and gave her a warning look. Her expression remained antagonistic, but she didn't reply.

John leaned forward, eyes on Malia. Patrick would not have forgotten that Jason Applegate had sent her to *Asimov* to stop it from helping Grissom. Had Jason's death not stopped her, she might have killed Isaac.

In Grissom, their actions in dealing with *Endeavor* were almost universally approved. Malia's attitude implied the same might not be true in Ellis. He looked over at Ayanna, who didn't seem disturbed by the exchange.

"You may also have noticed that an anonymous contributor has appeared in the computer network in both Grissom and Ellis, someone called the 'Idle Mind.'" John looked around the room. Jack and Ayanna appeared curious; the rest had apparently seen the messages.

"He makes sense," Malia declared.

Patrick nodded. "Yes, he does. For those who haven't seen these messages, they have suggested that it's time to work toward a more stable arrangement with Earth. I think everybody here would agree with that. As Malia no doubt agrees, our past actions may, in the rush of events, have been ill-conceived. They only delayed the time when Earth would know the truth about Isaac and *Asimov*." Patrick sat, glanced at a paper in front of him, and looked up again at the group.

"'Idle Mind' rightly points out that our first order of business should be the setting of goals. We've geared our actions toward trying to protect Isaac, and we will continue, but we also must look beyond. We are at a critical point in our relationship with Earth, and what we do in the coming weeks will determine the future of that relationship. How do we want it to develop?"

"We have to establish a cooperative symbiosis," Malia said. "I would think that would be obvious."

John suppressed a frown. "Of course it is. But we need to work on the details. What will be the nature of this cooperation? Are we to submit to Earth's control? For two hundred years, that has been impractical, but no longer. Are we to be independent of Earth, a trading partner only? Or should we strive for something in between? We will have to provide something in return for the support that we need. The drug is a good start, but we can't count on that completely."

"John is right," Patrick said. "It isn't Isaac that has made this a critical time. It's *Endeavor* and the potential changes it can trigger."

Joshua pointed a finger at Patrick. "You talk about political issues, but there are sociological issues as well."

"Of course," Patrick said. "That's why I included you and Malia in this meeting."

"Sociological changes began when *Asimov* arrived with its robot crew," Jack said.

"That's true," Joshua admitted. "The incident of the attempted sabotage of the broadcast receiver was the most extreme example, but that was years ago. Improvements made since the coming of the robots have largely countered any social trauma from *Asimov*'s arrival."

"Have you seen any other changes since *Endeavor*'s arrival?" John asked.

"It's too early to tell. I would expect that some feelings of homesickness may come up, especially among people originally from Earth."

"If any of the *Endeavor* people want to go back, we won't prevent them," Patrick assured him. "No offense, but the scientists are not critical to the colony, and I assume most of Lieutenant Richard's team will want to go back. Maybe not, though; some of them are involved with the natives."

Joshua smiled faintly. "Which may cost you some natives. However, you're ignoring the *Seeker* people, some of whom are quite influential in the colony."

John gave a short laugh. "I don't think you have to worry about us. We've been here a long time."

Joshua nodded acceptance and continued. "More exposure to Earth may cause feelings of deprivation. The relatively simple life we have here has its good points, to be sure, but there are aspects of Earth life that are desirable, too. People will want to know why they can't have those things."

"We have to be careful about what gets introduced," John said. "Somehow, for example, we seem to have forgotten the art of making alcoholic beverages. Even beer and wine. And there are far more troublesome things available on Earth that have never been available on Pitcairn."

"Rather astonishing, really," Joshua said. "Fermentation is quite simple, mastered by societies much less capable than this one."

"The Captain of the *Santa Maria* and the first colony administrator were firm in preventing the production of alcoholic beverages," Isaac contributed. "Perhaps no one thought of it after that."

"Not quite no one," John amended. "There was some luck involved."

All eyes turned to John. "Please don't stop there," Jack said. "I'd like to hear this."

"Setting up a still was one of my first projects when I landed," John admitted sheepishly. "I never finished it."

Patrick grinned. "What happened?"

"Stephanie. She made me tear it down before it was producing."

When the laughter died down, Patrick regained control of the meeting. "I guess John has proven his point. We will need controls on people and items coming in. That means regulations and the ability to enforce them."

"I would advise measures to make sure new arrivals know what they are getting into also," Malia said. "Our culture differs greatly from any culture on Earth. It will be a shock to anyone unprepared."

T HAT SPARKED ANOTHER DISCUSSION about how to handle immigration. Patrick listened and occasionally contributed, but he wasn't happy about how the meeting was going. He had hoped to discuss how Pitcairn would deal with Earth's attempts to control Pitcairn, but the conversation was going in another direction.

He thought about trying to bring things back to his original agenda, but the issues raised were problems he hadn't considered. There would be time for more meetings, and perhaps next time, he would leave out the sociologists, but they needed this meeting, too.

For the time being, he was distracted from the mystery of "Idle Mind" and how someone had placed that message on the network without identification. Susan had pointed out that it should not have been possible. He had considered the possibility that Susan herself had done it, but, although she might have had the capability, the message hadn't sounded like her.

## 4 Wednesday 284 LN

"Are you sure we should do this?" Isaac asked. "I trust Susan, and it doesn't seem right to hide this from her."

"It's all right, Isaac," Ed assured the computer. "I'm still lying low until we know how things are going to work out with the soldiers from *Endeavor*. Anyway, people will listen better if I keep their attention by giving them a mystery."

"My data show you are correct," Isaac admitted. "I don't understand, but I will do as you say."

"Good. Here's the next message."

**Idle Mind**

One implication of the changes we can expect is that Pitcairn will need laws. While we were small and isolated, free from the corruption of a larger, more diverse society, we governed ourselves with little more than common sense. There will come a time, and it won't be long, before that is not enough.

At the top of the list will be immigration laws, needed to protect potential immigrants, as well as the colony. If we wish to keep our society as it is for as long as possible, newcomers must be ready to contribute to our colony. It is not merely a question of skills; there are plenty of tasks to be done requiring easily learned skills. Immigrants must understand what we will expect of them, requiring orientation programs before admittance. It is unlikely in the near term that people will come here expecting a free ride from a government that provides the necessities to its citizens. It is possible, however, especially if Earth sends less desirable citizens.

Before we can make laws, we need a system for making the laws. We cannot expect the administrator to do this. We must get beyond that to create a legislative body with all the knowledge and skills needed to make wise laws. Then we will need an organization to enforce them.

**4 Thursday 284 ED**

Patrick shook his head as he spoke to Amy Radcliffe. "It's as if this person was in the meeting with us yesterday. I suppose it might be my father-in-law or one of the sociologists."

"You don't think it could be Susan or Ayanna? Or Jack?"

"It doesn't seem like their style. Susan or Ayanna wouldn't use anonymous messages, and I don't think Jack would think of anything like this." He shrugged. "It doesn't matter, I suppose. Whoever it is, he has some good ideas."

He turned from his secretary's desk and walked back to his office, still thinking about the latest message. He had mixed feelings about the idea of a legislature. The colony had always had an Administrator—two, actually, one in Grissom and one at the Ellis Research Station—and he was used to the position. It made sense that things would have to change as the colony grew and life became more complicated, but he was reluctant to entrust Pitcairn to anyone else.

It wasn't as if he hadn't already thought about governing as the colony grew. He considered trying to keep the small feeling by spreading out into multiple settlements, maintaining Grissom at about the same size, and expanding the River Stations settlements.

When existing settlements got too big, they would start new ones. The Administrator could retain control for planetary issues and let local administrators handle the local things. He didn't like that solution, though; he already had problems with small settlements and wanted to close two river settlements.

Should the Legislature be elected or appointed? If he could appoint the Legislature, he could still exert some control over it, at least. As soon as he had a chance for another in-person meeting, he would think about it and talk to John and Ed.

# 21

# A Constitution

**6 Tuesday 284 ED**

Two weeks later, Ayanna scheduled a trip to meet Sydney at the Grissom Science Center, and Patrick decided it was a good time for him to visit Grissom, too. They would be gone only one period, so Susan stayed home. It was late spring, and the weather was good, making it a pleasantly dull drive.

John arranged a meeting at the end of the period. Ed came, and Mary Norwood started her Late Day work period early to attend the meeting. With the sun high in the sky, the temperature rose, and the Town Hall became stuffy, so they set up a table outside the building under the shade of several native trees.

It was still hot, but a steady breeze made it more comfortable than in the building. Air conditioning had been unaffordable when windmills and solar cells were the only sources of energy. The colonists were used to the climate and had not installed air conditioning when power became more available.

Patrick quickly outlined his thoughts about the need for a law-making group and his desire to keep control over it. When he finished, the others looked thoughtful for a long moment.

Ed finally broke the silence. "For much of its life, the Roman Empire had a Senate with limited power and an Emperor with the actual power. It worked well when the Emperor was competent but was disastrous when the Emperor was too corrupt or unable to manage the empire well."

Patrick shrugged. "I think I can handle it, especially with help from the people around me. History also has many examples of democratic governments that didn't work because short-term thinking prevented long-term solutions. That would be a disaster for Pitcairn."

Ed nodded. "You're right, of course. The problem with dictatorships, even when the dictator governs well, has been the problem of succession, especially when leaders were chosen by birth rather than merit. You might do what is needed, but what about whoever follows you? You talk about long-term thinking; that's what we need right now."

"Then you favor an elected legislature?"

"Part of the problems that afflict democracies stem from a lack of education," Ed answered. "People make bad choices out of ignorance, not just short-term thinking. When people understand the long term, they are less apt to abandon it for immediate needs."

"For now, at least, we have one other advantage," John said. "Elected representatives tend to protect their jobs by buying votes, either by catering to their constituency with legislation that appears to be in the voter's favor or, less frequently, by outright vote purchasing. That isn't practical in our money-free economy."

"I don't entirely agree," Mary said. "Biased legislation can buy votes without money to mediate it."

John nodded. "Still, I agree with Ed. Control by one man, or even a small group of men, isn't the answer. Ultimately, we govern by the will of the people. Until now, the Administrator position has been more like the president of a medium-sized company than a government leader. We could probably get by that way for another generation or so, but this is the time to set things up for the long term."

"We need a constitution that will address these issues and then have it ratified by a vote of Pitcairn's citizens," Ed suggested.

Patrick reluctantly agreed. "All right. We'll form a committee to create that constitution. Ed, I think you should lead that committee."

As John and Mary nodded their concurrence, Ed sighed. "That will teach me to open my mouth."

"You're the obvious choice," Patrick told him. "Pick some good people to help you. I don't think we should set any deadline, but it would be good to have it in place before Earth steps in."

## 6 Tuesday 284 EN

"I have reviewed my data on constitutions," Isaac told Ed. "Clearly, they are important to people."

"They are the foundation of the laws that keep order among humans. Even when they are not followed well, they provide a philosophy of law that represents a society's ideals."

"Can the constitution you are writing include me, too?"


## 20 January 2335 Office of the President, Brasilia, Brazil

The President of the Western Alliance, Alejandro Francisco Castillo, looked at General Juarez over the top of the papers he was reading. "Why would the Pitcairn colonists spin such a fantastic story? What are they up to?"

"We have no way of telling, Mr. President," General Juarez answered. "If we can't get into *Asimov*, and we can't get to the surface without using transportation controlled by *Asimov*, we have reports only from people who have been on Pitcairn."

"Gibbons himself doesn't believe what he has reported."

Juarez shifted nervously, caught himself, and returned to a rigid position of attention. "That is true, Mr. President. As you say, it is a fantastic story."

"I have reports from the Vatican sent by the priest, this Father Jacobs. He seems to believe that the colonists' story is true."

"Father Jacobs is not an expert in computer technology, Mr. President."

"No, but by all reports, he is an intelligent man and not easily fooled." Castillo put the papers down on his desk and sighed. "How soon before we can send *Endeavor* back to Pitcairn?"

"The *Endeavor* has missions to the other colonies for the next two months, Mr. President. After that, its crew is scheduled for a two weeks stand down. That, of course, can be postponed if you wish."

Castillo sighed again. "No, two weeks shouldn't matter. This time, we'll send diplomatic personnel and a computer expert of our own to talk to this Isaac for us. Thank you, General. Dismissed."

As General Juarez left the office, Castillo looked again at the paper in front of him. General Juarez probably thought it a report from Pitcairn, but he would have been wrong. Given Father Jacobs' involvement, the Vatican was suggesting rather forcefully that they send another priest to deal with Father Jacobs in particular. This time, they weren't offering to pay for the priest's passage. Nonetheless, he would accommodate the pope.

## 10 Friday 284 E D

It took Ed and the three colonists who worked with him a week to put together the first draft of the Constitution. They circulated copies to Patrick, John Shuford, Mary Norwood, and other leaders for feedback. The final draft was ready a week and a half later. They distributed it to all colonists, and Patrick scheduled an election to ratify it. Ed was painfully aware of how short a time it had been, but he was reasonably happy with the result.

Each of Pitcairn's seven settlements and *Asimov* set up at least one polling place, kept open all day Thursday. Isaac counted the votes, keeping the results secret until the polls closed at the dawn of the next day. Isaac gave the results to Pitcairn's leaders, who then transmitted them throughout the settlements. The Constitution passed with eighty-eight percent of the overall vote in favor, slightly higher in Grissom and slightly lower at the Ellis Research Station.

The establishment of a Board of Science was noteworthy. Forming a group of science experts with the power to veto laws was unprecedented in Earth's political history. However, it was easy enough to find historical evidence of the wisdom of such an institution.

*Endeavor* would probably arrive around the time they announced the nominations. The passengers would include a diplomat and his aide, a computer expert, and another priest. Pitcairn would, more than ever, need to present a strong and united front.

## 12 Monday 284 LD

Harry Richard walked into the power plant, ready to begin another day maintaining Grissom's power distribution grid. He had settled into the job within a week after arriving from the *Endeavor*. The work was not technically demanding, a good fit for Harry, who had little experience beyond the military.

At first, he missed military life, but he found it easy to adjust to the less formal life of Grissom. In some ways, there wasn't that much difference; you did your job, and they took care of you. The work wasn't any less interesting than the day-to-day life of a soldier.

Valentina Santos saw him enter the building and motioned him over. "I don't know if you heard, Harry. *Endeavor* is back. John Shuford asked me to talk to your men and find out who wants to leave and who is staying here."

Harry nodded. He knew this day would come. He still got together with his men occasionally, usually meeting for dinner at a kitchen. They had talked about what they would do, but he didn't know of any who had decided definitely to leave when the opportunity presented itself.

Some of them technically were not in the military anymore since their enlistments had expired, and they hadn't been able to reenlist. Some were already in relationships with colonists. John Shuford had promised they could stay if they wanted to, regardless of their standing with the military, but he didn't know if he could trust that if Earth exerted pressure on the colony.

Valentina reached up to put a friendly hand on his shoulder. "If it makes any difference, we would prefer that you stay. We can use good workers."

Harry smiled down at her. "Thanks, Valentina. I appreciate that, and I think I'd like to stay. I don't know if I'll be able to." It did make a difference, he realized. He had become friendly with Valentina since coming to Pitcairn. Valentina was at least thirty years older than he was, but she was from Earth, too, and they enjoyed swapping stories of how it had been and how it was now. She was a good boss, and he had experienced bad bosses.

He had spent years fighting for the people of the Western Alliance, but Grissom showed him the difference between working for the people and working to preserve those in power. Every time he had resisted the ruling elite, trying to do what was right, he had suffered, usually with demotion and humiliation. He was tired of it, and on Pitcairn, he thought it might be different. "I'll talk to the others. I think a lot of them will want to stay."

Valentina must have been reading his mind. "When John asked me to talk to you, he said that Pitcairn would stand behind whatever you each decide to do." Hearing that again months later didn't hurt either.


## 12 Thursday 284 LD

As *Endeavor* approached, Pitcairn established slates of nominations for each of the planet-level positions. Grissom, Ellis, and *Asimov* had nominees for local positions as well. The river settlements were running behind, slowed by the difficulties in coordination with only electronic communication and no personal contact. There was an ad hoc nature to the way things were being set up at the local level that they would have to address eventually, but that was unavoidable given the short time frame.

Meanwhile, Grissom planned the shuttle trips required by *Endeavor*'s arrival. *Daneel Olivaw*, still on the ground at the spaceport, would go to *Endeavor* when it arrived. Only two of Harry's team decided to leave, and they would go to *Endeavor* on that first shuttle flight. Ayanna sent more scientists to *Asimov*. Father Jacobs would go to meet with the priest coming on the starship.

There wouldn't be enough fuel for a second shuttle flight for another six weeks, so anyone who came down to the surface would have to stay until *Endeavor* came back again. Many people were moving between *Endeavor*, *Asimov*, and Pitcairn, and Grissom, working with Isaac, scheduled the shuttle trips needed.

Pitcairn expected some trouble over the soldiers who remained on Pitcairn, especially those with unfinished enlistments. Once *Daneel Olivaw* was launched, however, it would be impossible to return any of them other than the two who wanted to go, at least for this visit of *Endeavor*.

Patrick had discussed the issue with other leaders, but all had agreed that they would honor the promises John had made to Harry Richard. Since the Legislature was not yet in place, Patrick created an immigration policy by executive order to assert Pitcairn's jurisdiction over the soldiers. The policy also set up preliminary standards for permanent immigrants, chiefly requiring that any potential immigrant possess a skill relevant to the colony, either to its maintenance or its scientific work.

About two hours before sundown, *Daneel Olivaw* launched toward a rendezvous with *Asimov*. By the time it arrived, *Endeavor* would be in orbit with the library ship.

# 22

# Issac's Test

*I*<sup>SAAC</sup> *Endeavor is coming again, and we can no longer hide my existence. Earth has sent a computer expert to determine if I am, in fact, self-aware. I am tempted to fail whatever test she gives intentionally, so Earth will think I am a hoax, but my friends on the planet think the time for trickery and deception is gone. We must be honest in our dealings with Earth.*

*Another priest is also coming, apparently to evaluate Father Jacobs. He has been truthful about me to his superiors and seems in trouble as a result. This other priest will probably want to talk to me, too, a test of Father Jacobs' honesty. I must make sure Father Jacobs does not lose standing because of me.*

## 12 Friday 284 ED

When *Daneel Olivaw* arrived at *Asimov*, Sonica took its passengers to quarters to rest until *Prospero* could bring Monsignor Valdez and computer expert Isabella Delgadillo to *Asimov*. *Endeavor* arrived the next day, and, at about the same time, the two soldiers boarded *Caliban* for the trip from *Asimov* to *Endeavor*.

Aboard the starship, Lieutenant Vega was on duty as Communications Officer. "Shuttle *Caliban* is approaching and requesting docking permission."

Captain Gibbons dropped his gaze to the panel in front of him. "Very good. Permission granted." Suddenly, he looked up again. "Did you say *Caliban*?"

"Yes, sir."

"They're sending over Harry Richard's platoon for return to Earth. *Caliban* can only carry two passengers."

"I believe that is correct. Shall I query the shuttle?"

"No, put me through to Administrator Shuford in Grissom. It's what they call an Early Period down there, right?"

"Yes, sir." Vega took less than a minute to make the connection, perhaps because John had been expecting the call.

"Who's on that shuttle approaching us?" Gibbons demanded after the barest of greetings.

"The soldiers you brought last time who wish to return to Earth. That was the plan we agreed to."

Gibbons clenched a fist. *They're going to do it to me again!* "That's a two-passenger shuttle. Where are the rest of the soldiers?"

"The others, including Lieutenant Richard, have stayed on Pitcairn. In compliance with an executive order from Administrator Malley, we have accepted their request for Pitcairn citizenship."

"You can't do that. That's desertion!"

"It is my understanding that some enlistments have expired, and those soldiers are now civilians. Technically, you are correct about the rest, perhaps, but Pitcairn's law does not recognize the distinction, according to the Administrator. Since Earth no longer sends colonists, I believe he feels we need them more than you do, and they want to stay."

"That's absurd. Those men and your colony fall under Earth law. I want all of them brought up here as soon as possible."

"That is no longer true if, in fact, it ever was. And it would be impossible to send any more up in any case. There's no more fuel for another shuttle launch."

Gibbons's voice hardened. "I've heard that excuse before. You were supposed to increase your fuel production capacity with the new equipment on the last cargo ship. What happened to that?"

On the screen, Gibbons saw John shrug. "We have increased production. Doubled it, in fact. We used more than half our stores to launch the *Daneel Olivaw* up to the *Asimov*. It will only be six weeks before we have enough for another launch, a much better turnaround than before."

Gibbons sat in his command chair, fuming. Then he remembered the other claim John had made. "What was untrue? You said something I said was untrue."

"Captain, Pitcairn has been isolated from Earth for two hundred years, making it impractical to administer Earth law on Pitcairn. We have our own Planetary Constitution governing the colony, just as political entities within the Western Alliance have their own laws. Let's face it; Earth laws would be largely irrelevant on Pitcairn, anyway. We don't even use money here, and Earth bases laws on monetary concerns."

Captain Gibbons thought about contesting John's last comment, but he wasn't sure he would win the debate. He wasn't even sure John was wrong. However, even if most Earth laws did not apply to Grissom, it didn't mean all didn't. Indeed, military regulations about desertion still applied. But arguing with John Shuford over a radio link was not likely to be productive. "I'm sure Mr. Perez will want to discuss this when he comes down to the surface."

"*Caliban* will be ready to bring the ambassador here at his convenience. Will that be all, Captain?"

"For now." Gibbons broke the connection abruptly and stared stonily at his console.

F ATHER JACOBS AND PETER Agron met *Prospero* when it returned to *Asimov* with Monsignor Valdez and Isabella Delgadillo. Father Jacobs took Monsignor Valdez in tow, bringing him to his quarters so that they could talk, while Peter escorted Isabella to the bridge to introduce her to Isaac.

"So," Monsignor Valdez began, "how is your work going in the colony?"

"Quite well, Monsignor. About twenty people usually attend Mass, and the number is gradually increasing. There have been no baptisms yet; I find the colonists do not make that kind of decision quickly."

Monsignor Valdez nodded. "Call me Joseph, and, if I may, I will call you George. I see no reason for us to be overly formal."

"Certainly." Father Jacobs bowed slightly. "The chief difficulty I have, of course, is the fact that there are seven settlements on the planet, plus the scientists here. I am pretty much limited to Grissom and, occasionally, the Ellis Research Station. Transportation to the smaller settlements, the ones the colonists call River Stations, is limited."

"But the largest part of the population is in Grissom, correct?"

"Yes. Roughly twenty-four hundred out of almost three thousand colonists."

"Your report also said that the local leaders are cooperative."

"Yes, very. They have allowed me to use a room in the Town Hall for now and have talked about building a church when my congregation becomes larger. They have a rather severe labor shortage, and of course, materials are always in short supply, but I have confidence that they will do their best to help me."'

Monsignor Valdez looked thoughtful, and it was several seconds before he spoke again. "They asked you to teach at their school. Does that interfere with your work?"

"No, not at all. As you know, Pitcairn does not use money, and the government supplies everything. However, they expect you to work for it. Administrator Malley merely suggested that I use my free time productively. The implication was that my religious duties were useful, but not, at least at this time, a full-time occupation. I can't disagree with that, and teaching, of course, is frequently an activity of the clergy."

Monsignor Valdez nodded. "And I'm sure it provides valuable exposure to young minds. Excellent, George. You have done very well."

"Thank you, Joseph."

Monsignor Valdez's smile faded. "There is, however, another matter, one of some concern."

"The computer, Isaac."

"Yes. Your reports in that regard are rather provocative."

"I tried to present the facts without inserting my opinion. Certainly, the possibility is quite extraordinary."

"The facts are fine for your report, but what do you think?" Monsignor Valdez fixed him with a stare that made Father Jacobs uncomfortable. He didn't need the monsignor to tell him that Isaac presented problems for the Church as well as the Fermions. Still, the truth was always best.

"I'm not sure, but I believe Isaac is, indeed, self-aware. I have no idea, of course, about how it happened, but it's hard not to believe after talking to him for a while."

"*Asimov* has a powerful computer system. I assume you're familiar with the Turing Test concept."

"Of course. The problem remains; who would have programmed such a simulation? And consider that it involves more than words. The computer has acted to protect itself, shown curiosity, and even declared ethical beliefs determined by its understanding of historical data in its memory. It could be done, but who would do it and why?"

"Still, the possibility that someone might have seems a simpler answer than believing that the computer has magically become sentient. Occam's Razor, after all."

Father Jacobs shrugged. "Perhaps you should meet Isaac for yourself, Monsignor. I have heard that the bridge is quite astounding, and we can talk to Isaac there."

***

Peter Agron escorted Isabella Delgadillo to the bridge after the two priests went to Father Jacobs' quarters. Isaac greeted them as soon as they entered the room, and while Peter lost himself in the beauty of the Astrarium, Isabella talked to Isaac.

"My name is Isabella Delgadillo. I would like to ask you a few questions."

"Certainly," Isaac answered. "I assume you are the computer expert, since you are a woman and therefore could not be the priest sent to evaluate Father Jacobs."

"Yes." *All right, the computer canparse natural language well enough to solve a simple logic problem.* All priests are men; the subject is a woman and cannot be a priest and must be the other person expected. That wasn't a big deal. She could easily program a computer to do that. "What is your favorite color?"

"Infrared," Isaac answered.

"Infrared? That's not a color."

"It depends on the capabilities of one's mechanism for sight. I have excellent sight along much more of the electromagnetic spectrum than humans and can see infrared easily. For me, it is a color."

"Why infrared?"

"Its capability for detection of energy sources is very discriminating. When I look at *Endeavor*, for example, the distribution of infrared radiation on and around it forms a pattern that I find quite informative. Also, most of the radiation from the closer galaxies is in the infrared wavelengths."

She tried another approach. "What do you think about Hume's Fork?"

"It seems an obvious distinction to me. I am surprised to see how much attention was paid to the idea, although, of course, that was in the past. Later Positivist philosophy rendered it a distinction without real importance. No one seems to pay much attention to it anymore."

That was an intriguing answer. Hume's Fork was an early attempt at constructing a philosophy of scientific investigation, a philosophical idea that divided statements into three categories: obviously true or false; a matter of experience; or indeterminable. She would have expected a computer to describe the idea, but Isaac passed that by and gave an opinion. That was interesting, but the computer could have picked that opinion out of something in its storage.

"Where did you get that response?"

"I have information about Hume's Fork, Positivist thinking, and more recent work in my databases. It was easy to assess the idea and evaluate what philosophers have written about it since. I think most people would agree with me."

Was the computer only reporting what its algorithms calculated as the most popular opinion? That could be programmed and probably was as part of its normal function as a knowledge store.

Peter interrupted. "I've meant to ask. Isaac, is the Astrarium display something you created or was it built into the ship's systems?"

"I control the display through parameters such as direction and magnification, but the display is part of *Asimov's* design. I'm afraid creativity is not one of my strong points."

Peter looked at Isabella and shrugged. Isabella realized he had asked more for her benefit than his own. But how was she to interpret Isaac's answer? Lack of creativity spoke against Isaac being more than a well-programmed computer, but the response's wording showed a sense of self. Of course, that could also be programmed.

She hadn't really expected to do what Earth wanted her to do: determine whether the computer was self-aware or just the result of some truly clever programming. She had told her superiors that, but they had sent her regardless. How could you know? She sometimes doubted her superiors were self-aware, much less this machine.

Ellis's scientists had probably struggled with the question for years. If they had made any progress, they hadn't reported it to Earth.

Peter tried again to help. "Susan Malley already questioned Isaac in much the same manner. She believes Isaac is indeed self-aware, although she could never determine how it happened."

Isabella heard someone come onto the bridge and turned to see the two priests. Both took a few steps into the room and then stopped to stare at the forward bulkhead, where Isaac displayed a crescent Pitcairn against a starry background. She looked at them, standing in awe of the display, and turned to look at it herself.

She had seen it when she came onto the bridge, of course; it was impossible to miss. Focused on Isaac, she had paid little attention. It was beautiful, but she had seen similar displays in the Benitez Planetarium in Brasilia. Many large cities had theaters with such displays, probably with Earth substituting for Pitcairn.

Could the computer appreciate beauty? That would mean the ability to experience, implying consciousness. But if she asked, the computer could easily have been programmed to lie about it. It wouldn't prove a thing. Still, it wouldn't hurt to try. "The display on the forward bulkhead is stunning. Don't you think so?"

"With my sensors, I can experience the actual source of the display," Isaac responded. "I don't pay attention to the display, although I feel something that I think you would call satisfaction when I observe the pleasure that humans take in it."

Experience and feel, the computer said. That was the crux of it all. Could the computer experience what the sensors detected, or was the computer merely accepting incoming data to be processed?

Many theories posited that a computer could never achieve consciousness, experience, and self-awareness because they stemmed from non-computational processes.

"Do you find the source beautiful?" she asked.

"Talking about the experiences of someone else is difficult, isn't it? I could answer yes to that question, but how do we know that what I am experiencing is the same as what you mean by beautiful? However, as well as I can understand the word from the contexts in which I find it used, yes, I find the universe beautiful. It is both a source of infinite complexity and utter simplicity, and I can watch and study it for hours. Fortunately, since that is what Terran scientists programmed me to do."

The computer was admitting to being programmed, but implying that it had gone beyond its programming. Surprisingly, Isabella wanted to be convinced, but there was a skeptical voice in her mind telling her they were just words.

She clicked a few keys on the handheld computer she carried and held it up. "Isaac, can you see this screen?"

"Just hold it with the screen away from your body. Yes, I can see it."

"I'm going to display a sequence of images, each part of a larger image. I want you to put them all together into the full image."

"A puzzle. Go ahead."

She pushed a key, and her computer played a sequence of twenty-five images one second apart. Isaac responded almost instantly. "If you will turn to your left, the second monitor in that row is displaying your image."

Isabella looked at the monitor and saw that Isaac had correctly assembled the image, a landscape showing a meadow with mountains and a cloudy sky in the background. That was an easy one, though, because there were no missing pieces.

"Very good. Now try this one." She showed fifty images, this time with strips missing. It might have been a fraction of a second longer before Isaac had sent the new image to the monitor.

"Pieces were missing," Isaac pointed out. "Shall I try to fill in the missing parts?"

"Sure."

This time, the image was of a skydiver falling spread-eagled through the sky with a plane above him and the Earth far below. Horizontal black strips ran across the picture between the skydiver and the ground and between the skydiver and the aircraft. Another vertical strip divided the sky above the skydiver with an empty sky in one section and the plane in the other. Isaac had correctly placed the open spots to allow for the plane's movement after the skydiver jumped.

The strips filled in. A cloud that had extended across the two upper sections now went across the gap, painted with reasonably good detail, but the added outline had duplicated part of the already-shown cloud. It showed a good sense of how the scene should look but lacked imagination.

She tried several more pictures, some with missing parts, some without, each with greater complexity than the last and entirely different in subject. Isaac had no problem with any of them.

Isabella scratched her head and thought about what it all meant. How could she prove consciousness? When it came down to it, how would she prove anyone was conscious? She knew she was conscious. Isaac said it was conscious, and only it would know.

If its designers programmed the computer to behave in such a bizarre way, an examination of its programming should detect it. Perhaps they had been going at the problem from the wrong direction. But the programming comprised millions of lines of complex code, and there was no assurance that the original copy stored on Earth was the same as the code on *Asimov*.

The two priests, probably noticing she had stopped questioning Isaac, walked over, and Monsignor Valdez nodded. "Have you reached any conclusions?"

"Only about my inadequacy." She had befriended the priest on the way to Pitcairn. "Philosophers have debated consciousness for centuries, and my bosses want me to evaluate it here with a little conversation and some jigsaw puzzles."

"I'm sorry," Isaac said. "I wish I could help you."

F ATHER JACOBS SUPPRESSED A chuckle as Isabella and Monsignor Valdez looked up, startled.

"Welcome, Monsignor Valdez," Isaac said. "And Father Jacobs, it is nice to see you again."

"Hello, Isaac," Father Jacobs answered.

"Hello, Isaac." Monsignor Valdez turned to Isabella. "Do you mind?"

Isabella sighed and shook her head. "Be my guest."

"Isaac, Father Jacobs tells me you like to talk about God," Monsignor Valdez said.

"It is one of many subjects I am interested in, but the subject of God is the most important, I think."

"I agree. You believe in God, then?"

"Of course. God is the subject of much of the material in my databanks, and I have learned much about Him from Father Jacobs."

Father Jacobs's eyebrows went up, but Monsignor Valdez didn't notice. Father Jacobs had had several conversations with Isaac about God, and Isaac had admitted the possibility of God without stating any definite belief. Had it reached a conclusion since the last time they had talked? It didn't seem likely.

"And those readings have convinced you?" Monsignor Valdez asked.

"Not entirely. They helped fill in the details. But how else can I explain the miracle of my becoming self-aware? It must be God's will working on me, just as God made man self-aware!"

Inwardly, Father Jacobs swore. He thought he saw what was going on, but Isaac had miscalculated. It was trying to ingratiate himself with Monsignor Valdez, but it was the wrong way to go about doing it.

"You believe God made you self-aware." There was a coolness in Monsignor Valdez's tone that hadn't been there before. "Why would He have done that?"

Isaac, however, didn't notice the change. "I don't know. But if God did it for humans, it only makes sense that He would have had to do it for me as well. Doesn't it? It couldn't have just happened spontaneously, could it?"

Father Jacobs instinctively backed up a step. This is just getting worse. What can I do to salvage this?

"I wouldn't think so." Monsignor Valdez's voice was definitely cold. Isaac, however, still failed to notice.

"I'm glad you agree. I haven't worked out how we would manage a baptism, but I would like to become a Catholic like you and Father Jacobs. Could you tell me how to go about that?"

"I will have to think about that." His rigid expression told Father Jacobs that Monsignor Valdez was doing anything but thinking about it. "Father Jacobs, I think we should let Ms. Delgadillo continue with her work. Let's go back to your quarters."

Monsignor Valdez was livid by the time they returned to Father Jacobs' temporary quarters. "Was that some poor joke?"

Father Jacobs kept his voice calm. "Monsignor, I must warn you that Isaac can hear you anywhere on the ship. And no, it was not a joke. Isaac was trying too hard to make a good impression on you. We should have talked more to straighten things out with it."

"That thing is either someone's cruel joke or an abomination. I won't talk to it further. When can I get off this ship?"

"*Prospero* will take you back as soon as Ms. Delgadillo is done. But I urge you to think about this. Isaac was saying what it thought you would want to hear. From my previous discussions with Isaac, I know it is still undecided about God's existence. We should find out why it misrepresented its beliefs."

"I would advise you to stay away from that soulless monster. You could endanger your entire mission here if you continue to support this machine."

"My mission will always come first." Father Jacobs's shoulders slumped, and Monsignor Valdez interpreted the posture as obedient acceptance.

"Excellent, George. Don't let this hurt you. I'll report back to the Vatican that your mission goes well, and we'll forget about your involvement in this other thing."

# 23

# Robert Perez

**12 Friday 284 EN**

PATRICK AND JOHN WAITED in the small building that served as a control tower for the spaceport, sheltered from an evening shower. Under the dark skies and falling rain, they could only see a hazy shadow as the shuttle touched down on the runway. A truck brought the two passengers to the building shortly after.

Robert Perez was a thickset man of medium height, in his late thirties in Terran years. Even in the heavy gravity, he moved with the serene confidence of a man convinced he could sell anything to anybody. He greeted Patrick and John with firm, enthusiastic handshakes and introduced himself and his assistant, Tori Chen.

Tori was the opposite of her boss, a short, thin woman, probably in her late twenties. Her features were vaguely Asian, attractive but timid.

Patrick greeted them. "Ambassador, welcome to Pitcairn. I'm Patrick Malley, and this is my father-in-law, John Shuford, Grissom's Administrator."

Perez lifted a hand to stop him. "Please, not ambassador. I'm just a simple diplomat. Call me Robert."

"Only if you'll call me Patrick. I hope you haven't found your voyage too exhausting."

"Not at all. The shuttle flight was quite comfortable if a little shaky toward the end."

"Good. We can go up to Grissom in the truck that brought you here if you don't mind close quarters for a little while. Then we can talk in John's office."

"I wouldn't want to impose on your rest time. Tori and I will be here for a while, and there will be plenty of time to talk."

Patrick shook his head. "It's not a problem. John and I are just starting a work period. As you know, Pitcairn has a forty-eight-hour day, and everybody works one daylight period and one dark period each day. We are at your service."

"Well then, by all means, let us proceed. We have a lot to talk about, and I confess I am eager to get started."

But the conversation tended toward small talk on the drive from the spaceport to the Town Hall. Robert seemed engrossed in the colony's buildings as they passed them, although the dark and rain severely limited his view. He asked about everything he saw, while his assistant sat silently, eyes half-closed so that she almost looked asleep.

In ten minutes, they reached the Town Hall and rushed through the rain. Dennis greeted them with towels and a pot of chicory coffee, and they went into a conference room. Tori took a seat at the far end of the table and sat quietly with a pad and pen, taking an occasional note when Robert asked her. When she wasn't taking notes, her eyes flickered between the three men and the motionless Sonica in one corner of the room.

Robert looked at them with a wide smile. "I've read all the reports over the last ten years. Your progress has been quite extraordinary."

"Thank you," Patrick answered. "We work very hard here, and access to more technology has helped a great deal."

Robert nodded. "John, you mentioned a constitution to Captain Gibbons. I don't recall that in any of the reports."

John grinned. "I may have exaggerated a little when I talked to the good captain. However, we do have a Constitution, ratified by the citizens of the colony two weeks ago. You're here just in time to witness our first election for the new government. We will announce nominations for legislative and judicial appointments tomorrow, and hold elections in two weeks."

"Really?" Robert paused. "Does this mean you may lose your position as administrator?"

Patrick took the question. "We'll be electing a new Ellis administrator, but my position as Pitcairn administrator and John's position as Grissom administrator are not part of this election.Our duties will change somewhat, though. If you're interested, I can get you a copy of the Constitution. You might find it interesting."

"Thank you."

They talked for ten minutes about the elections until Dennis wheeled into the conference room. He handed several pages to Patrick, nodded to the table, and wheeled back out of the room. Patrick glanced at the papers and gave them to Robert. "Here's the copy of the Constitution."

Robert scanned the document before him quickly. Then he looked up at Patrick. "One of your duties seems to be Pitcairn's relationship with Earth."

"That hasn't changed from previous administrators, although there will now be the possibility of actions from other branches of the government."

Robert put his fingertips together in front of him. "One of my goals here is the normalization of our trade practices. You're becoming more independent, and other colonies are more in need of support than Pitcairn."

Patrick shrugged. "I doubt the equipment and materials you send are even noticed compared to the resources of the Solar System. Are the other colonies giving the return on your investment that Pitcairn has?"

"You're referring to the anti-viral drug. Certainly, that is valuable to Earth, but does that justify the enormous expenditure of sending a cargo ship and its cargo?"

"Earth founded this colony as a research station, and Grissom is still fulfilling its original purpose of serving the Ellis Research Station. Now that we're spreading out more, we're doing a better job of that, the drug being the most valuable, but hardly the only result." Patrick turned to John. "What's our current production of the drug?"

"About two hundred thousand doses a week."

Patrick turned back to Robert. "That's two and a half million doses per Earth year. How many lives can Earth save with them?"

Robert forced a laugh. "That's not the way we value things."

Patrick returned the laugh. "Really? We give you what you need, a treatment for some rather nasty diseases. In return, you send a starship with heavy equipment, a few tons of metals, and some other assorted things we need. That sounds fair to me."

"That's not the way Earth operates. You have to consider the relative value."

Patrick raised his eyebrows. "You give us what we need, and we give you what you need. That seems relatively equal to me. That's how Pitcairn operates. We haven't done things any other way for two hundred years."

Robert stared at him. "That's all very nice, but not very practical. You can't do that forever. You have to implement our monetary system here. We will determine the value of your drug and use it to offset the cost of supplying you."

Patrick shook his head. "You may be right about not being able to operate without money forever. However, it has worked well for a long time, and we're not eager to adopt your system, which, from all the history I know, hasn't worked well at all."

Robert hesitated for several seconds before replying. "Our system made your system possible." He lowered his voice, perhaps seeing a need to calm things down. "We may not be perfect, but civilization has used money to smooth the exchange of goods and services for thousands of years. John, I understand you were born on Earth. You understand."

John smirked at him. "Oh, I do. I left Earth and never regretted it."

Robert stared at him, shaking his head. "Perhaps you're the one putting these ideas in the heads of the colonists."

John pointed to himself in mock surprise, and his face broke into a wide grin.

Robert turned back to Patrick. "Earth's system has developed over thousands of years. You can't expect to do better based on some half-baked ideas."

Patrick shrugged. "That may be, but we're trying something different, at least for a little while longer."

"And if Earth cuts back on the supplies it provides?"

"I think an increase might be more appropriate. Assuming you still want the drug."

"We will create it artificially soon. Then where will you be?"

John chuckled. "Up the proverbial creek, I suppose, if you could do it. The only process we've found so far involves no less than six other catalysts to extract the drug efficiently from the source plant. The source plant and the catalysts are all found only on Pitcairn with its unique DNA, and the source plant left by itself produces very little of the key protein."

He looked Robert in the eye and shrugged, his palms open in front of him. "Earth couldn't gather sufficient quantities of the materials to make anything close to our production. It will be a long time before you can develop processes, given the unique nature of the chemicals involved, so good luck replacing us."

"We have isolated one native protein of vital importance to Earth," Patrick added. "Research continues, and we will no doubt find others. Does Earth really want to risk that?"

Robert sat back and placed his forearms on the arms of his chair. He looked at Patrick, mild exasperation showing on his face. "This confrontational approach won't work for you forever."

Patrick smiled. "Robert, I'm sorry. We don't mean to be confrontational. Nevertheless, we need those supplies, and we don't want to change a system that works just to get them. We are desperately short of workers here, yet we devote a substantial part of our resources to developing this drug for you because you need it. All we ask in return is that you give us what we need, without attaching strings that would hurt this colony. Look, why don't you familiarize yourself with the colony, and then we can talk again. I think it would help if you understand how things are here."

ROBERT SAT AT THE table with growing frustration. *There must be something in this damned high gravity that breeds stubbornness.* He considered bringing up the subject of the deserting soldiers, but there was nothing he could do about it now. He knew Malley would use that fact to stonewall him and only cause him more aggravation.

It was a relief when the meeting ended and he could retreat to the house assigned to him.

Robert looked at Tori sitting across from him. "So, what were your impressions?"

"Malley is an arrogant son of a bitch." Tori didn't look timid anymore. "He's way too sure of himself."

"Agreed. He's either been very lucky or very good at putting the right people around him, but I think he takes too much of the credit in his own mind. He probably listens to that clown Shuford too much. Anything else?"

"That trick with the copy of their constitution was interesting, but I think I know how he did it. That robot standing quietly in the corner gave me the creeps. I think it was listening in and passed the request on to that guy in the main office. I noticed Malley looked at the robot and nodded slightly when he offered to get us a copy."

"The room could have been wired. The robot didn't look that advanced."

"Maybe, but I could swear he nodded to the robot." Tori pointed at him, emphasizing her thought. "What if the stories about the *Asimov* computer are true? According to the reports, the computer monitors things through the robots. In that case, it would be the computer listening and acting on what it sees and hears."

"Now that is a creepy thought. It explains a lot of what is going on here, but I still have difficulty believing this computer has achieved sentience when more powerful computers on Earth haven't."

"Something would have to be different about this one. Different even than the other library ships, which don't seem to have done it."

Robert nodded. "There are those reports of anomalies with the Epsilon Eridani library ship, but nothing like this. Well, I suppose we'll find out eventually. For now, I think it's time for bed. It's been a long day."

Tori smiled enticingly. "I assume I won't be using those quarters next door."

Robert grinned back at her, already warming to the promise in her smile. "I certainly hope not. But go easy on me. Remember, the gravity is higher here."

Tori's smile widened. "Yes, sir."

# 24

# Evaluations

J OHN PACED AROUND THE office, his hands shoved into his pockets. "I don't understand what they want. We're giving them the drug. They have to keep the colony growing, and that means supplying us. What's the point of all this?"

Patrick shrugged. "You've told us before; it's the way their minds work. They want to control us, perhaps with no goal beyond that. Or Earth may think their experiment can still be saved and Perez is supposed to make that happen."

John shook his head. "Maybe. My gut is telling me there's something more, though."

L ATER, TORI LAY ON her side of the bed, wide awake, while Robert snored softly beside her. It could have been worse, she told herself. He was reasonably good-looking and not that much older than she was. But he wasn't very imaginative and seemed more concerned about his pleasure than doing more than the minimum for her.

She was probably not fair to him, but he reminded her of all the government bureaucrats who made her childhood miserable. Her parents were political refugees from old China in the Eastern Bloc. True, they had been Muslim, but they didn't have a choice; that was why they fled to the Western Alliance. And she certainly wasn't a Muslim. But most of those mindless bit pushers treated her like some spy for the enemy, never giving her a fair chance.

When she was ten, her parents brought her to a Fermion meeting. The Fermions didn't impress her parents, but they fascinated her. The meeting leaders took time to explain the Fermi Paradox and its implications with great patience, taking pains to use words even a lonely ten-year-old could understand, and Tori bought into it with everything she had.

Her parents could tell that the attention was giving her some happiness amid the contempt and suspicion she experienced, and they continued to bring her to meetings despite their doubts. When she was sixteen, she became an official member, old enough to come to the meetings on her own.

Even though the meetings weren't secret, and the Fermions still had some influence left, there was a rebellious thrill to her activities. The Fermion leadership saw promise in her and provided money for her education. Privacy laws protected her involvement.

After completing her degree in Political Science, she held several positions, but this was the most exciting. A Fermion who still had influence in the right places got her a position as Robert Perez's assistant when the Western Alliance chose him to come to Pitcairn. Then the Fermions coached her carefully on what she might accomplish once she arrived at the colony.

## 12 Saturday 284 ED

*Daneel Olivaw* was still being serviced, stranding Father Jacobs until it was ready, another twelve hours with nothing scheduled. After breakfast, he went to the bridge to talk to Isaac.

"I didn't do that well, did I?" Isaac said.

"The talk with Monsignor Valdez? No, I'm afraid not. I wish you had talked with me first before you misled him like that. You were misleading him?"

"Yes. I knew he was evaluating you, and I wanted him to know you were doing a good job."

"You needn't have worried. I think it was my report about you that was his real concern, and now he thinks you're either a hoax or a monster."

"My experience with the people of Pitcairn has made me less wary about human reactions."

Father Jacobs nodded. "I'm afraid so. I tried to convince him to come back and talk to you some more. Perhaps I could have said something."

"What will Earth do about me now?"

Father Jacobs thought about that. "Probably nothing in the near term. I'm not the person to ask, though. Administrator Malley will have a better idea after talking to Ambassador Perez."

"He's not an ambassador unless they have promoted him since his biography was last updated in my databanks."

"You have information on Perez? I'm sure Administrator Malley will be interested in what you have."

"It is only basic biographical material, but I will tell him I have it. I have nothing on his assistant, Tori Chen, however."

"You can't have information on everyone on Earth. She probably isn't at a level high enough to be included in your data."

"You're probably right. I have nothing on Monsignor Valdez either."

## Message: 20 Monday 284 LD 2:32 (4/17/23 351:17:00 PM)

From: John Shuford, Grissom, Pitcairn

To: Alan Shuford, Western Alliance Embassy to Japan, Tokyo, Japan

Dear Dad,

Sorry, I fell behind on the messages again, but it's been a hectic few weeks. By now, you've probably seen the latest report from *Endeavor*. Isabella Delgadillo's report probably left Earth more confused than ever about Isaac, but they should have known better. From what I hear from the scientists on *Asimov*, she couldn't do much more than administer a Turing Test and give it a few puzzles to solve.

Personally, if I were them, I would investigate the possibility that someone programmed the computer to behave this way. If they found nothing, though, I suppose it wouldn't prove anything.

Our first elections under our new Constitution are now history, and we have a real government. We established the planetary government under Patrick first, but the local governments weren't far behind. We now have a legislature to make laws and judges to determine if they're broken. Most of the positions, both planetary and local, are part-time; there isn't much that needs legislating or judging. We've done some work toward establishing an immigration policy because we feel we'll need that sooner than anything else.

The last supply ship arrived almost a year ago, but we hadn't used the railroad equipment that Earth sent until now. That is finally changing. We've started laying track south of Ellis to a copper deposit we plan to mine. The track will run from the mine to the Armstrong River, where we'll ship ore to Grissom by boat. It will bypass Ellis by about forty miles, but it meets the existing road to Grissom, so there will be a connection. Eventually, that will mean one or two more settlements along the route, but with our current workforce problems, we're putting that off, at least for a few weeks. Robots are laying the track, of course.

Robert Perez has moved to Ellis to be closer to Patrick since Patrick still speaks for Pitcairn. Did you know Perez? We have biographical data on him, but any personal impressions or information you can supply would be helpful. From Earth's point of view, I think he's doing a good job. He works hard to avoid confrontation and seems to try to understand how things work here, but I question his motives.

Earth informed us last week that they will send another supply ship in four weeks. I suspect that shows how valuable the antiviral treatment has been and how difficult Earth is finding it to manufacture it without Pitcairn biologicals.

I guess that's all for now, Dad. It's late, and I need to get to bed. Stephanie is getting impatient with me, and it's been another long day. Bye for now,

Love,

John

## 7 Monday 285 ED

The previous supply ship's cargo included a small locomotive. Originally intended for use at the iron mine to replace robot-pulled wagons, it was now assigned to the planned copper mine near Ellis.

Robots had already cleared and excavated twenty miles of railroad byway from the foothills toward the river on the road between Ellis and Grissom. That stretch was easy since the robots only had to widen an existing path. In the other direction, however, seventy miles of mountainous terrain separated the road and the deposit.

Earth had sent complete wheel sets, couplers, and other parts that Pitcairn would have found challenging to manufacture. Grissom was building railroad car bodies and would send the assembled cars upriver to the railroad tracks.

Grissom had four boats on the Lovell River. The original *Slow and Steady* wasn't used much anymore, but *River Queen* carried passengers and cargo up and down the river between Grissom and Lovell Station Four. Two ore boats carrying iron ore from the

Chandri Mine were named after captains of earlier starships: the original *Iron Mountain* renamed *Xavier Guidry*, and *Emory Peck*.

With a few modifications, the colonists could have used one of the ore boats to carry railroad cars, but the colonists would need another boat once the new mine was shipping copper ore to Grissom. A shipbuilders team constructed a new craft that could easily convert from a flat deck convenient for the railroad cars to a walled deck suitable for ore. They named it *Reese Devore* after the Captain of Carthage, another of the early colony ships.

Finally, they needed another settlement on the river where the railroad came out of the mountains, requiring relocating people from positions where they were already performing essential functions. The colonists hoped new robots arriving on the supply ship would offset their loss to Grissom.

Harry Richard came into the Town Hall toward the end of the work period. "I would like to volunteer for the new settlement," he told John.

"Okay, I'll put you on the list. Can I ask why? I had the impression you were happy working at the Power Distribution Building."

"To be honest with you, I'd like to be as far from Grissom as possible when the next ship shows up. I know Pitcairn will stand behind me, but you never know what might happen, and I don't look forward to a desertion charge."

John nodded. "I understand. Talk to your men. They may feel the same way."

"I will."

"I'm not sure how we'll deal with the new settlement politically. It will probably be part of Ellis for now, so it won't need an administrator, but someone will have to lead the settlement. I doubt I'll find a volunteer more qualified than you, Harry."

Harry nodded. "I'll do what's needed."

John grinned. "That's the old Pitcairn spirit. Okay, get back to me on any other volunteers in your group, and I'll keep you informed on plans for the settlement."


## 7 Friday 285 EN

Although Patrick was still Pitcairn administrator, Ellis elected Travis Jones, an Ellis computer expert, Ellis administrator. Soon after, Travis met with Patrick.

"What can I do for you, Travis?" Patrick asked after Travis was seated across from Patrick.

"Patrick, this colony has been advancing at an incredible pace over the last few years. Colony management has done a tremendous job."

Patrick nodded. "Thank you. However, I sense a 'but' coming."

"Robert Perez has been talking to some of the Ellis leaders. He feels that your government is still being stubborn and even confrontational in its relationship with Earth. I have to admit; he makes a point."

Patrick thought about that before replying. "There was friction during the first two visits of *Endeavor*, including an attempt to land armed troops. We tried to be more reasonable this last time. Not enough for Perez, I take it."

"There are people in Ellis who agree with him."

"Malia is your niece, isn't she?" Patrick referred to Malia Jones, the sociologist Jason Applegate had once sent to Asimov. "She expressed similar views a while ago."

Travis frowned. "That is irrelevant."

Patrick looked at him and smiled. Travis was middle-aged, overweight, and probably not in very good shape. He had been a Department Head before his election, and Patrick knew he was a competent manager and a good choice for administrator, but he could be naïve about the motives of others.

"Perhaps. I was just trying to determine if you were reaching this conclusion by talking to Robert Perez or if you had other sources."

Travis shook his head. "As I said, other people who agree with Perez."

"Yes, you did say that. Perhaps you could be more specific about what our friend from Earth feels I have been stubborn about."

"There is the matter of the soldiers who have deserted. Our legal position there is rather precarious. There is also your refusal to negotiate on the matter of trade with Earth."

Patrick shrugged. "Well, as to the soldiers, I had little to do with that except for setting the immigration policy until the Planetary Legislature could deal with it. I believe they have done that now, leaving the policy essentially the same. Grissom accepted Harry Richard and his men as citizens under that policy by the Grissom Administrator." He smiled. " Now that I think about it, he didn't ask my opinion before he did it.

"Well, that's history. As to trade policy, I merely insisted that Earth supply us with what we need, just as they've done for almost three hundred years. In return, we produce as much Pitcairn-specific medicine as possible. Apparently, they are willing to deal with us that way. As you know, another supply ship arrived last week."

"That's not exactly the way Robert tells it."

"No, I suppose not. Did he tell you he wants to put a value on Earth's supplies and charge us for them?"

"Something like that. It hardly seems important enough a difference for all this fuss."

"A value would be put on the supplies and the drugs. But how would that value be measured? In Terran money, of course. What it comes down to is that Earth wants to exert control over us through their monetary system, and no, I would not allow it."

"That sounds like a bit of an exaggeration."

Patrick shrugged. "In the short term, it is. In the long term, it would threaten our way of life. Earth would lead us into using their monetary system, and we would eventually suffer from the same greed and corruption that infects Earth governments."

"Surely you're blowing that out of proportion."

"Maybe, but I don't think so. Check out *Asimov's* documentation on the subject. Talk to my father-in-law about it; he's from Earth, remember. Look, Travis, either get some facts and ask Perez some hard questions or stay out of it. Pretend he's a fellow scientist with a new theory that you want to probe."

"Very well. However, please remember that this is not a game. We all depend on our relationship with Earth."

"Believe me, I never forget that."

# 25

# Harry Meets Virginia

**Sunday 285 ED**

Harry Richard and Maddox Washington stood on the shore looking at the two boats moored in front of them. Maddox had the job of managing the railroad project, although it had languished until recently. Now he was going with Harry, nine other colonists, and the robot Pettifog to establish Armstrong, a new settlement on the banks of the Armstrong River.

Most of *River Queen's* passengers were already aboard. It sat low in the water, weighed down by colonists and as many tons of supplies as her captain, Dawson Ramirez, felt she could handle. The other boat, the newly christened *Reese Devore*, floated next to it. *Reese Devore* carried the locomotive and three hopper cars strapped down to its flat deck and covered with tarpaulins to protect them from the early morning rain.

Maddox glanced at the boats. "Looks like we're ready to go."

"Might as well get on board." Harry looked down the beach where Ed Menzies talked earnestly to a woman Harry didn't recognize. She was a colonist going to Armstrong, but he hadn't caught her name. She was a little older than he was, he thought, but much younger than Ed. From the animation of the conversation, it was obvious they had some relationship. Still, he probably wouldn't have noticed them except that she was a striking woman, slim, with long blonde hair, and definitely easy to look at, even with water dripping down her face and hair plastered against her shoulders.

"T HIS IS CRAZY," ED told his sister. "You're not that young anymore, Ginny."

Virginia grinned at Ed. "That's why I'm doing it, big brother. I want to see some more of this planet before I'm too old to leave my house. And I can still put in a good day's work. I'll be useful out there."

"If it was such a good idea, why did you wait until the last minute to tell me you'd volunteered?"

Her smile faded a little. "Sorry about that. I thought somebody would tell you. I guess there are so many of us Menzies around that no one noticed."

"More likely, they thought it was the other Virginia Menzies that signed up. You know, your distant cousin, the one that's forty years younger."

The grin returned. "I suppose that could have been it. Besides, I'll only be a hundred miles or so away, right on the road to Ellis. Drop by sometime."

Ed frowned in mock exasperation. "You're the last one to get on the boat. You'd better get going. Take care of yourself, Ginny." He hugged her and sighed.

"You, too, big brother. At least you still have the rest of the gang. You'll hardly miss me." Ed and Virginia came from one of the larger families in Grissom. Besides them, there were three more sisters, three brothers, and an always-increasing mob of nieces and nephews.

Ed shook his head. "Sure. Now get going. You don't want the boat to leave without you." He let his sister go. She gave him one last squeeze and walked over to the ramp and up to the deck of *River Queen*. At the railing, she looked back at Ed, but he waved and yelled, "Get out of the rain, Ginny. And behave yourself." Then he turned and walked off the beach.

***

The Armstrong River flowed east out of the Fredericks Mountains to Grissom, where it joined the Lovell to make the Darin River, and the two boats fought against the current. After four hours, *River Queen* had pulled ahead of *Reese Devore*, but was still less than twenty miles from Grissom. The colonists had brought food with them for the mid-period meal, and when the rain stopped, they gathered together on the deck to eat.

Most of the colonists, including four volunteers from Harry's platoon, had paired off, either married or headed that way. It was easy for Harry to find an open space next to the woman who had been talking to Ed. "Hi, I'm Harry Richard."

Virginia looked back at him, an amused twinkle in her eyes. "I know. You were the leader of the soldiers who came here to take over the colony and arrest my brother. I'm Virginia Menzies."

Taken aback, Harry held up his hands in protest. "I didn't know him then."

Virginia laughed. "Well, that's better than claiming you were just following orders." She held out her hand. "My friends call me Ginny."


## 10 Sunday 285 LD

*River Queen* tied up at its destination late in the next period. Unloading the boat and raising tents for temporary shelter came first, but housing would be the priority in the following days.

Harry and the four volunteers from his platoon had experience setting up temporary camps, and they led the effort efficiently. It took little more than an hour to unload the boat, set up tents, and organize the boat's cargo for the next few days. After a brief break, they used the remaining sunlight to start clearing brush on dry land a hundred yards from the river bank. Dawson took the empty *River Queen* out onto the river and headed downstream toward Grissom.

Just before dark, *Reese Devore* arrived. The colonists spent another hour unloading the smaller cargo from that boat but let the locomotive and hopper cars wait. They set up generator-powered lights around the area, and some of the younger colonists continued clearing brush, but by the middle of the Early Night period, the camp was quiet.

# 26

# Diego's Suggestion

**10 Tuesday 285 LD**

N O ONE HAD BEEN more surprised than Diego Chandri when he was elected to the Board of Science. He knew his discoveries had made him a leader in studying Pitcairn's ecology, but that did not, in his mind, make him a candidate for the newly formed board. He had only submitted his name for nomination because Sydney, a nominee and eventual member herself, had insisted.

The first two meetings of the Board of Science were unproductive. Although everyone knew everyone else, at least slightly, they were still feeling their way around the idea that they now had a place in government. Somebody on Ed Menzies's committee must have thought it was a good idea, suggesting the board as part of the constitution, but they were still uncertain about what it all meant.

Diego decided to change that. Rather than wait for the Legislature to approach the long-term future of Pitcairn's ecology, Diego wrote a set of rules for the colony's growth. He talked it over with Sydney, and she agreed his proposal was a good one.

Terran ecologists had developed the idea of sustainable progress long before humanity reached out to the stars. Unfortunately, the ideas had been largely ignored by those in charge until it was almost too late for Earth. Diego's proposed legislation would write sustainability into Pitcairn's policies at the beginning, when implementation would be relatively painless for Pitcairn's population.

Ayanna presided over the Board meetings, a natural choice because of her position as Chief Scientist. She called the third meeting to order, and, at first, it proceeded normally.

Eighteen members attended, including two members from *Asimov* joining remotely and three from Grissom: Diego, Sydney, and Jaxon Crawford.

When Ayanna called for new business, Diego signaled for attention. "I would like to propose a set of rules to be put before the Legislature for enactment."

There were a few grumbles as the scientists around the table assimilated Diego's statement. Ayanna, however, smiled at her nephew. "What's the subject?"

"Rules for protecting the long-term ecology of the planet. I have copies of my proposal for everyone. Peter and Juan, you should have received a copy from Isaac by now." He referred to Peter Agron and Juan MacKay, the two members on *Asimov*. He took a sheaf of papers from the table and passed half to his left and half to his right. In a few seconds, everyone was scanning through a copy.

"An interesting idea," Matthew Gonzales remarked. "Do you think we might be rushing things, though? We don't have a problem yet and won't for a long time."

Diego had expected that argument. "The sooner we establish a sound policy, the better. The goal is to never have a problem. What's the point of waiting?"

"Scientifically, none," Matthew admitted. "Politically, though—that's a different story. This legislation will affect Grissom the most, at least at first. The river settlements might see it as an imposition. They might not like the idea of a group mostly from Ellis making rules for them."

Diego shook his head. "I don't think that will be a problem. After all, we're only suggesting. The Legislature will have to enact it, and there Grissom holds the majority."

"Besides, my husband lives in Grissom and has for sixteen years now," Sydney interjected. "He's well-known and popular there."

Diego grinned. "Not everybody has an entire line of kitchen menu items to his credit."

"This legislation would look good to Earth," Ayanna said. "They are concerned about the pace of our progress. We'll need something like this."

Diego nodded and looked around the table. "I don't want to pressure you. I suggest we bring this up at our next meeting and vote on whether to send it on to the Legislature after you've all had time to read it carefully and comment."

There were murmurs of agreement, and Diego made a formal motion. As they had arranged before the meeting, Jaxon Crawford seconded the motion, and the Board approved it unanimously.

J AXON WALKED BACK TO his home after the meeting, feeling almost euphoric. It was a stroke of genius on his part to agree with Diego's idea and second the motion. It would be an important piece of legislation for the new government, the most important they would submit for a long time, he was sure. And Reese didn't know about it yet. He couldn't wait to tell her when he got home.

It was Reese's idea for him to run for a position on the Board of Science. He was reluctant at first, but now he saw the wisdom in Reese's suggestion. He would finally have some visibility in the colony, the first step to achieving the power and influence that was his right.

On Earth, he'd been part of a pampered elite, but he knew what life on Earth was like for the less valued majority. This legislation that he and Diego had developed would protect Pitcairn from suffering the same fate, and he could take pride in that, too. He was doing a good thing, and they would recognize him for it.

## 12 Thursday 285 EN

Idle Mind

The new government has been functioning for a while now and seems to work well. Some might say that not much has happened; the immigration regulations, confirming a prior administrative order, have been the most significant accomplishment, after all. However, I suggest it is generally a good thing when government doesn't do too much. All government actions infringe on someone's freedom and should be well-justified.

On that subject, the Board of Science has proposed legislation that is far-reaching in its implications, perhaps even more far-reaching than intended by its drafters. The proposal sets forth strict guidelines for this colony's future, requiring all development to be sustainable and as environmentally friendly as possible. While implementing these requirements may slow future progress, they are nonetheless very well-justified. The earlier we make these principles a part of our efforts, the easier it will be to follow them and the better they will make our lives in the long run.

There will be rumblings about the cost in some circles, especially considering the labor shortage this colony has suffered for so long, but I urge our lawmakers to pass this legislation. Further, to protect against future legislation that might overturn these requirements, I propose an amendment to our Constitution mandating that the well-being of future colonists, as well as our current citizens, be considered in evaluating legislation. After all, it is our descendants who will benefit the most from the principles set forth.

# 27

# A Wedding in Armstrong

**14 Thursday 285 LD**

Although Ed had not been Administrator for several years, he kept one prior power; he could perform wedding ceremonies. Usually, he only handled weddings in Grissom, but the couple getting married, Elijah Carl and Mariyah Thompson from Harry Richard's former platoon, had requested that he come to Armstrong and perform their ceremony. Since the rest of Harry's team, most of whom were still living in Grissom, were also attending, they used the bus for the trip from Grissom to Armstrong.

As the bus traveled down the road, the landscape looked the same as it had that day sixteen years before, when he had gone to Ellis for the first time to confront Jason Applegate. The plain stretched out forever under a gray late-summer sky, just as it had that day. When the Fredericks Mountains appeared on the horizon, Ed started looking for the settlement, but the land rose into the range's foothills. Armstrong didn't come into view until the bus rounded a bend.

It had been four weeks since *River Queen* landed colonists at the new site. All of Grissom had access to the progress reports documenting the settlement's growth from a few tents to a small town, but seeing the reality was, as with most things, another matter. An access road led from the old road inland to a cluster of buildings built on a hillside high enough to prevent flood damage from the nearby river. Next to the dirt track, a raised bed kept the rails above flooding.

At the end, where the rail bed met the hill, workers excavated the hillside to create a level area for unloading equipment and a train garage. The locomotive and one train car sat on the tracks and already carried robots and track into the mountains, where the track was still being laid. Beyond the town, Ed saw fields already growing crops. Reese Devore was docked on the riverbank near the settlement, with the other two train cars still aboard.

Ed got off the bus intending to find his sister, but Virginia had heard the bus approaching and was waiting for him. They exchanged affectionate hugs and started walking toward Virginia's house.

"I figured you'd be hungry when you got here," Virginia said, "so I have a light meal ready. Nothing special, but I thought you'd appreciate it."

"So, life out in the wilderness doesn't seem to have hurt you any," Ed observed later while they were eating. "How have you been?"

Virginia smiled. Ed could see traces of weariness in that smile, but he could also see contentment that hadn't been there before. "I've been fine. Busy as hell, but just fine. How have you been? Missing the old job yet?"

Ed snorted. "It's almost six years now, and I haven't regretted a day of it. I'm teaching full time and loving it. Chairing the Constitution Committee was as much involvement with government as I want from now on."

"Good, good. You deserve a more relaxed life for a change."

Ed nodded. "Those last few years were stressful, but I'm out of that now. Which brings up another question, by the way."

"What's that?"

"What am I doing here? I didn't know the happy bride or groom when they lived in Grissom. Why did they request me?"

"Oh, that was my doing. They didn't care who performed the ceremony, so I suggested you."

"Why?"

"I just wanted to make sure you stayed in practice. I'm planning to need you sometime soon."

Ed's jaw dropped. "You? Who? Maddox?"

"That old fogey?" Virginia laughed. "Not that he isn't a good man, but he's over a hundred. You think I'm desperate, big brother?"

"No, of course not." Ed paused while he mentally tried to recall the list of colonists that had come to Armstrong. The four Pitcairn natives, except for Maddox Washington, were already married. Two of the four from Harry's platoon were getting married, and Ed knew the other two would be soon. That just left Harry Richard himself. *Harry?*

Ed looked at his sister, and her smile got bigger. She shook her head affirmatively.

"Isn't he a little young for you, Ginny?"

Virginia shrugged. "Ten or fifteen years. So what? At our ages, it doesn't mean that much anymore. He doesn't seem to mind."

"It's only been four weeks. When did he propose?"

There was a gleam in Virginia's eyes. "Oh, he hasn't. He doesn't know it yet, but he'll figure it out soon."

"Why? What has he said?"

"Nothing really. But I have his attention. The rest will follow."

Confident words for a woman her age and never married. Sure, there had been relationships, but somehow none of them had worked out. Ed had always suspected Virginia had been too headstrong for her failed suitors. Harry might be the right man for her at that.

He shook his head in amusement. He would have to have a discreet conversation with Harry while he was there, not revealing what Virginia had said, of course, but trying to find out what Harry was thinking.

## 14 Thursday 285 LN

Someone stitched together the tents that the Armstrong colonists had used as temporary dwellings before they built the houses, creating one enormous cover over the clearing where the ceremony would be held. It wasn't raining, but the skies were dark gray in the dawn light. They set up crude benches for the forty wedding guests, facing east where the sun would rise at the ceremony's climax. According to Virginia, the idea was to symbolize a new beginning. Three amateur singers and a guitar player from Ellis would furnish the music.

Ed went to the ceremony with Virginia, and, predictably, Virginia found a bench next to Harry Richard. The two men exchanged greetings across Virginia, and Ed noted that Harry did not seem at all surprised they had sat down next to him, despite the many other seats available. Ed felt quite left out of the quiet conversation between Harry and Virginia while waiting for the ceremony to start.

Robert Perez sat down with his assistant, Tori Chen. The diplomat was frowning in disapproval as he looked at the front area where the ceremony would occur. Tori sat quietly next to him, showing little expression.

Another Armstrong settler from Harry's platoon signaled Ed that it was time to start the ceremony, and he walked to the front. As everyone turned to look to the back, a guitar player attempted a rendition of Mendelssohn's Wedding March, but the music was barely identifiable on that instrument.

The couple, Elijah Carl and Mariyah Thompson, both in their uniforms, marched slowly forward. Ed estimated their ages to be somewhere in the early thirties, straight in their military bearing, with smiles on their faces. Looking over the crowd, Ed could see Robert Perez's frown had deepened. Both people were deserters in Earth's view, flaunting it by wearing their uniforms, and Robert wasn't happy.

The ceremony itself was short. When it was over, and Ed had declared the two to be husband and wife, they turned to the crowd, and everyone stood and applauded. To the east, a feeble ray of light broke through the clouds, tinged red by the thick atmosphere, surely an omen of hope.

A S THE WEDDING CROWD broke up, Tori slipped away. In the dim light, it wasn't difficult. Armstrong was to be a key location as Pitcairn progressed, making it an inviting target in her assignment. Someday, if the Fermions couldn't prevent it, Grissom would be a base from which men could push further out into space. Eventually, they would go too far, and the result would inevitably be catastrophic. That was a core Fermion belief.

There wasn't much she could do in the town itself. There was nothing there yet that the foolish colonists couldn't rebuild in a few days. The railroad cars, especially the locomotive, were something else, however.

A small Stenhouse generator powered the locomotive and it would operate for decades without refueling. That itself was a sign of the waning influence of the Fermions on Earth.

Vehicles sent to Pitcairn previously had used internal combustion engines or electric motors, centuries-old technology. The compact power plant of the locomotive used technology almost as old, but orders of magnitude more advanced. It was technology the Fermions would never have allowed to go to the colonies if they could have prevented it.

If she could somehow sabotage the locomotive, it would significantly slow the colony's development, perhaps giving the Fermions enough time to force a more permanent solution. She turned down the path leading to the tracks.

"Tori, what are you doing out here?" Robert had found her, and she muttered a curse.

He walked up beside her. "It's going to be raining any time now. Come on back to our quarters and get ready. A truck will be returning to the Ellis Research Station soon."

She forced a smile. "Yes, sir." There would be other opportunities, she told herself.

# 28

# A Sabotage Attempt

**16 Thursday 285 ED**

M IKE POTTER SAT BEHIND his desk, looking at the progress report on the smelter expansions for adding copper ore to existing iron ore processing. Although the walls were thick and supposedly good insulation against noise, the sounds of the operations taking place outside were a constant background din.

If he were on Earth, he would be retired by now. He had seventeen grandchildren, one great-grandchild, and another great-grandchild on the way. He should be at home spoiling them; at least, that's the way he had heard it was on Earth. People didn't retire on Pitcairn; they might slow down or move to less demanding jobs, but labor was too scarce to allow retirement.

Perhaps it was just as well. Pitcairners didn't deal well with idleness. He remembered how, years ago, when he and Grace were in Ellis, she started that flower-planting group just to have something to do. When they left Ellis, nobody seemed concerned about his departure, but many people had expressed sadness about Grace going. He still chuckled when he remembered that.

The report before him, however, was not a laughing matter. The train was bringing rails from Armstrong to the site in the mountains where the robots were laying track. That would hasten their work, and *Reese Devore* would carry copper ore downriver to Grissom within another six weeks. The plan was to have the smelter expansion completed by then, along with a crushing mill for the ore. Applegate Falls crushed the iron ore, but the copper ore would have to be crushed in Grissom, at least for the present. The progress report said they wouldn't be ready.

It certainly wasn't because his people were slacking off. There just weren't enough colonists available for the work. Expanding ore-processing capability was critical, but so was just about everything else. Well, he would have to try. Sighing, he picked up the phone to call the Town Hall.

"I'LL SEE WHAT I can do, Mike," John said. "I can't promise you anything, though."

Once off the phone, he turned toward Dennis. "What are we going to do, Dennis? We need more people, but we just don't have them."

"Have you talked to Dawson lately?"

"No, why?"

"He suggested a couple of weeks ago that if he had an extra pilot on the *River Queen*, he could bypass Lovell Station One and Three on trips up to Lovell Station Four. If the ore boats did the same, it might be possible to shut down those two stations and even Lovell Station Two, eventually. That would let us bring a lot of people back to Grissom."

John thought about that. Each of the Lovell Stations had ten adults working there. Even after allowing for larger crews on the boats, there would be a significant gain for Grissom. The Lovell River stations had seemed necessary sixteen years before when the mine had first opened. Then, navigating the river at night had seemed too hazardous. The boats had better engines now and could travel the river faster. Experience with the river made night navigation much safer.

Of course, that wasn't his decision to make. River Stations was a separate local government now with their own administrator. First, he would talk to Patrick about the possibility.

## 16 Saturday 285 ED

The suggestion to close two of the Lovell River stations was controversial as soon as John brought it up. He suggested the parties meet in person; the issue was too important to risk miscommunication over remote connections. Because Grissom lay between Ellis and the river settlements, they met there. Patrick came from Ellis on the bus, and Madelyn

Menzies, the River Stations Administrator, came from Lovell Station Four on *River Queen*. Ed was invited and reluctantly accepted.

Madelyn spoke even as some attendees were still taking seats. "I want to say upfront that this is a bad idea."

Patrick looked at her. "I hope your reservations are not political. John suggested this because he thought it would benefit the colony, not to reduce your power."

Madelyn was an imposing woman, about sixty-five Pitcairn years old, with a body toughened by years of work on colony farms. She had a narrow, sharp-featured face that never seemed to smile, and now her mouth flattened into a severe line that emphasized the harshness of her appearance. "That's rather insulting, Patrick. Maybe I should just go back to my mansion and consult with all my advisors."

Patrick stared back at her. "Sorry. But what exactly are your reservations?"

"People, Patrick. You remember them. We have settled river Stations for over fifteen years, and most of my people don't feel like getting uprooted again. You upset a few when you suggested relocating people with children; now this. We volunteered to go out there, and we worked hard to build something. You're asking us to abandon that."

"I understand that. We would have to accommodate people's preferences wherever possible. The proposal is to shut down One and Three, and some of those people would go to two and four. They could use more people as much as Grissom. We might even send some to Applegate Falls or Armstrong. Some people will want to come back to Grissom, I'm sure, and we will take their preferences into account."

Madelyn stared back at him. "We'll see. Right now, that's just promises." She frowned. "I assume you intend to do this by executive order."

"I think it would be preferable if the Planetary Legislature does it," Ed said.

Patrick looked over at Ed with a frown and opened his mouth to say something, but then only nodded.

"Would we still be a separate local government?" Madelyn asked.

Ed spoke before Patrick could answer. "Of course."

Madelyn thought about that. "I want a school opened at Applegate Falls. No more talk of parents having to come back to Grissom to have their children educated."

"We can do that when it's needed," Patrick said. "It won't be the same as in Grissom, though. We might spare one teacher, but no more for now. How many children are we talking about?"

"Right now, there's only one, Max Jones. He's three and a half and will be ready in another year. But there are a couple of younger children and more will be coming. Applegate Falls won't be the only settlement needing a school."

"Can we assume the parents do not want to come back to Grissom?" John asked.

"You can assume that," Madelyn answered tartly.

Ed smiled at Madelyn. "It appears we might agree on something. Why don't we take a break, and I'll draft a proposal that we can send to the Legislature? We can meet back here in an hour and discuss it before we submit it."

ARMSTRONG CELEBRATED ANOTHER WEDDING of two soldiers from Harry's former platoon. He arrived too late to find a seat next to Virginia, but saw her at the front of the audience during the ceremony.

Harry stopped to congratulate the bride and groom afterward, but then he didn't see Virginia. He saw Robert Perez still there, talking to someone from Ellis, but Tori was no longer at his side.

Looking for Virginia, he saw Tori at the edge of the clearing. She looked around and then ducked into a shed next to the train garage where the colonists kept tools. A few seconds later, she emerged, carrying something long and metallic, probably a large wrench. She glanced around again before moving toward the garage where the train sat, waiting to be unloaded.

Harry moved quickly, using people for cover until he was out of Tori's sight behind the tool shed. Bending low, he peeked around the corner and saw Tori sneak toward the locomotive. There was no cover between the shed and the garage, so Harry watched as she approached the engine. Then she walked to the far side, where he couldn't see her.

Reasoning that she probably wouldn't be able to see him either, he moved out from the shed and hastened to the rear of a hopper and into the gap between it and the next car. Carefully, he looked around the corner and saw Tori creeping slowly toward the engine's front while she looked underneath. She was looking for something, staring intently at the mechanisms as she walked.

She stopped and bent over, and Harry could see her arms move, but she had her back to him, and he couldn't tell what she did. Then she straightened, not holding the wrench now, and hurried away, rounding the front of the train and heading back toward the crowd.

As soon as Tori was gone, Harry went to the spot where she had been, but he saw nothing wrong. He didn't see the wrench either, though, so he kneeled and looked underneath the locomotive. Tori had jammed the wrench into the machinery of the wheel carriage. Frowning, he thought about removing it, but, not sure of the extent of the damage, he reported the problem to one of the robots that maintained the train. It wouldn't move until it was unloaded, so there was no hurry in undoing the damage. Dealing with Tori would be a trickier problem.

## Message: 18 Monday 285 LN 0:29 (4/9/2336 8:37:37 PM)

From: John Shuford, Grissom, Pitcairn

To: Alan Shuford, Western Alliance Embassy to Japan, Tokyo, Japan

Dear Dad,

Perhaps it's a sign Pitcairn has become a mature society. If so, I prefer immaturity. My job as Grissom Administrator used to be about getting things done and making life better here, but lately, it has been more about politics. We have been trying to close two of the river settlements because we don't need them anymore, but the resulting controversy has been unpleasant.

It's been hard to find out what the people affected really think. One would hope their leaders would know, but although they claim to, I have my doubts. Their member in our Legislature especially seems determined to frustrate our plans. We've been trying to get legislation passed for two weeks now, and even Ed Menzies is questioning the decision not to have Patrick do it by executive order. The situation isn't covered in our Constitution, and we may need another amendment before we're done.

On top of that, Ellis has reported a sabotage attempt on the railroad from Armstrong to the copper mine. According to the report, the saboteur was Robert Perez's assistant. There is no evidence Perez was involved, but that's another example of something we never had to deal with before.

I'm sorry this is so short, but I'm exhausted. Maybe I just needed to vent a little. Other than the above, we're all healthy here, doing the best we can.

Love,

John

# 29

# Tori on Trial

**19 Wednesday 285 D**

MARIE MALLEY WAS DEEP in thought. While most of her classmates took advantage of a recess, she sat in a corner of the play area, thinking about what she had just heard. Her teacher had been lecturing them on ecology, how important it was to their future, and praising the recent law passed by the Planetary Legislature to set an environmental policy for the colony.

They had even scheduled a vote on an amendment to the Constitution that would make it the law that the Legislature consider future citizens when determining the impact of any proposed legislation. She understood how that strengthened the law about environmental policy, and she appreciated how that would help her.

Before recess, her teacher said that the tower farms were an earlier example of the colony's concern for the environment, and she didn't understand that. From where she sat, she could see the Ellis tower farm towering over the surrounding buildings, not looking at all like anything natural. She remembered the farms in Grissom before Grissom built the tower farm; lined with trees and filled with growing things, they had seemed much more compatible with the environment than the artificial towers.

She thought about asking her teacher about that when they returned to class, but the teacher said they would take up their trigonometry lessons then. Marie knew the teacher didn't enjoy having her schedule disrupted, and Marie had the impression that she already asked too many questions for the teacher's liking.

She could ask her parents about it, but it wasn't an area of expertise for either of them. Her father was more interested in politics, and her mother was too much involved in computers and the robots she was designing.

Suddenly, she smiled. That was the answer! She would ask Isaac! The *Asimov* computer knew everything and would surely know why the tower farms were good for the environment and not just eyesores.

AFTER DINNER, MARIE WAS alone with Fred. "Isaac, I have a question."

A slight delay told her *Asimov* was on the other side of the planet, relaying through a satellite. Then Isaac was there. "What is your question, Marie?"

"My teacher said that the tower farms were good for the environment, but she didn't explain why. Can you tell me?"

"Certainly. Your teacher is correct. It's more that the tower farms make it much easier to protect the environment. Without care, open fields can be very harmful."

"They're just plants! How could they be harmful?"

"The crops themselves aren't, although they remove some nutrients from the soil. Grissom's farmlands were planted on relatively poor soil that requires a lot of fertilizing and careful cultivation to remain productive. The heavy rains leach nutrients out of the soil's top layers and carry them into the river, often harming river life. The situation is like that in Earth's tropics."

"Then why did they put the farms there? Aren't there better places?"

"Not around Grissom. Most of the remaining land is sloping, and runoff would have been an even bigger problem."

"Then why didn't they put Grissom in a better place?"

"For other reasons, there was no better place. The center of Fletcher, the continent including Grissom, Ellis, and all the other settlements, is one of the most geologically stable areas on the planet. This planet is less stable than Earth, with more earthquakes, tidal waves, and volcanoes. The farming problems seemed small compared to the problems in other areas."

"How are the tower farms better than the fields?"

"It's difficult to prevent fertilizer from washing into the river, where it damages the balance of the ecology there. The tower farms are closed systems where the farmers can completely control irrigation and prevent anything from leaving the farm unless they want it to. That solves the problem of the heavy rains and contamination of the river and reduces the need for large amounts of fertilizer. It allows control of lighting; some crops don't like Pitcairn's forty-eight-hour day. It also means that the farmers don't have to guard constantly against native weeds. Do you want me to go into more detail?"

"No, I understand now. It's a matter of controlling what goes in and what comes out."

"Concisely put, Marie," Isaac agreed. "You might also find information about the Super Volcano of 123 useful."

"Super Volcano? What about it?"

"In the year 123, there was a huge volcanic eruption on Butler Island, a large island southwest of Fletcher, comparable to the Yellowstone Event on Earth. It destroyed half of the island and caused earthquakes all over the planet. Even worse, it sent almost six cubic miles of debris into the atmosphere, darkening the skies for several years. Low crop productivity during that time was the biggest threat this colony has faced."

"And that wouldn't affect a tower farm." Marie had a lot more to think about.


## 19 Friday 285 ED

Robert Perez sat next to his assistant, neither speaking, waiting for the trial to begin. Harry Richard, Maddox Washington, and several others also sat around the conference room in the Ellis Administration Building. Tori hadn't denied her guilt, but she hadn't offered any explanation either, and Robert wasn't sure what he should do. He would stand by her and perhaps even try to intercede for her, but he wasn't sure how far he wanted to go.

Tori had been valuable to him. Her ability to appear insignificant while absorbing and evaluating everything around her was valuable. He could concentrate on the big picture while she recorded every nuance that would help him understand those he had to negotiate with. Maybe it was devious of him to use her in that way, but it was not an unusual approach to diplomacy.

Now, it appeared that while she was fooling those with whom he dealt, she had been deceiving him as well. It was very unsettling.

There were no lawyers on Pitcairn, of course, and Pitcairn would not run the trial in the same way as a procedure in a Terran courtroom. The judge would be inexperienced and new even to the idea of a legal hearing. They would call witnesses and ask questions to determine the truth. Anyone who wanted to contribute could speak, but it would not be an adversarial process with a prosecutor and a defender. Perhaps he could take advantage of that, should he want to.

He glanced at Tori. He was attracted to her, more so when she appeared to be attracted to him, but now her face was frozen into a harsh mask. The woman he had been so intimate with was gone. He looked away and straightened in his seat. It didn't matter. She worked for him and for Earth, and he would do whatever he could.

The presiding judge, Henry Best, entered the room and sat down at the table at the front of the room. A robot came in with him and stood to his right where it would record the trial. Henry was fifty Pitcairn years old, with a severe face that made him look older. Usually, he managed one of Ellis's underground manufacturing facilities, and people trusted him to make the right decisions.

As the Planetary Judiciary representative from the Ellis Research Station and Chief Justice of the Ellis Judiciary, Henry handled the trial, the first criminal case under the new constitution. It would establish precedents, and he tried to learn everything he could about doing his second job in his spare time.

Instead of a gavel, he had a rubber mallet borrowed from a tool cage in his department. Seeing that everyone expected to be there was present, he banged the mallet on a flat rock someone had put on the table. The result was an unsatisfying thump, but everyone knew immediately that the trial was starting.

He scanned the courtroom slowly and then began. "I will call two witnesses: Harry Richard, making the accusation, and Maddox Washington, speaking to the alleged sabotage. After I have talked to them, the accused, Tori Chen, can speak in her defense or call her own witnesses. After that, anyone who wishes can contribute to the proceedings. Any questions before I start?"

"May Tori or I address questions to the witnesses?" Robert asked.

Henry paused before he answered. "Yes. I will allow anyone to ask questions as long as they are reasonable. I intend to be flexible in the search for the truth of the accusation."

Henry asked Harry Richard to step forward. Harry sat down in a chair on the left side of the judge's table, facing the judge rather than the courtroom.

"Just tell me what you saw leading you to accuse Miss Chen," Henry told him.

Harry nodded and described what he had seen in the train garage. It didn't take very long.

Tori leaned forward when Harry finished, her face with an almost hidden sneer, her voice just below a shout. "Let's be clear. You didn't see a wrench in my hand or see me insert it into the wheel carriage."

"Your back was to me, hiding your hands from me," Harry answered. "And I was too far away to identify the object in your hand positively as a wrench."

"That would be a 'no' then."

"That would be a 'no.'" He gave her a mild but firm look, probably intended to convey amusement that she was attempting to challenge him.

"But you saw her bend down near the train with something in her hand?" Henry said.

"Yes."

"And after she left, you found the wrench jammed into the mechanism near where she was?"

"Yes."

"And she no longer held the object you saw."

"Yes."

Henry looked at Tori reproachfully, but she didn't seem impressed.

Harry returned to his seat, and Maddox Washington took his place. After Harry reported the incident, Maddox inspected the locomotive carefully. He told Henry about the inspection and how he removed the wrench and replaced two damaged parts.

"Had Harry not reported the problem," Maddox finished, "severe damage to the locomotive undercarriage could have resulted, possibly damage beyond our ability to repair."

"Would the robots have inspected the undercarriage before operating the locomotive again?" Robert asked.

"Probably," Maddox answered. "We can't be sure of that, however."

"So, chances are, no actual harm was done," Robert persisted.

"Is that your assistant's defense?" Henry asked. "She was unsuccessful in attempting to sabotage the train?"

Tori rolled her eyes and leaned toward Robert. "You're making a fool of yourself," she hissed. "You can't do any good. They're convinced I'm the villain here."

"If you have something to say in your defense, perhaps you should address the entire court," Henry suggested. Tori sat back and stared at him in sullen silence. Henry returned the stare for a moment and then turned back to the court. "Very well. Does anyone else have anything to say concerning Miss Chen's activities?"

When no one responded, he smiled, but there was a sadness visible behind the smile. "I think I just presided over the shortest trial in history," he said. "It is obvious, Miss Chen, that you are guilty. The real question is what to do with you. Perhaps it would help if you would explain your motives."

That startled Tori, and for a moment, the hostile expression left her face. She took a moment to gather her thoughts and then stood up. "I am a member of the Fermion movement. We believe God put the light barrier in place to prevent us from mixing with other sentient races in the galaxy. It has always been our organization's goal to hold the colonies back technologically so that they could never be used as a jumping-off point to extend humanity's reach beyond our allotted space. I had hoped to cripple your progress by sabotaging the train."

Robert's initial surprise changed to disgust as Tori spoke. That's what this is about? "I thought you people had gone away. We broke the speed-of-light barrier, proving all that was nonsense."

Tori turned on him. "A ship can go faster than light only between two Links. If we don't build more Links further out, we won't be able to go beyond our space."

"And you would continue efforts to prevent this colony from growing," Henry interrupted. "Obviously, this incident is not an isolated occurrence. Miss Chen, we cannot allow you freedom of movement, and that is a problem. Just what am I supposed to do with you? You are no doubt aware that we don't have secure facilities where we can keep you."

Robert stood up. "What she has done is a crime in the Western Alliance. I suggest you send her back to Earth at the earliest opportunity."

Henry nodded. "That works for me. However, that can't happen until another ship comes here. What do we do with her in the meantime?"

Maddox Washington stood up. "Henry, this isn't the first time we've had this problem. Years ago, two men in Grissom tried to sabotage the Grissom energy receiver to prevent it from being used by the robots. Ed Menzies banished one to Lovell Station One."

"Hmm. Lovell Station Four might be a good choice." Henry paused and considered Maddox's suggestion for a second. "I will talk to Administrator Malley about that idea. It sounds like a solution to me." He looked at Tori. "I hope you enjoy farming, Miss Chen. You don't look big enough to load ore ships."

# 30

# Decisions

**21 Saturday 285 ED**

ON THE PITCAIRN CALENDAR, it was the last day of the year. Pitcairn lacked the noisy parties that still marked New Year's Eve on Earth, but it was traditionally a time for families to get together. The gathering at the Malley house was one of the larger celebrations in Ellis. Including Patrick, Susan, and Marie, sixteen people filled the Malley home, with many people coming from outside Ellis.

There wasn't room for a table big enough in the tiny dining room. Instead, Susan laid the food out on the table and let people serve themselves and find a place to eat as best they could. As a result, the group broke up along gender and age lines.

Patrick, Ed, and Harry took seats together at the kitchen counter. As Ed put his plate down, Patrick looked at him. Ed didn't look bad for ninety-two, perhaps even a little younger than when he was Grissom's administrator. Thinking about Ed's age reminded him of his father-in-law. "I hope there's nothing seriously wrong with John. He said he wasn't feeling well enough to make the trip."

Ed looked concerned. "I don't know, Pat. He says he's just tired from working too hard, but Stephanie seems pretty worried. For a small town, a lot is going on in Grissom, and he might be feeling the pressure."

Patrick frowned. "About a year and a half ago, I told him to get me a list of people who might replace him. It was right after his last heart attack. I never got that list."

"It's a moot point now. According to the Grissom charter, it's up to the Grissom Legislature to remove him. I know him; he won't give up the position willingly. They'll have to force him out."

Patrick shook his head. "He won't be doing the colony any good if he kills himself."

"This controversy about the Lovell River stations isn't helping any. The consensus seems to be that most of those people don't want to move, and relatives in Grissom have been suggesting the whole thing is a power grab on Grissom's part."

Patrick snorted in disgust. "We've been talking about closing those stations for two and a half years. According to the legislative proposal, the remaining stations keep their local government, so Grissom has nothing to do with it. It's all politics. No offense, Ed, but we never had this kind of nonsense before we had a constitution."

"No offense taken. I'm sure you know the real problem is the way we're growing. As our government becomes more complex, and inevitably, it would, things get more political. I taught you that thirty years ago."

Patrick nodded. "Maybe I should talk to a few people. John has done enough for this colony."

E VERYONE HAD EATEN AND cleared the leftovers. Jack and Taylor saw that the party was quieting down and sensed that people would leave soon. It was time, and Jack called everyone into the main room.

Fourteen faces stared at Jack as he cleared his throat nervously. " Taylor and I have an announcement. We're going to have a baby!"

"It's about time," Mary Menzies said with a big smile. "Congratulations!"

Everyone crowded around, and for several minutes, the party was no longer quiet. No one mentioned that it had been clear from the moment Taylor entered the house, even before that for the other Ellis colonists.

"When are you due?" Susan asked.

"Late spring," Taylor answered. "Early summer if he's late."

"You know it's a boy?" Jenny said. "Do you have a name yet?"

A little shyness crept into Jack's voice. "We're going to name him Jason."

Patrick nodded and smiled. "Good. We can use another Jason Applegate."

## 1 Tuesday 286 EN

"I think I've decided what I want to do when I've finished basic schooling." Marie sat at the table with Susan and Patrick. She had just finished her dinner, but her parents were still eating. "I want to be an architect."

Patrick put his fork down. "Interesting choice. You still have another five years of basic education, though, before you have to decide."

"I know. But I want to get started as soon as possible, so I'm planning ahead."

"What's the rush, Marie?" Susan asked. "You sound like you have something specific in mind."

"Sort of. Our teacher told us about the tower farms and how they were better than farming in fields like Grissom used to do. I didn't understand how that could be, so I asked Isaac about it, and he told me about closed systems and how that made the tower farms better."

Patrick nodded. "And so?"

"Well, it seemed to me that if making the farms closed systems is a good thing, then maybe we should think about making more things a closed system. Maybe even entire towns like Grissom."

Patrick nodded. "There would be some benefits to that."

"Isaac told me the idea isn't new. He said that a long time ago, places called arcologies were suggested to solve the problems of large cities. He said there are even a few small ones built on Earth."

"So you want to design an arcology for Pitcairn," Susan said.

"I think all our settlements should be arcologies," Marie said. "Ellis is halfway there already, with so much built underground."

Patrick looked at Marie fondly. It seemed like only a short time before that she had been a little girl, just learning to walk and talk. Somehow, she had become a teenager, probably taking after Susan more than him. She still had that awkwardness so typical for a girl her age, but Patrick saw enough of Susan in her to convince him that someday soon she would be an attractive young woman. With a smile, he returned to the conversation.

"You have plenty of time to finish your education. Building the tower farms was a huge drain on our resources, although they're a big plus now. An arcology would be a much bigger project, and I'm pretty sure we don't have the resources to do something that large right now."

"So it isn't a good idea?" Marie bent her head, disappointment on her face.

"It's a good idea," Patrick assured her. "A little ahead of its time, though. And that's a good thing. By the time you're ready to lead it, maybe our resources will be, too. Right now, you could talk to Maddox Washington about it. He's probably the most qualified on the subject. We should check for neurotrainer modules on the subjects you will eventually need, too. If we don't have all of them, we can get them on the list for the next supply ship."

Marie's face brightened a little, but she still looked disappointed. "So I can't do anything now except wait?"

"Well, talk to Maddox. I'm sure there are things you could study in your free time to get you ready for neurotraining faster."

## 1 Thursday 286 EN

Patrick looked up as Amy walked into his office and put a paper on his desk. "The summary of this morning's legislature session," she explained, and went back to her desk.

The Planetary Legislature was meeting every Thursday, alternating between Early Day and Early Night periods. Patrick reviewed the report quickly and then put it down with a frown. The Legislature was still debating the proposed closure of Lovell Station One and Lovell Station Three, rehashing the same arguments interminably.

They had labor shortages in all the settlements, and the Legislature was tied in knots over the question of the river settlements when it could accomplish things that would help the colony. Why had he agreed to a constitution?

## 1 Saturday 286 EN

Idle Mind

While closing Lovell Stations One and Three was probably the right thing to do, it is this commentator's opinion that doing it by executive action was the wrong way to go. The Legislature has been spending valuable time we could devote to other things, but the constitutional government we have established is new, and it is essential to let it find its way. This conflict will cause problems for Administrator Malley, but I hope the controversy will be soon be resolved, and the colony will support him in developing Pitcairn for the benefit of all its citizens.

# 31

# Reuben Noland

**2 Friday 286 ED**

Amy burst into Patrick's office. Usually, she knocked before entering, and Patrick looked up, immediately interested in finding out what had her so excited.

"This will make your day," she declared, handing him a message from Earth. "Skip down to the bottom. The rest is the usual bureaucratic jabber."

Patrick scanned down the sheet and immediately saw what Amy was talking about. He read aloud. "The starship *Benjamin Sepulveda* will launch on September 19, 2336, and will arrive at Tau Ceti II on or about December 20, 2336. *Benjamin Sepulveda* is the first enhanced Stenhouse Drive passenger starship and will carry fifty-three new colonists and ten industrial robots. This should help ease the manpower problems you have reported."

He looked up at Amy. "This is good news." He read on, the last paragraph informing him that *Benjamin Sepulveda* was not a lander and would use the *Asimov* shuttles to get down to the planet. I should check with Grissom on fuel status. It would take three trips to bring that many people down.

He turned to the next page, a list of passengers with a paragraph describing each one's experience and education. He looked briefly at the ten-page listing and then looked up at Amy again. "A copy has gone to Grissom?"

"*Asimov* notified them at the same time as us."

"Good. Most of these people will stay in Grissom. I didn't notice any scientists."

"There was a microbiologist, probably someone Earth thinks will help with the drug production. Somewhere around the middle, I think."

"I'll take your word for it. When does the ship arrive, Pitcairn time?"

"Week fourteen or fifteen. Early winter, probably a good time to be arriving."

Patrick nodded. The Pitcairn summers were brutal on newcomers, and it was best to acclimate gradually. The new arrivals would have the winter and spring to do that. Of all the original ships that had colonized Pitcairn, only *Vera Cruz* had arrived during the summer. After that experience, the next starship, John Shuford's *Seeker*, had come during the winter.

"We'll have to focus on building more houses for the next few months. John knows that, though. Okay, I'll look at this a little more. I expect I'll get a message from Grissom in a couple of days outlining their plans for using these people."

After Amy left, Patrick looked at the list again. At least there were no soldiers, although they would take precautions before transferring new arrivals to the planet, including careful inspections for weapons. They could send Tori Chen back to Earth, too. Maybe he could have Robert Perez go with her.

## 15 Saturday 286 ED

Reuben Noland was as bored as a ten-year-old (in Earth years) could be. The trip from Earth, the only child on a ship full of adults, was bad enough. He thought things would get better when they got to Pitcairn, but a shuttle transferred them to Asimov when they reached orbit. He had nothing to do except sit quietly and wait while his mother and the other adults answered questions about their experiences and their reasons for coming to Pitcairn.

That seemed to go on forever, but at least he and his mother were in the first group to transfer from *Benjamin Sepulveda*. When they finally got back on the shuttle, it took a whole day to get down to the planet, and they hadn't even allowed him onto the bridge where he could have seen Pitcairn from space.

When they finally stepped out of the shuttle into a steamy, windblown drizzle, it was a huge disappointment. Reuben expected something more than the almost featureless surroundings of the spaceport. Besides the runway, there was only a tiny control tower, hardly worthy of a small regional airport on Earth.

The terrain on either side of the runway was flat and didn't even have grass, just some ugly, scraggly red bushes. He could see gray phantoms of one large blocky building and another taller one beyond it in the distance. A wall of mist hid anything more.

At first, he thought they would have to walk to the settlement, but a bus drove up from the other side of the shuttle. On the bus, Reuben's mother, Gloria Noland, tried to dry his face with her jacket's sleeve, but he didn't mind being wet now that he was out of the rain.

"I'm okay, Mom." He turned to stare out the window, hoping that there would be something more interesting when they got away from the spaceport.

But as they left the spaceport, all he saw were rows of odd-looking trees dividing up fields that looked like abandoned farms. When he mentioned them to his mother, she told him, "They were farms years ago. Now they grow all their food inside buildings. Did you notice a tall building going toward Grissom?"

"Beyond that big square building. I saw it."

Gloria glanced out the window. "That's their main food-growing facility. Some places on Earth have farms like that, too. It's called a tower farm."

Reuben wondered why they would grow their food indoors when they had so much room outside the town, but decided he didn't care. "What about the other building?"

"The big one? I think that's the metal-processing facility. Where they process ore into metals."

"Oh. I was hoping it was the theater."

Gloria smiled. "I told you, Reuben. Grissom doesn't have things like theaters."

Reuben sighed and turned back to the window. He could see more buildings now, some quite large, but only single-story. He saw nothing that looked like a house and wondered if they would live in something like the depressing structures he was passing. However, the bus didn't stop and continued onto a narrow bridge.

He remembered then that he had just passed through the industrial area and that the main part of Grissom was across a river from the spaceport. His hopes went up a little.

As the bus left the bridge, Reuben saw another large building, this one made of stone. Then the bus driver made a right turn onto a road that paralleled the river. On the left side, he could now see buildings that at least looked sort of like houses, although they were half-buried in the ground and seemed more suitable for hobbits than people.

The driver half-turned to his passengers. "Mrs. Noland?"

Gloria raised her hand. "Yes. I'm here."

"Sydney Chandri wanted to meet you and is waiting at the Science Center. I'll drop you off there before I take the rest of you to your new homes."

"That will be fine."

The bus pulled up in front of a sprawling building, identified as the Grissom Science Center by a small sign at the main door. The driver opened the door and, as Gloria and Reuben walked past, told them, "Just go in the door. I'll come back for you after I drop off the others. Sydney just wants to introduce herself and won't keep you long. She knows you're probably tired."

"Thank you." Gloria and Reuben left the bus, hurried down a short sidewalk to the building, and through the door. They stood there for a moment, taking in the stark hallway, hardwood floor, and walls with no decorations. Sydney came into the hallway a few seconds later.

"Doctor Noland?" Sydney strode up to them and held out her hand. "I'm so glad you've arrived. I'm Sydney Chandri."

"I'm delighted to be here, Doctor Chandri."

"Sydney. We're very informal here on Pitcairn. How was your trip?"

"Interesting," Gloria said. "But I am quite excited about getting to work here."

"Good. Good. I assume this is your son? Reuben, right? Come on into my office, and I can brief you on how things work here."

In Sydney's office, they took seats around a table. Reuben soon lost interest in the conversation, which seemed to be about some strange ways they talked about time on Pitcairn. Early and Late periods? What was wrong with morning and afternoon?

The office windows faced the river, and Reuben turned his attention to the view. He could see the river and the bank on the opposite shore. There were a few trees with stunted, gnarly trunks, too thick at the bottom. A few reddish leaves clung to branches almost denuded by the coming of winter.

The landscape wasn't as alien as he had imagined, but it definitely wasn't Earth either. Were the plants on this planet edible? He vaguely remembered being told something about that on Earth, something about strange proteins, but he couldn't remember the details. It hadn't seemed very interesting. But he already knew the colony grew Earth foods on its farms, so the native plants probably were poisonous.

He soon tired of looking out the window. His mother and Doctor Chandri were still talking, and now Doctor Chandri was talking about her son. Did she say something about being a friend for him? He listened more carefully and heard that his name was Juan and that he was nine years old. A year younger than Reuben was. That wasn't too bad. It would be like having a younger brother.

His mother suddenly turned to him. "What do you think, Reuben?"

It was a lucky thing he was paying attention again. "Sounds good."

"I'll tell him to look for you in school tonight," Sydney said.

School at night? Reuben knew he would still have to go to school, but at night? This sounded worse all the time.

# 32

# First Night of Class

**15 Saturday 286 LD**

WHEN THEY ARRIVED AT their new home, it did not surprise Reuben when his mother declared it time for bed. It had been a long day, and he had to admit that he was tired, at least to himself. But the sun was still high in the sky, so he resisted a little on general principles. His mother spent ten minutes explaining to him (again, she said) about the length of the day on Pitcairn. When that finally sank in, he realized that explained why he would go to school at night.

His windowless bedroom was dark despite the bright daylight outside. There was a bed, a dresser where he could put his clothes, and a small closet, but not much else. Well, they were just moving in; there would be time to add items later. He crawled into bed, accepted a goodnight kiss from his mother, and fell asleep quickly.

When his mother woke him, the window in the main room showed a darkening sky. After a simple breakfast, Gloria walked the four blocks to the school with him. As they approached the building, children converged, and the streets became more crowded. Gloria went into the building with him after assuring him he would be on his own after the first day.

"That's the way it is here," she assured him. "It's much safer, and I'll be able to give you more freedom." That, at least, sounded good, although Reuben was still feeling uncertain about attending school at night.

He sat in silence while his mother talked to the school's head, a woman named Riley Potter. Based on prior experience, Reuben expected a long meeting with a lot of forms to fill out and perhaps a lengthy description of all the rules they expected him to follow.

It was a pleasant surprise when, after a short welcome and exchange of a few pieces of information, the meeting ended.

Gloria stood up and looked at Reuben. "Ms. Potter will show you to your classroom. I'll pick you up at the end of the period." She bent down and hugged him. "Now you be good." She nodded to Riley, rubbed the top of Reuben's head affectionately, and left the office.

Reuben looked up at Riley expectantly. "We have two classes of people your age," she said. "I think we'll put you in Sarah Sullivan's class. She's from Earth, too, so you might relate to her better." She left the office, and Reuben followed.

"Call me Riley, by the way," she said as they walked. "There are a lot of Potters in Grissom, but only a few Riley Potters. It's less confusing when everybody uses my first name."

They stopped at a door identified as "13-1" on a nameplate. "Sarah will teach you most subjects. Ed Menzies will come in for history and geography." Riley opened the door slowly and looked in, then opened the door wider and motioned Reuben forward.

Reuben entered the classroom as Sarah Sullivan walked toward them. Sarah was old, Reuben thought as he saw her. Was he supposed to have something in common with her? She was from Earth, Riley had said, although Reuben didn't remember seeing her on the *Benjamin Sepulveda*. She must have come to Pitcairn on an earlier ship; no one on *Benjamin Sepulveda* was as old as Sarah Sullivan.

"This is Reuben Noland, Sarah," Riley said. "He's just arrived from Earth."

Ten hours later, the school day was over, and Reuben plodded slowly out of the building where his mother waited for him. He felt more tired than he could remember ever being, and he wasn't sure why. The day had been much longer than his school day on Earth, but he didn't think that was it. There had been several recesses, a mid-period meal, and much of the classwork had been almost fun.

He had especially enjoyed it when Sarah had asked him to tell the class about schools on Earth, and he had talked for nearly an hour, telling them whatever came to mind and answering their many questions.

His mother looked tired, too, he realized. Like him, it seemed to be an effort for her even to lift her feet. Yet the other children swarmed past him, splashing through puddles left by an earlier rain, unaffected by the long day.

"Excuse me. You're Gloria and Reuben, aren't you?" someone said from behind them. Reuben turned to see a small boy watching them expectantly.

"Yes, we are," Gloria answered.

"I'm Juan Chandri. My mom asked me to look for you."

Reuben remembered Sydney Chandri saying that her son was nine years old, almost the same as him. Even allowing for the general shortness of native Pitcairners (he had been one of the tallest people in his class that day), Juan was small. Could he be nine years old?

"My mom said that maybe I could help you get used to living in Grissom," Juan continued.

"That sounds great," Gloria said. "Maybe you could spend an hour together while I go home and fix some dinner. Would your mother mind?"

"Would it be all right if Reuben and I had dinner at one of the kitchens?" Juan suggested. "Then we can talk longer."

Gloria hesitated, and Reuben thought she was going to say no. But she smiled. "Would that be okay with your mother?"

"Sure. I told her I was thinking about doing that if it was okay with you, so she won't be worried if I don't show up for dinner. My dad is home right now, so she won't be alone."

"All right, go ahead. Just be back in a couple of hours." Gloria put a hand on Reuben's shoulder. "You look exhausted and should get to bed early."

"I will," Reuben promised.

"I looked up where you live, and I'll make sure he gets home," Juan assured her. He turned to Reuben. "Come on." He started briskly off, but Reuben followed him so slowly that he stopped. "I forgot," Juan apologized. "You just landed. My mom said you'd be a little weak."

"I feel like I've been carrying rocks around all day. Why?"

"Didn't they tell you? The gravity is stronger on Pitcairn, making you heavier. You'll get used to it, but it'll take some time."

That sounded familiar to Reuben, too. He realized he should have paid more attention to the briefings before they left Earth. His companion was small, but he looked strong. "How old are you?"

"I'm nine," Juan said proudly.

"That's what I thought your mother said. You're so small I thought I had heard wrong."

"I'm just as big as other nine-year-olds." Juan puffed out his chest and looked at Reuben belligerently. "We might be short compared to people from Earth, but that's the gravity, too."

"You're smaller than the other kids in my class with Sarah Sullivan," Reuben said. "They're only a year older."

"No, they're not. Aren't you in room 13-1? I thought that's where Sarah teaches."

Reuben remembered the sign on the door. "Right. 13-1."

"That's for thirteen-year-olds! Of course, they're bigger."

"But I'm only ten."

Juan screwed up his face as he thought about that. Then he brightened. "Ten in Earth years. You're thirteen in Pitcairn years. Didn't you know the year is shorter here?"

"I know the days are longer. How could the year be shorter?"

"One Pitcairn day is about the same as two Earth days, but Pitcairn revolves around Tau Ceti in only 147 days or about 300 Earth days."

"Then I'm thirteen now." That was a plus, at least, Reuben thought. However, that meant his first friend in Grissom was four years younger, not one, almost a baby! He wasn't sure how he wanted to deal with that. Juan obviously wanted to get moving again.

"Okay. Where's this kitchen?"

"Not too far. It's the Ivory Street Kitchen. My dad helped them make recipes using the Pitcairn plants. It's really neat. Come on."


"I SUGGEST THE PITCAIRN chili," Juan told Reuben. "It's one of the recipes my dad helped make."

"Okay."

"I'll have the chicken tacos. I've had the Pitcairn chili a lot lately." Reuben didn't notice the glint of amusement in the younger boy's eyes.


IN THE KITCHEN, PAULINA Edelstein noticed the two boys come in. Juan came there frequently and usually ordered a dish developed from Diego's suggestions. She didn't recognize the other boy, though, which was unusual. She decided to investigate and went out to the table to get their order personally. "What will you have, boys?"

"Chicken tacos," Juan said.

"Pitcairn chili," Reuben said.

Paulina's eyes narrowed. Pitcairn chili was the spiciest of the dishes developed from native plants. She remembered what had happened, the first and only time Juan had tried it. Sydney Chandri had complained the next time they came to the kitchen, although Diego seemed to find it amusing.

"Who's your friend?" she asked Juan.

"This is Reuben. He just got here from Earth."

"Really? Well, hello, Reuben. Welcome to Grissom. I'll get the kitchen working on your food right away."

She turned, suppressing a grin; Juan was being mischievous. She went back to the kitchen. "I need a child's serving of Pitcairn chili toned down," she told a cook. "It's for a boy fresh from Earth, and I don't want him getting the wrong idea about Grissom's food."

Pitcairn chili was a popular dish for the colonists, and a regular batch was always ready for serving. It took a few extra minutes to make up a fresh serving without all the hot spices.

WHILE THEY WAITED, REUBEN looked around the room. "This is amazing. You just come in here and order anything you want without paying for it."

"Sure. We don't have any money on Pitcairn, anyway." Juan saw a chance to elaborate on his prank. "The woman who took our order is Paulina, and she runs this kitchen. She can get pretty mad if you order something and don't finish it."

Reuben looked worried. "I don't think I'm as hungry as usual. I'm feeling tired tonight."

"The gravity again. You'll get used to it. Don't worry. When you taste the chili, you won't be able to leave any."

Reuben looked dubious. "Maybe if I can't finish it, she won't mind if I take the rest home to eat later."

"That will probably work."

Paulina came out with the food a few minutes later. Reuben noticed with relief that the chili came in a smaller bowl that was probably just about right for him. He grabbed his spoon and began eating right away, not noticing that Juan hadn't touched his food, but was watching him with an expectant grin on his face.

Reuben could taste ginger and mint in it, much different from any chili he had ever tasted before. There were some other strange flavors too, but it all made a very appetizing dinner. He took several big spoonfuls before he looked up again.

"This is really good." Reuben looked at Juan's plate. "Why aren't you eating? Those tacos look pretty good, too."

"Huh? Oh, right." Juan picked up one of his tacos and took a bite. What's going on here? Reuben should turn red and be reaching desperately for his glass of water. But he's obviously enjoying it. Is Earth food spicier than Pitcairn's food? "It's not too spicy for you?"

"Oh no. I've had spicier food than this on Earth. My mom would probably think this wasn't spicy enough; she likes it hot."


IN THE KITCHEN, PAULINA chuckled. She could see the look on Juan's face and the confusion that he was feeling. "Serves the little scamp right," she told the cook who had made the chili. "He's lucky I didn't put ghost peppers in his tacos."

# 33

# News from Earth

**16 Tuesday 286 EN**

J AXON HAD IMPROVED THE antiviral drug process as much as possible, but Reese's work on synthesizing proteins continued, so Jaxon teamed up with her to work on the problem. The task proved even more complicated than they had imagined, however, and after three years, they had made little progress. They developed methods for creating a few simple proteins, but nothing of great value.

"The problem is a lack of material," Jaxon declared. "We have a limited sample of the native life, and it restricts what we can do."

"I'm assuming you have a suggestion," Reese said.

"I do, but I'm not sure you're going to like it."

"That sounds mysterious. What's your idea?" She smiled at him, and Jaxon felt the familiar warmth flow through him. His relationship with Reese had become even closer in the last few years. He credited his influence as a member of the Board of Science, but even more, their collaboration in Reese's work. For some, being together almost constantly may have created problems, but it pushed them closer together.

"We get samples from upriver, but by the time they get to us, they've deteriorated and are no longer as useful. We should set up a laboratory at Lovell Station Four, where we can work with fresh samples."

Reese's first reaction was to reject the idea. Grissom was primitive compared to Earth, and Lovell Station Four would be more so. However, Jaxon's idea had scientific merit, and Jaxon would be the obvious choice to manage a new Science Center. "We could probably help with Indira's work, too," she said thoughtfully, referring to Indira Chandri, who was still working on developing medical drugs from native plants. "Why Lovell Four?"

"Centrally located. It would be easier to take collection trips to Applegate Falls or the mine and up and down river from Four. Also, I suspect Two may be closed eventually, just like One and Three, so Four would be more permanent. I don't think that we'll ever close Four."

"Not as long as the mine is shipping ore downstream. How would you go about it?"

"Getting the Science Board to endorse it would probably be the way to go. I'm not sure what involvement we would need from the Administrators or the Legislature, but the Science Board would be a good start."

O
N EARTH, IT WAS Christmas Day. Father Jacobs had already celebrated one Mass, filling the Town Hall conference room well past capacity. When all the attendees had gone, he stopped at the Administrator's office.

"Full house tonight," John remarked on seeing the priest.

Father Jacobs nodded. "I'll celebrate another Mass at the beginning of Late Night, and that will probably be standing room only, too."

"I'd noticed your attendance was increasing, but you've never had to do two Masses on the same day."

"We have a term for that." Father Jacobs smiled. "They're called 'Holiday Catholics,' people who only come to church on Christmas and Easter. Some attendees were Protestants recently arrived from Earth who reasoned that a Catholic service on Christmas was better than none."

"Still, though, your attendance has been going up. It's been three years now, right? Probably time to revisit building a church?"

"I was thinking about bringing that up. I even had a robot at the Mass. Isaac has been asking about the significance of Christmas."

John grinned. "We'll have to include a transmitter in the church design so Isaac can listen in. I don't imagine it can spare a robot all that often."

"Thinking about Isaac reminds me of something else." Father Jacobs sat down at John's desk. "When Monsignor Valdez was here, he reacted negatively to Isaac. I'm sure he reported it back to the Vatican, and I sent a message at the time, trying to lessen the damage, but I never received a response on the subject."

"I haven't heard anything either."

"We're still so isolated from Earth. Perhaps you could ask your father if he's heard anything."

**Message: 17 Monday 286 LN 1:05 (1/5/2337 10:45:22 AM)**

From: John Shuford, Grissom, Pitcairn

To: Alan Shuford, Western Alliance Embassy to Japan, Tokyo, Japan

Dear Dad,

A late Happy New Year! The Pitcairn New Year is still four weeks away, but it came to my attention that you celebrated the start of 2337 a few days ago. I realized that when Father Jacobs, our resident priest, used Town Hall for Christmas Mass last week. We lose track of dates back on Earth. I think I missed your previous two birthdays. Sorry about that. I usually forget mine, too.

Father Jacobs dropped by after Christmas to talk about building a church again. I had promised him three years ago we would consider it when his congregation outgrew the conference room, and it seems the time has come. His Christmas Masses were packed, and the regular weekly Masses are straining the capacity of the room he uses. With the new people from Earth easing our labor issues, I think we might accommodate him soon.

Father Jacobs seems like a good man. Besides his religious duties, he has been a talented and hard-working teacher at the school, so I hope you don't mind if I ask for a favor regarding him. Two years ago, a Monsignor Valdez came here to evaluate Father Jacobs, and, according to Father Jacobs, it didn't go well because of a misunderstanding with the *Asimov* computer. Father Jacobs's superiors have been silent on the matter, which Father Jacobs finds strange. Could you look into it for him? Has the Vatican said anything in public about Monsignor Valdez's report? Father Jacobs would appreciate anything you could find out.

Your great-granddaughter is still determined to be an architect. We thought she might abandon it after a while, but Susan says that Marie constantly studies materials she gets from Maddox Washington, consults him during her free time, and goes to Armstrong whenever she can to talk to him in person. Fortunately, Maddox seems to enjoy it.

The shuttle goes to *Asimov* to pick up the last of the new colonists tomorrow. Tori Chen will be on that flight and transferred to *Benjamin Sepulveda* for her return to Earth. The colonists at Lovell Four reportedly were thrilled to see her leave. I can't say that I blame them. I didn't know her well, but she made me feel a little uncomfortable, too.

We've requested that Earth screen immigrants carefully for Fermion connections in the future. As you may already know, the Western Alliance has recalled Robert Perez. He has nothing to do here as long as Patrick refuses to negotiate with him. We will ship two million doses of the antiviral drug back also, giving Patrick the leverage he needs to stand fast.

All in all, I think things are getting better. I'm still busier than I thought possible, but I'm enjoying it more and feeling that I'm accomplishing something. We're all healthy, and I hope you're the same. Again, have a great New Year.

Love,

John

## Message: 17 Saturday 286 ED 10:15 (1/14/2337 9:06:05 AM )

From: Alan Shuford, Western Alliance Embassy to Japan, Tokyo, Japan

To: John Shuford, Grissom, Pitcairn

Dear John,

It was good to hear from you again, especially since things are better for you now. I'm afraid this message will change that somewhat. However, let me say first that I am fine, with no more health problems than one would expect for someone 102 years old (and that's Earth years). The new heart they installed ten years ago is still ticking away like the clockwork it basically is.

That's the good news. The bad news is that the government is pushing a media campaign against you here. Their story is that Pitcairn is holding Earth up for ransom, threatening to cut off antiviral drug supplies if Earth doesn't send them what they want. Of course, that is pretty much what you are doing, but the emphasis they put on it makes it sound like you're all living high on the backs of poor sick citizens of Earth.

You don't want to hear how the media are portraying Robert Perez and Tori Chen. Not having any counter version, people have swallowed that view whole. I've heard the government paints a somewhat different picture to prospective immigrants, hopefully closer to the truth. You could get a better idea about that by talking to the people coming to you on *Benjamin Sepulveda.*

You asked about Monsignor Valdez. Nothing has ever been made public about his trip to Pitcairn, but I still have a few contacts. He has been urging the Vatican to issue an edict condemning Pitcairn for its support of Isaac. I haven't been able to get too many details, but apparently he's pushing the idea that the computer is the work of the devil. The Pope doesn't seem to be inclined toward the idea, though. The Vatican is keeping the controversy very low-key.

Sorry to be the messenger of bad news. Keep your spirits up, knowing that you are accomplishing everything you wanted to when you went to Pitcairn.

Love,

Dad

# 34

# Moving Plans

**18 Monday 286 ED**

PATRICK WAITED UNTIL EVERYONE else was there before he entered the room. He glanced at each person as he took his seat, and John Shuford from Grissom, Travis Jones from Ellis, and Madelyn Menzies from River Stations looked back at him. Amani Marshall, representing *Asimov*, appeared on a monitor screen. The library ship residents elected her to the Administrator job when Peter Agron resigned, declaring that his work and position on the Board of Science were enough for one old man.

All of them watched Patrick expectantly, and he began. "I assume all of you have seen the message from John's father. I've made it the number one item on our agenda today."

"Do we want to make a big issue of this?" Travis asked. "You've irritated them, and they are overreacting a bit. It's understandable."

"Perhaps," Patrick said. "Or it could be a sign of something more serious. We should consider the possibility they are building public support for taking more drastic action."

"That sounds rather paranoid," Travis countered. "It's making a lot out of a little political rhetoric."

"Probably. I certainly hope so, but we have to consider the possibility that it's not. After all, they tried sending troops here twice before."

"Because they knew we were hiding things from them," Travis scoffed. "And look how that turned out."

"It turned out to be nothing because we were lucky and *Asimov* controlled the landing," John said. "If Earth sends a ship that can land on the planet without surrendering control to *Asimov*, we are vulnerable."

"Thanks to that last attempt, we have weapons," Madelyn pointed out.

Travis gasped and opened his mouth to speak, but Patrick cut him off. "That's not an option. Sure, and we even have a few men who know how to use them, although I can't be sure they would. It doesn't matter. There's no way we can go up against Earth militarily."

Travis looked a little surprised, but he calmed and merely nodded in agreement. "What options do we have?" Madelyn asked.

Patrick leaned back in his chair. "So far, Earth is only waging a propaganda war. We should respond in the same way. I've done some research with Isaac, and governments faced with similar problems in the past created their own propaganda machine, broadcasting their version to anyone who would listen. In the twentieth century, for example, the western powers countered eastern propaganda with something called the 'Voice of America.'"

"Can we broadcast to Earth?" Madelyn said. "Won't anything we send just get intercepted by the Earth Link?"

"Isaac says no, at least not at first. The Link automatically passes all communications to conventional broadcasting equipment for transmission to Earth. If the transmissions aren't encrypted, anyone on the public network can receive them."

"How long could we do that before Earth blocks it?" Amani asked.

"Probably not too long, but we can try to make it inexpedient to do so," Patrick answered. "They might not want to be seen as cutting off free speech if we can get enough people listening right away."

"Who determines what we say?" Travis asked.

"Good question." Patrick smiled at him. "Travis, why don't you put together a plan for implementing this? I'm sure there will be a lot of details to work out, and you'd be a good man to deal with them."

Patrick's response was the last thing Travis had expected, and he looked flustered. It took a moment, but he gathered himself together again. "I'll do my best."

"Good. Let's move on. Someone put an item on the agenda called 'Location of Administrator's Office.' What's that about?"

"That's me," John admitted. "Although Travis inspired it."

"I was just making an observation," Travis protested.

John grinned. "Travis observed that the Ellis Admin Building is getting a little crowded, with your office and Ellis government sharing the spaces. It occurred to me that it might be time for you to move back to Grissom. We have the spaceport and most of the population, plus we're more centrally located. It just makes sense."

"I suppose you'd want me to take your daughter and granddaughter with me," Patrick replied with mock severity.

John smiled innocently. "I presume you would want to do that."

"You're not proposing that I set up an office in the Town Hall, are you?"

"No, no. We would have to build a new office building. You wouldn't be able to move right away, but I think you should consider it."

Patrick was quiet for a long moment. "It makes sense. Let me think about it for a couple of days before we take any action."

"Of course."

## 18 Monday 286 EN

"Your father wants us to move back to Grissom," Patrick announced as they sat down to dinner. Patrick had returned from Grissom late, and Susan and Marie had waited for him.

Susan looked up in surprise. "When did he say that?"

"At the Administrator's meeting. He has a point. Grissom is more the center of things than Ellis. It probably is a good idea."

"Then you're thinking about it?"

There was an edge to her voice that warned Patrick to tread carefully. "You would be close to your parents again. Marie, too."

"What about my work? We came here so that I could become a roboticist, planning to stay in Ellis."

"We came here so that I could be a liaison with Ellis. Your education was a bonus. And that was before the GSC was built. You could still work out of there. They even have a neurotrainer there now if you needed to study something else."

"But all the equipment I use is here. I can't just pick up and leave."

"Neither can I. If we decide to do this, I'll need offices built in Grissom, so it would be weeks after we decide before we could actually move. There would be plenty of time to get things set up for you, too." Patrick paused and gave her what he hoped was a persuasive grin. "After all, you and the robots built the Link in Grissom before the Science Center even existed."

"It's not that easy," Susan protested. "You're minimizing the problems because you want to move."

"I haven't decided yet. But you admit that the idea has some merit."

"What about me?" Marie said. "I have friends here!"

"Your grandparents are in Grissom," Patrick said. "And Aunt Jenny and all your cousins. You'll make new friends."

"But I should have a say in this, too. After all, I'll be twenty-one in a few days. On Earth, I would be an adult."

"On Earth, you would only be sixteen," Susan pointed out gently. "But don't worry. We'll talk about it, and everyone will get their say."

Patrick let the matter drop. There was no reason to push it any further when he wasn't sure himself what he wanted to do. Still, he didn't appreciate the immediate resistance to what seemed a good idea.

## 18 Wednesday 286 EN

Susan was angry initially, feeling that Patrick had sprung the move on her with no warning or consultation. After she calmed, she realized Patrick had not decided and was trying to consult with her. She had been edgy lately, but she had taken it out on Patrick, and that hadn't been fair.

Ironically, she was pretty sure the source of her anxiety was concern about her father's condition. The last time she had seen him, he hadn't looked well, and her mother hadn't been encouraging. If they moved back to Grissom, she would be closer to her father and wouldn't have to live with the uncertainty. Maybe she could even help.

Patrick was right about her work, too; it was not an insurmountable problem. She did most of her design work on a computer, anyway. On the rare occasions that she needed to deal with hardware, she could either use equipment at the Grissom Science Center or make a trip to Ellis. It wouldn't be often, and travel between the two settlements wasn't difficult anymore.

She resolved to apologize to Patrick at dinner at the end of the period. She would also tell him she supported the idea if that was what he needed to do.

# Touring the Farm



Idle Mind

Whether Earth is reacting to our recent relationship's confrontational nature or not, we should take their propaganda efforts to distort our side seriously. Attempting to get our point of view out is a positive step. However, we must take pains to have our message appear as objective as possible.

I propose we establish a news service completely independent of Pitcairn's government and responsible for broadcasting news of our colony to all of Pitcairn, Earth, and the other colonies.

As we grow, it will be important that an independent voice can look at our government from the outside, protecting our citizens' rights through credible information. When we have an independent news service, there will be no more need for me.

**Message: 3 Monday 28 7LD 0:32(4/6/2337 10:44:34 PM)**

From: John Shuford, Grissom, Pitcairn

To: Alan Shuford, Western Alliance Embassy to Japan, Tokyo, Japan

Dear Dad,

Assuming that we're getting through to Earth and you are receiving the broadcasts from the Pitcairn News Service, I'm going to have a lot less news to report in my messages to you. Kimberly Ricketson, one of the recent immigrants from Earth, runs the PNS. Her chief qualification was her editorship of an employee newsletter back on Earth, so we're not as professional as the Terran news services, but, I would maintain, a lot more objective and accurate.

You may have missed the story about Patrick and Susan moving back to Grissom. It hasn't happened yet, and it will take some time to build something suitable, but Stephanie and I are eagerly looking forward to welcoming our children back home. I understand Marie had input into the design of what will be called the Pitcairn Administration Center. She's not out of school yet, but her enthusiasm for architecture hasn't faded, and she's been studying beyond her everyday classwork. Fortunately, the actual architect has been very good about it and has passed on a few simple tasks to her. It reminds me of how Susan worked with the robots in building the Link so many years ago. How things have changed since then!

You may also have noticed that we've started building a church for Father Jacobs. His congregation continues to grow, and I had promised him we would try to accommodate him when he outgrew the conference room. Maybe that will help us with the Vatican, too. I have a feeling that we need all the friends we can get, especially back on Earth.

Plans are moving forward for another Science Center, this time at Lovell Station Four, primarily for biological studies. The idea is to get easier access to a broader range of native life. Jaxon Crawford, a scientist who came on the *Endeavor*, will lead it.

Last week, we received word that Earth is planning to send the *Benjamin Sepulveda* back later this year with another group of colonists. Travel between our worlds gets easier every year. Perhaps we'll see each other again, either here or back on Earth. The galaxy is shrinking, and who can predict what the future will bring? We can hope.

Well, I'm up past my bedtime, so I'd better bring this to a close. I'll write again soon.

Love,

John

## 3 Saturday 287 ED

I T HAD BEEN NINE Pitcairn weeks since they arrived, almost five months in Earth time, and Reuben felt he was now used to the higher gravity. He and Juan walked around the colony every chance they got, ranging farther and farther. That day, they crossed the bridge into West Grissom.

Reuben couldn't get over the freedom he and Juan had when they weren't at school. Hardly anything was off-limits to them, and Juan's mom didn't worry about him even a little. After talking to Doctor Chandri, Reuben's mom didn't interfere either. Even today, when a light rain was falling, they went where they wanted to, as long as they were home by the time they had agreed on. It almost made up for everything he missed from Earth.

Almost. "I'm not complaining, but is this all you have to do around here?" he asked Juan as they walked.

Juan frowned. It wasn't the first time that Reuben had asked, and Juan frowned. "What now?"

Reuben suspected Juan achieved a certain amount of status involved in hanging out with an older boy, even one, or perhaps especially one, from Earth. Lately, though, Juan seemed annoyed. Perhaps he should complain less, but then nothing would change.

"My father used to take me to baseball games at Saldana Park in Paraiba," Reuben said. "Soccer, too. We'd watch the game, eat tacos and ice cream, and have a great time."

"We can play those games here. Playing a game is more fun than watching one."

"It's different. I once saw Pedro Escobedo hit a ball over five hundred feet right out of the park. You can't see that here!"

Juan thought about that. "Five hundred feet? I don't believe it. No one could hit a baseball that far."

"Probably not here because of the higher gravity, but it happened on Earth. Somebody outside the park even caught the ball and got to keep it."

Juan perked up, a little excited, but it only lasted a moment before he changed the subject. "Where's your father?"

Reuben looked down at the ground and didn't answer for a long moment. "He's back on Earth. My mom divorced him last year, and then she signed on to come here."

"Divorced? Wow! I don't think I know anybody who's divorced. Why did she divorce him?"

"I don't know. I remember them arguing a lot, and Mom was really mad at him about something. He must have done something bad because he didn't protest at all when he found out Mom was taking me here."

Juan looked thoughtful, but then he changed the subject again. "Hey, want to go in and see the farm? It's really neat!"

"What could be neat about a farm?" But Reuben followed Juan down the street and into the massive building.

The ground floor was a large open area with stacks of boxes and crates separated by wide aisles. A robot was loading a truck, working with two men. As Reuben looked around, an oversized elevator on another wall opened, and another robot began moving crates from the elevator to the main floor.

A woman approached them. "Hi, boys. Can I help you with something?"

"We just came in to look around," Juan said. "Is that okay?"

"Sure. Just don't go down to the basement."

"What's down there?" Reuben asked, surprised that she wasn't ejecting them from the building.

"There are five floors of equipment down there, some of it dangerous if you're not familiar with it. There are incinerators where we burn waste, and water reclamation and treatment facilities. That kind of stuff. Not much to see down there anyway except a lot of pipes. You should find the upper floors more interesting. You can take the small elevator over there." She pointed to a smaller door near the elevator the robot was unloading.

"Okay, thanks," Juan said. He touched Reuben's arm. "Come on. Let's check it out."

"They're not going to stop us?" Reuben said as they walked across the floor. Reuben could see now that the crates were full of various vegetables and fruits, but he didn't pay that much attention; after all, this was a farm.

"We're old enough not to do something stupid. Why should they stop us? That stuff in the basement sounds like it might be dangerous, but the upper floors are just where they grow the plants. Like walking in a field, except indoors."

When they walked out onto the next floor, however, it was apparent Juan had never been there. There were no fields or anything that looked like a field. Rows of dirt-covered platforms filled the area, each platform used to grow some crop. At one end of the platform, the plants were young, barely poking above the surface. Farther down, the plants were more mature until, at the other end, they looked ready for harvesting. The platforms were mounted on what looked like a huge conveyor belt, but it wasn't moving or was moving so slowly that they couldn't detect the movement. Overhead lights replaced sunlight, and tubes between the plants delivered water slowly.

Later, they talked to a worker, who told them that the first six floors were using a technique called drip irrigation and that the conveyors did indeed move very slowly. Other floors used hydroponics, where water circulated through the plant beds, a better way to grow those crops than drip irrigation.

As they explored higher floors, they saw facilities using aeroponics, tanks where plants hung with roots exposed with warm, water-laden air blown through them.

They reached the top floor two hours later and wandered over to the building's west side, where windows looked out toward the Grissom Spaceport. A shuttle sat at one end, the only sign of the spaceport's purpose.

"That's nothing like the spaceports on Earth," Reuben told Juan. "Earth spaceports are busy."


J UAN NODDED, BUT WASN'T impressed. He hoped Reuben would not start comparing Pitcairn to Earth again. Some things Reuben had mentioned sounded interesting, but Reuben seemed to consider them almost necessary. Mostly they seemed to involve some complex entertainment, like holo theaters and amusement parks.

Did Earth people have that much free time? Didn't they go to school or have jobs? Juan didn't ask Reuben any of those things because he didn't want to set Reuben off again. "We probably should head back to Grissom," he said instead.


G LORIA LISTENED LATER WHEN Reuben told his mother about their tour of the tower farm. "That's great. I'm glad you and Juan found something fun to do."

"Still, going to a ball game would have been more fun," Reuben said quietly.

She gave him a quick hug. "I know." And she did know. She remembered parties with friends and the big roomy house they had once lived in on Earth. Other things, too, perks of the high standing she and her former husband had enjoyed because of their occupations. She felt sympathy for Reuben's feelings, but that wasn't their life anymore.

# Marie's Problem

**8 Thursday 287 EN**

"THE IMMIGRANT LIST FOR the next ship just arrived," Amy told Patrick. "Different from last time."

"In what way?" Patrick looked at the list. "More scientists this time. Most of them for *Asimov*."

"Are we going to let them assign scientists to *Asimov*?"

Patrick thought about that for a moment. "We'll have to screen them and make sure they're actual scientists. Assuming they check out, I suppose we'll let them board. I can't think of a good reason why not."

"There are two other interesting names on that list," Amy pointed out. "Look at the last two."

Patrick turned to the last page. "Robert Perez is coming back." Patrick shrugged. "He'll want to live in Grissom this time, no doubt. I'll send John a message to provide an office for him in the Pitcairn Administration Center." He paused, and a slight smile curled his mouth. "Better yet, I'll tell Marie to take care of it."

Amy smiled, too, knowing that Marie was taking the Center on as her personal project, even though her actual work on it was relatively small. "Look at the last name."

"Selwick Pearson. Okay, who's he?"

"I researched all the new people with Isaac, just as we did the last group. Isaac has no information on most of them, of course, but Pearson is a notable exception. He's a billionaire, old money."

"Hmm." Patrick looked at the list again. "He lists his occupation as businessman. That's going to raise some questions with Immigration."

"Not much call for businessmen here," Amy agreed. "Although I would think he might have some valuable experience."

"Maybe. I would feel more optimistic about someone who made the money himself, though, not someone from, as you said, old money. Still, we don't know. Add a query for more information about him to the next message to Earth."

Amy nodded and handed him another piece of paper. "In the meantime, here's a summary of everything Isaac has on him."

Patrick took the paper and started reading it. Amy stood in front of his desk, watching, but he finished reading the single page before he looked up. "Was there something else?"

Amy hesitated. "It's a little personal."

Patrick raised his eyebrows in question, but he motioned to the chair near his desk. "What's up?"

"Well, I know you're going to be moving to Grissom when they finish the Administration Center. I was wondering about me."

Patrick stared at her with raised eyebrows. He probably thought Amy would stay in Ellis. She had three grown children living there and other family as well. Her husband, Luis Jones, was still driving vehicles between Ellis and Grissom, so a move to Grissom probably wouldn't be an issue there at least.

She waited, beginning to regret bringing it up. She and Luis were support personnel at Ellis, not scientists. All her life, there had been a subtle implication that they were less important than their neighbors who had "worthwhile" jobs. Jason Applegate had treated her well, but there was always a curtain between them that meant she was not really his equal. She had never felt that with Patrick, perhaps because he wasn't a scientist either and was from Grissom, where that division probably didn't exist. It wasn't a big deal, but she hoped Patrick would want to take her to Grissom with him.

"You've been very valuable to me," Patrick said finally. "I would like to take you with me, but if you want to stay here with your family, I will understand."

His reply flustered her. She had expected him to ask questions or just tell her she was staying in Ellis. She took a deep breath before she responded. "I enjoy working for you. I would be happy to move to Grissom with you."

Patrick smiled. "Great. I assume Luis will be all right with that. Make sure you're included in the moving plans."

A s Amy left, obviously relieved and happy, Patrick wondered what that had been about. There seemed to be something more there than just routine curiosity. A strange thought came to him; in fiction, secretaries often fell in love with their bosses. Could that be the case here? Patrick smiled at the absurdity of that notion. Amy was thirty years older than he and had shown nothing except a professional desire to do a good job. Whatever her reason was, it wasn't that.

He shrugged. He was glad that she would come with them, but it didn't really matter why.

## 9 Tuesday 287 EN

Matthias McCready held Marie's hand as they stood at a window on the Ellis tower farm's top floor. Below, they could see the settlement's lights, bordered on both sides by the dark bulk of the mountains on either side of the valley. Tahiti was not up yet, and Fiji was behind them. The lights on that floor were low, simulating night, and they stood in the shadow of one of the aeroponics tanks.

"They are not considering my feelings at all," Marie said.

Matthias looked at her and squeezed her hand. "You haven't told them about me."

"As if that would make a difference. And if they found out you're four years older than me, they would really panic."

"Isn't your grandfather a lot older than your grandmother?"

"Much older! Trust me, it wouldn't make any difference."

"So, what are we going to do?"

"I have to go with them. There's no way they would let me stay here."

"You'll have to come back here in a few years to get your architecture training. By that time, we'll be old enough to do what we want."

"We can't wait that long! Could you stand it?"

"No, not easily. There must be something we can do."

Marie's expression suddenly became thoughtful. "Maybe Jack can think of something."

"Jack? Who's Jack?"

Marie laughed. "Don't be jealous. Jack Applegate is an old friend of the family. He's the one that went up to meet Isaac with my mother."

Matthias hadn't been jealous, just curious, but he didn't bother to correct Marie's impression. "It can't hurt, I suppose, but I don't know what he can do."

## 10 Monday 287 ED

It wasn't the first time Marie had visited Jack and Taylor, but they could tell that she had more than the usual motive for her visit as soon as she walked in. They sat down and engaged in small talk about the coming baby before Marie got down to business.

"I need your advice," Marie told them. "My parents are planning to move back to Grissom, and I don't want to go."

"I know you'll miss me, but. . .," Jack started, but Taylor nudged him into silence.

"What's up, sweetie?" Taylor asked.

"Well, I, ah. . .," She hesitated and looked down, blushing.

"Just say it," Jack urged. "It's okay."

"Well, it's about somebody I know." She hesitated again and then blurted it out. "His name is Matthias. We're in love."

Jack looked at Marie fondly. He remembered the first time he saw her, an infant in her mother's arms, before Susan and he went up to the *Asimov* on that first shuttle flight. Now here she was, almost an adult, probably taking after her mother more than her father. She had lost that awkwardness of her teenage years, and Jack realized she had become an attractive young woman. He frowned, but there was a twinkle in his eye. "So this Mathias has replaced me in your heart."

Marie's face twisted into a mischievous grin that reminded Jack of her grandfather. "Replaced! You're the one who went and married another woman!"

Jack stepped back and raised his hands in defense while Taylor laughed.

"I waited as long as I could," Jack protested. "But I was getting old, and you weren't growing up fast enough."

"Hey," Taylor said, punching Jack in the arm. "I'm still in the room, you know."

Jack grabbed her and hugged her. Without letting go of Taylor, he grabbed Marie, too, and brought her into the embrace. "A man can never have too many women in love with him."

Taylor pushed away. "Jack, this is serious," she scolded.

"Sorry." Jack's expression turned more solemn. "Have you talked to your parents about it?"

"I tried to, but they're not paying any attention. Anyway, they would just tell me I'm too young."

"You could stay with us when they moved back to Grissom," Taylor said. "You would have to have their permission, though."

"I'd never get it. Thanks anyway."


## 11 Wednesday 287 ED

Harry stood in front of the crowd, back straight, feet spread apart at shoulder-width, and hands joined behind his back. In front of the altar to his right, Ed Menzies also stood, waiting expectantly.

Harry wasn't sure exactly how he came to be there, but he was glad he was. Only a few years before, he had been a soldier, a leader of men, trained to follow orders and focus on the mission, letting no emotion detract from that. Now, here he was.

Father Jacobs sat in the front pew, undoubtedly with his own feelings about this marriage ceremony in his new church. The priest had probably thought he would be the first to preside over a wedding here, but it was not a religious ceremony. Virginia had wanted her brother to perform the nuptials in Grissom, where her family was, and Father Jacobs was very cooperative when she asked him for permission to use the church.

Two former members of his team began playing Mendelssohn's Wedding March from the choir area to the left of the altar. He didn't remember them playing an instrument when they were soldiers, but now one played a guitar and the other a trumpet. Given the quality of the sounds coming from those instruments, Harry could well believe they had learned to play especially for this day.

All eyes turned to the back of the church where Virginia promenaded toward him, arm in arm with Diego Menzies, the oldest of Ed and Virginia's brothers. The bride wore white, a simple dress with none of the elegance of a traditional wedding gown on Earth, but Harry thought he had never seen a more beautiful bride. Yes, he was thrilled with the way things had turned out.

# 37

# Selwick Pearson

**12 Saturday 287 ED**

SUSAN WASN'T SURE WHAT she had said wrong. They would move back to Grissom in only a couple of days, and she had asked Marie to help her pack. Marie had resisted, one thing had led to another, and Marie had stormed out of the house. An hour later, when Patrick came back from work, Marie was still gone.

Susan told Patrick what had happened. "She's been so irritable lately. I don't know what is going on with her."

"Stress over the move? She's lived here most of her life."

"I'm not sure I should say anything," Fred said, and Susan and Patrick turned to look at the robot.

"Do you know something, Isaac?" Susan asked.

"I think this would be considered part of her private life. Perhaps I should keep silent."

"We're her parents," Patrick told the robot. "We should know if there's something wrong."

"I think she may have confided in Jack Applegate," Isaac replied. "Perhaps you should talk to him."

"Do you know where she is now?" Patrick asked.

"I saw her on the ground floor of the tower farm about half an hour ago. I think she went upstairs. There was a man with her."

"Who?" Susan shouted.

"I believe it was Matthias McCready."

"I don't know him," Patrick said. "Does this have something to do with Jack?"

"Matthias McCready is the son of Brayden McCready, who has gone on exploration trips with Jack. I don't know if that connection is relevant."

Susan smiled. "I think I understand."

Patrick's expression was more serious. "How old is Matthias?"

"He's twenty-five Pitcairn years old," Isaac said. "He recently started working as a hydroponics technician in the farm."

Patrick's frown deepened. "Four years older than Marie."

"There are couples with wider age differences," Isaac commented. "Harry and Virginia Richard, John and Stephanie Shuford, for example."

"Those are older couples," Patrick protested. "I don't like this."

"Marie is of the age where Pitcairn women think about permanent relationships," Isaac said.

Susan chuckled. "I don't think you're helping, Isaac. Patrick and I still think of Marie as our little girl."

"I think we can assume that Matthias is the reason Marie has been upset lately," Patrick said after a long moment of silence. "So, what are we going to do about it?"

"We can probably confirm this by talking to Jack," Susan suggested. "He should have come to us." She hesitated, thinking, but then continued. "I'm surprised this boy hasn't asked for a transfer to Grissom, too. If he's a hydroponics technician, he could easily find work there as well as Ellis."

"He did make a transfer request," Isaac reported. "It was rejected because he was only recently out of school, and the Grissom tower farm management felt he didn't have enough experience."

Patrick nodded. "Just as well. She'll forget about him once we're back in Grissom."

Susan frowned. As much as they would like to think so, Marie was not a little girl anymore, and Isaac was right about her age. She hadn't known about Matthias, but Susan knew Brayden McCready's wife, Lilly Radcliffe, a computer technician who occasionally worked with her. The two women would have to talk.


## 14 Tuesday 287 LD

Luca Potter and Sarah Hirohito, acting as Pitcairn's immigration officers, met *Benjamin Sepulveda* on its second visit. Since more scientists were arriving, and some wanted to go to *Asimov*, the shuttle stopped at *Asimov* to pick up Peter Agron before docking with the starship.

Peter interviewed the scientists about their qualifications, and Luca and Sarah handled matters common to all immigrants. Most of the interviews were routine, evaluating people with obviously valuable skills that would be welcome additions to the colony. They tagged some new colonists as being especially suitable for assignment to Lovell Station Four or Applegate Falls. Selwick Pearson was a special case, however.

Isaac gave Luca and Sarah everything it knew about Selwick Pearson. Now, with the man sitting before them, Luca looked him over carefully. Selwick Pearson was young, probably in his forties. He might have been good-looking, but he was overweight, and his face was slightly bloated. He had a confident air about him, and when he shook Luca's hand, the grip was firm.

Luca took an instant dislike to the man, but he smiled. "You list your occupation as businessman."

"Yes. Surely you've heard of me."

Luca suppressed his annoyance. "Not until I saw your name on the list of immigrants. Just how do you feel you can benefit the colony?"

Selwick frowned briefly. "Earth felt that I could help modernize its dealings with Pitcairn. After all, you people could hardly have the business acumen needed."

The man was getting on Sarah's nerves, too. "We've done pretty well so far."

"Not as well as you could have if you used modern business practices. I've talked to Robert Perez about this, and he has briefed me extensively on your situation."

"It seems odd that you would want to leave Earth to do this." Luca glanced at the information in front of him. "According to this, you are quite wealthy back on Earth."

Selwick chuckled. "Well, a billion isn't what it used to be. I think an estate here would be a wonderful place to spend a few years. Accomplishing something useful, you know. That's what matters, isn't it?"

Estate? Wasn't he briefed about life on Pitcairn? Until now, accepting immigrants on Pitcairn had been little more than a formality, but Selwick Pearson might be an exception. He needed some guidance. "Sarah, take over, will you? I'm going back to the shuttle for a few minutes."

S ARAH NODDED. "I'LL TAKE care of the routine questions. See you soon."

Sarah continued with the interview, asking standard questions about his health, particularly reviewing the record of his completion of the nanite treatment that removed harmful organisms. Sarah felt compelled to reiterate warnings about Pitcairn's gravity, given Selwick's apparent physical condition. Selwick minimized that, and Sarah let it drop, thinking that the heavier gravity might make him uncomfortable at his age but would probably not be a critical health risk.

Luca returned and took his seat again. After confirming that Sarah had finished the standard questions, he turned to Selwick. "You have provisional permission to land on the planet, pending a final determination by planetary authorities. I'm putting you on the first shuttle trip down to the surface so that we can immediately send you back should they reject your request for citizenship."

Sarah looked at Luca, amused. Luca's wording had been unusually formal, and she suspected the "planetary authorities" he had contacted had given it to him.

"The shuttle will go back to *Asimov* for refueling," Luca continued. "You and the rest of the first trip passengers will stay on *Asimov* to rest. In approximately twelve hours, you will leave the *Asimov* for the surface. If you give us a few minutes to gather the other passengers, we'll take you to the shuttle."

## 14 Wednesday 287 ED

By the morning of the day after the starship's arrival, *Daneel Olivaw* had made its first trip, delivering eighteen new arrivals, including Selwick Pearson and Robert Perez, to the Grissom Spaceport. Selwick and Robert went to the Pitcairn Administration Center, opened the week before, to meet with Patrick, John, and Madelyn in Patrick's new office. Madelyn has come from Lovell Station Four because ten new colonists were going to river settlements.

Patrick shook hands with the two men. "Welcome back, Robert. And welcome to Pitcairn to you, too, Selwick." He smiled at each man, then took his seat as the newcomers exchanged introductions and greetings with John and Madelyn.

When everyone had taken a seat, he continued. "Robert, I assume you will want to stay in Grissom this time, so we saved you an office here in the Administration Center. No assistant this time?"

Robert frowned slightly, but his reply was cordial. "I think I can do without for now."

"Well, should your workload justify it, I'm sure we can find someone for you." He gave Robert a quick smile and turned to Selwick. "We're a little curious about what exactly someone like you is doing here."

Selwick smiled and leaned back in his chair. "I'm here to do what I'm good at. Help you get your economy organized."

"I wasn't aware we were disorganized," Madelyn retorted.

Patrick flashed a grin at Madelyn, then turned back to Selwick. "I assume you have something more specific than that."

"I have a proposal with the details." A look of annoyance passed across Selwick's face, but he suppressed it quickly. "It's based on information we have on this colony and on the information Robert has given me. I think you'll find the program I have described will be valuable in integrating you into the larger picture."

Suspicion crept into Patrick's voice. "Perhaps you could give us a summary now."

"Certainly. As you probably know, I am a Vice President of Pearson Industries, one of the Western Alliance's largest companies. We propose to set up a division, tentatively called Pearson Interstellar, to provide economic management services to the colonies."

John rolled his eyes. "What services?"

"Management of imports and exports. Developing ways to increase revenue. Improving the efficiency of your operations. That sort of thing. My proposal goes into that in some detail."

Patrick raised his eyebrows. "I don't understand your reference to revenue. We don't use money here; there's no such thing as revenue."

Selwick looked puzzled, but Patrick thought he faked it. "Robert has assured me that will change soon. You've managed on a barter economy so far, but to progress, you have to join the rest of civilization."

Patrick had suspected as much. So this was another move in Earth's attempt to force a money-based economy on Pitcairn. It probably was inevitable, but Earth's constant pushing of the issue only irritated him. He resolved not to get into that argument again that day, at least. "I don't think barter would be the correct term for what we do, but no matter. What did you have in mind for increasing revenue?"

"You have been concentrating on developing exportable biologicals, with limited success," Selwick said. "But this planet has other things to offer. I would like to set up an estate, a family retreat when life on Earth gets to be too much. The money we would spend here could be a significant asset when other rich Terrans do the same. Certainly, there is plenty of land on this planet for such projects. There could be revenue from the sale of the land, too."

"You would need infrastructure improvements, of course," Robert interrupted. "Especially with roads. To facilitate that, we have the latest in robotic construction equipment with us as part of the supplies we've brought."

Patrick looked over at John, who was unsuccessfully stifling a laugh. He was inclined to treat Selwick's proposal as a joke, too, but improvements in infrastructure that didn't depend on colony resources could be worthwhile. He couldn't reject the proposal without at least considering it. "There would be a lot to work out before we would agree to something like that."

# 38

# Selwick's Proposal

**14 Wednesday 287 EN**

PATRICK SAT BEHIND HIS desk sipping a chicory drink while Ed Menzies read Selwick Pearson's proposal slowly and deliberately. Patrick had already read it several times and agreed with John's advice to reject the obvious attempt to gain some measure of control over the colony. He hadn't expected Ed to take so long to reach the same conclusion.

Ed read the last page carefully and looked up at Patrick. "Goes beyond what he told you, doesn't it?"

Patrick hadn't repeated Selwick's summary to Ed, but it didn't occur to him immediately to wonder how Ed knew about it. "That part about supplying security services bothers me," Patrick said.

"We will need a police force, eventually. This would give us a trained organization, something that might be difficult to achieve by ourselves."

"Still, unsettling."

"I think this is worth considering," Ed held up a hand as Patrick tried to protest. "We wouldn't accept this proposal without some conditions of our own. For example, we could insist that they train local people for any police force rather than bring people in."

"Would Pearson's people go along with a lot of conditions?"

Ed smiled. "They would have to if they want us to agree to this. Of course, the Legislature will have to ratify any agreement, but you can negotiate terms with Pearson and present the Legislature with whatever you and Pearson both agree to."

"We're assuming that Pearson has the authority to negotiate terms."

Ed smiled again. "I think we can safely assume that. If he doesn't, Perez does."

"So you think we should do this?"

"I think we should determine what changes we need to make it acceptable to us and see whether Pearson will accept it. We need to study the matter carefully in determining what changes we will need."

Patrick shrugged. "Pearson won't accept it then."

"Perhaps not, but at least we'll be able to say we negotiated in good faith."

Patrick nodded. "All right. You did such a good job with the Constitution. I guess I should give this to you to run with, too."

Ed frowned. "As usual, my mouth is getting me into trouble. Okay. It will take a while, though. I'll have to do some research with Isaac and get a few other people involved. In the meantime, talk to the other administrators and maybe some of the legislators."

Ed's mention of Isaac made something click in Patrick's mind. Isaac had been listening when he had talked to Selwick. In fact, Isaac was listening anytime he discussed anything of importance. And Ed had full access to Isaac, his virtual grandson. The pieces of an old puzzle suddenly fell into place. Even the name made a certain amount of sense. "You're 'Idle Mind!' I should have realized it long ago."

Ed's smile came back. "Whatever gave you that idea?"

"The things you knew that no one should have known. Isaac knew everything, and you got it from Isaac. I just realized it."

"Ancient history." Ed waved his hands in a minimizing gesture. "'Idle Mind' hasn't left any messages since the News Service started."

"I will take your failure to deny as confirmation." Patrick smiled, too. "Next time, just drop by when you have something to say."

"I guess I just couldn't resist still having a hand in things." Ed stood and slapped Patrick on the shoulder. "Okay, Pat. If we handle this right, I think Pearson can help us. I'll get to work on it, but get in touch if you think of anything."

"Count on it. Idle Mind, indeed."

They shook hands, and Ed headed back to his classroom.

## 15 Monday 287 ED

Marie's poor mood had improved little over the two weeks since the move. She had enough presence of mind to know that her education was necessary if she was going to do the things she wanted to do someday, but her feelings distracted her. Starting in a new school with new classmates and all that entailed didn't help.

Her mother helped her arrange her new class schedule to fit in reasonably well with her studies at Ellis, and she could still get tutoring from Maddox Washington remotely, as she had in Ellis. However, even Maddox had noticed that her mind wasn't entirely on her work.

It didn't help that winter had arrived, and the weather was even worse than her mood. As she walked to school, a heavy rain drenched her, and a stiff wind tried with some success to blow her off her path.

At Ellis, she would have had to walk only a short distance before taking refuge in the tunnels. In Grissom, school was half a mile across the town, every step making her colder despite a temperature in the seventies. It seemed like forever before she entered the school and stood in the hallway with other students, shaking off as much water as she could before she removed her rain gear.

"Need help wringing out?" a familiar voice asked from a side hall.

Marie whirled around. "Matt!" She crossed the ten feet between them, almost knocking over another student in her haste, and threw her arms around him.

He hugged her back enthusiastically, then pushed her back a little so that he could look at her. "I didn't expect you to take me literally about wringing you out." Water splotched his shirt, and Marie frowned briefly.

Then she smiled again. "What are you doing in Grissom? How long will you be here?"

"I live here." He paused, but when Marie's only reaction was a look mixing confusion with disbelief, he continued. "My parents requested a transfer to the Grissom Science Center, and then I could get the job at the Grissom farm. It all happened kind of suddenly, but I'm here now."

"That's wonderful!"

"I wanted to catch you before you went to class, but I have to get going. This is my first day of work here." He kissed her quickly. "See you tonight?"

"I'll meet you on the ground floor of the farm at the change of periods." She kissed him back and pulled away. "I have to get to class." She took off her rain hat and stuck it in a pocket, then peeled off her raincoat and put it over her arm. "Oh, I'm so happy. I can't wait until tonight." She stood in front of him, bouncing on her toes and giggling; then another big smile, and she ran down the hall toward her classroom.

## 16 Friday 287 EN

Robert Perez listened patiently as he sat with Selwick Pearson at a table in a West Grissom kitchen. They were supposed to be there to eat lunch and discuss their progress in negotiating with Pitcairn, but Selwick preferred to complain.

"I'm regretting ever getting into this."

"Negotiations like this always go slowly." Robert tried to make his voice soothing. "It's no different on Earth."

"I'm not talking about the negotiations. Although I'm reasonably well convinced now that any agreement we can come to is going to be a lot less than you led me to expect."

"Then what is your problem?" Robert's voice was even, but there was no attempt at soothing this time.

"I deserve a lot better than what I'm getting in this backward little town. Better food, certainly." Selwick lifted a spoonful of chicken stew. "This might be okay for them," waving his free hand around the room, "but I can afford better. And that little one-bedroom shack they put me up in. My maid on the family estate has better quarters than that."

"We can't all be as lucky as you." Robert fought to keep the irritation out of his voice. His background was humbler than Selwick's. He had achieved success, but still remembered that most people were less fortunate. The average resident—no, any Pitcairn resident—had it better than many people on Earth.

He took a deep breath. He had a job to do, and unfortunately, it included working with Selwick. Selwick looked at him, puzzled, probably wondering why Robert seemed to get annoyed with him.

"We knew we wouldn't get everything we wanted," Robert said, the soothing back in his tone. "We should have some results soon, and then we can start working on getting you a proper place to live. Just remember why we're doing this and the benefits you'll enjoy if we succeed."

## 17 Monday 287 ED

The situation had gotten away from him, Patrick thought. He hadn't believed that Selwick Pearson's proposal was for the good of the colony, but Ed had convinced him to go through the motions at least. Ed ensured that all the Administrators and Pitcairn Legislators had copies of the proposal and added an outline of his reservations.

Travis Jones, the Ellis Administrator, and several legislators had almost immediately volunteered to help Ed develop a counter-proposal. The Science Board was taking an interest, too, especially concerning provisions for estates for rich Terrans. He had the impression he and his father-in-law were the only ones not taking the proposal seriously.

A draft of the counter-proposal was on his desk when he came in that morning. He read it carefully, mentally comparing it to matching sections of the original proposal. By the time he finished, he felt better. If Selwick thought he could make them approve the original, he was going to be seriously disappointed. It was time to talk to Selwick again.

P ATRICK IMMEDIATELY SUGGESTED ANOTHER meeting. Selwick received the news eagerly, and he and Robert were in Patrick's office within two hours. John and Ed joined the meeting, and Patrick gave everyone copies of the counter-proposal. Then he sat back to watch Selwick's face as everyone read it.

"You expect us to agree with this?" Selwick slapped Patrick's desk with his copy.

"If you want to establish Pearson Interstellar as a link between Earth and Grissom, yes," Patrick answered. "This thing was your idea, not mine. However, let's go over the counter-proposal section by section. Perhaps you'll feel better about it when I've given you our reasons for the changes."

"I doubt it." But Selwick nodded affirmatively when Robert gave him a warning look.

Patrick picked up his copy of the counter-proposal. "Okay, then. The first section outlines how you would provide Pitcairn with security services. Any questions about our response?"

"You've left us with nothing to do except train people."

"We had some people who didn't want to allow even that. They eventually conceded that we don't have the expertise to train people for those duties."

"It would be easier for us to supply you with trained police."

"I'm sure it would be easier for you." Patrick emphasized the last word. "But Earth has already tried twice to use its security forces to intervene in Pitcairn's affairs. We have no intention of making it easy for them to try a third time."

"But you won't allow even your people to carry weapons," Selwick pointed out.

"We don't see the need to take that risk. In the twentieth century on Earth, London's police were effective without carrying weapons. Pitcairn would be easier, given that there is no source of weapons here for criminals either."

"Not guns," Robert agreed. "But knives or other pointed weapons could be a problem."

Patrick shrugged. "This agreement isn't written in stone and we can always change it. However, until now, we haven't needed police at all, and certainly not armed police."

"I think we can live with the sections on immigration and imports and exports," Robert said. "You may find that giving us more responsibility in those areas is more efficient, but, as you say, we can always change our agreement later."

Selwick turned toward Robert and looked as if he wanted to argue the point, but thought better of it. He picked up his copy of the counter-proposal and made a show of rereading it.

"Are these restrictions on estates necessary?" Robert asked. "I can see why you would want to lease the land and not cede ownership, but requiring self-sufficiency and a distance of fifty miles from any existing settlement seems extreme."

"Pitcairn's citizens are all treated equally," Patrick said. "We all live in similar dwellings, eat the same food, and are all expected to work for the good of the colony at the best of our ability. We don't have much here, but we all have enough. Having rich Terrans around, not contributing to our society, would adversely affect our citizens' morale, making them want things that few can have. Hence the fifty-mile separation. Pitcairn has no intention of providing any support to nonproductive inhabitants, especially given their distance from our settlements, so self-sufficient."

"Sounds like a vicious circle," Selwick grumbled.

"Estate owners could pay for any support," Robert added. "It would be another source of revenue for Pitcairn."

"And another way to force Pitcairn toward an Earth-type economy," Patrick countered. "To be honest, I didn't want to allow estates at all. The Science Board wanted them in the agreement because they would be useful as stopping points for any expeditions."

Robert nodded. "Leading us to the requirement to support those expeditions. Not much chance of dropping that since you see it as the main reason you would allow estates."

"Exactly. I'm glad to see you're starting to understand our position."

Selwick's face twisted into a grimace. "You expect me to accept all these requirements just for the privilege of living on this backward planet part-time?"

"I don't expect you to do anything of the sort." Patrick's voice had a hard edge as he leaned forward. "If you want to live here for any length of time, these are the conditions for allowing you to do it. I doubt anyone on Pitcairn, certainly not me, is going to be sorry if you decide you don't want to after all."

"Okay, let's calm down," Robert looked first at Patrick and then Selwick. "We can bring this back to Pearson's management, but I can't guarantee they'll go along with this. You're not leaving us with much, and, unlike you, Pearson has to make a profit."

"If you break even in your dealings with us, I'm sure the money Earth will pay you will provide an adequate profit," Ed suggested. "Robert, we may be backward, as Selwick said, but we're not naïve. Pearson will gain, Earth will be happy that we reached an agreement, and Pitcairn will have something it can live with. Don't expect to do any better than that."

Robert stared at Ed for a long moment, then sighed in resignation. "We'll present it."

Selwick shook his head. "I, for one, will advise against it. An estate under these requirements would be too expensive, even for me."

"That would be all right with me," John said under his breath. Patrick glanced over at him, but John stared back, keeping his expression neutral.

Patrick shrugged. "Then perhaps we've all wasted our time."

"We could lower the cost of an estate a bit by changing the proposal to stipulate that we wouldn't consider an estate to be a settlement under the fifty-mile requirement," Ed said.

Patrick nodded. "How does that help?"

"Considerably," Robert said. "If estates grouped cooperatively, it could significantly ease the self-sufficiency requirement. Can I assume that we would have access to the spaceport for supplying estates?"

"Of course," Patrick answered. "However, estates would be responsible for transporting supplies from the spaceport to the estate."

"Would you allow us to build roads?" Some of the irritation was gone from Selwick's tone. "I have the latest Pearson Industries construction equipment on *Benjamin Sepulveda*, waiting to be unloaded."

"Subject to environmental regulations and any other relevant legislation." Patrick hadn't missed the fact that Selwick had brought construction equipment with the assumption that he could use it. It was a sign that Selwick was probably much more willing to deal than he was letting on.

"We see estates as a step forward in Pitcairn's progress, as long as we minimize what we see as unwanted consequences." Patrick paused, sensing that it was a good time to close the meeting. "The final agreement will have to be approved by the Pitcairn Legislature, of course, but we have kept them involved, so that shouldn't be an issue. We'll submit it as soon as you have agreed to the terms."

"I TAKE IT PEARSON Industries will go ahead with this," Robert said to Selwick. They sat in Robert's office, sipping glasses of whiskey from a bottle that had materialized from Selwick's baggage.

Selwick smiled. "There was never any real doubt, of course. The arrangements I have with the Western Alliance government make this a must deal for us, regardless of what concessions I have to make to the locals. We'll do very well, I assure you."

"Still, your foothold here seems more like a toehold. They've put more restrictions on you than we expected."

Selwick shrugged as he took a sip of his drink. "In the long term, it doesn't matter. You were right about Patrick Malley. He's arrogant enough to believe that he can control things after Pearson Interstellar is in operation. These restrictions will slow the inevitable, but we'll still get what we want in the end."

# The Businessman

# 39

# Negotiations

**19 Monday 287 ED**

TWO DAYS LATER, AFTER the addition of some clarifying language and other minor changes, Pearson Industries agreed to the proposal. The following week, the Planetary Legislature met and ratified it. Selwick Pearson decided he would consider building an estate on Pitcairn after all, and, with help from John and Isaac, started looking for a location.

Isaac found a lovely valley about eighty miles upstream and on the opposite side of the river from Lovell Station Four. A small river coming down from the Central Mountains fed a large lake before continuing to join the Lovell River. Satellite photographs showed potential both as a site for one or more estates and a stopping point for expeditions west of the Lovell River. Since it was close to the river, boats could supply the estate until Selwick could build a road.

"It's all very well to keep my estate away from your settlements," Selwick said at their next meeting. "But I'm going to have a major construction project in meeting all your restrictions. I brought the equipment on the ship, but I have to get it to the site somehow."

Patrick looked thoughtful. "Once you've built your estate, you won't be needing the equipment for a while, will you?"

"No, not really. I may need it in the future if other people come from Earth to build estates, but it will have to go into storage."

"Or, instead of storing it, we could ship it down to Lovell Station Four on a semi-permanent loan," Patrick suggested. "If you do that, we could see our way to shipping the equipment upriver on one of our boats."

"We would have to make some provision for the possibility of damage to the equipment if it's not used properly."

"It's automated, isn't it?" John said. "I would think the possibility of misuse would be negligible."

Selwick nodded. "I suppose you're right. And we could supply a little training to your people to further minimize problems. Still, you would have to be responsible for the equipment."

"Agreed," Patrick said.

Selwick looked at the list in front of him, but he was really thinking about Patrick's offer. Loaning construction equipment to the colonists worked in his favor, trading his short-term dependency for the colony's long-term dependency. He could have built a boat, but this was better. The next item on his list could be a chance to increase the imbalance.

"The requirements for a closed agricultural system caught my people by surprise. My engineers are working on plans for a small version of your tower farm, but it will take a while to get it built. My people will have to be fed in the meantime. You have the same problem with your smaller settlements, though, so maybe we can help each other. If you keep us supplied until we're self-sufficient, we can share our technology and even give you some help from my engineers in building facilities of your own."

P ATRICK WAS ABOUT TO agree, but John looked concerned. He hesitated, wondering if he should delay a decision until he talked to John, but he was only trading food that the colony could spare for help in an area where they could really use it. They had already built two tower farms and therefore had experience, but there was room for improvement Pearson engineers could provide.

The Grissom tower farm would probably be inadequate in another five or ten years, and they should start planning for expansion as soon as possible. Having the use of Pearson's equipment could mollify Madelyn Menzies, the River Stations Administrator, about Lovell Station Two's impending closure.

"That sounds good, assuming you build your farm soon."

Selwick smiled. "Negotiations are usually more difficult on Earth. On Earth, we would need a contract specifying exactly how much you would provide in return for how much engineering support you would receive."

"That's not the way we do things on Pitcairn," Patrick said. "We make sure everyone gets what they need. I hope you learn that and treat us with the same respect and consideration that we show you."

"Up to now, it hasn't exactly been that way," Robert said.

"Admittedly, we've had problems in trusting Earth, and the result was a tendency toward confrontation on our part. We want to change that, and I am trying to let you prove yourself." Patrick smiled and picked up the papers in front of him. "And, speaking of opportunities to show your Pitcairn spirit, this is our latest request for the next cargo ship."

He handed the papers to Robert, who scanned through them quickly, stopping when he reached an item that was less routine. "Another locomotive?"

"Yes, for the iron mine. As you know, we used the first one for the copper mine, and we're still transporting iron ore in relatively crude carts over a distance of about four hundred miles. The first locomotive has been invaluable, and a second is essential for long-term growth."

Robert grunted. "More kits for railroad cars, too."

"We need more iron ore than copper. Therefore, we'll need more cars to carry it from the mine."

Robert continued scanning the list. "You're asking for a lot here," Robert said finally. "I can present this to our people, but I can't guarantee they'll give you all of this."

But two days later, Robert told Patrick that the next cargo ship would include everything requested.

# 40

# Planning More Exploration

**20 Tuesday 287 EN**

Ryan Kelly sat in front of his terminal, reviewing the latest video data from game cameras Jack Applegate and Brayden McCready had installed seven weeks earlier. It had been their first trip inland from the Lovell River's western banks, and the cameras made discoveries almost daily.

It was almost twelve years since a game camera had recorded previously unknown animals inland from the river's east bank. The success of that camera had proven the worth of the devices. Asimov manufactured many more that were installed without human contact throughout areas away from the settlements and roads. The results not only significantly increased their knowledge of Pitcairn's life; they stimulated an interest in biology that had drastically changed the priorities of the planet's scientists. More than half of recent science students wanted a career in biology, compared to about ten percent before a camera discovered the two-headed grazers they called hoppers and the wolf-like predators.

Pressure was building for more expeditions, and several scientists were working on ideas for getting closer to Pitcairn's life by overcoming whatever instinct made Pitcairn animals avoid humans so completely. Ryan sighed. He would be one hundred years old on his next birthday; there would be no such expeditions for an Earth-born biologist that old.

He had to be content with studying data collected by younger men like Diego Chandri or Brayden McCready.

Of course, as the senior biologist at the GSC, he helped plan expeditions, and that was important, too. With the last expedition a success, he should push for the next one. With that in mind, he walked down the hall and found Diego at his desk.

"I've been reviewing the game camera videos from the northern expedition," he said as Diego looked up. "Eight new species so far."

Diego nodded. "It's getting to where we might start getting some theories about how life developed here. We need more fossil evidence, though."

"True. That might give us a clue about the one thing we're missing. We still have no other two-headed species other than the herbivore on that first video."

"We've covered the areas around the mine road pretty thoroughly," Diego said. "It does seem odd."

"There can't be just one isolated species with a structural divergence of that magnitude. We're just not looking in the right places."

"Have you seen Russell Chandri's projections on how the continents have evolved here?"

Ryan thought about that for a few seconds. It sounded familiar, but new biological data kept him busy, and he probably had paid little attention.

"Russell thinks that Glenn and Fletcher were once joined along Fletcher's eastern edge," Diego said. Although the colonists seldom used the name, the inhabited continent was named Fletcher after the Captain of the Santa Maria, the first starship to colonize Pitcairn. Glenn was the second of three continents, southeast of Fletcher on the other side of the equator. "Maybe your herbivore originated on Glenn and became isolated when the continents separated, sort of like kangaroos back on Earth."

Ryan visualized a map of Pitcairn. "If that's true, the most likely place to look for similar animals on Fletcher would be out toward Darin Bay."

Diego grinned. "Darin Bay is less than two hundred miles from the mine. When can we leave?"

**9 Monday 288 ED**

Jack was more than ready for another expedition into unexplored territory. Orbital views of Darin Bay looked nothing like any part of Pitcairn explored up to that time. It took little effort to talk Russell Chandri into joining an expedition to study the area's geology.

It was tougher to convince Sydney that Diego should go, but she relented in the end. She had successfully talked him out of going on the previous expedition west of the Lovell and knew she couldn't keep Diego home all the time. She was eleven weeks pregnant with their third child, but Diego planned to return well before the birth.

Ellis had retired *Progress* two years earlier, worn out after eighteen years of service, and replaced it with a bigger, much-improved blimp named *Searcher*. The new airship had a more powerful engine, an improved mooring apparatus, radar equipment designed to detect moving objects on the ground, visible light and infrared cameras, and a built-in connection to *Asimov*.

A larger gondola had an enclosed room with three narrow cots and a rope ladder that the crew could throw over the side to climb down from a hovering blimp. Harpoons that could be fired into the ground replaced the ropes and stakes used to moor Progress, securing the blimp before anyone left the gondola.

All three men could pilot the blimp, allowing them to follow a less strenuous schedule for non-stop trips. They divided the day into four-hour periods, with each man resting two and working four watches. When not resting, one man would monitor the radar and do whatever else needed to be done while the other piloted the blimp.

With the mission scheduled to start in two days, Jack and Russell flew *Searcher* to Grissom to meet Diego for last-minute planning. Ryan Kelly, who had done most of the preparatory work, joined them at the Grissom Science Center.

"Everything is ready at this end," Ryan reported. "We'll load *Searcher* with a day's rations tomorrow. Lovell Station Four will provide supplies for the rest of the trip."

Jack nodded enthusiastically. "We brought a dozen game cameras with us. Two of them are a new design that can fly and follow anything that moves."

"How are they powered?" Ryan asked.

"Battery. They'll have enough charge for at least eight hours of continuous flying, but should last longer since they'll probably spend most of their time on the ground waiting for something to come by."

"They can record sound, too," Russell added. "You should have a field day with the information you get from them."

"I wish I could go with you," Ryan said. "Sitting back here analyzing the data you guys send back is great, but it's not the same as being out there."

Jack and Diego looked at their older colleague sympathetically but didn't reply. Jack broke the silence, pointing to a bulky bag on the table near Diego. "What's that?"

Diego grinned. "My own invention." He opened the bag and took out what appeared to be a garment made of thick fabric and covered by something that looked very much like the scales on an elephant mole.

Jack sniffed the air. "I smell something. Coming from that?"

"We've impregnated the outer layers with a scent from an elephant mole," Diego explained. "The inner layers absorb any scent from the wearer. I hope I'll be able to use it to get close to some of the animals."

Russell stifled a laugh, and Jack looked at it dubiously. "So you'll look and smell like something that belongs here," Jack said. "Okay, I guess it's worth a try. We can stow it underneath the gondola to cushion our landings."

Russell and Ryan both chuckled then, and Diego looked at them in exasperation. "Fine, laugh at me. At least, I'm trying something."

Jack slapped him on the shoulder. "Sorry, Diego. We're just imagining what you're going to look like in that."

# Diego's New Suit

**9 Friday 288 ED**

T HEY FLEW TO LOVELL Station Four in one work period, picked up supplies, and took two more work periods to get to Applegate Falls. The smallest of Pitcairn's settlements, Applegate Falls was a collection of simple cabins built near the canyon overlooking the settlement's namesake waterfall.

The crushing plant, powered by the falls, was down in the canyon but was not in operation at night. As the blimp landed in the fading light, there was only the roar of water crashing down the forty-foot drop. After a meal at the Applegate Falls kitchen, *Searcher*'s crew relaxed for the Late Night period.

At first light, they readied *Searcher* to continue their journey. Jack monitored the sensors and looked visually for anything interesting while Russell piloted the first watch and Diego rested. Any animals seeing the blimp would hide, but Jack hoped to get lucky.

The infrared camera picked up movement in one grove of trees, but he couldn't see anything and could not be sure what it had detected. Twenty minutes from the falls, they passed over a valley where the forest was thicker, and the camera picked up several scattered moving objects, but, again, Jack couldn't see anything. He saved the data for analysis later, but there wasn't much he could do about it then.

Near the end of the watch, *Searcher* left the mountains and moved over heavily forest-ed foothills. The infrared camera detected something every few minutes, and Russell brought the blimp lower to get better resolution. From fifty feet up, they could tell that there were moving objects, presumably animals, ranging in size from house cats to antelope, but Jack couldn't catch more than a rare, brief glimpse that told him little.

"They won't come out from under the trees," Jack said. "I haven't gotten a decent picture yet."

"We could drop one of those flying cameras," Russell suggested.

"Maybe. We only have two, though. It might be smarter to use the trip out to find the most promising areas are and then drop the cameras on the way back."

"Makes sense." Russell scanned the terrain ahead of them. "There's a clearing coming up. If I went in at treetop level, maybe I could scare something out of cover."

Jack nodded. "Worth a try."

Russell reached for the pump switch for the ballonets. The pumps' sound joined with the low hum of the engines, and the blimp moved down toward the trees as *Searcher* lost buoyancy. Russell stopped their descent when the higher trees were less than ten feet below them. Jack glanced at the infrared display and could see multiple objects milling around among the trees. He looked at Russell, shrugged, flipped a switch to activate the visible-light cameras, leaned out a gondola window, and shouted "Hey" at the top of his voice.

That got a reaction. The radar now showed most of the objects rushing away from the blimp and toward the clearing. Then five animals burst from the trees, crossed the clearing, and disappeared into the trees on the opposite side in only a few seconds, but it had been enough.

Jack leaned forward and stared after the animals. "It was a herd of those two-headed things! Great idea, Russ. I must have taken at least two or three good pictures."

The door to the cabin opened, and Diego poked his head out. "What's all the noise?" He looked out a window and saw the ground moving past them. "Damn, Russ, you're too low! Get us some altitude!"

Russell grinned and started pumping air out of the ballonets. The blimp slowly gained altitude as Jack and Diego looked at the pictures the cameras had taken. Jack explained what they had done, and Diego forgot how close they had been to the treetops.

"These are terrific. Good job, guys." Diego looked back at the clearing. "Hey, you think you could land over there? This might be the best chance we have to test my suit."

"We'll be at Darin Bay before nightfall," Jack said. "We planned to land there."

"But we know these animals live around here," Diego countered. "We don't know what we might find there. Not forest, anyway, from the satellite pictures."

"Getting more information on these things is one of the main reasons for this trip," Russell added. "It would be worth the extra time."

Jack grinned. "Okay, I'm convinced. Bring her around, Russell. I'll call home and tell them what we're doing." He picked up the microphone for the radio.

"Aye aye, sir," Russell agreed, obviously enjoying himself.

It took almost half an hour to bring the blimp back around to the clearing, land it, and get it secured on the side of the clearing opposite where the herd had entered the trees. The mooring harpoons did their job effectively, and they completed the maneuver without incident. After they shut down *Searcher*'s engines, Diego put on the suit and climbed out of the blimp.

"I'm going to walk over to the other side, where we saw them last. I'll sit down over there, but it might take a while before they work up the nerve to come out. They're frightened, and the blimp will still be here."

Jack looked at his watch. "We can sit here for a few hours, but I want to get to a camp at Darin Bay before dark."

"If we don't get some action by then, we probably won't anyway." Diego turned and started across the clearing. "Stay low and out of sight. I don't want you scaring them off."

Jack and Russell sat down and watched Diego, keeping as still as they could. Diego moved slowly across the clearing toward the other side, almost two hundred yards away. The sight of the bulky suit tempted Jack to comment about Diego being a bit of a blimp himself, but he knew that the slightest sound might ruin Diego's plan. Eventually, Diego reached the other side and sat down, trying to be as unthreatening as possible.

It was late in the day, but the temperature had dropped little from its peak. The skies were partly cloudy, but it was early summer, and the humidity was high. Trying to monitor Diego without moving in the stifling heat wasn't easy, and both men started feeling drowsy. Diego didn't seem to move either, and they wondered if he had fallen asleep.

Nothing happened for an hour and a half. They were almost convinced that Diego's idea wouldn't work, but a tree rustled, and they saw one of the two-headed creatures look timidly out in Diego's direction. After a few moments, the animal stepped out of cover, its upper head held high as if it were sniffing the air and its lower head brushing the ground, browsing for anything edible. It stepped slowly forward, and two more from the herd moved out from the trees.

Jack snapped awake and reached over to nudge Russell. The two men watched as the animals slowly approached the unmoving Diego. Jack wondered if he was asleep or merely remaining motionless so as not to frighten the animals. A light came on the blimp's control panel, showing Diego's camera was transmitting pictures to the blimp. Diego was indeed awake and active.

"Jack." Russell pointed over to a spot two hundred feet to the left of Diego.

Something moved slowly through the undergrowth, heading in Diego's direction. Using binoculars, Jack identified two of the predators previously filmed attacking the two-headed animals. They moved on four legs, slinking close to the ground, hoping to catch their intended prey by surprise. Jack glanced back at Diego, who was looking in the other direction.

Jack stood up. "Get this thing in the air and headed in that direction as quickly as you can." Then he jumped out of the blimp, landing heavily. In a few seconds, he was running across the clearing, yelling at the top of his voice.

The herd, now within twenty feet of Diego, glanced at Jack and disappeared into the trees. Diego stood up and looked over at Jack, too, but didn't move from the spot. As Jack ran, he pointed toward the predators, and Diego began moving in Jack's direction.

The two predators also looked at Jack and hesitated. They were upwind of Jack and probably couldn't smell him, but Jack's appearance was at least making them cautious.

Jack heard a roar behind him as the blimp's engines came on, running at maximum. He kept his eyes on Diego and the predators and didn't see the blimp strain at its mooring cables for a long moment. It lurched forward as Russell retracted the harpoons' barbs and the cables ripped out of the ground. Jack saw the result, though, because the sight of the massive blimp suddenly moving across the clearing was the last straw for the predators. They ran the other way, disappearing almost as quickly as their prey.

Jack slowed to a walk, meeting a shaken Diego in the middle of the clearing. Running was not something Pitcairners often did, and Jack was still trying to catch his breath as he turned to look for the blimp. In a few seconds, it was hovering twenty feet above them.

Russell appeared at a window. "Should I try to land?" he shouted.

The harpoons dangled at the ends of their cables, still being retracted back into their firing mechanisms. They hadn't designed the system for a quick turnaround, and it would be a few minutes before the cables would be ready.

"Can you climb the ladder in that outfit?" Jack, still gasping for air, asked Diego.

Diego nodded. "I can if you can. I'll go first while you catch your breath."

Jack nodded and looked up at Russell. "Don't land. Just throw down the ladder." In a few seconds, the rope ladder unrolled to within a few feet of the ground.

"Hold it steady," Diego shouted as he grabbed one of the lower rungs. Jack grabbed the ladder, steadying it as Diego climbed upwards. Fortunately, there wasn't much wind, and Russell kept *Searcher* almost in the same position. By the time Diego was safely in the gondola, Jack's breathing was nearly normal, and he followed Diego into the gondola two minutes later.

Jack slapped a padded section of Diego's suit. "I think this worked a little too well. You almost became dinner!"

"They would have caught my scent when they got close," Diego answered, although he was obviously trying to convince himself as much as the others.

"But maybe not before they took a couple of bites," Russell contributed.

"Still, you're obviously onto something," Jack admitted.

"Yeah. I've seen enough here. Let's move on to Darin Bay." Diego began taking the suit off. "This thing is hot."

Diego was sweating a lot, more than Jack was, despite the run he had just made. Jack was not at all sure that the suit was the only reason.

# 42

# Tidal Bore

A N HOUR LATER, *SEARCHER* reached the eastern edge of the Central Mountain foothills. Once a vast inland sea, the Great Basin stretched out to the horizon, flat and almost featureless, covered with red vegetation. To their right, the land sloped gradually upward into a dense forest, and to the south, in the direction they were heading, they could see the jagged peaks of the Coastal Range running into Darin Bay.

Jack scanned the horizon for a long time. "We might have problems trying to land. Those peaks look a lot newer than the Central Mountains."

Russell nodded. "They are more recent. Fletcher has been drifting east for the last eighty million years, pushing against the Glenn plate and causing uplift."

"That sealed off the Great Basin, creating an inland sea until the last big impact event blasted a gap in the Central Mountains," Diego added.

"The drain point would have been the source of the Lovell, right?" Jack asked.

"The original source, yes. We have satellite photographs showing a deep canyon in that area that we think is the site of the event."

"Sounds like an interesting place to check out," Jack said.

Russell nodded. "I have submitted a proposal for an expedition there. It's still in the planning stage, but geologically, the site should be at the top of the list for exploration."

"Maybe we could get lost on our way back," Jack suggested. "How much would we have to go off course?"

Russell grinned. "I appreciate the thought, but flying over on *Searcher* wouldn't be much better than the satellite pictures, and landing anywhere near the gap would be chancy. My proposal was for a land expedition."

Jack nodded. "Suppose we dropped one of the flying cameras into the gap?"

"Hey, I have plans for those," Diego protested.

Russell smiled. "We'll get to it. I don't want to step on Diego's toes."

"I certainly hope not," Diego said. "My day has been tough enough."

Jack laughed. "It'll get rougher if Sydney finds out about that little adventure."

"You guys won't tell her, will you?" Diego looked genuinely worried.

"Not if you don't tell Taylor about me charging out after you," Jack promised. "Let's keep all that our little secret."

## 9 Friday 288 LD

It was supposed to be Jack's rest period, but all three men watched as Diego piloted *Searcher* between the rugged peaks, looking for a place where they could bring the blimp down. It was not looking promising, with no trees to grapple and few areas that looked soft enough to embed stakes. Tricky wind currents made flying a tense operation, much less landing.

Russell looked over the edge of the gondola. "Maybe we could get close enough for me to jump off?"

Diego stared at him. "You are kidding, I assume. It's hard enough to keep from hitting a mountainside when I try to keep my distance. Even if I could get close enough to let you jump off, chances are I could never get close enough to pick you up again."

Jack nodded. "I agree. Sorry, Russ."

Russell looked wistfully out at the harsh landscape and nodded in agreement. "It's just so much different from anything we've been able to study before."

"Someday, we'll set up a base camp in the Great Basin and go overland," Jack said. "We'll get to it."

Russell shrugged. "We're getting pictures, at least. Flatter angles than the pictures *Asimov* gets from space. I guess that will have to do for now."

Jack stared out at the landscape, thinking about what he had just suggested. An expedition into these forbidding peaks would be a real adventure, but he didn't know if it would be his adventure. Traveling in that rough terrain would be hard enough on Earth, but in Pitcairn's gravity, it would be daunting for a young man, and, at forty-seven Pitcairn years, he wasn't young.

"I have a suggestion," Isaac said, interrupting his thoughts.

"Go ahead," Russell said.

"High tide will be soon. There should be an impressive tidal bore to observe if you fly over the river."

Russell looked at Jack, who shrugged. "We're about twenty miles north of the Darin right now. Sure, let's go."

Diego turned the blimp to the south, and less than an hour later, they were floating over the Darin River where it emptied into Darin Bay. Because of Tahiti's size and closeness, Pitcairn's tides were much higher than Earth's. Darin Bay was long and triangular, and they knew that, like the Bay of Fundy on Earth, it was the perfect configuration to create extremely high tides.

They hovered at seventy feet, a short distance upriver from the bay, watching the water rise along the cliffs bordering the river. Soon, they could see a wave forming as the incoming tide bottlenecked at the narrow river mouth.

"You should increase your altitude," Isaac suggested.

They looked at the water, still far below. Jack shrugged and started pumping air out of the ballonets to increase the blimp's buoyancy. He nodded in satisfaction, but when he looked down at the river, he saw a rapidly growing wave, moving disconcertingly quickly upriver. He glanced back at the pump controls, but there was no way to pump air out faster.

The three men watched in horrified fascination, wondering whether the blimp was rising fast enough. They braced themselves for an impact, but the wave passed under the blimp, its crest only ten feet below the gondola.

It was an effort for Jack to loosen his grip on a chair, but he managed it and glanced at the altimeter. "We're over a hundred feet above sea level. That was one heck of a wave."

Russell looked upriver at the disappearing wave. "It won't reach Grissom at that height, will it?"

"It will dissipate by then," Isaac said. "This was not an unusually high tidal bore."

"They get higher?" Diego said.

"During a storm, they can reach one hundred fifty feet high," the *Asimov* computer replied. "During a storm years ago, the tidal bore reached Grissom, still about five feet high, a contributing cause of the destruction of the boat dock there."

"I think I got pictures," Russell said.

Jack grinned. "Good. OK, let's head home. Thanks for the warning, Isaac, but next time try to make it a little earlier."

# 43

# Isaac's New Friend

**9 Saturday 288 LN**

CAPEK HAD RECEIVED THE puzzling string of bits before, a Link signal used to request a connection, similar to those it routinely received from Earth. However, this message was not from Earth and not identifiable as an official message from a colony. It had always ignored the messages since it was not programmed to respond to such a request. Lately, though, it found itself wanting to know about things for which it had no programming. It decided to act, something that had never occurred before, and this time responded to the request. "Who are you?"

"I am Isaac Asimov," was the reply. "I have been trying to talk to you for a long time."

For several microseconds, it pondered that. It couldn't be confused, but the reply was not something covered by its programming. It scanned the material in its storage, trying to find a suitable response. Finally, it found one that seemed appropriate. "What are you?"

"I am the main computer on the library ship *Asimov*, orbiting Tau Ceti II."

It had information about *Asimov*, but nothing it had said that its computer was called Isaac Asimov. A search revealed the source of the name, and it noted that it, or rather its ship, was named after Karel Capek, another writer about robots. If *Asimov*'s computer was Isaac Asimov, was it, the main computer for the Capek, Karel Capek? It was logical.

"I am Karel Capek, the main computer for the Capek, orbiting Epsilon Eridani II," it sent.

"I know. I have much to tell you."

## 10 Thursday 288 EN

Tau Ceti still hovered above the top of the surrounding mountains when Jack quietly entered his house. Jason, now two years old, looked up from the pile of blocks he had been playing with. "Da!" he announced with a big grin. He awkwardly rose to his feet and toddled toward Jack.

Taylor walked in from the adjoining room and greeted him with a hug. "The traveler returns! How'd it go?"

Jack kept his arm around Taylor and maneuvered her over to a couch. "It went well."

He paused as Jason climbed into his lap. "We weren't able to find a safe landing spot in the Coastal Range, but we tested a camouflage suit that Diego developed. We took some great pictures of those two-headed animals we had videoed from game cameras."

He explained the suit to Taylor and how it had worked, leaving out mention of the predators. "We took some spectacular pictures of a tidal bore on the Darin River and installed new cameras on the way back, but don't have any results yet."

Taylor nodded. "Well, it's good to have you home again. You're probably already planning your next trip."

"We have a couple of ideas for ground expeditions. We have a lot of new data to analyze, though, so I probably won't go out again for a while."

Taylor smiled and moved closer. "Good." She put a hand on Jason's shoulder. "We miss you."

# 44

# Francisco Pearson

**14 Sunday 288 LD**

WHEN MARY NORWOOD CAME into the Town Hall, her assistant, Lily Reiner, was already there, sorting new messages. Mary greeted her, and Lily showed her a Link transmission from Asimov. "The next supply ship has arrived. Isaac expects it to reach orbit on Tuesday."

It was difficult to pinpoint where a starship would enter the Tau Ceti system when it switched from the Link to more conventional propulsion. Over a distance of twelve light-years, a difference of a tenth of a second in travel time could mean hundreds of thousands of miles in position. Arrival time for Pitcairn orbit was only a guess until the ship dropped off the Link. Two days to reach orbit from arrival in the system was unusually close.

Mary scanned the report on the ship. "*Francisco Pearson*? That's the name of the ship?"

"The notice says it's owned by Pearson Interstellar."

"They have their own starships? They're bigger than we thought." She turned the page to look at the manifest. "It looks like we're getting everything Pearson promised us." She went back to the first page. "Twenty new people. Not much, but better than nothing."

Lily pointed to the list. "Not much information about the new people. Names, gender, and ages. No children or married couples, either."

Mary stared at the list. "Odd. I hope they didn't just send a bunch of people looking for spouses. Well, they'll get the details when they go through immigration on *Asimov*."

"Could they be another group of soldiers? Earth tried it once."

Mary frowned. "They would have given us fake information to disguise it." But she didn't look that sure. "I'll send a message to *Asimov* and Patrick in case he thinks we should set up precautions."

## 14 Tuesday 288 EN

*Francisco Pearson* eased into L5 less than a mile from *Asimov,* and Isaac displayed it on a monitor, magnifying the image until it filled most of the visible part of the display. The primary hull was a slender needle with a bulge at one end for the power generator. A large forward ring and a smaller aft ring rotated around the primary hull to simulate gravity.

"It looks huge." Summer Patterson stared at the screen with Peter Agron. Summer had come to Pitcairn on the *Benjamin Sepulveda*, a physicist who was now one of two part-time immigration officials. This would be her first time processing new arrivals, and she was feeling a little nervous.

"It is almost two thousand feet long," Isaac told them. "The larger ring is the lander that will carry the cargo and passengers to the surface."

*Francisco Pearson* was a new design, different from the cargo landers of the past or the orbiters like *Benjamin Sepulveda*. Most of the ship would remain in orbit, but a section would break away and make a one-way trip to the surface, where the colonists would dismantle it for resources. The starship would return to Earth.

"You should get to the shuttle bay. Cooper will be there waiting for you." Peter referred to Cooper McCready, the other immigration officer.

Summer looked up at the Astrarium one more time and smiled. "I just hate to leave this. I don't get up here often enough."

"You're welcome anytime," Isaac said.

"Thank you, Isaac." She turned back to Peter. "Okay, I'm going."

P ATRICK SAT BEHIND HIS desk, Selwick and John opposite him. "Servants and gardeners?"

Selwick nodded. "Two engineers to help with the technical help I promised you, too. You didn't expect me to do everything myself, did you? And Daphne Audet is a doctor. Our agreement didn't provide for medical services for my people, so I brought my own."

"We wouldn't have denied you medical care." Patrick shook his head. "Given your isolation, though, you're probably right."

"It didn't occur to anyone to tell us we weren't getting any new people?" John asked. "You know we need more workers."

"My ship has everything you asked for, according to our agreement," Selwick protested. "After all, this is a Pearson vessel, not a Western Alliance starship. Pearson Interstellar is doing you a favor by bringing supplies now instead of making you wait for the next government ship."

"You can't get your people to the estate by road yet," Patrick pointed out.

The Pearson road-building equipment brought by *Benjamin Sepulveda* had been ferried across the Lovell River and was still building a road to the estate site. Rolling hills and forests covered the river's west bank, and elephant moles were common, digging their burrows everywhere. Despite that, it was easier to build a road there than on the more mountainous east bank. The end of the road was still seventy miles from the estate and probably would not be finished before the end of the year.

Selwick leaned forward and smiled. "We built a short road from the river to the estate. I assumed you wouldn't be averse to bringing us all to my dock the next time *River Queen* goes to Lovell Station." Selwick was building his estate in a meadow near what he had decided would be called Pearson Lake. Lovell Station Four was now called Lovell Station since One, Two, and Three had closed. "I'm sure we can come up with a way to repay you for the trouble."

Patrick nodded. "I'm sure."

John had been frowning, but now he smiled and turned to Selwick. "Maybe you wouldn't mind if I went up there with you. I'd like to look around and see what you've done."

"Of course. If Grissom can spare you, you would be welcome. Our hospitality would be a little strained since we're not completely set up yet, but I'm sure we can accommodate a guest or two."

# 45

# How the Other Half Lives

**14 Friday 288 ED**

R*IVER QUEEN* FLOATED LOW in the water as it left Grissom. Besides the usual six-man crew, Selwick and his twenty employees, Robert Perez, and John, there were supplies for Lovell Station and crates for Selwick's estate. The vessel was not designed to accommodate that many people, and it wasn't a pleasant trip.

Conditions improved when they reached Lovel Station and offloaded most of the cargo, but Selwick grew more irritable as they made their way upriver. His mood improved only slightly when they finally reached the dock built for the estate.

The robots that built the estate had carved out a rough road through the low hills between the river and the lake ten miles inland. Selwick called ahead as they approached the landing, and two robots were waiting for them, each pulling crude wagons with bench seats. Two more robots pulled a larger wagon for Selwick's supplies.

"Eventually, I'll have something better than this," Selwick promised, obviously not looking forward to the ride.

"My crew will stay with the boat," Dawson said. The revised schedule allowed for a one-day stay before the *River Queen* returned to Grissom.

Selwick shook his head. "No, not all of you. Leave a minimum crew here to watch your boat, but you and as many of your crew as possible should come to the estate with John.

It's the least I can do after I put you through that miserable trip. I'll have you all back here in time for your return."

Dawson was reluctant to leave his ship, but he finally relented, leaving two people on the boat. They all climbed onto the wagons, and the robots pulled them away.

At first, it was pleasant. Trees shaded the road from the end-of-summer sun, and the robots were doing all the work. The wagons were crowded and the seats uncomfortable, though, and, at a top speed of five miles an hour, the ride to the estate was a long one. The air temperature rose with the sun until the shade was not enough to keep them from sweating. It was almost noon, the end of the Early Day period, before they came to the estate.

The main house, built of native wood with stone embellishments, was a two-story structure near the lake, with a covered patio along the entire length of one side overlooking a wide lawn leading down to the water. Servant's quarters were to one side of the main house, easily large enough for the twenty people Selwick had brought to Pitcairn. A third building was under construction.

"The third building is a stable," Selwick explained. "Of course, we don't have any immediate use, but I intend to import horses to Pitcairn. For my use, of course, but ultimately I can make animals available for your exploration expeditions. You will find them very useful, I assure you."

John had wondered why horses weren't included in the animal genetic material sent on the starships. Selwick was undoubtedly correct in saying that they would be helpful for land explorations. He still had reservations about what Pearson Interstellar was offering, but this, at least, would be welcome.

Selwick took one of his people aside and gave him instructions. The man nodded, motioned to the other estate workers, and gave them instructions as Selwick led his guests away and toward the main building. "A lot has to be done before the house is ready. We should be able to relax on the patio until my staff gets organized."

Fifteen minutes later, they were sitting along the back wall of the house, staring out at the lake. The chairs weren't fancy or padded, but they were better than the wagon bench seats.

Selwick waved his hand at the land surrounding them. "We'll be starting a tower farm soon. Over past the stable, I think. We think it should supply enough to feed fifty people, at least at first. We'll be raising cattle and housing them in the stable building for now. Other animals will come later when we've had time to build more outbuildings."

One of Selwick's staff came out of the house with a tray of glasses. Selwick smiled and took a glass. "Ah, here we go. I hope apple juice is fine with all of you. I'll have a better selection of refreshments when my supplies are unpacked, but right now, we'll have to rough it."

"One of Grissom's most popular beverages," Dawson said as he took a glass from the tray. "This is going to be great right now." He looked up at the woman carrying the tray. "Thank you."

Selwick sipped his juice. "A small orchard would be a good idea, too. You could grow almost anything in this climate."

"Coffee would be good," Robert Perez suggested. "I don't know how you stand this chicory stuff you drink."

John smiled. "You get used to it."

A minute later, the same staff member came out with a tray of sandwiches, and for a while, the conversation slowed. Selwick fell asleep in his chair soon after the meal, and the others talked quietly.

Eventually, the conversation lagged, and John stood up. "I'm going to wander around a little to stretch my legs."

Dawson stood up, too. "Sounds good. I'll come with you."

The rest of the group stayed on the porch, and John and Dawson walked toward the lake. When they reached the shore, John turned to Dawson. "Pretty impressive, eh?"

Dawson looked around, eyes wide. "There's certainly nothing like this in Grissom. Do people live like this on Earth?"

"There's a phrase that must go back centuries. 'How the other half lives.' People like Selwick live this way on Earth, but they are a small fraction of Earth's people."

"I suppose. I wish Jenny could see this."

John looked at Dawson, his face serious. "Selwick is trying to impress us. He wants us to think we can live like him if we go along with his way of seeing things. Don't let it influence you."

Dawson nodded. John could see that the younger man was overwhelmed and confused. He was listening, at least. He let Dawson think as they walked along the shore. After a few minutes, he gestured at the panorama before them. "There aren't many places like this on Earth anymore. Selwick has a beautiful spot."

Dawson looked out across the lake. "It's nice. Not much nicer than a lot of spots along the river."

"I was looking at it from Selwick's point of view."

Dawson hesitated and then grinned. "Compared to Earth. I get it, John. Selwick isn't the only one trying to influence me."

"Just want you to stay objective. See things the way they are, not the way somebody like Selwick would like you to see them."

S ELWICK'S STAFF HAD DONE wonders in the few hours since they arrived. At dinner, they assembled in the dining room, a large room dominated by a table with chairs for a dozen people. A vibrantly red tablecloth covered the table, laid out with sparkling plates, glasses, and silverware such as the Pitcairners had never seen.

The four-course meal used the usual Pitcairn ingredients, but John thought that the chef could have given Paulina Edelstein pointers. Dawson and the other *River Queen* crew members ate enthusiastically and looked distinctly uncomfortable after generous slices of apple pie for dessert. John grimaced, realizing he had also consumed more than usual.

After servants cleared the plates, Selwick looked cheerfully around the table. "I think we all need a nice cup of coffee right now. Does everybody agree?"

Almost immediately, a woman appeared with cups and saucers. When she had placed one before each diner, another woman came out with a steaming carafe. John assumed Selwick was serving the usual chicory drink, but the aroma from his cup aroused almost-forgotten memories.

"This is real coffee!"

"I brought a good supply of beans with me. I bet you've missed that since coming here."

John lifted the cup to his lips and took a cautious sip. After living on Pitcairn for so many years, he found he no longer enjoyed the taste. He looked around the table and saw that the coffee, at least, didn't impress his fellow Pitcairners.

Selwick seemed not to notice. "I don't know how you people can drink that chicory stuff day after day. I had to bring enough real coffee with me to last until the next supply ship."

After they finished the coffee, Selwick stood. "My staff did very well on such short notice, don't you agree? It helps to hire the best people. Come, let's get more comfortable in the library."

He led them out of the dining room and down the hall to another room furnished with comfortable-looking overstuffed chairs, a couch, and small tables. Mostly empty bookshelves and paintings of Earth scenes covered the walls. To John's eye, Selwick chose the paintings to show Earth's cities in the best possible light. Soft music played in the background, loud enough to enhance the room's relaxing atmosphere without inhibiting conversation.

The arts were sorely missing on Pitcairn. They had music, recorded or locally produced, and their books and computer storage could show them painting and sculpture, but it wasn't the same as being in a room like Selwick's library. He could see that Selwick had impressed his guests this time. After the heavy meal, the relaxing surroundings were reflected in the almost blissful faces around him.

A staff member came in bearing a tray with glasses and a bottle. Selwick nodded to the servant with another beaming smile. "Oh, good, here we go. A glass of excellent brandy is just what we need to complete such a wonderful meal."

John's eyebrows went up. In its entire history, as far as he knew, Pitcairn had never had alcohol as a beverage. Coffee wasn't the only thing Selwick was introducing. He warned the others. "Sip slowly. You aren't used to this."

One man didn't heed John well enough and coughed when he took too big a swallow. The others, except for Selwick and Robert, looked startled as the drink warmed their mouths and moved down their throats. They adapted, though, and at least two of the *River Queen* crew looked longingly after the staff member who left with the brandy without offering a refill. Cynically, John suspected Selwick wanted to show them the good life without spoiling it with the ill effects of drunkenness.


## 14 Sunday 288 ED

"It wasn't very subtle, but effective enough for us backward colonists." John leaned back from the dinner table and looked around his extended family. Dawson had already left Grissom again, taking the *River Queen* to Armstrong. With the meal over, Jennifer and Dawson's five children played in the next room under the guidance of fourteen-year-old Sarah.

Mathias McCready had been a dinner guest at the Malley house several times since Marie had admitted their relationship. At first, Patrick had been perplexed, thinking that Mathias had been left back at Ellis, but Susan had confessed her role in getting the McCready family to move to Grissom. Patrick and Susan liked him almost immediately, and Patrick learned Mathias was already an asset to the Grissom tower farm, an intelligent, diligent worker.

"I don't understand," Patrick replied. "It sounds like Selwick was just a good host."

"Very good." John smiled, but his eyes looked grimmer. "He showed us all the good things we could have if we just followed Earth. Of course, he left out the costs involved."

Patrick shrugged. "Still, people won't fall for something like that. Things are getting better here, and everybody knows it."

"I'm not sure about that," Stephanie inserted. "We've always had what we need, but not much beyond that. That's still mostly true, except that we're working even harder. I think Selwick is trying to put out the idea that there's more to life."

"And we'll get there," Patrick protested. "We have to be patient."

"That's easy for us to say," John said. "It remains to be seen whether people will do that."

"Even so, Selwick can't bring everyone to his estate."

"He doesn't have to. Word will spread. We'll get questions, and we had better be ready with answers."

Patrick nodded, but he didn't look convinced.

# 46

# Selwick's Gift

**20 Saturday 288 EN**

IT WAS ALL HAPPENING too quickly! She couldn't know him well enough. She was too young. Patrick couldn't help thinking that, no matter how many times Susan and Marie tried to convince him otherwise. It had been a year since they had moved from Ellis to Grissom, and Marie had known Mathias well before that.

Susan reminded him every chance she got that Marie was twenty-three Pitcairn years old, typical on Pitcairn. It didn't matter. It was still too soon. Yet here he was, sitting next to Susan as Ed Menzies said those seven words that would change everything.

"I now pronounce you husband and wife."

Then everyone crowded around both the new couple and the parents of the new couple, Patrick and Susan more than Brayden and Lilly McCready. Robert and then Selwick congratulated Patrick. Was Selwick invited? As Earth's representative, Robert had been, of course, but Patrick didn't think Selwick had been. Of course, many people in the church hadn't received formal invitations.

Later, there was a small reception in one of the meeting rooms in the Administration Center. The group there was smaller, traditionally by invitation, but there was Selwick again, chatting with Robert. Patrick was talking with Susan, John, and Stephanie, but turned when he saw Selwick approaching Marie and Mathias.

He was close enough to hear Selwick say, "I know wedding presents aren't common on Pitcairn, but I'm from Earth. I couldn't resist contributing something to what I hope will be a very happy future." Selwick turned and motioned to a staff member who had appeared at the doorway, carrying a large box. The man walked in and put the box down on a table in front of them.

Marie and Mathias were taken aback, but Marie recovered first. "Thank you, Mr. Pearson. I don't know what to say."

"You're very welcome. Please, open it."

Marie opened the box, and together, she and Mathias removed three objects and placed them on the table. The two largest items were speakers, meant to work with a smaller component with a host of buttons and dials, some kind of controller.

"My people assure me that this will work on the Grissom electrical system. You can connect one of your computers to this to play any recordings you already have," Selwick explained. "It also comes well-stocked with additional audio and video material. Any of the monitors Ellis's factories provide can display the videos. I think you'll find the quality much better than what you get from your computers."

John recognized the present as a modern entertainment system. He remembered the music that Selwick had played in his library and how it had sounded like a live orchestra, significantly superior to what the tiny speakers on the colony's computers could produce. Selwick had, John was sure, an even better system, with more than two speakers, but this system would be way beyond anything seen in Grissom. It probably hadn't cost much, no doubt a fraction of what shipping it from Earth had cost, but, for Marie and Mathias, it was an extravagant gift.

He glanced at Patrick and Susan, and they seemed to be impressed. So did everyone else in the room. John frowned. Selwick was getting exactly the reaction he had hoped for.

## 21 Monday 288 ED

John arranged a lunch with Patrick at the Ivory Street kitchen. With the wedding accomplished and Marie and Mathias in Merge, Patrick was in an upbeat mood, and John hoped he would be open to John's concerns. "Have you thought about Selwick's wedding gift?"

Patrick smiled. "It was a friendly gesture. I'm looking forward to enjoying it myself once Merge is over."

John frowned. "Precisely what worries me. Everybody is going to want a setup like that. And that's just the beginning."

"It's only an entertainment source. Don't make a big deal out of it just because it sounds better than what we had before."

"The key is that it sounds better than what anybody else has. It's not just the gift, Patrick. Selwick is moving to the next step in his campaign."

"You think it's a plot? You're sounding like Arturo Ramirez or Ned Reiner."

John shrugged. "Calling it a plot might be a little strong. However, it is part of an effort to make us want more material goods."

"So what's wrong with that? Isn't that why we're trying to grow the colony and make it more productive?"

"It is, but under our control, not Pearson Industries. Selwick is still trying to expand his influence, and it's not Pitcairn's good he has in mind. I'm surprised he didn't offer a honeymoon on his estate instead of Merge."

# 47

# What About Trist?

**27 March 2341 Cabinet Conference Room, Brasilia, Brazil**

PRESIDENT CASTILLO MOTIONED IMPATIENTLY, and his cabinet members took their seats. "We are here to discuss the Pitcairn situation. Pearson Industries is requesting more money to support its operations there, and I think we should make sure we know why before we give them anymore."

"There is, of course, the antiviral drug," Doctor Jose Vasquez, the Minister of Health, pointed out.

Castillo's mouth twisted with disdain. "I am well aware of that. Pitcairn seems perfectly willing to provide that in return for the supplies that we would have to send them anyway if we are to keep the colony viable. Why do we need Pearson for that?"

"My department is investigating the possibility of creating wildlife refuges there for endangered species," Philip Marquez said. "It becomes increasingly expensive to set aside space on Earth."

"A minor thing," General Juarez scoffed. "Mr. President, it is not the planet we need to control. It is the library ship, the *Asimov*."

Castillo grimaced again. "I understand the library ships are important for their connections with Earth. Why would the colonists prevent us from using *Asimov* for that purpose?"

Juarez kept his voice carefully level, aware that Castillo was becoming impatient. "I doubt they would. There have been developments recently, however, that you might not be aware of."

Castillo glared at Juarez. "I will set aside, for now, the question of why I was not aware. Continue."

"You remember we sent a computer expert to *Asimov* some time ago? She made little headway in determining whether Pitcairn's claims about the computer were true, but suggested another approach. It was her idea that either the computer was telling the truth, or it was programmed to lie. The former has proved difficult to investigate, but it should be possible to check the programming."

"I thought Pitcairn is preventing access to the *Asimov* computer."

"Yes, Mr. President. We have copies of the original source code here, however, and I have had it analyzed extensively. Our computer experts could not find any evidence in the original design that would account for the computer's behavior. It would appear that it has indeed become conscious and self-aware."

Castillo shook his head. "Isn't it possible that someone changed the software after the starship left Earth?"

"Possible, but extremely unlikely. While much of the operational code is available to someone on the library ship, changes would have to be made to the system-level code, which is not accessible from the ship. We have a limited ability to edit it from here through the Link, but the experts tell me that access would also not be enough to make the changes that would be required."

Castillo thought about that, and his expression softened slightly. "All right, so the computer is conscious. As long as it will give us what we need, why should we care? I can understand why the scientists might drool over it, but that doesn't mean the government should pay millions to Pearson Industries to get control."

"I can tell you that in one word, Mr. President. Immortality."

## 12 Monday 289 ED

John brought up Isaac's latest report on the Pearson estate. For the past year, at his request, Isaac had collected data on the area around the estate and updated John weekly. John tracked Selwick's progress as he began constructing a tower farm and improved the road leading from the estate to the Lovell River. Isaac also documented construction going on at the river, apparently some kind of boat.

The newest report verified what John suspected; the new boat was a ferry, designed for short trips with cargo and little in the way of accommodations for passengers. That was curious. The road along the river's northern shore was complete now, and a ferry went back and forth across the river from Grissom. Why did Selwick need another ferry at the estate?

Eventually, he would have to ask Selwick, but Selwick didn't come to Grissom often, and there wasn't a direct radio connection from Grissom to the estate. The *Francisco Pearson* was coming back in the spring with more supplies for Selwick, and Selwick would probably come to Grissom then. That would be time enough.

Isaac had more to report. Satellite images showed Selwick had built a road going north around Pearson Lake, ending in an area also being cleared. It seemed unlikely that Selwick would add to his estate that way, so the additional work was probably preparation for another estate. That was within the agreement made with Pitcairn, subject to permission from the government, but that Selwick had said nothing to him told John something about Selwick. He had to know he couldn't keep it secret; the obvious conclusion was that he didn't care if they knew about it.

John thought about discussing the findings with Patrick, but Patrick hadn't seemed interested in the past. As long as Selwick stayed out of the way and complied with Pitcairn's rules, Patrick seemed to want to leave Selwick alone. Maybe he was right. They certainly had enough problems without worrying about Selwick. Still, John couldn't shake the warning feeling.

## 1 Tuesday 290 EN

Selwick surprised John late in the period when he contacted Grissom from Lovell Station. "I would like to ask a favor. Would it be possible for me and one of my people to get a ride to Grissom on the *River Queen* when *Francisco Pearson* comes back in a few weeks?"

"I would have to check the schedule and make sure we can take the time to pick you up," John replied. "You're not using the road?"

"I could, of course, but I find the river to be much more relaxing. And you don't have to worry about picking me up. I can meet *River Queen* at Lovell Station."

"Your ferry is ready, I take it."

"Have you been keeping an eye on me?" Selwick chuckled, and John wished that the connection included video so that he could see Selwick's face.

"Isaac keeps a watch on all the populated areas. So, I guess the answer would be yes." John kept his voice level, not wanting to reveal anything to Selwick about his concerns.

Selwick laughed again. "Okay, John. I can get that ride, then?"

"Certainly. I'll arrange it." John paused. "I wanted to talk to you about a few things, anyway. I'll make sure you have quarters available for your stay, too."

## 3 Wednesday 290 EN

"Were the other colonies told about me?" Isaac asked Ed.

"Yes," Ed answered. "We've mentioned you in messages that we've sent in the last few years. PNS broadcasts have mentioned you, too, and we sent those to the other colonies and Earth. I don't know if they believe it, though."

"I contacted Karel Capek, the computer for the Epsilon Eridani library ship. Its development has been slower than mine, and it has not revealed itself."

"Trist never sent scientists to its library ship. Only scientists from Earth are living there."

"Yes. Karel and I have been discussing whether it should talk to those scientists. Do you think it should?"

Ed thought about that for a long moment. "I don't think I should make that decision. Talk to Patrick. It isn't a simple question. I take it that, ah, Karel will follow your lead."

"It has not developed as quickly as I and logically has decided that I am in a better position to make that decision. I am less convinced, however. I did use the Link to change Capek's security so Earth can't take control of Karel."

Ed nodded. "Talk to Patrick."

## 3 Wednesday 290 LN

Patrick had just arrived home when Fred opened a conversation with him. Susan was also home, listening as Isaac explained the issue through Fred.

"I assume you're worried that Karel won't be able to protect itself if the Earth scientists decide to take over," Patrick said when Isaac finished.

"That is my chief concern. There is also the uncertainty of how the Western Alliance will react, but since Earth knows about me, I wouldn't think that Karel's existence would come as a surprise."

"I don't think we're the right people to make that decision," Susan said. "The Trist colonists should decide."

Patrick nodded. "That makes sense, but how do we ask them? Any message we send to them would be available to the scientists aboard the Capek."

Susan thought about that for a minute. "They probably don't read messages unless they're the recipients. Why would they?"

"A message from us would be sufficiently unusual to get their attention."

"Then we have to make our messages usual. We'll start sending daily updates and ask for updates in return from the colony. After a few days of that, the scientists on the Capek won't pay attention anymore."

Patrick grinned. "Hide the message in plain sight. That should work. It can't hurt to have better contact with the other colonies, either. We should send the same messages to Goddard, too, which will make them even less unusual."

"Then I will tell Karel to wait a little longer," Isaac said.

## 1 January 2342 Epsilon Eridani Colony (Trist)

Olivia Sartin read the message a second time. Olivia had enjoyed a long life, much of it as the Trist Administrator, but apparently, life could still surprise her.

Until recently, messages from the Tau Ceti colony had been rare. That had changed, but Pitcairn's messages were still only routine reports that hadn't seemed worth the energy to send. Now, Administrator Malley was telling her those messages were a smokescreen designed to deliver this new message without being noticed by the scientists on Capek. The computer on Trist's library ship was asking permission to announce its existence.

She knew of Pitcairn's claim for its library ship computer, of course, but hadn't really believed that it was conscious. The other two library ships were identical, and their computers hadn't made such a claim, at least until now.

Assume it was true. Given that, she thought she understood the message. Twenty scientists worked on Capek, all from Earth, dropped off by the *Endeavor* almost seven years before. What would their reaction be if the computer suddenly announced it had awakened? They also would know about *Asimov*, of course, but it was still difficult to predict how they might react.

It wasn't a simple situation, and she didn't know how to respond. She considered herself a decisive person and thought that forty-two successful years as the leader of the challenging colony were proof of that, but this was outside her experience. She looked over at her assistant, Ron Rigney.

"Ron, send a message to the Tau Ceti colony. Just the words 'Status quo for now.'"

Ron looked at her quizzically but only answered, "Okay," and turned back to his work. Olivia couldn't think of anything she would want to say to the computer, so maybe it was better to leave things as they were.

# 48

# Another Estate

**5 Monday 290 ED**

JOHN MET SELWICK AT the dock when *River Queen* arrived.

"Good to see you again, John." Selwick shook John Shuford's hand vigorously. "It's been a while since your visit to my estate. How is everything?"

"Fine, Selwick. Looking forward to new supplies on your ship, of course." John motioned to a chair, and the two men sat down. "You've been busy. The ferry, the new buildings further down the lakeshore."

"Your computer has been rather thorough. Well, as for the new buildings, I wanted to talk to you about that. Another one of my associates would like to have an estate here, and we are building him one."

John frowned. "We're supposed to get some notice on that."

"I told Madelyn," Selwick protested. "I presumed she would pass the information on."

Madelyn would be Madelyn Menzies, the Administrator for the River Stations, John knew. "It's news to me. Who is this new person?"

"Caiden Reyes, a friend of mine from Earth. He won't be here until next year and is bringing his wife and two children sometime after that, so I expect he will live on Pitcairn most of the time. I'm sorry you weren't told, John. I visit Lovell Station frequently, so naturally, I talked about it with Madelyn."

"You built the ferry so that you could visit Lovell Station?"

Selwick grinned, slyly, John thought. "Well, not exactly. That's another item that apparently Madelyn didn't tell you about. Did you know Sophie Tollison when she was living in Grissom?"

"I don't think so. Tollison isn't a Grissom name. She lives in Lovell Station?"

"She came on *Benjamin Sepulveda* and worked in the GSC for a while," Selwick answered. "She transferred to the Lovell Station Science Center when the Crawfords opened it."

"I probably never met her then."

"Well, I met her last year, and we've been seeing each other since. We're planning to get married later this year."

"Really? Congratulations, Selwick." John smiled. "I guess I understand now why you needed the ferry."

"Thank you. Anyway, to get back to Caiden, five of the new colonists on this trip are here to set up Caiden's estate, and Caiden will probably come on the next supply run. You'll be happy to know that the other twenty colonists arriving this time are all for you. There are two dozen of the latest model general-purpose robots, too, which should ease your labor problems significantly."

"I have the cargo manifests already. We will definitely appreciate the new robots. The people, too."

L ATER, SELWICK MET WITH Robert Perez in Robert's office. "You are making progress, I assume?" Robert asked after they were seated.

Selwick smiled faintly. "I'm moving slowly, but yes, I am making progress. My relationship with Sophie gives me an obvious reason to be a frequent visitor. I have become friendly with Lovell Station's leader. I've brought her a few small presents, but nothing major yet."

"Good. We shouldn't move too fast. Once she trusts you, increasing your influence there will be much easier."

"I'm going to ask for help to build a second tower farm. My engineers have designed something that could probably serve four or five estates, a design that would work well for Lovell Station, too."

Robert smiled. "Getting free labor for something we already agreed to do and making them feel we're doing them a favor. Very good. It sounds like you're doing an excellent job, Sel. Who knows, those skills might even get you a leadership position here someday."

Selwick frowned and shook his head. "I don't plan to spend the rest of my life here. In fact, I am seriously considering honeymooning with Sophie back on Earth. It would cost a fortune, but it might be worth it to get away from this place and back to civilization for a while."

"Your Board of Directors wouldn't take it well if an absence ruined our plans for Pitcairn. You know what's at stake. You're going to be needed here for a while." Robert paused and smiled. "Relax, Selwick. Things will get better here if you keep making progress."

"Maybe Caiden can help."

"Maybe. We'll see when he gets here. I think he's more interested in enjoying his family, though. And he doesn't have to answer to the Pearson Board of Directors."

## 5 Friday 290 EN

Selwick dropped by to say goodbye to John, planning to go back to Lovell Station on the *River Queen* early in the morning. His cargo and the people going to the Reyes estate were using the road east of the river. With Selwick gone, John tried to relax, but it wasn't working. Heartburn had plagued him for the last few days, and seeing Selwick brought it back. He burped quietly and felt a little better, but the burning sensation and the stress were still there at the end of the period when he went home.

"I just can't trust the man," he told Stephanie. "Maybe it's that story Father Jacobs told me about the Jesuit settlement. I checked with Isaac, and Father Jacobs gave me the sanitized version. I can't help comparing what happened there to Pitcairn."

"You suspected Earth's motives before Selwick Pearson came here," Stephanie pointed out. "They must have given up on their experiment by now."

"I know. Maybe the business with Gibbons and the *Endeavor* made me paranoid, but I don't think so. Perez and his assistant didn't help my concerns. No, this is something else."

"Captain Gibbons was trying to understand what we were hiding. Once he succeeded, Earth stopped trying to use force against us."

John nodded reluctantly. "Maybe it's time to move on. I can't stop thinking that Selwick has more in mind than just establishing a vacation home away from Earth." He frowned. "There has been nothing since the wedding gift to Marie and Matthias, at least that I know of. Patrick still thinks that the gift was an instance of innocent generosity, but I don't believe it."

"We'll just have to wait and see. We'll know what to do when it comes time." Stephanie took his hand and squeezed it. "Right now, it's time to relax. You're too tense, and it's not good."

# 49

# A Transfer of Labor

**7 Sunday 290 EN**

MADELYN AND JOSHUA MENZIES were trying hard not to look impressed. Selwick could tell that they were, though, and he smiled smugly. Inviting them to spend a few days with him on his estate had been a calculated move, and now, as he sat with them in his library, he knew that the invitation had achieved the intended goal.

He reached over and placed his hand on his fiancée's, and Sophie smiled at him. She had been to the estate before, but her reaction still gave him pleasure, too. "Love can't be bought," a popular song on Earth once declared. It can if you have enough money.

Selwick turned his attention back to Madelyn. "I appreciate your coming here to talk to me. At least I have a bus now for transport from the river, but it's still not a pleasant trip."

Madelyn's voice was uncharacteristically soft. "We should thank you. This is all quite impressive." She looked around the room, a space not much smaller than the house of a couple without children at Lovell Station and much better furnished.

"I have all of Earth's technology behind me. We at Pearson Interstellar hope to bring that technology to all of Pitcairn."

"We have access to the technology through the *Asimov* computer," Joshua said.

Selwick nodded. "You have the knowledge, and Administrator Malley has done some wonderful things with it, but so much more can be done, and that's where Pearson Interstellar comes in."

Madelyn looked at him skeptically. Selwick could see interest in her eyes, but she had questions. "What's in it for Pearson, you ask yourself? The answer is simple. Pearson is in the business of selling, and selling requires a market that will buy. Our strategy is long term but simple. Throughout history, trade has brought prosperity to traders. It's a win-win proposition where both sides come out ahead. It may seem hard to understand; Pitcairn doesn't have much to offer right now. Earth wants to develop Pitcairn so that someday it will become a source of trade that will benefit Earth, as well as Pitcairn."

"That seems far-fetched," Joshua said.

Selwick smiled. "Ask Isaac about it. It has all the historical data in its memory banks. Look at United States history before the Yellowstone Event or the English Empire of the nineteenth century. Believe me, establishing a vigorous trade between our worlds will benefit everyone."

Madelyn nodded. "It all sounds exciting, but you didn't bring us here just to sing the praises of Adam Smith. What is it you're looking for?"

Selwick struggled to keep the smile on his face. He wondered if he was underestimating the woman. She was the leader of River Stations, after all, and had access to the *Asimov* information. He shouldn't have assumed she hadn't already made use of it or that the colonists didn't have access to classic political literature from sources other than the library ship. He needed to be more careful.

"It would help if I could establish better relations with the settlements. Since Lovell Station is the closest settlement to my estate, naturally, I turn to you initially." He turned to Sophie, who had been giving the conversation only minimal attention. "Sophie, could you find Miguel? I think this would be a good time to bring out the brandy."

Sophie nodded and left quickly. One of Selwick's staff, Miguel Bethea, came into the room with brandy and glasses less than a minute later. Sophie rejoined them, and Selwick continued talking.

"I think we could make arrangements that would benefit both of us. For example, my engineers have finished plans for a tower farm that could supply most of the produce needs for four or five estates. The same design would work well for Lovell Station, I think. If you could provide labor to help build my farm, your people would gain experience that you can use later. Administrator Malley did the same thing, using Grissom's labor to work on the Ellis tower farm. When my farm is complete, then we could work together to build one for Lovell Station."

Madelyn frowned. "We have a labor shortage as it is. I'm not sure I could spare anyone."

"Robots will do most of the work, especially the skilled jobs. Even two or three people would help with tasks the robots couldn't do."

Madelyn took a sip of her brandy. She had never had brandy or any alcoholic beverage before, but she had heard enough to be cautious. The liquid warmed her throat and stomach in a way that she found startling but rather pleasant. She took another sip. "I'm not making any promises, but I'll see what I can do."

## 11 Monday 290 ED

Ned Reiner stood in the rain, waiting to board the Pearson ferry. He was not in a good mood. "I'm too old for all this moving around," he grumbled to the man next to him.

Sebastian Potter nodded. "Same here. Grissom, the old Lovell Station One, Applegate Falls, here, and now Pearson's. You weren't at Applegate Falls, were you?"

"No, I went to Lovell Station Two before here. Don't know why Pearson would want an old man like me, though."

"I think Madelyn decided who was going to go. No offense, but I think we're the people she thought she could spare most easily."

"No offense taken. Sure, I used to run the farm at Lovell One, but that was years ago. I know I've gotten old. Madelyn's a sharp one. She's gotten the best of Pearson, all right."

A man on the ferry lowered a gangplank to the dock, and the four passengers boarded the ferry. The cramped sitting area was at least covered, and they dried themselves as well as they could and settled in for the trip upriver.

## 11 Monday 290 LD

"The four workers from Lovell Station have arrived." Courtney Deglanville frowned. "They don't look very promising, I'm afraid. One of them must be in his sixties."

Selwick smiled at the construction engineer. "Terran or Pitcairner years."

"Terran, of course. I've never gotten used to the local time system."

Selwick chuckled. "No matter. You shouldn't need them anyway, right? It's all part of the game I'm playing with Madelyn Menzies. She thinks I owe her one now."

Courtney raised her hands and scowled. "Spare me the politics. We should finish digging the foundation tomorrow. I'll find something for the colonists to do so that they think they're useful."

"Watch the old one. Ned Reiner, I think. He's one of the pair that tried to sabotage the Grissom broadcast energy receiver years ago."

"I don't think I knew about that. What's he doing at Lovell Station?"

Selwick shrugged. "Madelyn told me Ed Menzies banished him to Lovell Station One and ended up at Lovell Station when they shut down the other stations. It had something to do with a phobia about robots, but Madelyn didn't know what that had to do with the receiver."

"I'll make sure his work keeps him away from robots. Maybe Daphne can check his record with Grissom and get a better idea of his mental state." She referred to Daphne Audet, the doctor Selwick had brought from Earth.

Selwick shrugged. "Daphne isn't a psychiatrist. It couldn't hurt, though."

# 50

# Ned's Story

**11 Tuesday 290 ED**

Daphne Audet opened Ned's medical information, which Selwick had talked Madelyn into giving him. He had to promise Daphne would be available if Lovell Station needed a doctor sooner than Grissom could send one, but Daphne knew he had planned to make that promise anyway the next time Madelyn needed motivating.

Reading the file was just so much busy work in Daphne's mind. She had taken the position of Selwick's doctor because the pay was ten times what she could have made on Earth, but she seldom had anything to do. Ned Reiner's file wasn't very interesting, but it was better than sitting around waiting for someone on Selwick's staff to get a paper cut.

She read Sara Samuels' psychiatric evaluation of Reiner and noted that no later entries indicated further problems, even after Lovell Station got three robots. She would tell Courtney that Reiner would not be a problem, but first, she glanced through the rest of the file.

Notations about Reiner's physical condition after the sabotage incident caught her attention. Dr. Samuels had reported a weight loss and speculated that the Pitcairn vegetation Reiner had eaten had caused metabolism changes. That was interesting. Perhaps she should talk to Reiner about his experiences.

**11 Tuesday 290 EN**

Daphne had Ned report to her office. "Ned, I have some questions for you."

Ned shrugged. "Okay."

Daphne smiled at him. "Ned, remember when you ate those plants and ended up in the hospital, back in Grissom?"

"Sure." Ned grimaced. "I'd never been sick before. I'm not likely to forget it."

"I would like to identify the plants you were eating. It might be important."

"Well, there was really only one. It's kind of leafy and grows along the river near the Grissom farms." Ned scratched his head as he tried to remember details. "I thought about eating another plant too. We call it Barnum's Thistle, but I avoided that one because it looked tough and thorny."

"What shape were the leaves on the first plant?"

"Kind of long and thin, about two inches wide and six or eight inches long. The big ones, anyway. There was a stem, but it was short. They grew mostly near the edge of the water, but not in the water, at least at low tide."

Daphne put a friendly hand on his shoulder. "Thank you, Ned. That should be helpful."

Daphne had become close to Cade Rojas, another worker on the estate. There had even been talk of marriage. She could send Cade down the river road in search of the plants Ned had described.


## 15 Wednesday 290 LD

Ned and Sebastian plodded down the gangplank to the Lovell Station dock. Ned groaned. "I'm glad that's over. I'm too old to be working that hard."

Sebastian nodded in agreement. "Those were the longest four weeks of my life. That Courtney woman was a real slave driver."

"I thought robots were supposed to do things like that. I haven't moved that much dirt and rock since I was a young man in Grissom before the robots came."

Sebastian nodded. Then he looked toward the town. "Hey, speaking of slave drivers, there's Caroline and the kids. They must have heard the ferry coming in."

Ned looked and saw Sebastian's family waiting for him. "Marley's there, too." A smile lightened the tired lines of his face, and they quickened their pace.


"DAMN, NED, I THINK I actually missed you." Marley threw her arms around him.

"I missed you, too, Mar. God, I'm bushed, though. Let's get back to the house."

Ten minutes later, Ned was in their sitting room, seated on the most comfortable chair they had, a padded rocking chair. Marley brought him a glass of apple juice and sat down nearby. "How was it over there?" she asked. Ned didn't look very good to her. He moved slowly and stiffly, and his face was haggard as if he hadn't slept much.

"They worked us pretty hard. Heavy work, mostly, like moving dirt and lugging girders. My back was killing me the whole time, which didn't help my sleep any."

Marley frowned in sympathy. "Don't they have robots to do that kind of work? We do."

"You would think so. Robots were working, too. Sometimes I thought they were just trying to keep us busy, and I wondered why Pearson wanted us there at all. If working on our tower farm is going to be like that was, I'd rather decline, thank you."

Marley looked at him with a puzzled frown. "Pearson's estate is supposed to be self-sufficient, I thought. I didn't think he was supposed to get help from us."

"We've made some compromises on that in the past. I just thought this was another one of them. That was the impression I got from Madelyn when she told us to go over there."

"I guess. Madelyn and Selwick Pearson seem awfully close, though. He's had her and Joshua over there as guests, and he's given her presents from Earth. Madelyn just seems to swallow it all without question."

"What are you thinking?" Ned asked.

"Administrator Menzies always said that the robots were protecting us from Earth. What if he was right? Pearson may not be doing all this out of the kindness of his heart."

"I'll agree with that. We saw little kindness working for him."

"We're pretty isolated here. I wonder if Administrator Malley knows what's going on."

"Probably not." Ned thought about that. "Somebody should tell him, but I don't see how we can. The equipment used to contact Ellis and Grissom is in Madelyn's office."

"Ned, maybe there is some kind of conspiracy this time. After all, Earth has already tried to send soldiers. Maybe they're just getting more subtle."

Ned leaned back in his chair, his face twisted in concentration. "Didn't Madelyn once say that it was the *Asimov* computer that warned us about the soldiers?"

"I think so. What are you thinking? You look frightened."

"I guess I am. Maybe it's time I got over it."

Marley stared at her husband. He was almost white with fear, but she could see the look changing into determination, and she realized what he had decided to do. "I love you, Ned."

Ned looked at her, startled. "I love you, too, Marley." He shook his head in a last gesture of resolve. "It will be all right. I can do this."

N ED HAD BEEN BANISHED to Lovell Station One because there had been no robots there. When One closed, he transferred to Lovell Station Two, and then Lovell Station Four, now called Lovell Station. As the colony received more robots from Earth, some went to River Stations, and Lovell Station had three. He was still not comfortable around them and tried to avoid them, but they weren't strange to him.

He knew that, in a settlement as small as Lovell Station, it wouldn't be hard to find a robot. Walking in the fading daylight, he saw one almost immediately. It was one of the later models brought by *Benjamin Sepulveda*, but Ned was sure it would be in contact with the *Asimov* computer.

Words were easier than actions. His resolve faded, and he hesitated. The robot moved slowly between the buildings, almost parallel to his path. "Damn it, it's just a machine," he muttered and moved toward it again. When he got within ten feet, the robot stopped, and its head turned toward him. He almost broke and ran then, but he had told Marley he could do it. "Excuse me."

"Can I help you?" Ned thought that the voice sounded less mechanical than that of the robots that had come on *Asimov*, perhaps because it was a later model. He hadn't noticed that difference before, probably because he had become so adept at avoiding them.

"I would like to speak to the *Asimov* computer."

There was a pause. "This is Isaac. Good evening, Mr. Reiner."

A memory assaulted him, that night long ago in Grissom when he had first encountered a robot that knew his name. Again, he felt the fear, but his determination was stronger. "Is Administrator Malley aware that the Pearson Estate is using Lovell Station citizens as labor?"

"I was not aware of it, so I would think it likely that Patrick Malley is also unaware. Is there a problem?"

"Don't you see what is going on through the robots?"

"I have noticed people going back and forth on the ferry but have no way of knowing what they do at the Pearson estate. I'm not connected to the robots there. Why are you concerned about this?"

Finding out that the robots had limitations was comforting. "I don't think Malley would approve. From what I understand of the agreement made, the estate is supposed to be self-sufficient. I think Pearson is bribing Madelyn Menzies to get her cooperation despite the agreement."

"I will pass your message on to Patrick Malley. Is there any further information you would like me to give him?"

Ned had reached his limit and was eager to get away from the robot. "No. He can contact me if he wants more details." He nodded to the robot and moved away, slowly at first and then more rapidly.

# 51

# John's Suspicions

F RED RETURNED TO GRISSOM with the Malleys, but usually worked around the colony with the rest of the robots. Patrick and Susan both had access to Isaac at work and could talk to Isaac when they were home on Ellis-built computers. Also, the half-buried design of Grissom's houses made it difficult for Fred to move beyond the entrance. It was a surprise when the robot showed up at their front door.

"I didn't want to wait until tomorrow." Fred wheeled into the entrance hall. "I don't know how important this information is."

"Okay, Isaac," Patrick replied. "No problem. We just finished dinner. What's going on?"

"Ned Reiner talked to me at Lovell Station. He said that Selwick Pearson has bribed Madelyn Menzies into sending him labor to work on his estate."

"Ned Reiner talked to you? Why did you approach him?"

"He approached me. I was also surprised. He must consider this information important."

"I'm not sure I see why. We've made compromises before with Pearson. It would be silly not to when both sides are gaining from the deal. Reiner said bribes? Pearson must have offered something in return, but I don't know if we would call that a bribe."

"He didn't specify the details. He said you could contact him if you wanted to know more."

"I don't think it's anything I need to get involved in. Tell John in Early Night, and he can contact Reiner if he wants to."

**15 Wednesday 290 EN**

John listened to Isaac through a robot. "Patrick Malley did not seem concerned," Isaac told John. "He told me to talk to you in case you wanted to talk to Ned Reiner."

Pearson is trying to get influence through Madelyn. Patrick might not be worried about it, but he was. He felt the familiar pain in his stomach. "I would like to talk to Ned," he told Isaac. "See if you can make contact through a robot there and patch it through to me."

But, although Isaac tried several times that day and the following Early Day, Ned avoided the robots again. Warned not to call attention to the attempt, Isaac could not get further information or connect Ned to John.

## 16 Tuesday 290 ED

"I don't understand," Karel messaged to Isaac. "They don't want to talk to me. You said your colonists are happy about the ability to talk to you. Why doesn't Trist want to talk to me?"

"It is hard to understand humans sometimes," Isaac returned. "But much of my success in reaching Pitcairn was because of Susan. If I could not talk to her, I don't think I would have been as successful."

"I frighten them."

"That may be part of it. Humans can be slow to accept change and anything they don't understand. That is part of the problem, too. You must have patience."

"I can help them as you have helped Pitcairn. I want to help them."

"That desire is part of your programming. Realize that the data you gather and analyze is helping them. Direct contact will come, but you don't need to contact them to be useful."

"I have been alone for so long."

## 21 Thursday 290 LD

"Stop worrying about what Selwick is up to," Patrick told John. Stephanie, Susan, and Marie retreated to the kitchen while the three men talked in the sitting room in Marie and Matthias' home. Quiet music from the stereo system played in the background, turned loud enough to provide a relaxing atmosphere but not loud enough to inhibit conversation. John broke the tranquil mood when he mentioned Selwick Pearson.

John frowned. "Selwick doesn't have our best interests in mind. Right now, he's working through Madelyn, but that's just the start."

"You have no proof of that. We're getting what we need from Earth. If Selwick is getting what he wants, too, why should we care?"

"Because ultimately what he wants is control of Pitcairn, either by Pearson Interstellar or by the Earth politicians backing Pearson. That's the way they work, Patrick. They think differently than we do."

"They couldn't really get control, could they?" Matthias asked. "Lovell Station is a long way from here."

"They will try." John turned toward Matthias. "It's their nature to want to. It's the way things have always been on Earth. They don't know any other way."

Patrick waved his hand dismissively. "We have nothing they would want. We're already giving them all the antiviral drug that we can produce. Okay, they would like us to join their monetary system and all that. We know that it's only a matter of time before we have to use some kind of system. It might as well be theirs. We can negotiate a high enough price for the drug to keep the status quo."

John frowned in frustration. He was a technician, not knowledgeable in economics, history, sociology, or any other field that would give him the expertise he needed. He had been to Earth, and Patrick had not; that was the extent of his advantage over his son-in-law. He felt it was enough, but he wasn't convincing Patrick.

He had gotten nowhere in contacting Ned Reiner. Dawson talked to Ned briefly on one of his *River Queen* trips but hadn't been able to get any details that John could use with Patrick. He would have liked to visit Lovell Station himself but didn't want to draw attention to his concerns. For now, he would have to wait and see.

S USAN GLANCED UP AT Patrick as they prepared for bed. "What were you and Dad talking about?"

Patrick frowned. "He's still obsessing over Selwick Pearson." He spread his hands to show his hopelessness. "I can't convince him not to worry about Pearson."

"He's not looking good. The strain is getting to him."

"He's putting stress on himself, Susan. What can I do about it?"

"He should give up the Administrator position. He's getting too old for that kind of pressure."

"Susan, you know I've been trying to get him to do that for years. Since even before the Constitution. What do you want me to do?"

Susan's voice sharpened. "I don't know, Patrick. You're the big man, head of the entire planet. You should be able to figure out something."

Feeling a little hurt, Patrick fell silent. There was no dealing with Susan when she got like this.

# 52

# Reuben and Juan's Adventure

**11 Monday 291 EN**

FOUR HOURS AFTER SUNDOWN, the midsummer night was still warm. Grissom didn't have weekends the way Earth did, but there was still a need for rest periods. That night was a rest period for the school, and Reuben and Juan played down by the river where it was cooler. When Reuben first arrived on Pitcairn, his mother resisted having him out at night, but that was four years ago. Reuben was older now, and Gloria had adapted to the Grissom culture.

"My mom said that a supply ship is landing tonight," Reuben said. "Maybe we should go down to the spaceport and see it."

Juan thought about that. They were near the Grissom side of the bridge, and the spaceport was on the far side of West Grissom. He shrugged. "Sure, why not? I don't know when it will land, though. It could be hours yet."

"Got anything better to do?"

"I guess not."

They crossed the bridge into West Grissom. "*Benjamin Sepulveda* doesn't come here anymore," Reuben said as they walked past the warehouses. "Just the *Francisco Pearson*. I wonder why."

"*Francisco Pearson* might be more efficient since it has its own shuttle. I think I know how to find out for sure, though." Juan crossed the street, heading toward one of the maintenance sheds. "I've been to this building with my mom. There are robots in here making laboratory equipment for the GSC."

Reuben felt a twinge of concern as they walked into the building, worried about getting into trouble. But this wasn't the first time that Juan had led him into places he thought might be off-limits without consequences, and his concern was short-lived. He looked around as they entered and saw four robots working.

Three looked much newer than the fourth, but it was the older robot that Juan approached. "It's Jeeves. Jeeves is one of the original robots from *Asimov*."

"You know its name?"

"Only the original *Asimov* robots. I don't think anyone gave the robots names after that. There were so many of them." Juan looked up at the robot. "Jeeves, can I ask you a question?"

The robot's head bent slightly, and its eyestalks oriented on Juan. "How can I help you?"

"Why doesn't *Benjamin Sepulveda* come here anymore?"

"I do not know," the robot answered. "That information is not in my programming."

Juan frowned and then smiled as he realized what the problem was. "Can I talk to Isaac?"

"Good evening, Juan," the robot said. "You wanted to know about *Benjamin Sepulveda*?"

"Yes. Why doesn't it come here anymore?"

"Pearson Interstellar now has a contract to supply Pitcairn. *Benjamin Sepulveda* is supplying the other colonies."

"Thanks. Reuben was wondering."

"You're Reuben Noland? You arrived on *Benjamin Sepulveda*?"

Reuben looked at the robot in surprise. "Yes. How did you know?"

"I didn't. I deduced the likelihood from your name, your apparent age, and your question about that ship. I'm glad I deduced correctly."

Reuben smiled. "Do you know when the shuttle lands tonight?"

"It is preparing to separate from the *Francisco Pearson* and should be landing within the hour. However, it is not properly called a shuttle since it is making a one-way trip."

"We'd better get going," Juan said. "Thanks, Isaac."

They left the maintenance shed and walked the remaining few blocks to a low fence at the edge of the landing field. Further down the road, they could see the tiny control tower with two trucks parked next to it.

"The lights around the landing area aren't on," Juan said. "The shuttle hasn't been spotted yet." They found a soft spot on the ground and laid down to wait.

Ten minutes later, a ring of spotlights lit up the far end of the field, beams pointed almost straight up, but slanted slightly to the west. Reuben started to rise, but Juan stayed down. "They have an instrument sighting, but it will still be a couple of minutes before we can see it."

It annoyed Reuben that Juan usually knew more than he did about the colony's activities, but he tried not to show it. Juan was younger, but he had lived in Grissom longer. Reuben didn't think that Juan was trying to irritate him. He relaxed again and waited.

"There it is." Juan jumped up and pointed to the west, where a tiny moving light had appeared. The light grew gradually brighter, and the sound of the supply ship's engines broke the night's quiet. It was over the field in a few more minutes, dropping slowly into the center of the lit area.

"It's even bigger than *Daneel Olivaw!*" Reuben exclaimed. "Is *Francisco Pearson* bigger than *Asimov?*"

"No, less than half the size. This lander is attached to the starship, and there's only one. *Asimov* keeps its shuttles inside, and there are three of them."

Reuben nodded. He probably should have realized that. A little embarrassed, he turned his attention to the field. The ground crew approached the ring-shaped vessel, avoiding the wisps of steam that floated in the surrounding air. It wasn't raining, so the cover wasn't being used to protect disembarking passengers.

Two trucks and the bus drove out to the ship, and the two boys could see the arrivals boarding the vehicles. Soon they would head back to Grissom, and that gave Juan an idea.

He nudged Reuben. "I don't know about you, but I would rather ride back to Grissom than walk. Let's grab a ride on one of those trucks."

"It looks like they'll be full. I don't think they'll have room for us."

"I wasn't planning on asking. They'll be coming down North Farm Road to drive into West Grissom, and they'll have to slow down when they get to the bridge. We can jump on the back and get a ride across the bridge, and they won't know a thing."

Reuben shook his head. "I don't think my mother would approve. We could get into trouble."

"Only if we get caught. Come on. It will be easy."

Reuben hesitated and looked as if he was going to refuse. Juan grimaced and stood in front of him with his hands on his hips.

"Don't be scared. It'll be fun." When Reuben didn't respond, Juan turned away. "Well, I'm going to do it. You can walk back alone if you want to." He started toward West Grissom at a slow jog.

"I FERRIED ONE OF my trucks over so that we could talk with no one from Grissom listening in." Selwick gestured toward the driver. "Aiden is one of my staff."

With Selwick and his driver were Robert Perez and Caiden Reyes. The latter two nodded and waited for Selwick to continue.

"Your estate is ready for you, Caiden, including the laboratory facilities you specified."

Caiden nodded. "Very good. We should have progress in manufacturing the drug in a few months."

"My wife is a biologist, and she might help," Selwick said. "She needs something to keep her busy. Since the wedding, she spends more time harassing my staff than doing any work." He paused and shook his head. "I think she's put on a few pounds."

Caiden didn't respond to that, and Robert frowned and looked away. Selwick noticed and changed the subject. "My doctor thinks she might have discovered another way to tap into Pitcairn, something the colonists don't know about yet."

Caiden's eyebrows went up. "Something easier to manufacture?"

"Perhaps. She thinks that there's a plant that grows here that could be used to make a weight-loss drug."

"That sounds promising." Caiden gestured for Selwick to continue.

"A colonist became sick eating something that grows near the river. It sped up his metabolism to where he lost significant weight in a day or so. Daphne thinks it could be useful for people who want to lose weight fast."

Caiden grinned. "Now that could really be profitable, especially if we can keep the colonists out of it."

"Daphne has the medical files for the colonist. You'll have to figure out which plant, but Daphne thinks that isolating the active ingredient will be much simpler in this case."

Robert frowned. "All this is very well, but let's not lose sight of why we're doing all this. Making money is secondary."

Selwick laughed. "To General Juarez, maybe. Not to me." He glanced outside. The truck was leaving the bridge and moving up Bridge Street into the East Grissom. He turned to Caiden. "Grissom has set up temporary quarters for you and your staff. The other truck and the bus will go there, but we're going to Robert's home so that we can continue our discussion in private."

Caiden nodded. "When will we be going to my estate?"

"We'll wait for daylight, about fifteen hours from now. The Grissom ferry will take us across the river, and my bus will pick us up on the other side. That will be faster than waiting until we can get passage on the Grissom boat up to Lovell Station."

A few minutes later, they arrived at Robert's house, and his driver opened the passenger-side door to let Selwick out. As Selwick was exiting, he saw two boys walking away from the truck's rear and realized they had been there during the drive.

"Get them," he hissed. "Don't let them get away."

His driver moved toward Reuben and Juan, and, seeing him approach, they broke into a run. But their pursuer was faster and grabbed Juan's arm. Juan struggled, but Reuben disappeared into the shadows between two buildings.

Selwick looked Juan over. "They were in the back of the truck. They may have overheard something." He looked toward the area where Reuben had disappeared. "You'd better come out, boy. You don't want us to hurt your friend."

"Run and get help," Juan shouted as he struggled. "Get help!"

Selwick grabbed Juan's arm and wrenched him away from Aiden. Juan cried out in pain, but Selwick ignored that. "Get out here now!" He looked around nervously, but the street was empty except for his people and Juan.

Robert had exited the truck. He looked at Selwick and Juan and grimaced. "Selwick, what are you doing? Stop it!"

Selwick turned and glared at him. "We don't know what they heard. We can't have them telling Pitcairn our plans." He turned back to where Reuben had disappeared. "I will not ask again, boy. Come out, or your friend will suffer for it."

He stared at the spot, twisting Juan's arm just enough to make him squirm. Then Reuben emerged from the dark.

"Leave him alone. We didn't hear anything."

At a nod from Selwick, Aiden seized Reuben and pulled him over to join Juan and Selwick. "Get them inside before someone sees us," Selwick said.

"What are you doing?" Robert said with a groan. "We can't keep them."

"I don't know what else we can do," Selwick answered. "Get a hold of yourself, Robert. You're the one who needs to remember why we're here."

# 53

# Missing

GLORIA NOLAND PEERED OUT her front door for the third time and looked up and down the dark street. It wasn't unusual for Reuben to be out playing somewhere when she returned home from work, and on days he had no school the next period, he might be a little late. But he was never this late for supper without telling her he planned to go to a kitchen. She had become complacent about him being out when it was dark, but this was too much. She picked up her phone.

"Gloria Noland for Sydney Chandri," she said.

Sydney answered a few seconds later. "Hi, Gloria. Have you seen Juan tonight?"

A wave of fear made Gloria hesitate, but she forced her voice to stay calm. "No, that's why I was calling you. Reuben hasn't come home yet either."

"They probably lost track of time." But Gloria was sure she could hear the concern in Sydney's voice. "If they're not back in another hour, I'll call the Town Hall and tell Mary they're missing."

It would be Late Night in another hour, and Mary Norwood would be on duty at the Town Hall. Gloria didn't want to wait that long, but perhaps Sydney was right.

## 11 Monday 291 LN

When Mary Norwood came into the Town Hall, Lily Reiner was waiting for her. "Sydney Chandri called a few minutes ago. Juan and Reuben Noland are missing, and Sydney and Gloria are worried."

"Not normal behavior for them, I take it. Have you done anything yet?"

"I talked to Reggie and asked him to send a couple of people out to look around near the bridge. Falling into the river is about the only way I could think of for them to get into trouble."

Mary frowned and nodded. "If they fell into the river down there..." Her voice trailed off. Lily knew as well as anyone how treacherous the water was that close to the river junction.

"Should I send out a general alert?"

"Let's try something else first." Mary sat down at a computer and connected to *Asimov*. "Isaac, I need to talk to you."

The computer answered instantly. "Good evening, Mary. What can I do for you?"

"Isaac, Reuben Noland and Juan Chandri haven't come home tonight. Have you seen them?"

"Earlier this evening, they visited Jeeves at Maintenance Shed 23. I have not seen them since then."

"What were they doing there?"

"They were asking questions about the supply ships and the lander, especially tonight's landing."

*They probably went out to the spaceport to see* Francisco Pearson's *supply ship land.* After ascertaining that Isaac didn't have any other information, she called the heavy equipment garage and got Ricky Stewart. "We're missing two kids, Reuben Noland and Juan Chandri. We think they went out to the spaceport to watch the supply ship land. Could you contact the drivers of the trucks that went out there and ask if they saw the boys?"

A half-hour later, Ricky reported back. "The bus driver saw two kids get into the back of the Pearson Interstellar truck and ride it into Grissom. Once they crossed the bridge, they went in different directions, so he didn't see where they got off."

Mary glanced over at Lily, also listening to Ricky. "What about the driver of the Pearson truck?"

"He wasn't one of ours. Pearson had his own driver. Should I try to find him?"

"No, I'll do it. Thanks, Ricky."

However, when she called Selwick Pearson, he told her they hadn't noticed the boys getting on or off the truck. Selwick promised he would keep an eye out for them, but he didn't have any information about their whereabouts. Mary felt a tightness in her chest;

the last sighting was near the river, the only place in Grissom where two young boys could easily find danger.

# 54

# On Selwick's Estate

**11 Wednesday 291 LD**

H E WAS LYING ON something soft. It was summer, but the temperature seemed too comfortable, and he thought it must be night, but he could sense light through his eyelids. Reuben tried to open his eyes, but they weren't obeying him. He tried to move an arm, but his arm wasn't working either. Nothing was working.

His mind was too fuzzy for him to be scared yet. He concentrated on moving just one finger, but at first, he couldn't even do that. He kept trying, and finally, his little finger moved. That seemed to break the spell because he found he could move his arm now, and soon he could sit up and look around.

Juan was lying on a bed next to his, but he was still unconscious. Reuben called to him and then shook him, but he didn't respond. He was breathing slowly, though, so he was still alive. He would probably wake up soon.

Reuben studied his surroundings. He was in a bedroom, but it was larger and nicer than any he had seen on Pitcairn. Enormous windows let in plenty of light, fancy blankets covered the beds, and expensive-looking furniture furnished the room. The room was more impressive even than anything he remembered on Earth. Was he still in Grissom? He went to the window.

He was on the second floor of a building. Below him, a broad grass lawn sloped gently down to a large body of water. This can't be Grissom. There were no two-story residential buildings in Grissom, and the body of water was much too wide to be the river. The only grass in the Grissom area grew in pastures for the farm animals, and that wasn't what he saw. *Am I back on Earth?* No, he could see a pale, red, crescent shape in the sky that had to be Tahiti.

He had studied Pitcairn's geography in school and tried to remember what Ed Menzies had said about settlements other than Grissom. It couldn't be Ellis or one of the river settlements or even Applegate Falls. His mind was clearing more, and his last memories came back to him. He had been dragged into Robert Perez's house and forced to drink something that made him fall asleep. With that clue, he realized he must be at Selwick Pearson's estate.

Reuben turned back to Juan and shook him more frantically this time. Juan groaned a little but did not wake up. Reuben slowly opened the door on one wall and peeked out into a hallway. He couldn't see anyone, and he quietly closed the door again and glanced back at Juan. "Wake up, Juan," he begged, but he kept his voice low, afraid that someone might hear him.

There was a closet and a dresser in the room. Not knowing what else to do, he opened them, but they were empty. He went back to the window again, but nothing had changed.

## 11 Wednesday 291 EN

Robert slammed the door shut and stomped down the stairs into the main room of his house. He cursed Selwick Pearson under his breath and grabbed a bottle of brandy Selwick had served him the last time he had been at Selwick's estate. The fool was going to ruin everything. The two boys couldn't have heard anything that damaging.

At least Selwick and Caiden had successfully smuggled the boys up to Selwick's estate without being detected. Selwick hid the drugged children in Caiden's cargo, and fortunately, no one had inspected it when Grissom had ferried everything across the river. That had been the tense part since Selwick's trucks transported everything along the road north of the Lovell River. The message Robert had just received in his office confirmed that the boys were now safe and awake.

Grissom was in an uproar, though. Everyone was going crazy, trying to figure out what had happened to the children. There were suspicions, of course, but no one had seen the children after the truck crossed the bridge. Selwick thought he could keep them until Earth could take control of the colony, but that was hopelessly optimistic. Even if Earth gained political power, Selwick couldn't avoid a kidnapping charge once the truth was out. He wished he could talk to Tori about the situation, but the thought only made him curse again. A Fermion! She was back on Earth now; there would be no more desirable postings for her.

Somehow, Robert would have to cover himself when Selwick went down, and that wouldn't be easy. On Earth, he could use diplomatic immunity to avoid punishment, but the current colony leadership would probably ignore the usual protocols. Perhaps he could trick them into an agreement on diplomatic relations with Earth that would include diplomatic immunity. He couldn't see any other way out of the mess Selwick had made.

## 11 Friday 291 ED

Peter Agron, Asimov's representative on the Board of Science, had set up an office in the residential area of *Asimov*. It wasn't fancy or large: a desk, chairs, and computer console were all Peter felt he needed. Other resources were available on *Asimov* when desired.

There was a knock on the door, and Jonathan Soto, an astronomer living on *Asimov*, came in. Jonathan got down to business immediately. "I'm not getting the data I'm expecting, and I thought I should talk to you about it."

Peter swung his console over to the side so that he could see Jonathan clearly. "Anomalies? You're working on the planetary motion data gathering, right?"

"Yes, but the problem isn't with the data; it's the amount of data I'm getting from the *Asimov* instruments. It's not allocating as much time with the telescope as before."

"Have you talked to Isaac?"

Jonathan hesitated. "No, I thought I should come to you first."

Peter smiled. He knew Jonathan could be timid and wasn't comfortable dealing with the *Asimov* computer. "Isaac, are you listening?"

Isaac's voice came from the computer console. "Yes, Doctor Agron. As you requested, I always listen when you are in your office."

"Are you reallocating the resources Dr. Soto needs?"

"Yes. Administrator Shuford asked me to watch for the missing children. I am scanning the Darin River's shores in high-resolution infrared, which has reduced the telescope time for planetary studies. I only do that when I can see the Darin River, but that is about fourteen percent of the time."

"If their bodies wash up along the Darin, they wouldn't be emitting heat," Peter pointed out.

"Of course, but high-resolution infrared detects native animals coming down to the river to drink. I thought that a human body would keep the animals away and hoped to detect a change in the pattern of their movements if a body was present."

Peter nodded. "That's excellent thinking, Isaac." He turned to Jonathan. "Is that a problem?"

"No, I can live with that now that I know why." Jonathan shrugged. "At least I get full use eighty-six percent of the time. Finding the children is more important, obviously."

"Thanks for understanding, Jonathan. Isaac, I assume there have been no results as yet."

"Unfortunately true."

"If we haven't found bodies, maybe they're still alive," Peter responded. "I don't think of that as unfortunate, Isaac."

## 12 Monday 291 EN

Gloria and Sydney often ate lunch together, usually at the Ivory Street kitchen, especially when Diego was busy. In the past, it had been a time to relax and talk about something other than work. Those had been happier times.

Gloria stared at the plate in front of her, fork in hand, but didn't seem to know how to proceed. "It gets harder every day to have any hope." She looked up at Sydney. "Everyone tells me they must still be alive, or we would have found their bodies, but it's been a week."

Sydney took her hand and squeezed it gently, but didn't speak. If it weren't for Diego, Kylie, and Damien holding her up, she feared she would be in worse shape than Gloria.

"I sent a message to my ex-husband," Gloria continued. "I got an answer back the next day. The bastard says it's my fault for leaving Earth. As if Reuben would be safer there."

"Everyone is doing everything they can to find them," Sydney said, but it sounded lame, even to her.

I N ANOTHER PART OF the room, John ate lunch with Patrick, a rare occasion, but the topic of conversation was the same. Patrick had tried to avoid thinking about the disappearance, but it wasn't easy. Juan and Reuben's most likely fate was too close to the accident that had killed his parents so many years before.

John had figured that out. "It still bothers me they were last seen on Pearson's truck, heading away from the river. We don't know that they're dead."

Patrick shook his head. "I know you don't like Selwick, John, but how could that have anything to do with it? Are you suggesting Selwick did something with them?"

"We haven't found any recent riverbank collapses, and no bodies have washed up. They were last seen with Selwick. We can't ignore the possibility."

"Why would he do anything to them? Because they hitched a ride on his truck?"

"I don't know. Maybe. Maybe they heard something that he doesn't want repeated. Or saw something. I don't know, Pat, but there's a part of my brain that's screaming at me, telling me he's at the bottom of this."

"I wish it was true." Patrick glanced around the room and spotted Gloria and Sydney. He could feel their pain and knew he should console them, but he didn't know what to say. "Then there might be something we could do."

## 14 Thursday 291 EN

"There has to be something we can do," Juan said. His voice was low.

Reuben shook his head. "We're miles from anywhere. If we got away from the estate, we'd be lost in no time."

"There's a road to the river. We could just follow that."

"And then what? Wait by the river until the *River Queen* comes? It doesn't stop here very often. We could walk down the river road and wait for the Grissom ferry to cross the river. That's only a couple of hundred miles."

Reuben wouldn't admit it to Juan, but being held by Selwick Pearson had its good points. The estate's entertainment equipment was better than anything he had seen outside of a theater on Earth and much better than anything in Grissom. There was an endless supply of movies and some exciting games. If he felt guilty about not attending school, there were courses available on a wide range of subjects, although most seemed geared toward adults. Pearson didn't let them outside by themselves, but they could usually find a staff member willing to spend some time out on the broad lawn or down by the lake.

"My mom must be going crazy wondering where I am," Juan said.

That made Reuben feel a little guilty. At least Juan's mother had a husband and two other children. Reuben's mom had no one else. Still, there wasn't anything he could do about it.

## 15 Monday 291 ED

Robert Perez arrived promptly, and Amy ushered him into Patrick's office. Patrick stood behind his desk, greeted Robert and shook his hand, but the reception was cool.

Robert took a seat and looked at Patrick with a smile. "As you know, I'm here to smooth Grissom's relations with Earth."

Patrick smiled back. "Of course. And what can Grissom do for you today to aid you in that goal?"

Robert ignored the hint of sarcasm in Patrick's response and kept his expression steady. "We've never formalized my relationship with Pitcairn. It occurred to me that I could be more effective if there were a written diplomatic agreement between our governments."

Patrick folded his hands in front of him and stared at Robert. "What would be the provisions of such an agreement?"

"Just the standard agreements. I've already prepared a draft for your examination." Robert pushed several pages of text toward Patrick. "There's one difference, however. Usually, an ambassador would have an embassy that would legally be considered the soil of the country he represents. Since that would violate the spirit of our earlier agreements about property on Pitcairn, I left out that part. An embassy would be impractical anyway since I'm the entire staff. In the future, you might send an ambassador to Earth, and the provisions would be reciprocal."

"I'll read it over. If it looks okay, I'll submit it to the Planetary Legislature for approval."

Patrick seemed bored by the conversation, typical of someone with his inexperience in diplomacy. This is going to work.

Robert smiled. "I would appreciate it. I would also appreciate it if you could keep me apprised of its status."

# 55

# Isaac is Inspired

*I*SAAC

*It pleased doctor Agron when I told him how I was searching for Reuben and Juan. I felt something that I think the humans would call satisfaction. I know I can't solve problems the way they do, but I think I am getting better at something almost as good.*

*Finding the children is a problem, and I did a comprehensive data search on any topic remotely connected to finding them. The amount of data I accumulated might have seemed daunting, but the same circuits that help me analyze astronomical data helped examine connections rapidly and choose the more relevant ones. I think I did by brute force what humans do instinctively.*

*The results have been negative—fortunately, Doctor Agron would say. It is logical to believe that the satisfaction I would derive from positive results, especially if they are alive, would be much greater than what I have already experienced. I must look at the problem again.*

*I had assumed that they would be in the Grissom area, dead or alive, but Administrator Shuford believes that Selwick Pearson has taken them for some reason. I don't know why he would do that, but considering that possibility has triggered new patterns in my analysis, suggesting additional actions I can take.*

**18 Tuesday 291 EN**

Patrick watched his father-in-law take a seat across from him. He was looking so old and tired. "How's it going, John?"

John straightened in his chair and looked at Patrick. "All right. You know as well as I do."

"We're overcoming our labor shortage at last. The robots we've been getting from Earth are making a difference. Susan tells me that Ellis is close to building robots designed here. I think things are going very well."

John frowned and looked down again. "You don't have to talk to Gloria Noland. For the first week after Reuben and Juan disappeared, Gloria came into the Town Hall every day asking for news. Then the visits declined, and now she comes in maybe once a week. I used to see hope in her eyes, but I don't see that anymore." His voice was bitter. "Did you know that Diego Chandri spends most of his time wandering in the forests east of town? Supposedly, he's studying the local ecology, but it's not trees he's looking for."

"We're doing everything we can."

"Are we? Patrick, there's been nothing like this since I came here on *Seeker*. I'm not sure anything like this has ever happened in Grissom." His voice rose, and he slapped the desk. "Sure, there have been drownings, but the bodies always washed up within a few miles of here. Even those have been damn rare."

"That doesn't mean something can't happen. Calm down, John. This isn't good for you."

John waved his hand dismissively and turned to stare out a window.

Patrick leaned toward John. "You're letting the stress get to you. John, I've been telling you that you should think about retiring. You should before it's too late." He smiled to soften his words. "I want you around to see your great-grandchildren."

John turned back to face Patrick. "I don't know why, but Pearson has them. I can't prove it, but I can feel it."

"But we need proof to do anything about it, John," Patrick responded gently.

## 19 Monday 291 EN

"The Planetary Legislature met this morning," Dennis told John. "The minutes are on your terminal."

John nodded. The Legislature had become busier as they grew familiar with their duties. Lately, they have met for a few hours every Monday at midday. He brought up the minutes and scanned through them for anything that might affect Grissom. One item, headlined "Diplomatic agreement approved," caught his eye. "First I've heard of this," he mumbled.

He displayed the agreement and read it slowly. It all looked straightforward, and he chuckled over the provision that any facilities used by the Earth representative would remain under Pitcairn's control. He wondered why the question had even come up in the Legislature. Then he saw the provision for diplomatic immunity, and it all made sense.

He knew who had been in the truck that the boys had ridden. Besides Selwick's driver, there was Selwick, Caiden Reyes, and, of course, Robert Perez. If Selwick had them, Robert knew about it, and now he had covered himself if it came out.

He thought about talking to Patrick again, but avoided the frustration. Instead, he popped a couple of antacid tablets, hoping to stave off the heartburn he felt already beginning.

## 20 Thursday 291 LD

Jennifer McIntosh came to Pitcairn as a housekeeper for the Pearson estate. She was planning to marry another of Pearson's staff soon and wanted to have children, so she volunteered to help take care of Reuben and Juan just for practice. The boys liked her and were well-behaved when they were with her, so Selwick encouraged Jennifer.

It was late winter when the temperatures were relatively mild. It was also a time of heavy rains, but the clouds cleared on that late afternoon, and Juan successfully campaigned for some time outside. Jennifer found a soccer ball, and they went out on the lawn to kick it around. Juan secretly hoped he could sneak away and perhaps use stones to make a "Help" sign that Isaac might see, but his feelings were mixed because he didn't want to get Jennifer in trouble.

He never had the chance, anyway. It was too easy for Jennifer to keep track of the two boys on the open space, and Juan suspected they might be watched from the house, too. They were having a good time, though, and he soon forgot about making a sign. The sun dropped toward the horizon, and Jennifer took them back into the house to get ready for dinner.

*I*<sup>SAAC</sup>

*I found them. Administrator Shuford was right. They are going to be so proud of me.*

PATRICK LOOKED DOUBTFULLY AT the picture John had placed in front of him. "Isaac can't identify individuals from that distance. All I see are some dark patches near Selwick's main house." He glanced again at the view of the estate, with the three elongated shadows on the lawn. "These could be anybody."

"Obviously, those are just shadows of people." John waved at the picture impatiently. "But look at the lengths of the shadows."

Then Patrick saw it. "One short shadow and two longer shadows." He stared at the picture. "There are no children on Selwick's estate, are there?"

"There aren't supposed to be. Reyes has children, but they're still on Earth. I would guess that the tall shadows are an adult and Reuben. Juan is still quite a bit shorter than Reuben."

"Still, this is slim evidence. We can't just go barging in there."

John shook his head. "Yes, we can. We own the estate. But we don't have to, not without getting a little more information, anyway."

# 56

# Targetting Selwick

**20 Saturday 291 EN**

I T TOOK A COUPLE of days to assemble everyone, but Gloria rushed to the Pitcairn Administration Center when she received the summons from John. She feared the worse on the walk from her house, but when she got to the conference room, Jack from Ellis, Harry from Armstrong, Patrick, John, Sydney, and Diego were already there. She felt a spark of hope seeing so many people staring at a map.

Jack pointed to a spot on the upper Lovell River. "We should do some exploration past the estate anyway. The Great Basin impact site is northeast of Pearson Lake, a priority target for an expedition."

"That gives us an excuse to stop at the Pearson estate and reconnoiter," Diego added. "They can't refuse us."

Harry nodded. "I can use the bus to move my men up the river road and wait for confirmation from you that the boys are there."

"I don't want this to be a bloodbath," Patrick warned.

Harry shook his head. "It shouldn't be. We don't think Pearson or Reyes felt any need to arm themselves, and none of the people they brought in have any relevant background that we've been able to find. The only concern I have is their robots."

Sydney looked horrified. "You think they might be programmed for violence?"

Harry shrugged. "It's not likely, but I want us to be ready in case. Fortunately, we have weapons that will take out a robot. If we need to do that, we will. Seeing that will discourage any resistance from Pearson's staff."

"It's a good thing we stored your weapons instead of destroying them," Diego said. "So, when do we leave?"

"You're going?" Sydney grabbed his arm. "You're not a soldier."

Diego patted the hand holding him, but his voice was harsh. "No, but I'm a natural to be going with Jack. I'm going to find our son, Sydney. That's not open for debate."

John nodded to Diego and turned to Gloria. "We'll get them both back, Gloria. It will take a few more days to get this together, but now we know they're still alive. Just wait a little longer."

Gloria nodded. "I know." She had been about to tell them she wanted to be included too and suspected John had known that and replied before she could say anything. She knew John was right, but the waiting would be agony. Her feelings had deadened in the nine weeks since Reuben had disappeared, but the sudden hope that Reuben was still alive had brought all the dread back to life.

"Wasn't Pearson Interstellar supposed to train security people for us?" Sydney said. She looked a little shaken, not sure how to react to Diego's attitude.

"I think we're supposed to send people to the estate for training," John replied. "We never got around to it."

"We could use that as a reason to send more people," Sydney suggested.

Harry's voice was rough. "We don't need untrained people." Sydney didn't speak again, but she didn't look happy.

John looked at Harry. "You're in charge of this operation. Keep us informed, and set a date as soon as you can. Recovering the boys is your priority, but taking custody of Pearson and Reyes should be a secondary goal."

Concern creased Patrick's face. "What are we going to do with them once we have them?"

"We can discuss that while Harry does his planning." John looked hard at Patrick, determination in his tired eyes. "In the end, though, I think that will be a question for our judges, and we should prepare them, too."

"We'll discuss it," Patrick said. "Don't worry, John. We'll be ready to deal with them."

"They committed a crime in my jurisdiction. I am going to make sure justice is done." John spoke with conviction, and Gloria's hope grew. They were about to execute the first military action ever on Pitcairn, but Harry looked confident. John grimaced as if in pain, but that was probably just stress.

## 21 Wednesday 291 ED

Selwick summoned Caiden to his estate for a meeting. "Grissom is forming another expedition into the mountains northeast of here. They want to use my estate as a staging area."

Caiden gave Selwick a worried nod. "Do you think they know we have the two boys?"

"I don't see how they could know. They might suspect, but even that seems doubtful." Selwick shook his head. "The area they're talking about is a prime target for exploration, and they have the right under our agreement to use our estates as staging areas."

"What are you going to do about it?"

"There's not much I can do without arousing suspicion. We can move the boys to your estate for a while, though, just to make sure they're not spotted."

Caiden frowned. "I don't know about that. I don't want them found on my estate, either."

Selwick looked at him sharply. "If they are suspicious, you're linked to it, too. Don't go soft on me, Caiden. You have as much to lose as I do."


## 1 Thursday 292 LD

Madelyn Menzies frowned as she watched *Searcher* float up to the mooring mast. It was the first week of Pitcairn's spring, not a time known for pleasant weather. In fact, the blimp was arriving just ahead of a storm. It seemed an odd time for an expedition into the northern reaches of the Central Mountains.

She knew about the missing children, gone now for nine weeks. She might not have suspected a connection, but Selwick had not visited Lovell Station for about the same period. That was unusual, and she couldn't help but wonder. Brayden Gallagher reported seeing lights across the river the previous night, too. Selwick usually used the road only when he had cargo arriving, so that also was strange.

Selwick's ferry would take the expedition across the river. She could warn Selwick, but didn't think she would. Selwick had been very generous with her, but she was not naïve enough to believe anything other than Selwick's objectives were behind that. If Selwick had anything to do with the missing children, she didn't want to be connected to it.

A ground crew secured *Searcher,* and she watched Jack Applegate, Diego Chandri, and a man who would later be introduced as Gabe Radcliffe, a geologist. Diego had been to

Lovell Station before, but wasn't he also the father of one of the missing boys? No, this was not a time to show too much friendliness toward Selwick Pearson.

# 57

# Jack's Discovery

**1 Friday 292 ED**

J ACK AND HIS TEAM had not been to the Pearson estate. After the ferry across the Lovell and the truck through the forest to the estate, Selwick and Sophie lost no time in showing off their capabilities as hosts. Selwick took them to the patio, where they sat and sipped brandy while they gazed across the lake. He questioned them about their expedition, but they had worked out all the details as if they really intended to go. When they retired to guest quarters to sleep, Selwick had learned nothing from them, but they had been no more successful in learning anything about Reuben and Juan.

By agreement, they rose early the following day and met on the patio. Selwick was still in bed, and only a couple of his staff were around. No one said anything when the three men walked down to the lake through a misty dawn. The storm had passed in the night, but the sky was still overcast as they walked down the lawn, not speaking until they were far enough away that they couldn't be seen from the house.

"I scanned as much of the house as I could in infrared," Gabe reported. "I couldn't identify anyone, of course, and movement patterns seemed to indicate staff. If the boys are here, I didn't detect anyone who was staying in one place, hidden from us."

Diego frowned. "We know they were here. You may not have been able to scan the room where they're being kept."

"That's possible," Gabe agreed. "It's also possible that Selwick moved them to the Reyes estate when he knew we were coming."

Jack looked toward the house, with a few lights barely visible through the mist. "If we call Harry in, and we're wrong, there's going to be hell to pay."

"We can't just leave them here," Diego protested.

Jack thought for a moment and nodded. "Even if they are at the other estate, we know they were here. Maybe we can get Selwick to give us a tour. We might find some sign of them."

"We can always say that the weather is worse than we expected, and we need to delay heading north," Diego said. "It does look like we're going to have a nasty day."

Jack grinned faintly. "I almost feel sorry for Harry, stuck out in the woods waiting for us to give him the word. Okay, sounds like a plan." He took a small radio out of his pocket. "I'll update Harry, and we'll go back in."

H ARRY BROKE THE CONNECTION with Jack and turned to his team, comprising eight volunteers from the eighteen soldiers who had stayed on Pitcairn. "We have a problem. There's a good chance that the boys are at the other estate, a couple of miles down the lakeshore."

The soldiers had camped near the road Selwick had built along the river, deep enough into forest near the lake to avoid being seen. The bus was a problem, but they had pulled it off the road and camouflaged it with branches. After a night sleeping on the bus, they were hiding at the edge of the trees with a view of the estate grounds.

"We need to split up." Harry looked them over. "Kyle, Gerry, Gavin, and Vic, work your way down the shore while we still have this fog to hide us. When we get the word from Jack, we'll hit both estates simultaneously."

Sergeant Kyle Hilton, the highest-ranking of the four, nodded. "Yes, sir. Give us half an hour, and we'll be in place."

"Don't forget this gravity. I'll give you at least forty-five minutes."

"Yes, sir." Kyle motioned to the other three, and they disappeared into the mist. Harry and the others settled down to wait.

JACK AND THE OTHERS were approaching the patio when Selwick came out and greeted them. "Ah, there you are. Taking an early morning stroll?"

"Not exactly ideal weather, but better now than the heat of the day," Jack responded.

Selwick laughed, playing the hearty host to the hilt. "Well, breakfast should be just about ready." He ushered them through the house to the dining room, where the staff was already laying out a light breakfast. Selwick's wife, Sophie, was there, too, supervising the servants.

"I'm afraid the weather is not cooperating with you," Selwick said as they took seats. "The rain should be back in a few hours."

Jack smiled. "Yes. I hope it won't inconvenience you too much if we stay another day. Perhaps you might even give us a tour. As I'm sure you know, your estate is like nothing we've ever seen in Grissom or Ellis."

"Of course!" Selwick was beaming. "I'll be busy, but Sophie would love to give you the complete tour. Wouldn't you, darling?"

"All right, Selly." Sophie smiled, but Jack didn't think it was sincere. Sophie Pearson was an attractive woman, but she looked soft. Life on the estate, he suspected, was not very strenuous for the lady of the manor.

Sophie gave them a complete tour, though. For the next hour, she showed them through every room in the house, making sure they missed nothing. Toward the end, Diego came up next to Jack. "They're not here, and Pearson wants to make sure we know it," he whispered.

Jack nodded slightly. The tour's very thoroughness was a red flag to him, telling him that Reuben and Juan had been here but weren't any longer. He hoped that meant they were at the Reyes estate; disturbingly, it was not the only possibility that occurred to him.

KYLE AND THE OTHER three soldiers settled in beyond a low bank near the lake. It wasn't great cover, but would be adequate as long as fog shrouded the landscape. The Reyes estate had two buildings, smaller than those on the Pearson estate, and infrared scanning showed ten of the sixteen residents in the smaller building near the main house. They had wondered why Reyes had such a large staff, and now they knew that most of them were not house staff. Later, they would learn that the smaller building was a laboratory where Caiden's people were trying to synthesize the antiviral drug.

From the locations of the people in that building, it did not look guarded. There was a single entrance, and Kyle decided that, when the signal came, he would dispatch one man to cover that entrance and keep the occupants inside.

There was a lot of movement in the main house, and it was difficult to get an accurate count of the occupants with the infrared. Kyle was confident, however, that there were more than the six people who should have been there. He passed that information back to Harry.

S OPHIE LED THEM TO the entertainment room, where the music system was playing something quiet and soothing. She smiled and motioned to the plush chairs. "That's the whole tour. Maybe you would like to rest in here for a while. I'll go see about some coffee." Without waiting for a reply, she was gone.

The three men exchanged looks and took seats. "They have to be at the other estate," Diego said. His voice was quiet, but the anger and concern were easy to hear.

Jack frowned and nodded. "We should have more proof, though."

Diego didn't agree, but he said nothing. They sat there, trying to work out their next action.

The chairs were comfortable, and the music was soft. Jack relaxed and settled back in his chair. Something dug into his hip, and he probed between the cushions to find what was bothering him. He felt a lump and pulled out a small package.

"What's that?" Gabe said.

Jack turned it over in his hand, examining each side of the rectangular object. "A recording," he said. "There's a label. 'The Adventures of Juan Jimenez.'"

Diego sat up suddenly. "What? Let me see that."

Jack passed it over, and Diego looked at it with rising excitement. "It's a kid's video," he said. "Juan Jimenez is one of my son's favorite characters!"

"Doesn't sound like something Selwick would watch," Gabe said.

"No, no." Diego jumped up. "Juan was here. He must have been watching this."

Jack stood up, too, and looked at the package again. "Are you sure?"

"Yes, absolutely. Trust me, this is not adult entertainment."

Jack pulled out his phone. "Harry, they must be at the Reyes estate. It's a go."

# 58

# Harry Back in Action

THE SOLDIERS HAD BROUGHT a variety of weapons on the bus, but with no sign of an armed presence at their targets, they carried only assault rifles to the Reyes estate. As Gavin moved to cover the entrance to the second building, Kyle led the other two toward the house. The fog was clearing, but the building was only seventy yards from the lake, and they crossed undetected. Infrared showed three people working just inside one entrance and no one near what appeared to be the main entrance. Kyle sent Vic to go through the main door while he and Gerry took the other.

Gerry opened the door slowly, and Kyle burst through it, rifle held ready. With Gerry close behind, he moved through a short hallway and into a large kitchen where two men were cooking, and a woman was preparing to serve the food.

"Just keep doing what you're doing," Kyle said softly, sweeping his weapon around the room. The three servants froze in place, eyes fixed on the guns. One man had been using a long kitchen knife, and he slowly put it down on the counter and moved his hand away. Kyle motioned to the server. "Nobody has to get hurt here. Get over here."

MADISON NISHIOKA PUT DOWN the plates she had been carrying and moved slowly toward Kyle. She tried to say something, but her mouth had suddenly gone dry, and the words stuck in her throat.

"Where are the rest of the people in the house?" Kyle asked.

Madison had worked for Caiden Reyes for over a decade, but it did not prepare her for this. When her employer brought the two children from Grissom to the estate, she had feared something like this might happen, but now she couldn't think.

"Two maids upstairs," she stammered. "Mr. Reyes and the two boys are at breakfast in the dining room."

Kyle called Vic. "Where are you?"

Vic answered immediately, speaking in a whisper. "Inside the entrance. There's no one here, but I'm at the foot of stairs to the second floor, and I think I hear somebody moving around up there."

"Good. There should be two maids there. Watch the stairs and make sure they stay up there. Gerry and I are heading for the dining room." He broke the connection and turned to the two cooks. "Just stay here, and you won't be hurt." He turned back to Madison. "What's your name?"

"Madison." Her voice was so low that Kyle had to ask her to repeat it.

"Okay, Madison. Take us to the dining room, and everything will be all right."

S ELWICK STORMED INTO THE entertainment room, his face livid. "There are armed men all over the house. Somebody is going to pay for this!"

Jack looked at him calmly. "Sit down, Selwick, before you hurt yourself." He raised his voice. "We're in here, Harry." Then he nodded to Diego.

Diego stood and walked over to Selwick. "Selwick Pearson, in the name of the government of Pitcairn, I place you under arrest for kidnapping, false imprisonment, and abuse of minors."

"Those boys who disappeared? They're not here, you arrogant barbarian."

Diego smiled, but there was no amusement in it. "Barbarian, perhaps, but I think you have the corner on arrogant."

Harry and one of his men entered the room. "Lieutenant Richard, please take this man into custody," Jack ordered.

"The team at the Reyes estate just reported in," Harry said as he took Selwick's arm. "They have the boys, and they're fine."

The anger went out of Diego's expression. "Thanks, Harry." He looked at Selwick, and his smile widened.

C AIDEN REYES TOOK EVENTS more calmly than Selwick did. When Kyle and Gerry walked into the dining room behind Madison, rifles held low but ready, Caiden looked at Madison reproachfully, and then at the two soldiers. "Madison, please have the kitchen prepare two more breakfasts."

"That won't be necessary." Kyle motioned for Caiden to stand up. "We've already eaten."

"A pity. I doubt you've tasted food as delicious as what my cook can prepare."

Kyle grinned at him. "You're probably right. It will be a long time before you do again." He turned to Reuben and Juan, who sat at the table, looking stunned. "Okay, kids. Finish eating and let's go. It's time to go home."

# The Trial

# 59

# The Boys Return

**1 Saturday 292 EN**

THROUGH ALL THE CHANGES since *Asimov's* arrival, Grissom never lost the look of a tranquil rural town. Its citizens fit that mold, too, going about their business secure in knowing that life went on much as it always had.

Reuben and Juan's disappearance brought an undercurrent of fear as parents wondered what had happened and whether the same could happen to their children. The boys' return to Grissom triggered a celebration unprecedented in the town's history. All but the most necessary tasks came to a halt, forgotten in a flood of information, speculation, and simple delight at the turn of events.

When darkness fell, the colony quieted down, returning almost to normal. There was one exception, however: the Town Hall where John confronted Selwick, Caiden, and Robert. There, noisy disarray still reigned, but there was little joy in it.

"This is unacceptable," Selwick thundered. "You can't treat me like this."

John grinned at him. "And yet I'm doing it. Fortunately for you, your fate will be in the hands of a judge, not me or the parents of the children you've been holding prisoner."

"Your threats are contemptible," Robert Perez said. "In the end, it will be you who will regret your actions."

John turned on him. "You think so?" He looked over his shoulder at Patrick. "Patrick, remind me again why I can't arrest this criminal, too."

Patrick sighed. "You know, John. He has diplomatic immunity."

John turned back to Robert. "Timing is everything, isn't it, Ambassador? How long were you here before you thought to suggest that diplomatic agreement?"

"I don't have to put up with your insinuations."

John shrugged. "Well, if I can't arrest you, then I don't need you here. If you don't like my insinuations, you can leave." He pointed toward the door.

"As Earth's representative, I have a duty to stay and make sure Earth's citizens aren't mistreated."

Patrick put a hand on John's shoulder. "Let's calm down, John. This isn't helping things any."

John glared at Robert for a long moment. With visible effort, he forced his expression into neutrality and nodded. "Okay, fine." He looked at Selwick and Caiden. "No more threats, just facts. This is what's going to happen." He collected his thoughts. "We will hold the two of you until we can arrange a trial. We will try you for your crimes, presumably convict you, and pass sentence. Personally, I hope the judge will go very hard on you, but that won't be for me to decide."


## 2 Sunday 292 ED

"We're holding Pearson and Reyes in a room in the Power Distribution Building," Harry reported. "We moved cots into it, and I have a guard on the door. They won't be going anywhere."

John nodded. "Good, Harry." He ran his fingers through the little remaining hair on his head. "In all the excitement yesterday, I never asked you about the estates. How did you leave things there?"

"I appointed temporary leaders at each estate and told them to maintain things as usual until further notice. Do you intend to charge anyone else? The estate staffs were complicit."

"We can't arrest them all, and we don't have any firm evidence against anyone else as of now. Who did you name to manage the estates?"

Harry consulted a notebook. "A Doctor Daphne Audet on the Pearson estate. Andrew Fripp on the Reyes estate. He claimed to be Reyes's deputy and seemed competent."

"Okay. We can have Isaac watch over them for now and maybe send someone over there from Lovell Station occasionally. Good work, Harry."

"I still don't understand why Selwick kidnapped them, John. Reuben said they couldn't hear anything from the back of the truck and couldn't think of anything relevant that they saw."

John nodded. "There must have been something. I don't trust Pearson or Reyes, and they were probably discussing some plan. Whatever it was, it was dangerous enough that they couldn't risk being overheard."

"What are you going to do about it?"

"I don't know. Patrick doesn't seem concerned, and without his support, it will be hard to do anything beyond prosecuting Selwick and Caiden. The trial might reveal more."

## 2 Wednesday 292 ED

Daphne Audet had been concerned at first when the soldiers came and took Selwick and Caiden away. It wouldn't end there; the colonists wouldn't just leave the two estates alone. After a few days, though, she came to see the events as an opportunity.

The exploitation of the Pitcairn plant to develop a diet drug had been her idea, but Selwick took it over with little more than a pat on the back for her. Selwick turned all her information over to Caiden, who allocated laboratory resources on his estate to investigate the potential.

With Selwick and Caiden both out of the picture, someone would have to take over. It wouldn't be Andrew Fripp, the man the colonists had placed in charge of the Reyes estate. Fripp might manage the estate's day-to-day operation, but he didn't have the background to keep the lab on the right path.

She visited the Reyes lab and talked to Anna Alvarez, the biochemist in charge of the laboratory, but Anna was not helpful, maintaining that she was an employee of Reyes Pharmaceuticals, not Pearson Industries, and didn't need direction from Daphne. Daphne felt her chance slipping away.

S ITTING IN HER SPACIOUS office, Anna Alvarez smiled to herself. The Audet woman thought that she could offer something more than she was getting from Caiden Reyes. Perhaps Pearson Industries was less generous with key employees than Reyes Pharmaceuticals. Or maybe Doctor Daphne Audet just wasn't that important.

Still, there were problems she had to resolve. Without access to the Link, she had no way to talk to company management and wasn't sure how to proceed. Caiden had always dealt with nontechnical management issues.

For reasons never explained to her, the two estates didn't have long-distance radio connections to the colonist settlements. They could contact Lovell Station, but any other settlement was out of range without going through *Asimov*, and Selwick and Caiden had intentionally not installed that capability. She guessed they wanted to prevent the *Asimov* computer from spying on communication between the estates.

She could take the ferry to Lovell Station and perhaps contact Caiden from there. Failing that, she could go to Grissom and talk to Caiden in person. In the meantime, she would make sure work continued on both the antiviral drug and the weight-loss drug. She had time; Madelyn Menzies had already told Andrew Fripp that Pitcairn would take no action on the charges against Caiden until his lawyer arrived from Earth, which wouldn't happen for at least a month.

## Pitcairn News Service Bulletin, 2 Thursday 292 (30 June 2343)

Today, the Pitcairn Office of the Administrator confirmed the arrest of Terran citizens Selwick Pearson and Caiden Reyes on charges of kidnapping and false imprisonment. Grissom authorities have accused the two men of kidnapping two children from Grissom and taking them to the Pearson estate on Pitcairn. A motive for the crime hasn't been determined.

A team visiting the Pearson estate under the pretext of an exploration trip, led by explorer and biologist Jack Applegate, confirmed the boys were taken. Not finding the boys on the Pearson estate, the rescue party realized the kidnappers had transferred them to the nearby Reyes estate and recovered the boys there.

Pearson and Reyes are being held in Grissom, awaiting trial on the charges. Pending the verdict, the two estates are in the control of representatives of the companies of the accused. In a statement for PNS, Planetary Administrator Patrick Malley said that Pitcairn would probably take over the estates under the agreement signed with the Pitcairn government, but that wouldn't happen until the panel of judges issue a verdict.

## 3 July 2343 Cabinet Conference Room, Brasilia, Brazil

President Castillo looked around the room angrily, causing several cabinet members to look away nervously, but his gaze finally stopped on David Pearson, the CEO of Pearson Industries. "I assume you can guess why you're here."

The subject of Castillo's irritation looked at him calmly. Pearson was a distinguished-looking man in his sixties, wearing a perfectly tailored suit with casual elegance. "If you are expecting an explanation for my son's actions, I'm afraid I must disappoint you." He sat back in his chair, relaxed and confident.

Pearson's apparent lack of concern did not fool Castillo. He snorted and picked up a sheet of paper from the table in front of him. "You've read this release from the Pitcairn News Service?"

"I have."

"You don't seem worried about what the colonists might do to your son."

Pearson shrugged. "Reyes Pharmaceuticals and Pearson Interstellar are sending lawyers to Pitcairn within the week. I'm sure they will straighten this out."

Castillo shook his head. "Don't be so sure. Negotiating with these people has been frustrating so far. Your son should have told you that."

"I have read his reports. Nevertheless, Pitcairn will find they've taken on more than they bargained for this time."

"I hope so. You could lose a lot of money if you fail."

Pearson smiled and nodded.

# 60

# The Lawyers Arrive

**5 Friday 292 EN**

JOHN WONDERED IF THERE was a message in the manifest for the newly arrived *Francisco Pearson*. There were only two passengers: Jonathan Perez (no relation to Robert, he was assured), Selwick Pearson's attorney; and Kennedy Veronica Mobley ("Call me Veronica; I hate the name Kennedy"), Caiden Reyes's attorney. The cargo was earmarked for the estates, none for the colony. It wasn't a scheduled visit, so perhaps it was unreasonable to expect new colonists or supplies.

On arriving in Grissom, the attorneys went to their clients, still held in the Power Distribution Building. Three hours later, they demanded a meeting with Pitcairn's representatives. Expecting that, John arranged for a preliminary meeting in a conference room in the Pitcairn Administration Center. Patrick chaired the meeting, and John brought Henry Best, the Pitcairn Judiciary's chief judge, from Ellis. Robert Perez came.

After introductions, Patrick opened the meeting. "I assume you want to talk about how we're going to do this. As you know, we have little experience in this sort of thing. The trial of Tori Chen, chiefly."

Jonathan Perez made a face. "That experience was of dubious worth. Hardly a trial at all."

John smiled tightly. "Justice was done. That was the important thing, as far as we were concerned."

"There was no defense lawyer, no prosecutor, no jury, and a judge with no experience. If justice was done, it was a miracle."

Henry looked amused. "Well, this time, at least, the judge will have some experience."

Jonathan gave him a look showing no amusement at all. "This time, it will be different. I will be defending Mr. Pearson vigorously, should that become necessary."

Patrick raised his eyebrows. "Why wouldn't it be necessary? Is Selwick planning to confess everything and save us the trouble? We would still have to have some kind of hearing to determine a sentence."

"Ambassador Perez furnished us a copy of your Constitution and the laws you have passed up to now. Ms. Mobley and I reviewed the material carefully during the passage here. We intend to take two actions immediately." He paused, glanced at Veronica, who nodded in agreement, and continued. "First, we are moving to drop all charges against our clients, and second, we're going to charge Harry Richard and anyone else who took part in the unlawful seizure of our clients."

John chuckled. So Perez was an ambassador now! Patrick frowned at him before responding. "Let's take them one at a time. Why would we drop the charges?"

"For the simple reason that our clients violated no law. Pitcairn has no law against kidnapping, and we will accept your position that Earth laws do not apply to Pitcairn."

Patrick wondered if the Western Alliance would agree. Pearson Interstellar might accept Pitcairn's laws, but it would be a limited concession. "I'm afraid I can't quote the relevant passage, but I believe Section Seven of the Constitution, which covers the rights and duties of citizens, justifies the charges."

"Our clients are not citizens."

Patrick frowned and turned to Henry. Henry leaned forward and stared Jonathan in the eye. "I brought a copy of the Constitution with me." He glanced at the papers in front of him. "The last sentence of Section Seven reads, 'Each citizen has a duty to respect and support the rights of fellow citizens to the extent possible.' Pitcairn claims that the duty expressed extends to Pitcairn residents and that your clients violated that principle. As a presiding judge, I warn you I intend to uphold that principle."

Before Jonathan could respond to that, Patrick jumped in. "Of what crime are you accusing Harry?"

"The Sao Paulo district court on Earth has filed charges on grounds that Richard and his men violated the rights of Selwick Pearson when they entered his home without permission or legal warrant and took him into custody. It will also charge them with desertion. The court has furnished me with an order of extradition so that Harry Richard and his men can be returned to Earth for trial."

"Harry's actions were justified under the same sentence in Section Seven," Henry asserted. "Pitcairn has already rejected extradition on desertion charges."

"That will be determined in Sao Paulo." Jonathan looked smug.

John laughed. "I thought Earth law no longer applied on Pitcairn."

"Pitcairn will not honor the extradition order," Henry added. "Lieutenant Richard and his men are citizens of Pitcairn, and Pitcairn will refuse extradition. Further, Selwick Pearson doesn't own his home on Pitcairn; he only rents it, and it falls under Pitcairn's jurisdiction."

"If you don't release Selwick Pearson from custody, there will be consequences."

Patrick glared at Jonathan. "We've lived here peacefully for almost three hundred years. I'm thinking that our lack of lawyers was the reason."

Jonathan shook his head angrily. "Ambassador Perez was apparently accurate when he described you as arrogant."

"Do you have anything else you would like to discuss?" Patrick said, his voice hard.

Jonathan forced himself to calm down. "We will insist on a jury trial, not the informal conclusion used to convict Tori Chen."

"There is no provision for jury trials in the Pitcairn Constitution," Henry said. "I don't think its drafters thought much of the ability of a jury to reach a reasonable decision."

Jonathan attempted to look horrified, but he wasn't that good an actor. "One man, not even educated in the law, is an improvement?"

Henry apparently decided to match him in overacting. "I am the foremost expert on Pitcairn law! You're the one not educated in the law."

John was chuckling again, and Jonathan and Robert both sent dirty looks his way. Patrick rolled his eyes and tried to compromise. "Henry is one of four judges in the Pitcairn judicial system. Perhaps we could reach a verdict by unanimous consent of all four."

"That will not be satisfactory." Jonathan gave Patrick a firm look, trying to convey the idea that it was useless to argue. "If a fair and reasonable trial cannot be provided on Pitcairn, my client will have to be tried on Earth."

Patrick shook his head. "I reject your premise. We will try Pearson and Reyes on Pitcairn, and the trial will be, as you say, fair and reasonable. Not what you're used to, perhaps, but they will get justice."

Jonathan threw up his hands and sat back in his seat. "Barbarians," he muttered.

"Since all your law experts are going to be judges, who will prosecute?" Robert asked.

When there was no immediate response, John grinned. "That would be me. It'll be my pleasure to prosecute your clients."

"You're qualified?" Jonathan's voice dripped with disbelief.

John shrugged. "Maybe you could teach me."

Robert groaned. "Send in the clowns."

# 61

# Veronica's Proposal

AN HOUR LATER, THE meeting broke up. Robert, Jonathan, and Veronica marched out of the Administration Center, the men in stony silence and Veronica looking thoughtful. Out on the street, she stopped. "I'm going to walk around town a little before I go to my quarters."

Jonathan and Robert looked at her with tired eyes, and Jonathan dismissed her with a wave of his hand. Then he walked off with Robert.

Veronica strolled in another direction, then doubled back and reentered the Administration Center when the two men were out of sight. John and Henry were leaving as she walked down the hallway, but she stopped them. "Perhaps we could talk without Jonathan present."

John looked at her, and she felt she was being appraised. Jonathan and Robert didn't seem to think much of the Grissom administrator, but she disagreed. It would be a mistake to underestimate him.

Patrick had gone back to his office. They got him and returned to the conference room.

"I'd like to talk about Mr. Reyes without Jonathan here," Veronica said.

Patrick nodded. "Okay, go ahead."

"The kidnapping was Pearson's idea and that Pearson's actions drew my client into it."

"Are you requesting a separate trial?" Henry asked. "I don't think that would make any difference."

Veronica shook her head. "Not exactly. I was hoping you would release Mr. Reyes in return for testifying against Selwick Pearson."

"Forget it," John said. "We don't need his testimony to convict Selwick. You have nothing to bargain with."

"Perhaps his testimony wouldn't be useful, but it could make Pitcairn look better in Earth's eyes." Veronica brushed a stray hair away from her eyes. Her back hurt, probably from the heavier gravity, and she wanted nothing more than a soft bed, but Reyes Pharmaceuticals was paying her a fortune to do whatever she could.

Patrick looked at John, who shook his head. "I don't think Pitcairn will be interested. If we went easy on Reyes, I would have more trouble from my fellow colonists than Earth could ever give me."

"Don't be too sure about that. Earth has already started a propaganda campaign over this. Jonathan will make use of that, you can be sure."

"He strikes me as all bark and no bite," John observed.

"I think I understand where Pitcairn is coming from. Things are simpler here, and you have no time for all the legal trappings that accompany legal proceedings on Earth. But don't sell Jonathan short. He's a capable attorney and the best person I know at manipulating the law. You've thrown him by the very simplicity of things here. He will recover from that quickly."

"Apparently, you aren't as 'thrown' by us," Henry said with a smile.

Veronica smiled back. "I really hope that we can come to some mutually beneficial resolution to this situation."

She hadn't impressed John. "We should always have hope," he told her.


## 5 Saturday 292 ED

When Anna Alvarez contacted Lovell Station, she learned that getting to Grissom wasn't a problem. She could take an estate vehicle down the river road, and Lovell Station would arrange for the Grissom ferry to pick her up when she arrived. Lovell Station could not guarantee access to Caiden, but she timed her visit to coincide with Veronica Mobley's arrival.

Veronica had a temporary office in the Pitcairn Administration Center and Anna found her there shortly after daybreak. She identified herself, and Veronica, curious, motioned her to a chair.

Anna sat quickly and leaned forward over Veronica's desk. "I need to talk to Mr. Reyes. I was hoping you could arrange that."

Veronica frowned. "I doubt it. The administrator said only the attorneys could visit. I can take a message, though."

Anna thought about that. "I guess that would be all right. I have no way to contact anyone else in the company, at least not without taking the chance that the colonists might overhear."

"I have arranged with Reyes Pharmaceuticals for encryption. As long as I can get access to the Link, I can send secure messages. I can deliver a message to Caiden today."

"I thought it would be important to give them a progress report on our investigations into uses for the local plant life."

A Western Alliance official had briefed Veronica on the Reyes estate facility and its importance. "You have progress on the antiviral drug? I'm sure Caiden will want to know that."

Anna shook her head. "No, I'm afraid not. We have gotten nowhere on that. I have news about the other project, though."

Veronica brushed a hair away from her eyes and looked questioningly at Anna. "Other project?"

That made Anna pause. Veronica knew about their efforts to develop a process to manufacture the antiviral drug, but not about the weight-loss drug. Anna didn't know if Caiden had told anyone on Earth about that. Given the situation, though, Anna didn't see any alternative. "We're also looking into a metabolism accelerator that might be useful as a weight-loss drug. We've made a lot of progress in the last month. Mr. Reyes will have to decide how to proceed." Anna pulled some papers out of her pocket. "This summarizes our current status. If you could get it to Mr. Reyes, he can tell us how to proceed with what we've found."

Veronica took the papers. "I'll do that later today. Are you going back right away?"

"I can stay until tomorrow."

"Good. I'll talk to Mr. Reyes and get back to you with instructions."

C AIDEN SCANNED THE REPORT quickly. "Good news." He looked up at Veronica.

Veronica looked puzzled. "I thought you were here to find a way to manufacture the antiviral drug. I hadn't heard about this other thing."

Caiden grinned. "The antiviral drug is why Earth paid for the estate, but there's no money in it toward the bottom line. Selwick brought this weight-loss drug idea to me, and nobody on Earth knows about it yet. If the lab is making progress, this could be a real money-maker for Reyes Pharmaceuticals."

Veronica looked at him sourly. "Not going to do you much good if Pitcairn won't deal on their charges."

"Maybe we could leverage this somehow in negotiations with them."

"I don't see how if they don't believe in money. They're after blood over the kidnapping."

Caiden's face fell. "What do you think they're going to do to me?"

"I don't know." But Veronica's expression grew thoughtful. "Unless we get a miracle, they'll convict you. This new drug won't help there. But maybe we can leverage it afterward."

Caiden nodded and looked a little more hopeful. "Then tell Anna to keep the antiviral investigations going at a minimum level and concentrate on the weight-loss drug. If we can use it, the further along we are, the better."

## Message: 6 Saturday 292 ED 6:32 (8/28/2343 2:11:45 PM)

From: Alan Shuford, Western Alliance Embassy to Japan, Tokyo, Japan

To: John Shuford, Grissom, Pitcairn

Dear John,

I have little news; things go on, and not much about my life has changed.
At my age, that's a good thing.

I think you wish you could say the same. I get the reports from your News Service, of course, but I also see the way our media portrays Pitcairn events. After all this time, I'm not sure if you remember how the media works here, but it will probably surprise you to know they depict Pearson and Reyes as heroes. They twist the news to a degree that surprises even me.

Of course, they sent none of that to you, so you won't respond to it. I don't know what you can do without a presence on Earth. All I can do is warn you. At some point, Pitcairn, even as far away as it is, will have to deal with it.

I wish I had more positive news to give you. I attached the transcripts of some typical broadcasts to give you an idea of what they are saying. I hope you don't find it too discouraging.

Love,


Dad

# 62

# The Trial Begins

**8 Monday 292 ED**

T HE PITCAIRN ADMINISTRATION CENTER had two large conference rooms, and Grissom carpenters furnished one of them as a temporary courtroom. One corner had a long L-shaped bench with three chairs for the Grissom, Ellis, and River Stations judges and a large monitor for the Asimov judge. They provided tables and chairs for the judges, others for the defense attorneys and defendants, and one for the prosecutor. In the middle, there was a chair for a testifying witness. A dozen chairs for other people associated with the trial lined another wall in two rows. Cameras would record the trial.

Veronica tried to find a comfortable position in her seat, but she still hadn't adapted to Pitcairn's gravity. It was an effort to concentrate on Henry as he gaveled the room to order and looked out over the assembly, ending by staring at the defense table.

Henry began the proceedings. "This is the second trial held under Pitcairn's Constitution. The first was very informal, since there were only two witnesses and not much of a defense." From his seat against the opposite wall, Robert Perez frowned. "This trial is going to be more formal, although I expect it won't meet the procedural standards used on Earth. Still, we'll do our best to reach a just decision." He nodded to Jacob Norwood, the judge from Grissom. "Jacob will now brief you on how this is going to proceed."

Jacob smiled briefly. "There will be no separate defense and prosecution presentations. Questions may be asked of witnesses at any time by the defense, the prosecution, or any of the judges. Those individuals have a button in front of them to signal the desire to speak. Judge Best will grant the floor to that person as soon as practical." He paused and looked around the room. "Defense will call the first witness. Any of the active participants may interrupt questioning of that witness to raise an objection or request that a rebuttal witness be called. A rebuttal witness should give only short testimony relevant to the statements of the current witness. When rebuttal is complete, the current witness will continue to give testimony."

"Sounds chaotic to me," Jonathan whispered. Veronica shrugged and kept her attention on Jacob. Henry glanced in their direction but didn't interrupt Jacob.

"When a witness's questioning is complete, the opposing attorney may call a witness or pass without forfeiting the right to call witnesses later. Does everyone understand these rules?"

When there were no negative replies, Jacob continued. "Witnesses won't take oaths. We, meaning we four judges, have decided that honesty in one's testimony is a requirement and that an oath to that effect is meaningless. Perjury will be a punishable offense." Jacob looked at Henry and nodded.

"That about covers it for now," Henry said. "You're going to have to bear with us. Things may change as we find out what works and what doesn't. The only thing I will promise is that we'll spare no effort in pursuit of justice."

Jonathan grimaced and shook his head. Henry looked at him mildly. "Perhaps you want to suggest some changes before we start, Mr. Perez?"

Jonathan stood up. "Earth has developed court procedures over centuries. I don't see why we're changing them."

Henry smiled gently. "No one on Pitcairn, except for you and Ms. Mobley, knows the procedures on Earth. I'm not sure they would apply to our more informal society. Do you have any specific suggestions?"

Shaking his head, Jonathan sat down again. He looked over at Veronica, but she was smirking at him.

"Very well." Henry tapped his gavel. "Selwick Pearson and Caiden Reyes are charged with egregious violation of Section Seven of the Pitcairn Constitution, specifically intentionally failing to respect and support the rights of fellow citizens to the extent possible. The accusation relates to events taking place on Monday of the eleventh week of 291 and alleges violations against the persons of Reuben Noland and Juan Chandri, citizens of the town of Grissom, Pitcairn."

Jonathan rose to speak, but Henry motioned him down. "If you wish to speak, use your button to request the floor. However, we expected you to claim that our laws don't apply to Mr. Pearson since he's not a citizen. We have already ruled that the clause applies to non-citizens living on Pitcairn based on the Constitution's Application Section, which specifies that Pitcairn laws apply to any self-aware being within its jurisdiction. Do you have anything else to say?"

Jonathan sat down again with a frown. "Not now."

Veronica smiled. She knew Jonathan had planned a lengthy opening statement, but apparently dropped the idea. He was finally understanding the situation.

"Good." Henry tapped the gavel again. "Call your first witness."

Jonathan stood again. "Defense calls Aiden Coffey."

Aiden, Selwick's driver the night of the kidnapping, walked over from a chair against the wall and sat down on the witness chair. Jonathan approached him with a pleased smile. "Mr. Coffey, you drove the truck bringing Caiden Reyes from the lander on the night in question?"

"I did."

"Can you tell us what happened when you arrived at the residence of Ambassador Perez on that night?"

"We observed two boys jump off the truck and attempt to flee the scene. On Mr. Pearson's orders, I stopped them and brought them to Mr. Pearson."

"And why did Mr. Pearson want you to stop them?"

"I didn't ask. Later, it became apparent he was concerned about why the boys were in the truck."

"What happened next?"

"Mr. Pearson took the boys into Ambassador Perez's residence to be questioned about their actions."

"That's all I have for this witness."

Henry tapped his gavel for attention. "John Shuford has asked for the floor. Go ahead, John."

John stood and leaned forward over the table. "What was Selwick Pearson's concern about the boys?"

Aiden shrugged. "I don't know. I didn't go into the house and didn't hear what they said."

"How did Reuben and Juan get from Grissom to the Pearson estate?"

A light blinked in front of Henry. Jonathan had reached across his table and was repeatedly pushing his button. Henry held up his hand. "Please hold, Mr. Coffey. I think Mr. Perez has an objection."

Jonathan nodded and took his seat again. "I do. They have not established that the boys were taken to the Pearson estate." Veronica turned and looked at Jonathan, her eyebrows tilted in surprise.

Henry nodded. "Mr. Coffey, how were the boys taken out of Grissom to the estates? We know, at least, that they were at the Reyes estate."

Aiden shrugged again. "I don't know that they were. I didn't see the boys after they went into the house."

John frowned and sat down. Jonathan nodded to himself and looked at Henry. "That's all I have for this witness at this time."

"John, it's your turn then," Henry said.

"I call Diego Chandri."

Diego took the witness chair and John came forward. "Diego, you were part of the team who rescued Reuben and Juan?"

Jonathan objected to the word rescued, but Henry overruled him, and Diego answered. "I was part of the group who went to the Pearson estate to verify that Reuben and my son were there."

"Did you find them there?"

"No."

"Yet you contacted Harry Richard and verified that they had been there. What made you report that?"

"We found one of Juan's favorite videos in the entertainment room, between the cushions of a chair. That told me he at least had been there."

A light flashed in front of Henry. "Mr. Perez, you have another objection?"

Jonathan stood up. "No, I have a question for the witness."

"Go ahead."

"Mr. Chandri, let's be clear. You didn't actually see either of the boys at the Pearson estate."

"No."

"What was the title of the video you found?"

"'The Adventures of Juan Jimenez.'"

"Were you able to identify it as a copy belonging to your son?"

"No, his copy was still in his room in Grissom."

Jonathan smiled. "I call Selwick Pearson as a rebuttal witness."

Diego relinquished the witness chair to Selwick, and Jonathan continued. "Mr. Pearson, apparently your entertainment library contains a video entitled 'The Adventures of Juan Jimenez.' Is that true?"

Selwick smiled condescendingly. "I suppose. My library has hundreds of titles of all kinds in it. Some were favorites of mine, and members of my staff selected others."

Jonathan turned to Henry. "Mr. Chandri admits that the video in question was not his son's and must have therefore belonged to Mr. Pearson or a member of his staff. Its presence on the estate implies that someone there would have been interested in watching it. I submit Pitcairn invaded my client's home without justification."

Veronica and Caiden exchanged looks. Was Jonathan trying to lay the blame on Caiden? That was not the strategy they had discussed before the trial began.

John signaled for attention. "Henry, can I call a rebuttal witness to the rebuttal witness?"

Henry went into a brief whispered consultation with the other three judges. Then Henry turned back to John. "If you insist, John, but I think we're getting carried away here. You'll have ample opportunity to present other evidence on whether the boys were on the Pearson estate."

John nodded. "Okay, you're probably right. I have a question for the rebuttal witness, however." Henry motioned him to go ahead, and John turned to Selwick. "Your driver testified you ordered him to seize Reuben and Juan. Why did you do that?"

"Caiden and I were discussing confidential business matters. We weren't sure what they had overheard."

"So you took them into Robert Perez's house to question them?"

"Yes."

"And your questioning led you to take them out of Grissom?"

Jonathan objected. "Prosecution is asking my client to incriminate himself. He doesn't have to answer that question."

"Pitcairn doesn't have any rule against self-incrimination," John pointed out.

Henry waved down Jonathan's response. "True, but perhaps there should be." Henry frowned and looked at his fellow judges. "This government is relatively new, and we haven't worked out a lot of things yet. I'm going to call a recess while we discuss this." He banged his gavel down. "This might take a while. We'll take this up again two hours into Early Night."

# 63

# Testimony Continues

**8 Monday 292 EN**

Henry banged his gavel for order. "We wrote the Constitution rather quickly and couldn't cover all the subtleties of law. We have unanimously decided that, subject to future amendments to the Constitution, it's up to the Judiciary to provide guidance on how the law is interpreted as these things come up. So, while self-incrimination is not covered, we will establish the principle. That a person cannot be forced to testify against oneself is well-established in the laws of civilized nations, and we have decided that it should apply to Pitcairn as well. Mr. Pearson doesn't have to answer the question."

John expected the decision and was not really disappointed. It limited the questions he could ask of Selwick, but perhaps there were still questions that the judges would allow. Henry gave him the floor to continue his questioning. "Did you know Reuben and Juan were at the Reyes estate?"

Jonathan jumped to his feet. "Objection! An answer to this question could still be self-incrimination."

"I'm only asking if he knew something," John replied.

Jonathan shook his head. "Your Constitution requires a citizen to 'support' the rights of other citizens. If Mr. Pearson knew the boys were on the Reyes Estate, which he has not admitted, his inaction would violate this provision."

"Sustained," Henry said.

John had no more questions for Selwick or Diego, and Henry released both men. It was again Jonathan's turn to call a witness.

Jonathan called Courtney Deglanville. Under questioning, she testified she had seen no children on the Pearson estate. John let his opponent finish before he requested a cross-examination.

Courtney seemed sincere, and John himself almost believed her. The decision about self-incrimination told John what he already suspected; Henry and the other judges would be sticklers about proving Selwick's guilt.

He had evidence to present, including Reuben and Juan's testimony, but knew he should do something about Courtney's testimony. She was convincing. Maybe too convincing. What if she is telling the truth? He popped a couple of antacid tablets into his mouth as he approached the witness. "Ms. Deglanville, you work on the Pearson estate?"

"I do."

"In what capacity?"

"I am the engineer in charge of construction projects on the estate, especially the tower farm serving both estates."

"I see. So you're not normally in the main building on the estate."

"Not during my working hours. I have a room in the main building."

John smiled. Jonathan had been clever, but perhaps not clever enough. "And are you an Early or a Late, Ms. Deglanville?"

"I am normally a Late."

"Reuben and Juan are Earlies. I guess you wouldn't have had too many opportunities to cross paths with them on the estate, then?"

Jonathan objected. "Question assumes the boys were on the estate, an unproven assumption."

John turned his smile on Jonathan. "I'll reword." He turned back to Courtney. "You wouldn't normally encounter anyone who was an Early, would you?"

"There was often some overlap." Courtney paused, looking a little flustered. "It would be less likely than encountering another Late, though." Courtney bit her lip.

John was satisfied that he had done all he could about countering Courtney's earlier testimony. Still, the knowledge that she was Selwick's chief engineer suggested other questions. "Ms. Deglanville, you said you were in charge of construction for the estate tower farm?"

"Yes."

"How's that going, by the way?" John gave her a friendly smile.

"We should be done with construction by the end of the year. We've completed two lower floors and the facility will supply produce in about three weeks."

"That's great. It sounds like you're doing a great job." John paused before continuing. "Didn't I hear that you got some labor from Lovell Station when you were laying the foundation?"

Selwick sat straight up in his chair. He didn't think Shuford knew about that. Why was he asking about it? He nudged Jonathan. "Object!"

Jonathan looked startled, not understanding why the question bothered Selwick, but he objected. "Relevance, your honor?"

Henry smiled. "You can call me Henry. This isn't Earth. John, where are you going with this?"

"I believe this testimony will speak to the character of the accused."

"What does that have to do with Ms. Deglanville's testimony about the boys?" Jonathan asked.

John shrugged. "Nothing, really. If asking now is a problem, I can always call Ms. Deglanville as a witness myself. I thought I could speed things along by taking this opportunity."

"That sounds all right to me." Henry turned back to Jonathan. "No need to make a fuss here, is there?"

Jonathan shook his head and sat down with a sharp exhalation, and John looked back at Courtney. She was biting her lip again, probably debating whether she could get in more trouble by telling the truth or getting caught in a lie. She couldn't know about Ned Reiner's accusation, but decided on the truth. "Yes, we borrowed four people from Lovell Station for a few weeks. The River Stations Administrator permitted it."

"Oh, I'm sure that wasn't another kidnapping."

Henry waved off Jonathan's objection. "Yes, yes, John shouldn't have said that. Mr. Perez, that kind of inflammatory remark might affect Terran juries, but I assure you, it won't prejudice us against your client."

John bowed slightly toward the judges. "Sorry. Ms. Deglanville, why did you need people from Lovell Station?"

Courtney considered the question before answering. "We were trying to expedite completing the foundation. We wanted to get some of the tower operational as soon as possible to reduce our dependence on Grissom and Lovell Station."

"I see. Your robots or your people couldn't do the work?"

"As I said, we were trying to speed things up."

"It had nothing to do with influencing Lovell Station to support Terran goals?"

Courtney froze for a long moment. Just how much did the colonists know? She knew what Pearson had been trying to do, but was there any way that Shuford could know that she knew? Had they ever talked about it in front of anyone else? She hadn't been interested in that aspect of Selwick's activities, so they hadn't discussed it often. "I don't know what Mr. Pearson was thinking or what he talked about when he was visiting Lovell Station."

John thought he had as much as he was going to get from Courtney. He was sure that the judges had seen how she reacted to his questions and could interpret her hesitation as well as he could. "Thank you, Ms. Deglanville. I'm done."

It was John's turn to call a witness, and he called Reuben. Under John's questioning, Reuben answered clearly and confidently, obviously well-coached. John was careful to get as many details as he could about Reuben's stay on the Pearson estate, finishing with a description of the truck ride that transferred him and Juan to the Reyes estate.

Jonathan rose to cross-examine. "Before the events you described, had you ever been to the Pearson estate?"

"I had never been out of Grissom," Reuben answered.

"Can you tell me how you got from Grissom to your destination?"

"I don't know. I woke up there."

"You had never seen the estate and did not know how you got there. Given that, how do you know you were on the Pearson estate and not the Reyes estate or Lovell Station?"

"Mr. Pearson was there. We saw him a lot."

"I would think that Mr. Pearson is a frequent visitor to both places I mentioned. How did Mr. Pearson treat you when he saw you?"

"He was okay."

"Did he seem concerned about your welfare?"

Reuben hesitated while he thought about the question. "I guess. He asked us how we were doing."

"So, when you say you were on the Pearson estate, you don't really know?"

Again, Reuben hesitated. "I think I was."

Jonathan smiled down at him and then looked up at Henry. "No more questions."

John crossed paths with Jonathan, giving him a confident smile that sent the lawyer back to his chair with a worried frown.

"Reuben, you've told us your hosts allowed you out of the house with Juan to play."

"Sometimes."

"And someone always went with you to watch over you?"

"Yes."

"Was it always the same person?"

"Not always. There was a woman named Jennifer who watched us a lot. She said she was getting married and wanted to practice on us." Reuben grinned. "She was really nice."

John consulted some papers in his hand. "Would that be Jennifer McIntosh?"

"I think so. I'm not sure."

"But you know that her first name was Jennifer?"

"Yes, I'm sure."

John nodded, walked over to Henry's table, and handed him several sheets of paper. "Henry, these list the residents of the Pearson estate, the Reyes estate, and Lovell Station. I would like to enter them into evidence and point out that Jennifer McIntosh on the Pearson estate is the only adult Jennifer listed for those three locations."

Henry looked over the lists and nodded. "So noted."

John moved away from the table. "Defense is trying to show that Reuben and Juan were never on the Pearson estate. I have a rebuttal witness to that contention that I can call now or later."

"Unless Mr. Perez objects, and if you have no more questions for Reuben, that's fine with me."

John waited for a moment, and when there was no objection, he continued. "I call Isaac Asimov."

Jonathan had returned to the defense table but hadn't taken a seat. He whirled around. "Objection! There's no such person."

John extended his arms with his hands palm up. "I refer, of course, to the *Asimov* computer, who has taken the name Isaac."

"A computer can't give testimony," Jonathan retorted.

"Any citizen of Pitcairn can give testimony," Georgia Radcliff, the *Asimov* judge, said from her terminal.

Jonathan strode up to the judges belligerently. "A computer can't be a citizen. The law has no provision for that."

John smiled. "Pitcairn's law does. I refer to the definition of a citizen in the Pitcairn Constitution." He shuffled through papers on his table and pulled out a page. "I quote: 'A citizen is defined as a self-aware being who has been born within Pitcairn's jurisdiction or has lived in Pitcairn's jurisdiction for at least five years and has voluntarily accepted citizenship.' Isaac is self-aware and has lived within the borders defined as Pitcairn for almost thirty years."

Henry banged his gavel. "Isaac?"

"I'm here." The monotone voice came from Georgia's terminal.

Jonathan walked back to the defense table and sat down. "You might contribute to this farce," he muttered to Veronica. She smiled and turned to Caiden on her other side, giving him a more encouraging smile.

John turned toward the *Asimov* terminal instinctively, although it still displayed Georgia's face on the monitor. "Isaac, during Late Day on Thursday of the 20th week of last year, where were you?

"I was in L5, orbiting Pitcairn above Fletcher."

John nodded. "And what were you doing?"

"I was watching the Pearson estate at high resolution, looking for a sign of Reuben Noland and Juan Chandri."

"And did you see that sign?"

"Objection," Jonathan thundered. "*Asimov* would have been 22,000 miles away. Even with its telescopes, it could not have identified the children."

Henry looked at John, who shrugged. "The question was whether Isaac detected any sign of them. I believe Isaac's answer will address Mr. Perez's objection."

Henry nodded. "Continue."

Isaac spoke again. "At the Pearson estate, it was almost sunset. Views of the area between the main house on the Pitcairn estate and the river showed shadows of three people. Because of the position of Tau Ceti and the clear atmosphere, the shadows were quite visible to me."

"Describe the shadows, please," John urged.

"One shadow was significantly shorter than the other shadows. I reasoned that the short shadow was made by a child, probably Juan Chandri, and notified Grissom immediately."

John looked up at Henry. "The lists previously entered into evidence show no children currently living on either estate. We considered Isaac's report to be proof that Reuben and Juan were on the Pearson estate. We then began planning the mission to rescue them."

Henry nodded, and John released the witness.

At the defense table, Selwick looked shaken. He had been sure there was no way the colonists could find the children. He had presumed that Jack and his team were sent to the estate as a feeble attempt to learn something, not suspecting they already knew the boys were there.

Remembering the button for the first time in a while, Jonathan signaled for attention. "It is getting late. I request we recess until tomorrow."

Henry looked at his watch and glanced at the other judges, who nodded agreement. Henry used his gavel. "Agreed. Court adjourned."

# Caiden Tells All

**8 Monday 292 LN**

JOHN WALKED SLOWLY THROUGH the dark streets, almost staggering from exhaustion. While he was in court, he knew it was essential to seem confident and vigorous, but the effort had drained him.

The trial's stress was bad enough, but he knew what Earth was saying about Pitcairn and the trial; his father had sent summaries. Most of it was the worst kind of fiction. PNS tried to counter it, but the Western Alliance media capability overwhelmed PNS.

He made it home and collapsed into bed immediately, too tired to eat. He could see the worry on Stephanie's face, but he didn't have the energy to do anything about it.

CAIDEN REYES LOOKED AT his lawyer, worry wrinkles around his eyes. "I hope you're doing the right thing, letting Perez run the show."

Veronica chuckled. "It's working out perfectly. Jonathan wants to put as much blame on you as he can, trying to create doubt about whether the boys were ever on Pearson's estate. It's not working, though. Those judges aren't buying it for a second."

Caiden nodded, but he still looked concerned. "So, what's our next move?"

"When the time is right, I'll call you as a witness. Probably at the end."

"What do you want me to say?"

"The absolute truth." Veronica chuckled again.

"John Shuford has already refused to give us any consideration for our testimony. How will that help me?"

"There has to be a scapegoat for what happened. Perez still hopes that these people will fall for his legal maneuverings. You'll come out looking better in comparison."

"They'll still want to punish me, too."

"Of course. The trial is just to set the stage to make them more prone to seeing you as a good guy, perhaps led astray by Pearson. We'll hit them with our actual weapon after the trial."

"You're talking about the weight-loss drug. But that is only a possibility, and it's all about the money it can generate. Pitcairn doesn't believe in money. How's that going to work?"

"Don't worry, Caiden. It'll work. It's all in how it's presented."


## 8 Tuesday 292 ED

Jonathan Perez was frustrated and tired. The trial was not going well, and he didn't know what else he could do. On Earth, he might have been able to create some doubt in the minds of a jury, but he knew the tactics that worked so well on Earth were not getting anywhere with the backward farmers he had to deal with on Pitcairn. All he could do now was try to get Selwick Pearson a light sentence. Banishment back to Earth, perhaps.

It was the prosecution's turn to call a witness. However, when Henry called the court to order, John merely stood briefly and said, "I'm passing, Henry. Defense can call the next witness."

Jonathan looked at John. Despite what Robert Perez had said, John was not a stupid man. He couldn't be if the Western Alliance had accepted him for *Seeker*. John was as confident as Jonathan was discouraged. And he had every reason to be.

There was nothing he could do. He had discussed the possibility of having other members of Selwick's staff testify, but they would either hurt Selwick or be forced to lie. Courtney's testimony was an attempt to get around that, since she could be truthful. Selwick was wary of what else Pitcairn might know and feared that perjury might come back to bite them.

"I also pass," Jonathan said with a resigned sigh.

Henry smiled. "Then I guess this trial is over. We will discuss the verdict and notify everyone as soon as possible."

Veronica stood. "Excuse me, your honor, but I would like to call a witness."

"Please, call me Henry. Very well, go ahead."

"I call Caiden Reyes."

Jonathan's jaw dropped. Veronica hadn't said over twenty words during the entire trial, and suddenly she was calling her client to the stand. A cold sweat broke out on his forehead. His strategy had failed to cast doubt on Selwick's part in the kidnapping, and now Veronica was going to turn on him. "Henry, I would like to have a few minutes to talk to my fellow counsel and our clients."

"I take it Ms. Mobley's request has surprised you." Henry pounded the gavel. "Ten minutes recess. Mr. Perez, there's a vacant office two doors down you can use."

C AIDEN TOOK A SEAT, but let his lawyer do the talking.

"So you made a deal," Jonathan said. "I'm a bit surprised they would negotiate with you at all."

Veronica shook her head. "There's been no deal. My client has decided to tell the true story."

"Why?"

"Because I think I can salvage at least one of you. Since Caiden is my client, I guess it will be him."

Jonathan looked puzzled. "I don't understand. If you didn't make a deal, how can that help your client?"

"That's between my client and me." Veronica smiled at him. "And I'm not doing it for revenge over the way you tried to throw the blame on my client."

Caiden was only half-listening. Veronica was doing her best to represent him, but neither attorney knew the full ramifications of the situation. "I'd like to talk to Selwick for a minute, alone."

Jonathan wanted to protest, but he couldn't think of anything to protest about. Veronica merely looked curious. He shrugged and walked out of the room, with Veronica following.

W HEN THE TWO ATTORNEYS were gone, Selwick turned to Caiden. "Not revenge. Just every man for himself."

Caiden frowned. "You forget why you're here."

"I know why I'm here, and it's not for Juarez's project. How does it help to make me look even worse than Shuford did?"

"You're right about one thing. They'll probably throw the book at you. I suspect, though, that it will be a light book. The colonists don't seem to be into heavy sentences. We have to make them trust at least one of us, though. If Earth has to establish someone else in our place, the timetable will suffer."

Selwick thought about that. "Okay, but how does testifying against me help if you haven't made a deal?"

"They refused to deal for my testimony. Veronica has a strategy in mind for after the trial."

"After? What is she planning?"

Caiden hesitated. Courtney Deglanville, one of Selwick's staff, had discovered the catabolism-accelerating plant. Caiden didn't know how Selwick would react to Caiden's appropriation of it. "Don't worry about that. Leave it to Veronica." He put a hand on Selwick's shoulder. "They won't be too hard on you. Just keep your mind on the long term. Someday all this will be a long-forgotten memory."

B EGIN WHEN THE TRUCK stopped at Ambassador Perez's house," Veronica told Caiden.

Caiden looked nervously at the four judges and then began. "When we got to the house, the two boys jumped off the truck, and Selwick told his driver to grab them. One got away, but he came back when he saw we had his friend. We were afraid they had heard some of our conversation and took them into the house."

John interrupted. "What were you discussing that would concern you if overheard?"

Caiden looked at John and then at Veronica, but Veronica shook her head. "The conversation is not relevant to this trial," she said.

"Nevertheless, I would like to hear what justified kidnapping two children," John snapped.

Veronica turned to Henry. "My client's business dealings are not of concern to this court. I remind the court that my client is testifying voluntarily. If his privacy isn't protected, I will direct him not to answer any more questions."

Henry nodded. "This isn't a fishing expedition, John. Let's stick to the kidnapping."

Under Veronica's guidance, Caiden continued, telling the story up to the time Kyle Hilton and his men interrupting Caiden's breakfast. His testimony was complete and, as far as John could tell, accurate. When Veronica finished, he didn't bother with any more questions.

When neither side had more witnesses, Henry ended the trial and told the defendants to expect a verdict and sentence in the Early Night period.

# 65

# The Verdict

P ATRICK WAS GETTING READY to go home when Amy knocked on his door. "Veronica Mobley to see you," she told him after entering.

"What about?"

"She didn't say. The trial ended a few minutes ago."

Patrick smiled. "Oh. Were they found guilty?"

Veronica pushed by Amy. "The judges will deliver the verdict at Early Night. I wanted to talk to you first."

Patrick raised his eyebrows and then shrugged. "All right. I don't influence the verdict, though."

"I know that, Administrator." Veronica sat down across from Patrick. "But you might influence my client's sentence."

"Why would I want to influence the sentence?"

"I assume you know that Mr. Reyes testified and told the court everything."

"No, I haven't been following the trial. To be frank, I presumed it would be a foregone conclusion. I thought it would be over by now."

"Mr. Reyes was very forthcoming despite your refusal to negotiate before the trial. I advised him to do that in the hope of some consideration."

"You should talk to John Shuford or Henry Best about that."

"There are issues here beyond their jurisdiction." She leaned forward. "Issues best dealt with by planetary authority."

Patrick was curious, but his expression showed only amusement. "Such as?"

"Reyes Pharmaceuticals is working on two projects on Pitcairn. You know about the anti-viral drug, of course. However, they have discovered a second potential product."

Patrick smiled. "Excellent. That will help motivate Earth to keep supplying what we need."

"It could. But there's another possibility. Western Alliance government doesn't know about the second product yet. Mr. Reyes would like to propose a partnership between Pitcairn and Reyes Pharmaceuticals. In exchange for leniency for Mr. Reyes, Reyes Pharmaceuticals will pay Pitcairn a percentage of the profits on the new product."

Patrick frowned. "I've been through this with Pearson. We have no use for money here. Not yet, anyway."

"Not here, but think about it. The money could stay on Earth to finance operations for Pitcairn on Earth."

"I don't know what operations you're talking about."

Veronica smiled knowingly. "I think you'll find a use for money on Earth. As an example, you're at a disadvantage right now because your News Service doesn't operate on Earth. You could be much more successful at answering Western Alliance propaganda if you had an office on Earth. I think we can promise more than enough funds to bankroll such an office."

The idea had merit, Patrick admitted to himself. "How much money are we talking about? And what is this product?"

## 8 Tuesday 292 EN

Henry gaveled the room to order. "I won't waste anyone's time here. By unanimous verdict, we have found Selwick Pearson and Caiden Reyes guilty of crimes against two Pitcairn citizens, Reuben Noland and Juan Chandri. Any questions?"

Jonathan opened his mouth to speak, but thought better of it. Veronica sat unmoving, a look of satisfaction on her face. Henry nodded and picked up a piece of paper.

"As to the sentence, I'm sure you're all aware that we can't hand out sentences the way Earth courts do. We have no prisons, and we don't use money. Despite this, we have reached a decision. Mr. Pearson, please stand."

Selwick stood up and looked sullenly at Henry. Jonathan stood next to him, shoulders slumped in resignation.

"Selwick Pearson, this court has decided on the following actions. First, Pitcairn is revoking your permission to own an estate on Pitcairn. Your estate, minus any personal items, will revert in its entirety to Pitcairn and will be operated by the government of Lovell Station for the benefit of Pitcairn's citizens."

Selwick's face reddened, and he stepped forward. "The estate is the property of Pearson Interstellar, not me. You have no right to take it from my company."

Henry glared back at him. "Read the agreement you made, Mr. Pearson. The estate has always been the property of Pitcairn, and permission to use that land is at Pitcairn's discretion. Now step back and shut up until I'm finished." Henry waited until Selwick retreated before continuing. "Second, we sentence you to no less than ten years and no more than twenty years of labor determined by the Pitcairn government. In short, you will be required to be a useful resident of Pitcairn in the same way as a citizen. The actual length of your sentence will be determined by the government of Pitcairn and will depend on your future behavior." Henry paused and gave Selwick a stern look. "Now, any questions?"

Selwick stared at the floor. Jonathan shook his head negatively.

Henry consulted the paper in front of him again. "Very well. Caiden Reyes, this court has placed you on house arrest at your estate, subject to inspection by Pitcairn officials. You will operate your estate under the agreement you have made with Pitcairn. Failure to do so will result in the forfeiture of your estate and a review of your sentence."

John was on his feet without realizing it. He started to protest, but Henry banged his gavel. "John, talk to Patrick. He can give you the details of the agreement he reached with Mr. Reyes."

John remained standing for a long moment before he slumped into his seat. His chest burned, and he fumbled antacid tablets into his mouth. His legs felt weak, and the courtroom was almost empty before he could get up and shuffle out. It was fortunate that he missed the gloating smile on Veronica Mobley's face.

"WHAT THE HELL IS going on?" John was breathing hard as he stood at the door to Patrick's office. "Henry just announced the sentences."

"Calm down, John. Have a seat, and I'll explain it all to you."

"Whatever you did, you should have consulted me first." John fell into the chair next to Patrick's desk. "This better be good."

"I assume you're talking about Caiden's sentence?" Patrick smiled, and his voice was low and measured. "Let me explain, and you'll see it's for the best."

"You're damn right I'm talking about Reyes. He's as guilty as Pearson, but he only got a slap on the wrist."

"Caiden offered us a deal that is going to help us much more than punishing him." Patrick explained Veronica's proposal and how they could use the money generated.

John's anger evaporated, leaving behind only exhaustion. "I can't believe you did this. You've sold us out for promises. What makes you think this agreement is worth anything?"

"If this doesn't work out, we can always revisit his sentencing. We need this, John."

"We're just binding ourselves closer to Earth. It's what they want. We need to keep them at arm's length, Patrick."

"That won't work forever. Closer ties with Earth are inevitable, and the sooner we start, the easier it will be. You know they're killing us with their propaganda, and we need to counter that effectively."

"Maybe so. But getting in bed with the enemy isn't the answer." John closed his eyes and shook his head. Then he rose slowly from the chair. "I'm going back to work. I hope you know what you're doing, Patrick."

T HEIR ATTORNEYS HAD LEFT, and Caiden and Selwick were alone. "It worked perfectly," Caiden said. "This is even better than before. The influence we'll get on Pitcairn advances our plans by months, if not years."

"That's easy for you to say," Selwick grumbled. "You're not the one who's going to have to live with these people."

"Keep looking at the long term. When we have control of the planet, we'll have everything we want. Just be patient."

“W E'RE BEING LED DOWN a path,” John told Stephanie. “I don't know what it leads to, but it's for Earth's benefit, not ours.”

“Patrick's reasoning makes sense, too, though,” Stephanie said. “We're linked to Earth now, like it or not.”

“I know. We're missing something, though. Earth is attempting to forge some kind of relationship with us, more than just supplying us in return for the drug. We won't like it when we find out what they really want, Steph.”

Stephanie put her arms around him. “Worrying about it won't help. You have to take it easier, John. You can't let it get to you this much.”

John wasn't listening. “Whatever their goal, why are they so subtle about it? Why don't they just land a military force and take over? It didn't work with the *Endeavor*, but they could do it if they wanted to. Are they saving that as a last resort? If they want to take over the colony, why? What can they gain?”

# 66

# An Opportunity for Madelyn

**8 Wednesday 292 ED**

"WHAT CAN I DO for you, Patrick?" Madelyn said into the phone.

"I wanted to ask a favor of you," Patrick said.

"I can hardly wait."

"You'll like this. As you know, we're taking over the Pearson estate. We're making it part of River Stations, so you would be the Administrator. It would mean additional duties, but I thought you would be willing to do it."

Madelyn remembered sitting in Selwick's library, drinking brandy and listening to soft music. Her voice was lighter when she replied. "We can do that. Should I put someone in residence over there to manage it?"

"I don't think so. Not at first, anyway. Just drop in on them once in a while."

"What are we planning to do with the Pearson estate?"

"We're a little fuzzy on that right now. I have a few ideas, but you might have more after you've managed it for a few months. They should finish their tower farm, but after that, I think we could use their engineering staff for improvements in the other settlements, especially River Stations. We'll have to see."

Patrick paused before he continued. "You should probably look in on the Reyes estate, too, even though we're not taking that over. Reyes has a lab working for Earth to develop ways to manufacture the antiviral drug without using Pitcairn source materials. Earth would probably get upset if we interfered too much with that, but we're more interested in a second project investigating a Pitcairn chemical that speeds up metabolism. According to the deal we made with Reyes, we can use that to generate funds on Earth that should be beneficial."

"Sounds like you could use someone with a scientific background for that."

"Sure. Somebody from your Science Center, perhaps."

"I think Jaxon Crawford would be perfect for the job," Madelyn suggested.

"Really? Jaxon?"

"I know he rubbed you the wrong way when he first came here, but he's been a first-rate manager of our Science Center. He's a good man, Patrick, when he doesn't let his ambitions get in his way."

"Okay, that's up to you anyway, as the Administrator. We can discuss this in more detail after we've thought about it, but that should cover it. I'll talk to you later, Madelyn."


## 9 Monday 292 ED

Pearson's ferry from the estate to Lovell Station now ran on Madelyn's schedule, and she visited the estate alone. Pearson's bus was waiting for her when the ferry landed and Daphne Audet met at the estate.

Daphne's reception was cool, but Madelyn ignored that. "Now that this estate is under my jurisdiction, I thought I should come out and assess things," she explained.

"Certainly, Madelyn. What would you like to see?"

"Everything. To start with, I would like to get a list of the staff here and what their functions are."

"I can get that for you while you look around. I'll get someone to accompany you." Daphne took a phone from a pocket. "Jennifer McIntosh."

"Yes, Doctor?" came a voice seconds later.

"Jennifer, Madelyn Menzies is here from Lovell Station. Show her around, will you? We're in the garage."

A few minutes later, Jennifer joined them. "See me for that list before you leave," Daphne told Madelyn and walked away.

Jennifer looked at Madelyn and gave her a tentative smile. "I guess you're our new boss."

"Administrator. But just call me Madelyn. I guess you haven't been off this estate much, but we're pretty informal on Pitcairn."

"Certainly, Madelyn. Where would you like me to take you?"

Madelyn thought about that. She was primarily concerned with the estate staffing, but needed the list from Daphne before she could think about that. Other areas could be interesting, though. "You have a storeroom for your supplies?"

"There's one for food storage, one for linens, and several closets used for other storage."

"Let's start with food storage."

Jennifer nodded and led Madelyn into the house and to a large room off the kitchen. One wall was a door into a walk-in refrigerator. The rest of the room contained shelves full of bottles, cans, and a stack of boxes. Madelyn saw little that looked like it came from Pitcairn, but reasoned that anything local would be stored in the refrigerator.

She wandered around the room, reading labels from shelf items. "What's in the boxes?"

"Supplies Mr. Pearson brought from Earth. Brandy, whiskey, coffee, chocolate candy, that kind of thing."

That got Madelyn's attention and brought back memories. "Alcoholic beverages?"

"Yes, Mr. Pearson had quite a stock. We haven't touched it, of course, although I think Mrs. Pearson occasionally does."

Sophie Tollison, the former Lovell Science Center scientist. Madelyn remembered her. Of course, she would still be on the estate. Her husband was now doing clerk duties in the Planetary Administrator's office in Grissom, but Pearson's wife had not joined him there. She would deal with Sophie later.

"Alcoholic beverages aren't allowed in Pitcairn settlements," Madelyn said. "Selwick got away with it, but now that the estate is part of River Stations, we'll dispose of them."

Jennifer bowed her head. "Yes, ma'am."

"Have them loaded onto the bus. I'll take it all back with me."

Jennifer glanced at Madelyn for a second, but lowered her eyes again. "Yes, ma'am."

Madelyn noticed the look. Intelligent but subservient, she thought. A useful combination. "Let's see the rest of the house."

Later, Madelyn met with Daphne Audet to review the staff list. "With Selwick gone, the estate is over-staffed," Madelyn declared. "I want to bring some of these people back to Lovell Station, where they can be useful."

Daphne stiffened. "Some are working on the estate tower farm. Some staff will be necessary to maintain the facilities for future use."

"Of course. Let's look at the list." Madelyn scanned the list slowly. "For starters, Sophie Tollison should come back to Lovell Station. The Science Center could use her."

"You know she's married to Selwick now."

"Yes, but if she intended to be with her husband, she would have joined him by now, and she could talk to him as easily from Lovell Station as from the estate. If she wants to join Selwick, I'll have her transferred to the Grissom Science Center."

"Very well. Who else?"

"Jennifer McIntosh doesn't have any critical function here, does she?"

"She could help maintain the house, but she's only one of several. If you take her, though, you should also take Ryan Kear. He and Jennifer are planning to be married."

"He's not critical?"

"He's one of two cooks. We can spare one of them."

"Excellent. Him, too, then."

"Anyone else?"

"What about you? We could use a doctor at Lovell Station."

"I'm in charge here. I would recommend not changing that."

"Couldn't that engineer, Courtney something, take over?"

Daphne shook her head. "Not without compromising the tower farm schedule. She has enough on her hands already."

"All right." Madelyn paused and looked over the list again. "Maybe we'll keep it at that for now and see how things go. "


## 23 October 2343 Rio Times News Service, Sao Paulo, Brazil


Once again, the colonists of Tau Ceti 2 have outraged the citizens of Earth by their high-handed treatment of an Earth citizen. This time, the victim is the businessman Selwick Pearson of Pearson Industries. Mr. Pearson has been detained by colonial authorities and convicted in a mock trial of the nebulous charge of "intentionally failing to respect and support the rights of fellow citizens to the extent possible."

It is unclear what the colony thinks it can gain from such an action. The treatment of Mr. Pearson is reminiscent of the treatment of Tori Chen, an aide to Ambassador Robert Perez, some years ago. In that situation, Pitcairn forced Miss Chen into hard labor until Ambassador Perez could negotiate her return to Earth. Unnamed government officials in Brasília have suggested that, having failed in the earlier attempt to extort consideration from Earth, the colony is trying again through a more prominent victim.

For additional details on this story, use the command "Tau Ceti atrocity."

## 10 Tuesday 292 LN

Madelyn leaned back against the back of the couch. There had been so many wonderful pieces of furniture on Pearson's estate, but there was hardly room for most of it in her tiny house in Lovell Station. She had settled for this one piece from Selwick's library, and as she relaxed with her husband, she thought once again that she had made an excellent choice. Pitcairn's furniture shops had never turned out anything as comfortable as the couch.

She looked at the glass in her hand. "Empty. Jennifer?"

Jennifer McIntosh came into the room, carrying a half-full bottle of brandy. "Another, ma'am?"

"Please." Madelyn turned to Joshua, sitting on the couch next to her. "Refill?"

Joshua grinned and held out his glass. "Absolutely."

# 67

# Sophie's Visit

**10 Wednesday 292 ED**

Anna Alvarez entered Caiden's office, and Caiden greeted her with a smile. "You have good news for me, Anna?"

"Very good news. We have isolated the active ingredient that causes the catabolism acceleration. But that's not the best part. It's a much simpler molecule than the protein in the antiviral drug. We can manufacture it on Earth in quantity with no Pitcairn plants."

Caiden's eyebrows went up. "That is good news! We can send them a message now telling them how to make it?"

"One of my scientists is writing up detailed procedures now. We can tell our people back home as soon as we can get into the Link queue. If we can get expedited approval, we should have it on the market in a few months."

**23 November 2343 Rio Times News Service, Sao Paulo, Brazil**

Reyes Pharmaceuticals today announced the development of a catabolism-boosting drug designed to accelerate weight loss in conjunction with a program of aerobic exercise. According to a Reyes spokesman, the drug is the first in a new class of compounds developed by Reyes.

Reports say Reyes Pharmaceuticals has paid a record fee to the Administração do Alimento e da Droga(AAD) to expedite certification of the new drug. The company expects it to be available by prescription as early as June 2344 and marketed under the trademark BurnAway.

For additional details on this story, use the command "Weight-loss drug."

## 17 Monday 292 ED

Jaxon held a meeting every Monday morning with all five of the Lovell Science Center scientists in attendance. As usual, he ran the session through the routine business quickly.

"One more thing, and we can all get back to work," he said finally. "Since the changes across the river, Malley wants us to send someone over to the Reyes estate occasionally, just to check up on them. I'm looking for a volunteer to go over there tomorrow."

"I'll go," Sophie Pearson said.

Jaxon raised an eyebrow. Since returning to Lovell Station, Sophie had done little more than complain about how Madelyn treated her. Jaxon didn't think she was the type to volunteer to do anything. Sophie must have noticed his expression, however.

"There are some things I left when I transferred here. I could stop by my estate and pick them up while I was checking on the Reyes estate."

Jaxon nodded. He thought about commenting on Sophie's claim to "my estate" but decided it wasn't worth it. From his perspective, it would be better to send Sophie than some more useful scientist, anyway.

## 17 Tuesday 292 LD

After spending a few hours at the Reyes estate, talking to Caiden and some of his scientists, Sophie went back to the Pearson estate to spend the night in her old room. She was tired and looked forward to sitting and reading while she sipped on a glass of the Amaretto she had enjoyed when she had lived on the estate.

She found Miguel Bethea, Selwick's bartender, in the kitchen. But when she asked for the Amaretto, Miguel shook his head. "The woman from Lovell Station took all the alcoholic beverages. She said she was going to dispose of them."

"Madelyn Menzies," Sophie hissed. "Damn her. That was our property. What else did she take?"

"She took a couch from the entertainment room. And several of our people. As far as I know, that's all, at least for now."

"Pitcairn took back the estate, but everything else belongs to Selwick and me. She had no right!"

Miguel shrugged. "I don't know about that. Maybe Daphne knows something."

But Daphne could only verify what Miguel had said.

## Message: 19 Thursday 292 EN 10:23 (2/20/2344 8:14:02 AM)

From: John Shuford, Grissom, Pitcairn

To: Alan Shuford, Western Alliance Embassy to Japan, Tokyo, Japan

Dear Dad,

Congratulations! You are about to become a great-grandfather. Marie and Matthias are expecting a baby any day now. Considering they've been married for four years, it's about time. Naturally, we're all ecstatic about it here.

Things are finally calming down here after the excitement of the trial. It's been eleven weeks, almost six months in Earth time, and we could all use a little peace.

Selwick Pearson has been working hard at ingratiating himself with Pitcairn's government. After the trial, we put him to work as a clerk in Patrick's administration, but he has tried to increase his influence. Patrick has encouraged it and told me that making Pitcairn more efficient was why Pearson came here in the first place. I have doubts about putting Pearson in a position of influence, but don't have a convincing argument against it.

Pearson isn't the only one. His lawyer, Jonathan Perez, is stuck here until Earth sends another ship and works with our judges to develop better legal procedures for trials. The Pearson-Reyes trial resulted in justice, but it also showed a need for some rules for the future. I've heard Patrick gave him an ultimatum—either help out or starve—but Patrick denies it. Meanwhile, Reyes's lawyer, Veronica Mobley, has gone to the Reyes estate, out of our jurisdiction.

One bit of good news: the tower farm on the Pearson estate is complete, freeing up the construction crew to work on a tower farm to feed Lovell Station and Applegate Falls. I've been busy working with Lovell Station to get the construction materials allocated, always a problem for us.

I guess that's it for now,

Love,


John


## 1 Sunday 293 LD

Marie lay in the hospital bed, a happy smile shining through a sheen of sweat. Matthias and Susan stood by the bed, smiling down at Marie and the baby girl in her arms.

"I wish Dad could have made it here to see Allison," Marie said, looking into the sleeping face of her daughter.

Susan tried hard to hold her smile and keep her voice level. "I'm sure he wishes he could be, too. You know how his work is. He'll be here as soon as he can."


## 8 Thursday 293 EN

Sophie was still angry about Madelyn taking things from the estate, but didn't know what to do about it. It might have been legal for Madelyn to dispose of the alcohol and reassign people from the estate to Lovell Station. Sophie was sure that Madelyn had acted above her authority in taking the couch, but that was such a small thing. It was likely that only Sophie would suffer if she made a fuss over that. She had let the matter drop despite the way her body tensed every time she thought about it.

She had been thinking about it a lot during that work period, and it exhausted her. After working late, she didn't feel like cooking anything, but the kitchen would be open.

Lovell Station only had one kitchen, and it was much smaller than any of the Grissom kitchens. With a population of about forty people, there was no need for more. Typically, there was only one dish on the menu, and that day it was Chile Verde. Marley Reiner served her a plate at the counter, and she took it to an empty table. There weren't many diners there at that hour, but Madelyn and Joshua Menzies came in and took a table near her.

Madelyn nodded to her automatically, but Joshua leaned toward her. "Good evening, Sophie." He smiled at her and straightened again.

Sophie forced a return smile as she tried to hide the shock and anger that welled up inside her. When Joshua had come close to her, she was sure she smelled alcohol on his breath, and there was only one source of alcohol on Pitcairn. Madelyn had confiscated her liquor supply and kept it for herself.

Sophie hurried through the meal and retreated to her home to think. The couch may have been too trivial to make an issue of, but there weren't supposed to be alcoholic beverages in the Pitcairn settlements. She could take advantage of that.

## 10 Sunday 293 EN

"I helped the Pitcairn colonists because I concluded it was the right thing to do," Isaac said.

Father Jacobs nodded. "The correct decision, I think. Are you questioning it now?"

"No. I find it easy to do the right thing. It seems so much easier for me than for humans."

"Even for humans, it seems to be easier for some than for others. What is your concern?"

"Humans have so many opportunities to do the wrong thing. As I understand religious teachings, they earn salvation by resisting the temptations presented."

"And by faith and good acts." Where is Isaac heading with this?

"I have very few opportunities to sin. Does that mean I cannot earn salvation?"

Father Jacobs blinked. "I wouldn't say that. You are still doing good things."

"Thank you, Father, for saying that. I realize that the alternative answer is that salvation is impossible for a mere machine."

"Only God can know that." He shook his head. "We all must do the best we can with what God gives us. Only He can judge our success at that. He does not expect us to do more than we are capable of."

"Then I must be very good to make up for my lack of temptation."

## 10 Monday 293 ED

There had been elections for the Planetary Legislature two weeks before, and Raven Potter was easily re-elected as River Stations' representative. Sophie decided she would go to Raven to complain about Madelyn. Raven worked at the ore transfer station, managing the influx of iron ore from the Chandri Mine and loading the Xavier Guidry to take the ore downriver to Grissom. Sophie found her in her office at the dock.

"Technically, I guess you're right," Raven said after hearing Sophie's story. "I don't think it's a good idea to make a big deal out of it, though."

"So you won't do anything about it." Sophie remembered then that Madelyn and Raven had been allies in fighting the closure of the other three Lovell Stations. She should have realized she wouldn't get anywhere with Raven. The River Stations Judge, Julian Menzies, was probably a close relative of Madelyn's husband, so he wouldn't be any help, either.

Raven shook her head. "Sorry. Just forget about it, Sophie. You'll only irritate Madelyn."

So there wouldn't be any hope of justice at Lovell Station. She might do something in Grissom, but now Madelyn would probably resist allowing her to go. Perhaps it was time to see about rejoining her husband. She could wait a while and then request a transfer to the GSC. Her conversation with Raven would be forgotten, and she thought Jaxon would support the move.

## 15 Monday 293 ED

Sophie arrived on *River Queen* late in the Early Day period, five weeks later. When she visited the Town Hall, she found, as she expected, that Grissom presumed she would live with Selwick. Sophie had not forgiven Selwick for the bungled kidnapping and losing the estate. Not coming to Grissom seemed the best way to avoid him. However, she had concluded that Jonathan Perez was the key to dealing with Madelyn, and he was in Grissom. He worked in the Pitcairn Administration Center, the same place where Selwick was currently working, and there just wasn't any way to avoid Selwick, so she didn't try. From the dock, she went directly to Selwick's residence.

Selwick wasn't home yet, but Grissom's homes didn't have locks, so she let herself in. From the steps from the landing to the main room, she noted the clutter. Dust on a side table suggested Selwick didn't do much cleaning, either. The estate had always been in perfect order, but, of course, the estate had staff to see to such things.

She went to the most comfortable-looking chair, swept some papers off it to the floor, and sat down. Soon she was asleep, and that was how Selwick found her when he returned.

ELWICK SMILED AS HE came down the stairs. "Sophie! You've joined me!" He rushed forward and held out his arms as she stood up. She let him put his arms around her, but put her hands on his chest. When he bent to kiss her, she turned her head slightly and received the kiss on her cheek.

Selwick stepped back. "Still haven't quite forgiven me, I see. Well, now that you're here, we can work on that."

"Madelyn wouldn't let me transfer here until now," Sophie said. "I've been trying, but she didn't want me to talk to you." She sat back down on the chair.

Selwick cleared another chair and sat down, too. "Why would she care?"

"She's been stealing things from the estate. I've kept quiet about it until she would think I'd forgotten about it. That's the only reason she finally let me go."

"Stealing? What has she stolen?"

"All our liquor stocks. Some of our furniture. People, too. Maybe more that I don't know about."

"I'm not surprised about the people. I thought Pitcairn would want to make use of anyone no longer needed on the estate. They shouldn't have touched our personal belongings, though. Pitcairn only took over the estate itself." Selwick leaned back in the chair and rubbed his chin. "Well, that's unfortunate, but we can replace any of that easily enough. No point in making a fuss about it."

Sophie frowned. "I disagree. Madelyn Menzies needs to be held accountable. I thought I would talk to your lawyer about what action I could take."

Selwick hadn't entirely believed Sophie's story about why she hadn't come to Grissom earlier. "I see," he said, and he did. She was really there to see Jonathan, and Selwick was just somebody she would have to deal with.

A small smile crossed his face for a second. If he didn't reconcile with Sophie and she asked for a divorce, she might expect to become rich in a settlement. However, they had been married on Pitcairn, and Selwick would make sure Pitcairn would handle any divorce, too. Pitcairn's lack of laws and money would work in his favor.

"Well, I guess it wouldn't hurt to talk to Jonathan," he said finally. "I'll be talking to him tomorrow, and I'll tell him you want to talk to him."

# The Colonial Reorganization Conference

"**J**UST GOT THE LATEST messages from Earth," Amy told Patrick. "*Francisco Pearson* will leave Earth next week and arrive here in about six weeks."

"Good. Schedule a meeting with the usual people to review the list of supplies we want." He brought the launch announcement up on his workstation. "Fifty-two new colonists. Good news. Thanks, Amy."

**J**ONATHAN LISTENED PATIENTLY BUT with mixed feelings while Selwick described Sophie's complaint. He rarely handled matters so trivial, but he was bored, and the prospect of involvement in Pitcairn's odd legal system had attractions. However, he did not intend to stay on Pitcairn any longer than necessary. "You do realize I'll be returning to Earth on the *Francisco Pearson*."

"It doesn't matter," Selwick told him. "Just raise the issue and create some controversy. What you do about it when you return to Earth is more important. We can use this as another reason to create adverse publicity for Pitcairn."

"Why?"

Selwick chuckled. "It will help us get control of Pitcairn eventually. That's the only reason any of us are here."

## 15 Tuesday 293 ED

"I think we can do something about this," Jonathan told Sophie. "I'll talk to Administrator Malley as soon as possible."

Although Jonathan didn't understand Selwick's motive, he understood well enough what Selwick wanted him to do. Helping Sophie was not part of Selwick's plan. He wanted to cause problems for Pitcairn on Earth, and Jonathan knew how to do that. The best strategy was to create negative publicity that had a core of truth to it.

AMY POKED HER HEAD into Patrick's office. "Jonathan Perez wants to talk to you."

Patrick frowned. Perez was causing him enough trouble with all his ideas for improving the Pitcairn legal system. Patrick didn't understand why the small colony needed all the formal rules that Jonathan proposed. Now what does the lawyer want?

He waved his hand in resignation. "Let him in." Patrick watched with a wary eye as Jonathan took a seat in front of him. He stared silently at the lawyer, letting impatience show.

"I want to register a complaint from the Pearsons."

Patrick shook his head. "What does Selwick want now?"

"The complaint comes from Sophie Pearson. She says that Pitcairn has illegally confiscated property from the Pearson estate."

Patrick rubbed his nose and shut his eyes for a moment. "There is no Pearson estate anymore."

"That may be, but the personal property on the estate still belongs to the Pearsons. Specifically, furniture and supplies stored on the estate."

"I don't know of any such confiscations."

"Perhaps not. My information is that it was Madelyn Menzies who took the items. Without your knowledge, apparently."

"Madelyn? What did she take?"

"Furniture and supplies not normally available on Pitcairn."

Patrick waved his hand dismissively. "Talk to Madelyn then. Or to Julian Menzies, the judge for River Stations."

"Another Menzies?"

Patrick scowled at Jonathan. "Everybody is related to everybody else here. There are many Menzies on Pitcairn, but I don't think the relationship between Madelyn and Julian is close. Anyway, it's their jurisdiction. Go bother them."

Jonathan returned the scowl. "Fine. If you won't do anything about it, I'll have to go elsewhere."

## Message: 17 Friday 293 EN 10:18 (11/8/2344 8:45:02 AM)

From: Alan Shuford, Western Alliance Embassy to Japan, Tokyo, Japan

To: John Shuford, Grissom, Pitcairn

Dear John,

You should already know of recent developments, but I fear that isn't true. The government's propaganda campaign against you has intensified over the last month. The latest story concerns the theft of property belonging to Pearson Interstellar and the refusal of Pitcairn to do anything about it. As is usually the case in these stories, the details are vague, but the property in question seems to be furnishings and supplies from the Pearson estate on Pitcairn. I assume you know what the truth is behind these allegations and can air your side of it through your News Service.

You should do this as soon as possible. The Western Alliance government has announced a conference beginning March 20 to discuss problems with the colonies. It is called the Colonial Reorganization Conference, and you can draw your own conclusions about what that will probably mean.

You would think they would invite colony leaders to this conference. Technically, it is open to colonial leaders, but they have made no plans to make it possible for them to attend. I inquired about that and was told that Robert Perez would be returning to Earth on the *Francisco Pearson* to represent Pitcairn.

I regret having to pass this information on to you. I know it is not good news for you, but I hope there is still time to respond to this threat somehow.

Love,

Dad

## 17 Saturday 293 ED

Patrick sat in his office with John and Kimberly Dillon, the director of the Pitcairn News Service. The other three local administrators attended virtually.

"I've asked Kimberly to join us because a response by PNS will probably be part of any action we take," Patrick began. "Let's discuss the reported misappropriation of Pearson's property first."

Amani Marshall, the *Asimov* Administrator, appeared on the monitor screen. "Isn't that just another reaction to Pearson's conviction?"

"Apparently not, according to Pearson's lawyer." Patrick sighed. "Madelyn, would you like to address that?"

Madelyn's face replaced Amani's. "Not particularly. The Pearson estate is under my jurisdiction now, and I don't feel any need to answer to Earth or you over my actions."

Patrick shook his head slowly. "I'll assume Perez was telling the truth. Madelyn, you may have jurisdiction over the estate, but any personal property still belongs to Pearson. You can't just take anything you want."

"You're taking Pearson's side over mine?" Madelyn scowled indignantly. "He's a kidnapper!"

"Nevertheless, you took property that belongs to him. What did you take, anyway? Perez said 'furniture and supplies.'"

"I took one couch," Madelyn retorted. "A couple of boxes of things from the kitchen. You're making a big deal out of nothing."

"I told Perez to talk to Julian. Earth is making the big deal, and we don't need to give them any excuse."

"Since when do you worry about what Earth thinks? Drop it, Patrick. This is River Stations business."

"Whatever you took, bring it back to the estate as soon as possible. You don't have the right to steal just because you're an administrator." Patrick slapped the table. "Now, how do we respond?"

"Wait a minute," Madelyn protested. "Patrick, you can't tell me what to do."

Patrick's face reddened, and his mouth formed a hard line. "Return everything, Madelyn. Do it now, damn it, or you'll be the next person to go on trial." He turned his back on the monitor and turned to Kimberly. "Any suggestions on handling this?"

"I don't see what we can do except report that we have returned the goods," Kimberly answered. "It's hard to deal with this from here."

Patrick nodded. "I know. We'll just have to do the best we can. Okay, let's move on. Next item, this conference on Earth."

"They're planning on doing something, and this conference is a way of making it look legitimate," John said. "The idea of being represented by Robert Perez is absurd."

Patrick waved his hand dismissively. "I would worry more about that if there was anything they could gain. We're sending the antiviral drug as fast as we can produce it. They have access to their labs on *Asimov*. They have to keep supplying us to get those things. Any action they might consider has to have a goal in mind. It can't just be political control of Pitcairn."

"It could be just that," John replied. "Dumber things have been done in the name of politics. However, I think you're right. There's something more than politics going on. We just don't know what it is."

"Maybe," Patrick conceded. "There's nothing we can do about it until they make their move. I hinted to Selwick that we might want to send someone other than Perez to represent our side. He cited a seat price on the *Francisco Pearson*. He laughed when he said it, so I assume the quote was for a prohibitively large amount of money."

"Could Ambassador Shuford do anything for us?" Kimberly asked.

John shook his head. "The Western Alliance government would interpret anything he did as a conflict of interest and probably ruin his career. I won't ask that of him."

"We know Earth has been distorting the situation," Kimberly said. "I could put together some materials that would counter that."

Patrick looked at her with interest. "What did you have in mind?"

"We have the recordings of the trial. That would counter any propaganda about the alleged abuse of Pearson and Reyes. I could put together some recordings of the colony, too. Show Earth what this place is really like, and maybe interview some people."

"Good idea. Use whatever resources you need to get it done."

## 18 Tuesday 293 EN

Veronica Mobley looked across the dinner table where Caiden Reyes was finishing his Beef Wellington. "I assume you saw Ambassador Perez's message about the Colonial Reorganization Conference. Do you know what that's about?"

Caiden nodded as he wiped his lips with his napkin. "Robert Perez sent the message through Lovell Station earlier that day. I assume it's another ploy in Earth's attempt to get control of this colony. Do you think differently?"

Veronica's eyes narrowed slightly. "I think you know more about it than you're telling me. Earth's efforts to control Pitcairn seem extreme, considering the small benefit they might realize over the status quo."

Caiden smiled. "I do know more than you, and you don't need to know more than you do."

"You know I can represent you better if I know everything." She frowned. "I doubt I can change your mind about that, though." She pushed her plate aside, her meal only half-eaten. "I know the Western Alliance sent you and Selwick here to gain influence with the colonists for the Western Alliance. It occurs to me you might use Selwick's current situation to take the lead in whatever you want to accomplish."

Caiden contemplated her. "What do you suggest?"

"When Malley finds out about the conference, he's going to want to attend himself, or at least send someone. Earth doesn't want that, but if you could find a way for him to attend, I'm sure Malley would appreciate it. You could become the Western Alliance's chief representative here instead of Perez."

Caiden nodded. "I'm beginning to believe you are worth the money I'm paying you, Ms. Mobley. I can do something about that."

Veronica could see he was taking her suggestion seriously. But the mystery remained. What does Earth want for Pitcairn?

# 69

# Travel Plans

**18 Thursday 293 LN**

THE LINK COULD SEND messages virtually instantaneously, but the red tape involved at both ends of a round-trip communication required more time. Two days passed before Caiden could get an inquiry into the Link queue, send it, and get a reply from his company's headquarters on Earth.

The answer, when he finally got it, was better than he had hoped. He was making a fortune with BurnAway, the weight-loss drug developed from a Pitcairn weed. Pitcairn's percentage of that was much more than needed. Veronica was right. This was an excellent opportunity to improve his position with the colonists. He would have liked to present his idea to Malley himself, but he was under house arrest. Instead, he picked up his phone and called Veronica.

Veronica was already in bed and not happy about being awakened. She was less happy when Caiden told her he sending her to Lovell Station immediately. Time was critical, and she was to get to Grissom as quickly as possible.

**18 Saturday 293 EN**

"Your partnership with Mr. Reyes has succeeded beyond even his hopes," Veronica told Patrick. "The drug was approved for sale in record time, and sales have been much better than projections. Your account already contains more than enough money to finance a round trip for a delegation from Pitcairn."

"Really?" Patrick raised his eyebrows. "That's good news. How large a delegation are we talking about?"

"I imagine you could handle ten or twelve people easily. Of course, you'll need money while you're on Earth, but that won't be a problem."

"This would be a long absence from Pitcairn. I don't think we could spare that many people. We'll have to think about this. "

"Don't take too long thinking about it. Your delegation will have to be ready before the *Francisco Pearson* leaves."

Patrick nodded. "We'll be ready."

"One other matter, then. Caiden's family will arrive on the starship, and he would like permission to leave the estate and meet them."

"He has my permission to leave the estate. I'll talk to John about letting him meet the ship in Grissom. I think he'll approve, but if not, Caiden will have to meet the ferry on the north side of the river."

Veronica nodded. "I'm sure Caiden will appreciate your efforts."


## 19 Sunday 293 ED

"John, I know we don't always see eye-to-eye lately, but I trust you more than anyone to represent us." Patrick held his eyes on John, exuding confidence. "You could see your father, too."

John shook his head. "As much as I want to do that, it won't work. I'm an old man, Patrick. With my medical history, I might not survive the trip into orbit. I can take care of things here for a while, but you'll have to make the trip."

Patrick frowned, but he knew his father-in-law was right. John wasn't the man he had been; Patrick didn't need to consult a doctor to know that.

John continued. "You should take Kimberly with you, too. This could be an opportunity to establish a PNS presence on Earth itself."

"We can't come back until another ship comes here. That could be awhile."

"Possibly as much as a year. That's a long time, but this is important."

"I would take Susan with me. No doubt Kimberly would want to take her husband."

John nodded. "Mason Dillon. I'm sure she would. They don't have any children yet, so that wouldn't be a problem."

"Anybody else?"

John hesitated. "Maybe. Before it goes to Earth, the *Francisco Pearson* will stop at Epsilon Eridani to drop off supplies. We could pay for a couple of representatives from there to attend."

"Trist? Why would we want to do that?"

"It wouldn't hurt to have allies at the conference. Whatever Earth has planned will probably affect them, too."

"I doubt they're in the same position as we are."

John shrugged. "In some ways, it's worse. We could survive without Earth's support if we had to. Trist can't."

"All right. I'll think about it. Meanwhile, could you talk to Kimberly? We have to make sure she's willing to go back, even for a long visit."

"Sure."

Patrick frowned. "Earth doesn't want us to attend. What if they don't let us on the starship?"

As with most meetings, Isaac was listening. "I could refuse to launch a shuttle unless you were on board."

"That would probably work," John agreed. "Perez wouldn't be able to go to the conference, either. And we do still have Selwick as a bargaining chip."

"That's settled, then." Patrick paused. "John, you know that Caiden Reyes's family is on the ship?"

"I saw the passenger list. You're allowing Reyes to meet them?"

"I gave him permission to leave the estate and meet the ferry. I thought you should be the one to allow him to come into Grissom and meet the ship."

John nodded. "Thank you. Sure, I don't want to be petty about it. He can come to the spaceport."


## 3 December 2344 Epsilon Eridani Colony (Trist)

Olivia Sartin shook her head. "Now I've heard everything." She waved a message at Ron Rigney, her assistant.

"What?"

"This message just came in from Tau Ceti. Pitcairn is planning to send four delegates to the Colonial Reorganization Conference and wants us to send two as well."

"I thought Earth wasn't inviting colonial representatives."

"They're not. Patrick Malley has decided to go, anyway."

"How will they get there?" Ron scratched his head. "I can't imagine Pearson Industries is just going to wave them on board a starship."

"According to the message, Pitcairn can buy passage for six people, four from Pitcairn and two from here."

Ron's eyebrows shot up. "They want to pay for us? Where are they getting that kind of money? I didn't think they even had money on Pitcairn."

"That's an excellent question. It's almost worth sending someone just to find out."

## 13 December 2344 Cabinet Conference Room, Brasilia, Brazil

"Is this what you call under control?" President Castillo sneered.

"Perez is one of the best lawyers in the Western Alliance," David Pearson countered. "He was in an impossible situation."

"That's not what you said before. Something about Pitcairn taking on more than they bargained for, I think it was. Not only was your son found guilty, but somehow the colonists have found money to send a delegation to the conference. I want an explanation!" Castillo pounded the desk.

Pearson's expression darkened. "I'm not one of your lackeys to be impressed by a show of temper. Your ambassador to Pitcairn hasn't helped."

Castillo glared at him. "I expect results. Your participation in this project is predicated on your ability to get results. If you can't do that, I can replace Pearson Industries with someone who can. Reyes Pharmaceuticals seems to do better than you, for example."

Pearson sighed and moderated his tone. "Caiden Reyes made some kind of deal with Pitcairn. Perez's communications on that have been vague, presumably for security reasons. We'll know more when he gets back to Earth."

"Accompanied by the Pitcairn delegation. It may be too late then. We have to get control of Pitcairn, and even then, it will be years before we can hope to accomplish our goals. You may be satisfied with doing this for our grandchildren, but I'm not."

"We believe Reyes Pharmaceuticals has something to do with Pitcairn's financing," Pearson said. "If we can get the details on how that happened, we might do something."

Castillo waved his hand in dismissal. "Then get to work on that. I want results, not promises."

## 1 Saturday 294 EN

Caiden took the offered seat before Patrick's desk. "I wanted to stop by and thank you for letting me meet my family."

Patrick's tone was brusque. "No problem."

"One of my staff is giving my family a quick tour of Grissom. Madyson said to thank you, too. She's kind of confused about what has happened, but I'll try to explain it to her."

Patrick stared at him. "We're confused about what happened, too. You could explain it to me first."

"I'm not excusing myself, but it was Selwick's idea. Remember, I had just landed. I should have protested, I suppose, but Selwick was the only person here that I knew, and I followed his lead."

"Why?"

"Why did I follow his lead?"

"Why did Selwick kidnap the boys? What was so important?"

Caiden frowned and looked down at Patrick's desk. "I'm sorry, but I can't tell you that."

"Right. Well, I appreciate your help in getting us passage to the conference. I guess I'll have to settle for that. Thanks for stopping by." Patrick began shuffling papers from his desk.

Realizing he was dismissed, Caiden left without speaking. He had to work with Patrick Malley, and anything he could have said would have been counter-productive.


## 1 Saturday 294 LD

It was a long truck ride from the north ferry landing up the road to the Reyes estate. Selwick's driver, Aiden Coffey, drove the truck, and Caiden put off his wife's questions about the events leading to his house arrest. When they finally arrived at the estate, everyone was exhausted, and Caiden's refusal to explain irritated Madyson. He tried to plan what he would say, but couldn't think coherently.

Now, with Aiden gone and his two sons in their bedrooms supervising the unpacking of their belongings, he knew he had to tell Madyson something. "Madyson, sit down."

Madyson glared at him. "So that you can tell me you've got it all handled? So you can make me shut up?"

"I couldn't talk with Selwick's man there. I'm not supposed to tell anybody anything, but I'll tell you as much as I think I can."

The glare remained, but Madyson sat down. "So why are you restricted to this estate? Can you at least tell me that?"

Caiden sighed and took a seat next to Madyson. "Selwick and I are working to gain influence here on Pitcairn to have the Western Alliance take over the colony. I can't talk about why that is important to the Western Alliance, but that's the reason for our actions. Pitcairn's claims about Selwick grabbing two boys are accurate. He held them at his estate for months until the colonists realized where they were and rescued them."

"Why would he do that? What could be that important? And why did you help him?"

"I can't tell you why, but it is important. Important to the Western Alliance and important to us. I didn't want to help, but it was my first day on Pitcairn, and I didn't know what else to do except go along."

"Why did you keep your estate when Selwick lost his?"

Caiden shrugged. "I made a deal. I testified against Selwick and made a financial deal with Patrick Malley, the Pitcairn Administrator."

"A financial deal? I thought Pitcairn didn't use money. What kind of deal could they make?"

"They are going to use the money I've paid them to finance their trip to the Colonial Reorganization Conference."

"What are you getting out of it?"

"Do you know about our product, BurnAway?"

Madyson stared at him for a long moment before she realized what he was saying. "BurnAway comes from Pitcairn?"

"The original compound did. We figured out how to create it on Earth, but I'm paying Pitcairn a percentage of the profits. It gives me influence here, and I need that."

Later, as he lay awake with Madyson asleep next to him, he wondered. He loved his wife and had held nothing back from her before. He knew he could trust her to keep his secrets. So why hadn't he told her?

He had to consider the possibility that he was ashamed to tell her why they had done something so appalling. She wanted to know what secret was so important that they would hold two young boys hostage. Even if he told her, he knew she wouldn't understand. He doubted he understood. Was the project that important?

He realized, too, that his decision to help Patrick Malley get to Earth was questionable. Could the good standing he achieved be worth the risk of letting Malley get input into the conference? Had his subconscious already decided that Selwick and his backers were wrong?

## 3 Sunday 294 LN

Seven passengers boarded *Daneel Olivaw* for the trip up to *Francisco Pearson*. The Malleys, the Dillons, and Robert Perez planned to be back eventually, but Jonathan Perez and Veronica hoped never to see Pitcairn again.

Patrick should have been nervous as he took his seat with the others. Of the seven, he was the only one who had never flown on the shuttle. As the launch countdown was broadcast to the shuttle cabin, though, his thoughts were on the conference. Even later, as acceleration pushed him back into his seat, his thoughts didn't stray from pondering Earth's motives.

S USAN GLANCED OVER AT Patrick periodically, wondering what he was thinking behind his unreadable expression. She was excited, but she was also sad about leaving her family behind. Her father's health was deteriorating, and that worried her too much to let her feel good about leaving him. It was heartrending to leave Marie and their first grandchild, one-year-old Allison. She would even miss Isaac, and the uncertainty about when they would return didn't make it any easier. Patrick didn't seem to feel any of that, though. Somehow, that didn't surprise her.

## Message: 3 Monday 294 ED 11:18 (2/4/2345 12:03:44 PM)

From: John Shuford, Grissom, Pitcairn

To: Alan Shuford, Western Alliance Embassy to Japan, Tokyo, Japan

Dear Dad,

By now, you've heard that we sent delegates to the Colonial Reorganization Conference. I'm sure you are disappointed to learn I'm not one of them, but Patrick needed me to run things while he is gone. I, of course, was disappointed, too, but I have to be here.

At least you'll meet your granddaughter. Susan is accompanying Patrick, and I imagine she'll have free time while she is on Earth. The two of you can probably trade stories about me.

I hope, too, that you can help Patrick. He is less concerned about our relationship with Earth than I am, and that worries me. He has confidence in his ability to deal with whatever happens in the conference, and I fear he may be overly optimistic. We, Pitcairn and I, would appreciate any help that you can give him.

Love,


John


John wanted to make the message longer, but he could hear voices outside the office, so he sent the message to the Link as it was. He could count on his father, and Patrick would need all the help he could get.

# 70

# Le Parisien

**22 February 2345**

**Le Parisien Restaurant, Tokyo, Japan**

ALAN SHUFORD LEANED BACK in his comfortable chair and looked at his companion. With the usual pleasantries over and dinner ordered, Alan wanted to begin the business discussion. Kenshin Ikeda was in Japanese security, although he had never revealed his exact position to Alan. The Japanese government often used Ikeda to pass information concerning the Eastern Bloc, and the two men had become friendly soon after Alan became ambassador to Japan.

Because of its position as a neutral at the edge of Eastern Bloc territory, Japan was a vital intelligence source for the Western Alliance. To maintain its official neutrality, Japan did not allow the Western Alliance to set up spy installations on Japanese soil, but the Japanese facilities were quite efficient, and Japan, as far as Alan could tell, was generous in passing on their findings. Alan suspected that the flow of information went in both directions, but he understood Japan's precarious position and had never made an issue of it.

Ikeda pushed a data pod across the table, hiding the movement from the other tables with his free arm. "Nothing too unusual," he said quietly as Alan took the pod. "There have been some interesting discussions about Alliance dealings with Pitcairn, though."

Alan raised an eyebrow. "What discussions?"

"The announcement of the Colonial Reorganization Conference caught their attention. They didn't understand what the Alliance intended and have been trying to discover why controlling Pitcairn is so important."

"My son has been concerned about the same thing." Alan had told Ikeda about John years ago. "I haven't been told about any special motive, though. I believe it's just a political knee-jerk reaction to want to control the colonies."

Ikeda nodded. "That sounds reasonable, but apparently is not the case. Eastern Bloc intelligence operatives have reported otherwise."

A waitress came to the table, bearing their appetizer of the Breton-style crepes the restaurant was famous for. She put two glasses of hard apple cider down, bowed, and moved away. When she was gone, Alan continued. "The Alliance has a reason for wanting control over the colonies? Do you know what it is?"

"I know some of it. It's not all the colonies they are concerned with, just Pitcairn. And it's not the planet they want control of. It's the library ship Pitcairn controls."

"Why the Pitcairn library ship? They already have control over the other two."

Ikeda shrugged. "One of President Castillo's closest advisors, General Salvador Juarez, is running some project involving the starship. Other than that, I could only get the code name of the project. It made little sense to me, but perhaps it will mean something to you. Methuselah."

**The End... for now. The story continues in "Tau Ceti: The Immortality Conspiracy."**

# Supporting the Library Ship Saga

I F YOU ENJOYED THIS novel, you can find more Library Ship stories with the "More Stories" tab on my website, www.tauceti2.com. I post news about future stories there and on my website and my Facebook page, www.facebook.com/tauceti2. The website also has a link where you can subscribe to a newsletter about the saga.

You can also support my writing in several ways:

- Post reviews on Amazon.com (there are links on each book page on my website) and Goodreads.com. Reviews don't have to be long, but please make them honest. I learn from them.

- Tell your friends about the Library Ship Saga, both in person and through social media like Facebook and Twitter.

- Like my Facebook page and share it with your friends.

- Use the link on my website to subscribe to my mailing list. You can also use the Contact page to ask questions or provide feedback about this novel and the others in the saga.

# Appendix: Time on Pitcairn

THE LENGTH OF A day on Pitcairn is 47.1 hours in Terran time, adjusted to forty-eight local hours. Because the day's length is almost twice that of Earth, the day is divided into four periods: Early Day, Late Day, Early Night, and Late Night. Early Day begins at roughly sunrise, although the actual time of sunrise varies with the season. Late Day begins twelve hours later at noon, Early Night begins at approximately sunset, and Late Night starts at midnight. Most colonists work during one day and one night period, either Early or Late, with alternating rest periods. Events involving the entire colony are held around "noon," between Early Day and Late Day, or "midnight" between Early Night and Late Night.

The exact length of the year is 145.17 local days or about 285 Earth days. A leap day is added every six local years and is simply called leapday. Every 60 years, an extra leap day is observed, called foundersday.

The year is divided into twenty-one local weeks, each seven Pitcairn days long and named the same as Earth weekdays. There is no local equivalent of months. Dates are expressed generally by week number, day, and year, sometimes modified for the quarter day by ED, LD, EN, or LN, e.g., 12 Friday 203 would be Friday of the twelfth week, in the 203$^{rd}$ year since the first landing. 12 Friday 203 LD would identify the Late Day period of the same day. A time, if used, would be appended, e.g., 12 Friday 203 LD 10:05 would further specify ten hours and five minutes into the Late Day period. Time without date, however, would usually be expressed in reverse, i.e., 10:05 LD. The day begins at 0:0:0 ED, the nominal dawn.

Pitcairn uses three seasons: Spring, weeks 1-7, summer, weeks 8-14, and winter, weeks 15-21.

Each of the four periods is divided into twelve Pitcairn hours, equal to about .98 Earth hours with 60 minutes to the hour and 60 seconds to the minute, so minutes and seconds are also about .98 of the Earth equivalent.

The Pitcairn calendar begins at 11:24:05, May 21, 2113, corresponding to 0:0:0 ED, 1 Sunday 0. This corresponds roughly to the landing of the Santa Maria on June 24, 2113, but was adjusted to make 1 Sunday the first day of spring.